CONSTANCE

WARLOE

THE LEGEND OF OLIVIA COSMOS MONTEVIDEO

A NOVEL

THE ATLANTIC MONTHLY PRESS
NEW YORK

Published simultaneously in Canada
Printed in the United States of America

FIRST EDITION

Library of Congress Cataloging-in-Publication Data

Warloe, Constance.
The legend of Olivia Cosmos Montevideo: a novel / Constance Warloe.
ISBN 0-87113-564-7
1. Women—New Mexico—Santa Fe—Fiction. 2. Vietnamese Conflict, 1961–1975—Casualties (Statistics, etc.)—Fiction. 3. Mothers and sons—United States—Fiction. I. Title.
PS3573.A7618L4 1994 813′.54—dc20 93-29523

Design by Laura Hough

The Atlantic Monthly Press
841 Broadway
New York, NY 10003

3 5 7 9 10 8 6 4 2

For my husband, Roger,

and my sons, Stephen and Charles,

who offered love and space enough

to grow this novel

ACKNOWLEDGMENTS

Every writer knows. No one writes a novel alone. I, too, owe. I have received support from too many people for this list to be complete, but names left off are written in my heart.

Mary Knowles, Harlan Bower, John Knowles, the late Lillian Brown, Jan Littman, Stuart Northam, the late John Gardner, Richard Bausch, Tess Enroth, Harold Schneider, Clysta Kinstler, Denise Chavez, Joy Harjo, Kathryn Hohlwein, Jan Haag, Judy Painter, Mary Mackey, Karen Bijlsma, Elizabeth Stewart, Helen Mills, Marilyn Mills, R. G. Guches, Judy Rakela, Candace Cave, Betty Nelsen, Lora Allen, Betty Duke, Mary Anne Linane, Michael Montoya, Soila Solorio, Pauline McCleary, Gale Saastaad, Richard Hough, Dr. Craig E. Johnson, the Reverends Bert Sikkelee, Victor Matson, David Ellis, and Steven Smith, Margaret Swan-Levine, Howard Levine, Carol Klattenhoff Mullen, Barbara Henrioulle-Stein, George Kokis, Dan Hatfield, Ruth Cohen, Felicia Eth, Luther Nichols, Judith Regan, Aurora Salazar and her late husband, Max Salazar, citizen of Santa Fe and storyteller extraordinaire, whose happy heart and sad-sweet stories inform the pages of this novel, stories within stories within stories. I think I can hear him now . . .

Special thanks to Anton Mueller and my editors at Grove/Atlantic, Joan Bingham and Allison Draper, and to my angels—my heaven-sent agent, Linda Chester, and her divinely inspired associate, Laurie Fox.

Thanks also to the Museum of New Mexico; the Museum of Indian Arts, Santa Fe; Arlington National Cemetery; the Smithsonian museums of American History and Natural History; the University of New Mexico; American River College; California State University, Sacramento; the University of California, Davis; the Santa Fe Writers' Conference; the Mendocino Art Center; and the Bread Loaf Writers' Conference.

CONTENTS

Any bullet from wherever it comes is shot at the mother first, not at the son who is killed.

—Van Le, Vietnamese poet and novelist, from
Flashbacks: On Returning to Vietnam by Morley Safer

THE LEGEND OF OLIVIA COSMOS MONTEVIDEO

PROLOGUE

1991

Try to see me the way I see myself, an Indian woman wrapped in her blanket by the fire telling you a story she has to tell. But you might as well know, you will find out soon enough, that I am a redheaded gringo woman living in Santa Fe under an assumed name.

I was never a healer or an artist, but now I study with a woman at the pueblo, learning to make healing potions and the pots to put them in. And though I did not always believe, I go to the Catholic church of the Spaniards, saying novenas for my loved ones, living and dead. I have studied the history and laws of my people at the university in Albuquerque; I am a guide who has herself had many guides on her journey. Indian, Spaniard, Anglo. Does all of this make me a mestizo, a mixed breed? I like to think so; I see myself that way.

I see myself as a storyteller who should have spoken sooner. Now I hear war drums pounding again. My dead son has begun to come to me in dreams, dressed in his green soldier clothes. Of all the stories I would like to tell you, this is the one that must be told. The time has come for me to speak.

I

VISIONS

There whispers, for a moment, the wild voice of the unconscious self—using the disturbed language of the dream and the jest, as well as the language of tragedy.

—"The Meanings of Comedy" from *Comedy* by Wylie Sypher

1

Arlington, Virginia
July 4, 1970

I wake on Saturday morning to curtain-filtered sunlight that turns the twisted bedsheets into shadowy mounds of gray. Andrew has been up for hours; I hear the lawn mower sputtering below the window. Lawns have to be mowed, I tell myself, rolling away from the light. Someone has to tend the lawns and the laundry.

Unconvinced, I strip the bed, stuff the sheets into a pillowcase, and make my way to the laundry chute in the hall. I toss the bundle down the chute. A helicopter loaded with soldiers appears in a whirring cloud of red dust. It's something I've seen on the news, a visual fragment now detached from its source and broken loose in my mind.

In this helicopter the wounded lie on stretchers, which are piled atop the dead, who are in body bags. In this scene a body bag falls through the air and onto a concrete landing strip. I see it almost every day, that body bag or the one beneath the stretchers where something has ripped the plastic and a booted leg protrudes at a grotesquely unnatural angle. People in camouflage clothing usually enter the scene, some emerging from the helicopter, others apparently already on the ground. They always say the same thing; over and over their strained male voices shout, "FORGET THE FUCKING DEAD. WE'VE GOT WOUNDED ONBOARD." And then, after the stretchers are lifted into a white funnel of mist in the center of the red dust cloud, the voices speak again. "FORGET THE FUCKING DEAD."

In the shower I breathe deeply of hot steam. I've discovered that slow, deep inhalations can sometimes break the bands of tension that grip my chest when the body bags appear. I decide, as I have on many days recently, that Andrew is the real problem here. Every time I try to tell him about the body bags and the helicopters, he leaves the room. My mother is long distance in Potsdam, New York. She could hardly look at me during the funeral. She keeps telling me to come up to Potsdam; her cure for everything is to come up to Potsdam. But I know who this sorrow belongs to—the parents, husband and wife. And what did Andrew say to me last night? "I don't want to know what goes on in your mind." I would not, he assured me, want to look inside of his.

If we aren't going to share these terrors, can't we at least go to Arlington and remember our son? I need to remember my son.

Right now, this is all I can remember:

The doorbell ringing on another Saturday, May twenty-third, not even two months ago. I am vacuuming. Andrew has been reading the paper to me from the kitchen. He has read a few minutes before that the 1968 Tet Offensive was "a final blow to the failing U.S. Search and Destroy policy, and the reason that Vietnamization will fail, too." That is why I have started vacuuming, to hear no more about searching and destroying and failures. When the doorbell rings, I shut off the vacuum cleaner and walk toward the foyer. The instant I set foot on the tiles I know, though I don't know why, that I should not answer the door. Time has slowed and I have noticed the grain of the wood beneath the paint of the door. I am breathing abnormally, consciously performing what I know to be an involuntary bodily function, *thinking* about it. I glance through the small windowpanes in the upper part of the door and at the same time my hand touches the doorknob. I see army green, a wool gabardine sleeve with brass buttons; I see a clean-shaven jaw and neck, closely cropped hair, then the hat with the brim, the kind they save for special occasions. This is a dress uniform. And there are two of them. I call for Andrew as I open the door, then slam it shut and try to shout at them. "No," I say, too breathless to get any volume. "Get away from this house," I whisper, my back against the door. They remain on the porch. Andrew pulls me away from the door, propping it open with his shoulder as he holds me. "Mr. and Mrs. Andrew Masters?" the older one asks, his voice deep, restrained. He says he is a chaplain; he looks about thirty.

The one with him is a lieutenant, but he looks as young as Gary. And Gary is dead. The uniformed soldiers step carefully around my Electrolux and sit on the sofa. Hats in hands, heads lowered, they pass with us through strange moments of hospitality (ours) and guilt (theirs), and into some sort of shared complicity. "I'm very sorry, Mrs. Masters, Mr. Masters," the older one says. "Sorry," the younger one echoes. Andrew and I nod our acceptance of their apologies, offering them coffee, seating ourselves on the other sofa, bobbing our heads into our hands, reaching for each other, feeling each other's arms, legs, not finding what we're looking for. Unable to breathe, I can sit no longer. I start walking, bending at the waist, up and down, along the front wall of the living room. This news is a puncture wound. Air has begun to leak from my lungs; the pacing and bending serves a pumping function. "We knew this could happen, I suppose," Andrew says. "In a *war,*" I whisper from near the window. "Yes ma'am, yessir," the soldiers say, their polite words tumbling over each other. "You can never be ready for it," Andrew says, his voice rising. "I'm not ready for it." The men shake their heads in regret, ashamed of our lack of preparedness. A pause, and then Andrew asks, "Night mission, you say?" The second telling relieves the soldiers of their burden. They straighten up, move their round hats to their knees. "Yessir," the younger one says. "He was part of the Search and Destroy they're still doing over there. He hit a mine and . . ." He avoids our eyes. "You know, instantly. Killed instantly, the way it goes with those things." The older one picks up the narrative thread, watching me because I'm still walking the floor. "The report we have indicates they were on a night patrol, in a ravine near Pleiku. Hilly area. Three of the men were lost there to enemy mines planted along the slopes of hillsides, and another man was wounded. A report from his sergeant will be sent to you, along with his personal effects." They tell us a lot about money—insurance, back pay, something they call a gratuity check. Gratuity check, I'm thinking. Gratuity check! My pacing gets faster. There will be a body escort, they say. They quickly add that they will be available to us twenty-four hours a day, they'll even stay with us in our home, but we tell them we'll stay alone for the time being. It is no longer their fault; they *said* they were sorry. They leave with their hats on their heads and their jaws set firm. Andrew and I are numb, staring at the grain of the wood beneath the paint as we close the door behind them, both of us pressing to be sure it's shut.

This is what I remember:

Looking at Andrew and feeling numb. Seeing his face collapse as if inside there's been a cave-in. Noticing in the hall mirror that my face, too, looks as if some sort of demolition is going on behind it. Feeling nothing but a dull, distant, brand-new pain to which I do not respond. Resurrecting, instead, old hurts. Picking a fight with Andrew. Thinking that old scar tissue can muffle the noise of new wounds.

"No fair," I say, turning off the shower. Andrew and I were together in our numbness, at first. Now something is different. I seem to be feeling again and wanting to talk about it, and he does not. Today will be different, I tell myself, wrapping a towel around the lumpy, freckled body I see in the mirror. I brush my hair, I get dressed, I feel more reasonable. Two a day probably is too many cemetery visits.

I don't trust what I feel. I don't trust my memory either. Lately, in trying to remember Gary, I can picture him with me but I cannot for the life of me remember Andrew being a father. I bring up a scene and it looks like a photograph with the head cut off where Andrew is supposed to be. I know my memory is telling me lies or half-truths about father and son. I know I don't want his pain. Yet we each placed a flower on Gary's grave the day we buried him. Dazed with my own misery at the time, I didn't know what he felt. Now he seems like an inaccessible shadow I can never bring to light. He must have those sudden flashes of Gary's face and gestures, his voice. How different can this be for him? What is he remembering, or trying to forget? I'll go downstairs. I'll ask him . . . again.

He'll stop mowing if I ask him to, and we can go to Arlington. We'll take a lunch. We'll look like tourists from towns like Birmingham, Omaha, Iowa City. People out there live in white frame houses with big porches where grandfathers nod in sleep and women in cotton house-dresses hang laundry on backyard clotheslines. We'll look like that. Lies. All lies.

I leave an open package of lunch meat on the counter and sit on a chair near the window. Maybe I can come to believe it. Maybe we could look that way: me, a tall woman whose hips bulge beneath her kettlecloth skirt and whose hair is dyed too red for her thirty-nine years. Andrew, a slender, almost handsome man whose attempt to be stylish got stuck in the middle of the past decade with muttonchop sideburns and crepe-soled shoes. I know how we look, but we'll bring a lunch. We'll find a table. At Arlington or, if the air has become too thick with heat and humidity, across the way at Lady Bird Johnson's Memorial Grove. At the grove, then. We'll sit across from each other in the shade of those trees. We won't have to say much because, after nineteen years and one month, we don't seem to bring up new subjects. Or old ones, I realize gloomily. But that's acceptable to me. I wish to bring up only one subject. I want to know what is keeping Andrew separate from me.

From the screened porch I can see him in the woods, dumping a bag of grass onto the mulch pile. I walk outside. I catch the moist scent of decaying grass and leaves, observe the wave of nausea and the constriction in my chest. I try to keep the whine out of my voice. "I want you to come along this time," I say.

He slaps his hand against the stained canvas bag and replaces it on the mower. "I have to edge after this," he says.

"But I *need* you," I whine.

"I'm not going again, Roberta."

"Andrew . . ."

The voices might be right—FORGET THE FUCKING DEAD—but I cannot. I take a step toward him. He pulls at the starter rope. The mower sputters, stops. A bird chatters in a birch branch. Mowers chug in distant yards—threats to his lawn-mowing prowess. He yanks again. Beads of sweat roll from his forehead and down his cheeks. He is suffering. I know it and I can't stand it. Suddenly I focus on his skin and find it repulsive. Little pockmarks scatter here and there on his cheeks. Like the dark side of the moon, gray-white ash. Whose father could *this* be? Am I trying to eradicate his existence as a parent? This is not making me feel any better. I know I have to stop thinking this way.

The mower starts on the next pull. He cuts a path toward the screened porch, begins a new swath as he comes toward me. Two strides and I'm standing beside him. I grab the chrome handle and flick off the switch. He flings his arms away from the mower, narrowly missing my jaw, and pushes me aside with a shove to my shoulder. His voice is a growl. "I'm not staying around for shit like this, Roberta."

He's staying around? He's staying home on a Saturday? He's staying married to me? Our son is dead less than two months and we, the only two human souls who can properly remember him, are staying around for some idle purpose? Maybe *I'm* just staying around. Maybe I don't have to stay around. I know I'm not very original. If he hadn't said *he* was staying around, I know it would never have occurred to me that either of us could leave. Yet I sense that some other part of my brain has gone into action: I could go away.

I walk back to the house. I sort laundry in the basement where Gary played grocery store, run the sweeper in the living room where I read with him on rainy mornings. I go outside and hose down Andrew's freshly edged sidewalk, where we gathered with our neighbors in those long-lost years. I come back in the house and collapse on the sofa, aware of a new sensation, a sudden, wavelike breathlessness that washes relentlessly over me in the form of rage. I have to learn. More important than waiting in an empty house for my dead son's father to crack his shell, I need to ask the questions, find the answers, whatever they may turn out to be. Why? I have to ask. What happened? Who were these people who called themselves by words that no longer surrender to definition: Family? Father, Mother, Son?

I must learn new words . . . or new definitions.

It's Monday morning. On the phone I give the AAA travel agent instructions that are undeniably vague: "I want a guided tour. I am interested in visiting historical sites."

"With a group?" the agent asks.

"Oh, no!" I say quickly. "But with guidelines. A plan."

When I arrive at the AAA office, I know the agent has misunderstood. She has created a travel packet describing a month-long excursion to what seems like every battlefield of the War Between the States. No more war. Home war, foreign war. I want no more of war.

"Thank you," I say. I hesitate, then leave the office and return to my car. I realize I have put the agent at a disadvantage. I should have told her more about me. Maybe travel agents match tours to tourists; maybe travel agents can *tell* people where to go. I walk back inside.

I return the packet to the woman. "It's a fine tour. Really," I say. Palm trees wave confidently from wall posters while I search for words. "But I've just finished the, uh, Civil War."

"Oh," the agent says. Young, obviously cheerful by nature, she hardly blinks as she dumps the carefully marked maps and typed itinerary into the wastebasket. "You just want to go on the road, is that it?"

That could be exactly it. I resist the idea of rolling along in a Volkswagen bus or camping beside shaggy, migrating college students, but I am definitely going on the road. The thought of going away, when I've thought of it at all, has been a circular concept. Now my vision has gone suddenly linear. This is happening too quickly, I think, unable to examine the idea further.

We unfold a map of the United States. The agent pops the cap from her felt-tip marker and draws a jagged green line across the northern half of the country. Pulling maps from her shelves, she snips enlarged portions of Ohio, Indiana, Illinois, Wisconsin, Minnesota, South Dakota, Wyoming, Nevada, and California. She stamps red arrows on Primary Routes. She stamps blue arrows on Alternate Routes. She draws red circles around descriptive material for historical sites in the Scenic Guides for each region through which I will pass. She goes off for a moment, leaving me to contemplate the huge sheets of paper that delineate the U.S. of A. She returns, having created a steno pad sort of notebook, map strips bound across the top with a round plastic spiral.

"Your Trip-Tiks," she says, placing the pad in my hands with the certainty of a nurse placing a scalpel in the hands of a surgeon. Her confidence in my itinerary is impressive.

"Thank you," I say, enjoying the solidity of the notebook in my hand. Trip-Tiks. Tickets. Legitimate entry. The implication is that I know where I'm going . . . and why.

"Your Scenic Guides," she says, her voice musical and sure. She sets the booklets on the desk in front of me.

"And maps." She adds to the pile. Then she sweeps the whole stack into a plastic shopping bag with handles. She adds a litter bag with a hole for hanging from cigarette lighter knob or window crank.

"All set," she smiles, leaning back. "Are you all right?" she asks, coming forward again at the sight of my quivering face.

"Just tired, I guess." I get up from the chair and put my fingers through the handles of the plastic shopping bag, getting my grip. "I'll go on the road," I say.

After supper Andrew goes out on the screened porch. Alternating between moving the sprinkler and playing his guitar, he seems intent on using up, in solitude, the cool green hour that's left of the day. After a while, he comes inside. We reach for the refrigerator door at the same time. He makes his intentions clear: "I just came in for a beer," he says.

I hand him a can, then put a bowl of leftover salad greens on the refrigerator shelf. He sets about opening his beer with absurd concentration, placing the can on the counter, wiping off the top with a dishrag, drawing his head back as the tab seal breaks and hisses. I shrug and go back to the sink, pouring into the garbage disposal, with equal concentration, floating macaroni elbows and bits of whitish cheese. He heads for the door.

"I think I need to go away for a while, Andrew," I say, swishing the casserole dish with a scrubber. "I'll be leaving tomorrow," I say, startled at myself for saying it.

He pushes the screendoor open, pretending not to hear me over the noise. I shut off the grinder.

"I said I'm *leaving!*" I yell, my voice shrill in the silence.

He steps inside, lets the screendoor bump against his shoulder. "Why? Where are you going?"

I don't know where I'm going. My going has something to do with finding what's lost. "I'm going on a rest-and-relaxation tour. Kind of an R&R. To figure things out." To find America, I want to say, but I know I'd regret the words.

He seems to swell up, rise from the floor in anger. "It's your history thing, isn't it?"

"Yeah, history," I say, stupidly defensive. "I see things better if I look at what's happened before." I move closer to him by a yard or two. He stays in the doorway.

"You dragged that kid to museums," he says. "You shoved history down his throat with all your books. You signed the *paper* for him to join the army, for God's sake. Oughta be enough history for anybody. . . ."

We face each other, puzzled. The house is still; even from the upstairs rooms, it seems, the stillness hovers. "I have nightmares," I say, whimpering into the stale sponge. "I don't sleep well. I need to get away."

"I hear you sometimes, Roberta," he says, sitting down at the table with his back to me. His forearms rest on the table, the beer can between them. His shoulders, broad and bent, seem to have gone through a transformation. He is thin. His spine is outlined beneath the dampness of his T-shirt. "You have to let it go," he mumbles toward the table.

I try once more to explain. "It doesn't matter how he died so much as . . ." I watch Andrew swallow more beer. "To remember is . . ." My voice breaks again. I understand what my crying is doing to him. I stop.

"Look, Roberta. I go along. I go to work, I get nothing but shit. Some days I figure I'll just walk out of there. . . ."

"Why don't you?" I say. "I wouldn't blame you if you never . . ."

He starts to say something, then hesitates.

I join him at the table. I look at his eyes, translucent in the light from overhead. I read his thoughts in his tawny eyes, certain that he is reviewing, as I am, the disappointing smallness of our lives. An accountant working on the budget at the Pentagon? Andrew, I want to ask, what good has it done you? You told me once the Pentagon could be converted into the largest evacuation hospital in the world. Why? So nurses could wheel you down the ramps if your wounds start to show?

"But then I come home. I mow the grass. I run my sprinkler, right? I stand out there on the porch, everything's washed off clean. I wish I was playing guitar in a dark bar, but I gave that up . . ."

What's left? Acres of mowed green grass and miles of black cul-de-sac pavement? I recognize the pattern with a start: Gary buried at Arlington, me living on Branchview Court, and Andrew, the reluctant groundskeeper, mowing the grass! I am energized by the horror of the vision. Panic travels along my skin like electrical current.

I get up and march to the dishwasher. I ram the lever to START. The dishwasher hums. I am humming, rumbling. I swab the dishrag across the countertop to the familiar rhythm of words a little bit like "The House that Jack Built": Andrew counts the money that builds the bombs and here is the bomb that Andrew sent to 'Nam. A dud that didn't go off. The Andrew Masters Dud Bomb. Ah, but the VC found it and used the metal—I correct my thoughts—the shrapnel. The VC found the Dud and used the shrapnel that came from the Dud that Andrew built and built the bomb that Gary felt. The Gary Masters Side-of-the-Ravine Booby Trap Bomb.

"You did your part, Andrew," I say.

As if hit in the midsection, he folds in half. "Nobody's fault," he mutters to the table.

"Everyone's fault!" I cry, waving the dishrag like a protest banner. "You count the dollars that build the bombs and tell me I caused it with history? You say I signed the paper? You're a fungus, Andrew." A filthy fungus growing between Uncle Sam's toes, I think, a second later.

This must be the lowest point in my life. What has happened to me? What am I saying?

When I've stopped shaking and can lean calmly against the counter, I'm ashamed at having called Andrew a fungus. But I'm so slow. I never was any good at extemporaneous speaking. Look at all I never said to Gary. God, I'm slow, I think, hanging the dishrag on a nail beneath the sink, a nail I pounded there almost nineteen years ago. The rag droops.

I have to go away.

The next morning I hold my breath like a smuggler going through Customs. Andrew is examining the Trip-Tiks from the travel packet that I have carelessly, unthinkingly, left lying on the table. "These cut-up sections should be real handy. They're bound like a steno pad," he says.

"Can you take this thing?" I ask, hoping to distract him with my suitcase.

If he so much as looks at my itinerary or offers one helpful suggestion, I might lean, ever so slightly, on his judgment. If I lean, I won't leave. At last, he sets the Trip-Tiks down and takes the suitcase from me. I walk casually to the table and then hurriedly scoop them into my purse. I yank the zipper closed, pat the bulging leather bag as I swing it under my arm. I hook my fingers into the plastic AAA shopping bag. I look up. Andrew is watching me from the doorway.

"I have to do this myself," I explain.

He seems to be thinking it over.

We walk to the garage; he puts the suitcase in the trunk; I get in the car and close the door. It occurs to me, as I switch on the ignition and mash the accelerator to the floor, setting up a high-pitched squeal that is deafening in the close space of the garage, that we need help: a minister, a priest, a witch doctor. I back out, thinking there must be a hundred things we could have told each other, knowing we have already plumbed the depths of our resources. We can't help each other, but we do need help.

"I'll call every few days," I say from the driveway. I blow my nose in a tissue. "So you'll know where I am," I add helpfully.

"You're going, then?"

"Yes."

The engine dies halfway down the block. I restart the engine, jerk to the stop sign at the corner of Branchview and Woodland, look back to see if he is still there. He's gone inside, apparently unable to watch.

I turn onto Woodland. I'm going off to find what's lost, with a driver's license in my purse that reads Roberta Patterson Masters. What if the driver's license is lost, too? Quickly, I pull to the side of the road and rummage through my purse. I find the driver's license and sigh with relief that it's there, proof of something, though the expressionless face in the photograph gives no clue. "Roberta Patterson Masters?" I whisper, stricken by the enormity of that question.

It's nine-thirty by the time I reach the gates at Arlington Cemetery, but the tourists haven't yet begun arriving. What I see, as I walk toward the entrance, are patterns. Clean asphalt roads and black tarmac pathways cut the green into manageable sections. Clumps of maple trees and pines soften the angles and muffle the voices of mourners, but Arlington is a sea of death that would overwhelm anyone who came here if it weren't for the patterns, the comforting perfection of geometry.

I know this cemetery well, its white crosses planted in rows. I have made it my mission in the weeks since Gary's death to know the business of Arlington National Cemetery. My natural inclination toward research, I suppose, but the people here readily answer my questions. They know, in their military or government-worker mentality, that I have The Need To Know.

This cemetery has become my intimate space. I've looked it all over like a mother choosing a school for her child. I have discovered a rotating system of maintenance, four or five different sections scheduled for mowing, clipping, and cleaning. Newly filled graves have only fading, plastic-coated cards typed with name, serial number, hometown, dates of birth and death, and plot number, but the headstones do arrive. Gary's did.

The flowers are left too long. Flowers are often left until their petals pass through stages of discoloration akin to the fading of a bruise. The bouquets left lying around can whisper in the wind like brown brittle paper. The grave next to Gary's seems always to have withered flowers. Sometimes the dry petals blow onto Gary's headstone. At first I would look irritably at that grave, the way I might have glanced at an unruly child's mother in the park. Then one day I met the parents, a farmer and his wife from Missouri. He commented on the rows and how that was the way a good orchard was, in rows no matter what angle you looked from. We smiled and nodded, appreciating each other's need for order. Over the weeks and now months I've created various scenarios as I've watched the flowers arrive and then fade on that grave: Corporal James Lee Storey's family must have been in Washington for several days at the time of his services, having made the difficult decision to place his remains in Arlington and not in Warrensburg, Missouri. The father probably went home first. The mother must have stayed on a week longer, bringing flowers daily, then gone home and wired flowers every week or two. It occurs to me that I am leaving my son, too, but I'm not going "home" to anywhere. Yet my perspective has changed somewhat because of that neighboring headstone. Sometimes I take a communal view of loss.

My footsteps on these walkways have the familiarity of my own heartbeat, even and rhythmical and occasionally erratic—as now, when I stumble and take a few quick steps to recover my balance. I hear my ragged breath as I reach the path leading to Gary's section, his grass. I raise my forearm to shade my eyes as I look down the hill and count the granite headstones that have arrived since his was placed almost a month ago. I count twenty-two. I try to multiply four sections times twenty-two new stones, but I stop at four times twenty. Today I'm worn out by the numbers.

I kneel and dust dry grass clippings from the sun-warmed granite marker. I sit on the grass between Gary Andrew Masters and James Lee Storey. I am weeping, but the tears feel warm and sweet on my face. I mutter words to Gary, mother-to-son words that hold more memory than meaning, more air and light than sound or image. There are no years now: no days, no time. "Remember when we . . . ?" I am laughing but I cannot recall what has brought my laughter. "Wait! You forgot your books," I call. "There, there," I whisper. "It's just a dream."

I stand, then look again at the headstone next to Gary's. I kneel once more and run my hands across the letters carved on that other woman's son's grave, brush the grass and petals away as tenderly as I would brush the hair from his forehead. Then I walk away.

2

On the road near Towson, Maryland, a sun-baked flagman waves me down with an orange and black sign: S L O W. My first, irrational, hopeful reaction is to think that Andrew has called out a search for me. But the flagman directs me to a narrow column of cars heading north. I see a sign saying something about road construction on a new five-mile section of the Beltway. Maybe it said ten miles. Single-lane traffic, anyway. Okay by me. On the radio the 5th Dimension sings a song I haven't heard before: "One less phone to answer. One less egg to fry. . . ." I turn up the volume, try to sing along, learn these new lyrics, and conclude, like the abandoned lover in the song, that less is really not more.

The swirl of activity diverts me. I watch as great mounds of earth, future multilane highways, are sculpted onto this once green, tree-dotted landscape. Dump trucks three times the size of my car appear as ants offering their meager loads of dirt to even larger orange-yellow earth-movers that in turn appear as toys on the mountainous slopes. A driver in a business suit slips his Jaguar in ahead of me. I marvel at his impatience, at his having a place he feels he has to reach. I glance at my Trip-Tiks, only slightly reassured that I have a destination.

Suddenly a gust of wind sends red dirt swirling from the top of a loaded dump truck rumbling along the road shoulder. I see the cloud coming and quickly roll up the window, but I feel the dirt settle in my mouth and on my skin. The next thing I know, the familiar helicopter is landing in the red dust-cloud and I am shaking, gasping for breath, rubbing at my skin, my tongue. I hold onto the steering wheel and weep. Forget the fucking dead? Not when the wind runs sniper operations.

The road construction ends, double-lane traffic resumes. I follow the signs to Columbus, Ohio, the first stop on my itinerary, but I have the dawning sensation that the time since Gary's death—yesterday, this morning, all of it—lies on my skin, a greasy film that won't wash off. My eyes go wide with the fear; I drive hunched over, bug-eyed, watchful.

I reach Columbus by early evening. I sigh, I yawn, I stretch, not in an effort to relax but to make more room. For something else. Anything else. My body, bloated with memory, recalls what my mind tries to forget. I want to move out of this body, leave behind this cellular disturbance that is my life. I ache.

After dinner, reluctant to go into the room just yet, I sit on the curb at the edge of the Ramada Inn parking lot. The sun is setting behind a hill overgrown with heather and Queen Anne's lace. The sky is going hazy and gray, permitting only thin strands of reddish orange to emerge at the horizon.

Wait a minute, I think suddenly. I wanted more! What happened?

It's a difficult question, what happened.

"Accidents happen," I tell the cars in the Ramada Inn parking lot in Columbus, Ohio. Sad, sweet accidents like babies, ugly ones like war. But how could *this* have happened, two accidents, Gary's birth and now his death? Weeds scratch against my legs as I walk into the field, the question insinuating itself with an obscene will of its own. "What happened?"

I have always asked questions. Virginia, my mother, claims I asked too many as a girl. Once I asked her, "What is time?" "Oh, Roberta," she sighed, placing her hands on her round hips. "You ask such difficult questions." "But what is it, Mother?" I persisted. "What is time?" "Time is like the wind," my mother finally said. "We can't see it but it's always moving." Like most of the information I received from my mother, I have found her answer to be generally true, as far as it goes, but definitely lacking in specifics. Something in my body eases as I think of Virginia: that memory of looking up at her, asking for answers, and she finally tucking a long strand of my wiry red hair behind my ear and saying, "Go along, now."

I turn, as if inviting my mother to join me. If I were traveling with her on this trip we would already have walked through the field and over the hilltop. She would have discussed the way blooming things sometimes give off their richest perfume "when the radiant earth and the gathering moisture come together." I enjoy the distraction of noting her words, heard so often that they've become my own, familiar and known. Hers, mine. Past, present. Marriage, babies. Youth, age. Life, death. Everything happening in the right order. But whatever the direction of Virginia's nature commentary, I would stop her in mid-sentence if she were here and ask the same question: What is time? Same question, but maybe different phrasing: What happened? It is not as if I haven't asked these questions before.

"What happened?" I say again, walking back toward the parking lot. I turn to see the sky now giving up its last glow of light. I do the only thing that has felt good all day. I get lost in time, whatever it is, noting that in September of 1950 something *did* happen.

This is what I remember:

In September of 1950 the band at the Freshman Orientation Mixer Dance at West Virginia Wesleyan College plays a song made popular by Faron Young: "I wanna live fast, love hard, die young/And leave a beautiful memory . . ." Beneath a white pointelle sweater tossed across my shoulders and a pink, peasant-top sundress, I wear the Merry Widow my mother has insisted no young woman should be without. My breasts resemble the parallel prows of two cruising battleships. Not everyone in the gymnasium stares at my bulging and pointed breasts—I just imagine that. But during the steel-guitar solo, the part where the lyrics would be, "I wanna leave a lot of happy women/Thinking pretty thoughts of me . . ." there is an extra slide on the strings when Andrew Masters looks up and sees me standing by the bleachers near the stage. In the months that follow, we begin walking from classes together. We go to a football game. We almost hyperventilate on the steps of Agnes Howard Hall. We steam up the car windows, parked behind the snowbanks near Maggie's Cafe after my weekend waitress job. That's when he tells me that the corset did not cause his momentary lapse on the steel guitar, it was the drawstring on my peasant-girl blouse and the thought of untying the bow . . .

* * *

I am chilled by the pleasure these recollections are giving me. I resist their pleasure, partly because I know I didn't ask Andrew the right questions, or enough of them, or at the right time. And I have other reasons to resist: My son is dead. I have left my husband. I'm afraid of everything, including pleasure. I stand here shivering in the Ramada Inn parking lot. I walk to the car, holding myself in my arms. I take a sweater from the trunk and slip it on.

I have asked Andrew plenty of questions, mainly, Why? I know what he did *not* tell me in the fall of 1950, nor in the winter or spring of 1951—not until 1967, when we were at war in our bedroom and I asked him yet another question.

"Why did you want me in the first place?"

"I think the drawstring on your sundress connected with my peasant-girl fantasy," he tells me as we lie there in the dark. "My mother read *Heidi* to me and my sister."

"Oh, right," I say. "That explains everything."

"Actually, it was more like a peasant girl–goat herder–soldier fantasy."

"What about the soldier part of your 'affliction'?" I ask.

"That started after the war in Europe ended and I read about American GI's marrying French peasant girls. Just seeing that RKO newsreel when the Yanks marched through the streets of Paris . . ."

He stops to recall for me his hometown of Scranton, Pennsylvania, describing in minute detail the movie theater, the main street, his car, while I wait for information. "The soldiers were covered with flowers thrown from windows. And women, girls really, were running alongside them and they wore these drawstring blouses."

The newsreel left him with an erection that, as he puts it, "defied ordinary solutions." The trumpets sounded, the excited, patriotic voice announced THE NEWS OF THE WORLD. "You must have seen that newsreel, Roberta," Andrew says, squirming suspiciously on his side of the bed. "That French girl runs up to an American soldier and pulls his face down to hers and . . ."

My room at the Ramada Inn welcomes me with an Arctic blast. On the wall beside the light switch is a sticker showing a polar bear sitting on melting blue ice cubes. I shut off the air conditioner and turn on the shower, contemplating, as I undress, the dogged persistence of memory and the unreliability of human perception: the higher the retention rate, the greater the chance for error. I conclude that a person in my state of mind should not be allowed to consider such a paradox. But I step into the shower, the water too hot, the soap too small, the 1967 Bedroom War too near the front of my mind.

Andrew asked me that night in 1967 why I came to college in Buckhannon, West Virginia, in the first place. I came to the little Methodist college for a lot of reasons. I won a scholarship, and in a speech to the Rotary Club at the White Horse Restaurant in Potsdam, New York, I said, "I want to learn as much as I can, as quickly as I can. I want to learn about God and man and. . . ."

I groan and bend to pick up the soap for the third time. "What a speech," I say.

I came to West Virginia Wesleyan to study Civil War history with the eminent Dr. Walter Glackin. I came to please my mother who had said, "The church school is a nice idea . . . but in West Virginia?"

Implicit in Andrew's question was another, more pertinent issue: How could I, how dare I have come into his life? I came to the Appalachian hills under false pretenses. I told him so in 1967.

This is what I remember:

"I think it all started in 1946, Andrew," I say, my head propped, my elbow jabbing into his pillow. "I was fourteen. We were visiting my uncle Eugene in Kentucky. On our way home we stopped for lunch at a white frame building with a sign out front that read 'Aunt Mae's Diner.' We were in West Virginia by then."

Ever impatient with my digressions but always indulgent of his own, Andrew asks, "What does your Uncle Eugene in Kentucky have to do with anything?"

"I was catching fireflies with my cousins next to the back porch when we heard my uncle telling jokes about traveling salesmen and farmers' daughters, that's what!"

"I just asked," he says, momentarily willing to wait.

"When I got out of the car, the air tasted bitter," I say. "I imagined a coal mine nearby. I stood around after my parents had gone up the steps, waiting to see if a black-faced miner with a light on his helmet and a silver lunch pail in his hand would come walking out of the forest. Green covered everything," I tell him. "Like it was poised for a takeover if Aunt Mae ever got careless about chopping saplings out of her parking lot.

"Three girls came walking up the road to my right. Barefoot. Their hair was thin, so thin I saw sunlight dappled by the trees shine through it. They were laughing, holding hands as they walked. I guess I was dazed by the sight of them. Mom called to me, but I ignored her and she finally went inside. Then two boys carrying fishing poles and tackle boxes appeared from the other direction. The road just wound away behind them. It was strange, almost mystical."

"Come *on,* Roberta," Andrew says.

"Then the boys called out to the girls. I felt invisible, leaning against the fender of our new green postwar Packard. Watching, listening. 'Hey, Silva Lee,' one of the boys shouted. 'I heard tell you was out at Drunkard's Roost last night. With Eddie Prater, no less." I sit up. I imitate those easy, drawling syllables: "Sil-va Luh-ee."

Andrew laughs.

"So they met in front of the diner, and the girl who was Silva Lee of Drunkard's Roost fame put her hands on her hips, planted her dusty feet on the black soil, swayed her body defiantly and joyfully, and said, 'Cain't believe everything you hear, John.' The two younger girls twittered around her like moths around a porch lamp. He set down his fishing pole and tackle box. He grabbed her arm. . . ."

Andrew turns his head, ever so slightly, and raises an eyebrow. I raise my eyebrow right back at him in the way a child sticks out her tongue. I know he's listening more carefully; there may be evidence for his side in his war on my ever-increasing sexual inhibitions. "He grabbed her arm," I say again. "Gently," I say. "Because she didn't resist."

Andrew is staring at me. I stare back.

"He was a car-length away from me then."

Andrew is hoping to hear more. He raises up eagerly on his elbow, expecting a confession I've never made before. I consider telling him that I sneaked off with the boy and became pregnant and had to be sent away to my Aunt Caroline's, but I know he'd never believe it anyway.

"Then the boy noticed me," I say. "His eyes seemed to widen at the outer edges. He looked at me over the girl's shoulder. He jerked her arm, but he kept on looking at me. I would have fallen over without my thick ankles and chunky knees holding me up. I leaned a little more on the car. He looked at my eyes, then lowered to my mouth, my shoulders, my breasts, and kept on staring."

I am burrowing under the sheet to cover myself from Andrew's eyes. He knows it.

"It seemed like his chest rose and fell in that moment. And I felt a bursting cluster of sensations." I think a moment for an analogy, but there really isn't one. "My lips felt puffy; I put my fingers to my lips. My abdomen contracted . . . *you* know. I turned and walked toward the diner and up the steps. I was never the same after that."

Andrew's eyes are half open.

"My underpants were damp, and I knew that was related to the eyes of the boy. I knew it."

Whether he knows it or not, Andrew has the answer to his question: I chose West Virginia Wesleyan College because the possibility existed that farmers' daughters, even upstate New York pharmacists' daughters, and coal miners' sons might meet on cinder roads and share clusters of sensation.

"Jesus," Andrew says, awake again.

"I was a nerve ending," I say. "Roberta Patterson, fourteen in 1946 or eighteen in 1950, was a walking nerve ending. A ganglion on legs. My possibilities were seriously limited."

We throw back our heads and laugh.

"And *you* offered to walk me back to my dorm after the Freshman Orientation Mixer Dance!"

He'd been appealing to me. Tall. Wiry. Sandy-haired. His deep voice held a mixture of the sandpaper rasp in some downtown cab driver's throat and the sweet rumble of Johnny Cash. His face seemed even then kind of thin, weasel-like. But my two friends just twittered and stood back as he approached. And his chest rose and fell. I put my hands on my hips, swayed neither joyfully nor defiantly, and said, "Okay."

"My pants were damp before you opened the gym door, put your hand on the back of my neck, and said, 'What's your major?' "

Remembering, he says, "You were *always* wet. . . ." He tries to touch me. I push him away.

"What did *I* know? Nothing," I say, answering my own question.

"Jesus," Andrew says.

We lie in silence for a long time, stunned by our respective revelations, commenting into our pillows, flopping around on the bed. "A peasant girl and a coal miner's son," Andrew says, pulling me against him so that my head is on his shoulder and my breasts press against his side.

"She gets pregnant, natural as fallin' off a log," I say, vicious in my sarcasm and regret.

We look at each other, one night in the many nights of our 1967 Bedroom War, and shake our heads. "My God," we say, each of us, and negotiate a temporary truce . . .

I finish my shower at the Ramada Inn, vowing to buy a family-size soap first thing in the morning. As I pull on my nightgown, I realize my skin is red and mottled. How long was I in the shower? I consider checking my travel clock, but I don't have the energy to dig it out of my suitcase. I turn out the light and crawl beneath the stiffly clean motel sheets. I sit up suddenly with the thought that I haven't even called Andrew. But as I lie back and think about picking up the telephone to call him, I fall into a fitful sleep.

I dream of a woman who turns into a girl. The girl finds a tiny ship on the seashore. She carries the ship, a gray plastic model rough with glue at its seams, into a beach cottage. She sets it on a wooden table. Then the table turns to crashing ocean waves and the tiny ship becomes a great troop carrier like the ones that transported soldiers to Europe in the only war the girl seems to know about. Suddenly the girl in the dream is inside the quarters of the ship, running from bunk to bunk, where old men older than her grandfather and young men younger than her cousins lie sleeping. "Mayday!" the girl shouts. "Mayday! Mayday!" Then the ship is empty and only one sailor is left, a boy who sleeps in a bunk far off in a corner.

The dream comes toward morning. I know this because I am

awake enough to want to change it around. I try to coax the girl out of the ship. The boy sleeps, as Gary often did, on his belly under the covers with only his tousled hair and reaching hand visible at the head of the bed. "Who is he?" I ask. "Who is he?" the girl echoes back. But I am awake by then, and I'm not a girl. I know who he is, and I know why he doesn't wake up.

I get out of bed and I cannot find the Trip-Tiks. I look in the AAA shopping bag. I search the room in a panic, pulling the sheets and blankets from the bed and dumping the suitcase on the floor before I discover them in the bathroom, slightly damp, beneath the clothes I was wearing yesterday. I cannot understand how the Trip-Tiks got there, but I carefully return them to my purse and zip it. I smash all my clothes back into the suitcase and take it to the chair by the front door. I place the shopping bag on top of the suitcase and put my purse beside the suitcase. Keeping my eye on the whole pile, I get dressed and leave too early to take advantage of the free continental breakfast promised by the Auto Club and the Ramada Inn.

3

Early on, well before seven, eating breakfast at a truck stop near the Ohio-Indiana border, I read the Illinois Scenic Guide. The Guide describes the state of Illinois as "rolling to level farmland." Suddenly I'm tangled up in mental gymnastics, examining the transition that the mind must make from "real" land to a map showing an oblong shape on a flat piece of paper. It's too early in the morning for this, but I keep arguing with myself. What should I believe about Illinois? Certainly not my own eyes. My eyes are going bad. When I read maps I must hold them right up to my eyes; distant road signs are a blur until I'm already too close to slow down or make turns. But being nearsighted or farsighted isn't the half of it. Finally I assign my own clinical classification. I call it Perception Distortion Syndrome. PDS.

On my way through Indiana, I stop at several greenish-bronze historical markers, at a weed-infested battlefield of the French and Indian War, at a tidy farmhouse museum, all of them recommended by AAA. I keep to the estimated driving time on my typed itinerary. I slow down a bit when it seems I am running ahead of schedule and might arrive early for the discount dinner at the combination restaurant/Motel 6 in Bloomington. This timeliness has nothing to do with any efficiency in my driving. It's just that everywhere I've stopped, other than restrooms, I have stayed in the car. I cannot trust myself in the world outside my windshield. Locked in the car, careening through space, I have decided to just keep moving and follow directions. Besides, I tell myself as I drive along, I was a docent at the Smithsonian for years. "Why tramp through another museum?" I say aloud.

Depressed or perverse or both, I am making this strategy of

noninvolvement difficult for myself. Out of the entire Illinois Scenic Guide I read in the morning, I retain only one statistic: Ten thousand Indian burial mounds exist in the state of Illinois. I stop for lunch, open the Central States map, and, morbidly clairvoyant, locate a site close to Bloomington—only slightly out of my way—called the Dickson Mounds.

And I'm having trouble with statistics. All day, radio newscasters chatter in my ears, reading body counts from Vietnam on the hour. I turn them off before they recite their numbers because I already know the numbers. Gary was one of the numbers. My mind can't accommodate ten thousand burial mounds. I keep seeing him lying beneath them.

The car finds its way to the Dickson Mounds almost on its own, but driving there is one thing—getting out and walking among the dead is another. I stay in the car, muttering that the guides in the museum could not tell me much I don't already know. Mound builders come in two groups—tomb builders and temple builders. From what I can see of the grassy shapes rising and receding on the level landscape, I have come upon the first variety.

Gary made salt maps when he was little. For a moment I think of Illinois as a salt map on a plywood slab, but ten thousand bumps in varying shapes and sizes refuse to take form. Then the image of an oblong shape on a flat piece of paper returns, this one with countless ink-drawn curves darkening its surface. I see the map; I see Illinois and those dark curves. The image, though allowing me to successfully form the concept of ten thousand burial mounds, severely darkens my thoughts. I consider getting out of the car, but my legs are unwilling to move.

Not very long ago, just months ago—while reading descriptions in Gary's letters, or listening to his tapes from Vietnam, or squinting at photographs he had sent—I struggled to compare the real thing to paper maps I had of Vietnam. Now, when I want to make the comparisons again, I've left the pictures and letters and tapes back home. Damn! What made me think I should leave those tapes with Andrew? As if reality matters with PDS. The radio's off, but the car is filled with voices anyway. I am hearing things, and this is what I hear:

"Hi, Dad. Hi, Mom."

Gary's deep but ever-young voice speaks. He is always doing fine on the tapes. His unit is staying near a firebase and going out on night patrols but always doing fine. The countryside around Pleiku can be beautiful and rolling, and he often thinks of the hills around Manassas when he sees it early in the morning.

"I think about that trip we took with Gramps and Gran Patterson, Mom. Remember?"

His scratchy voice tears at me here in the car.

"Like Civil War battlefields, you know?"

Oh, God, yes, I know.

He makes intelligent comparisons between the two—hills where maples, birches, elms, and grasses are replaced by terraced rice paddies, green in the spring. Then he talks about reddish brown clay that won't wash off his skin; he seems to grind his teeth in the telling, as if he might start to cry. He writes about slogging through rain-soaked, washed-out roads. He talks about the smell of oiled gunmetal and leather and blood and how it's everywhere there at the War. The comparisons to home fall apart, stretched too far. He changes the subject. I am always relieved when he changes the subject.

"The only thing we talk about much is just coming home. And it's odd, Mom, but when somebody does go home, and we get a replacement . . ."

I'm losing the connection. I can't hear him. I have to cradle myself in my arms to hold back my own moaning voice until his voice returns. I rock, one arm at my waist, one hand on my mouth. It's as if someone is out there in the mounds with a landmover, excavating, digging up the mounds, and from every excavation voices are emerging. His voice begins again:

"We get a replacement and the first thing we ask the Green Bean is why he's here. I don't know why, but his first answer is always a lie. Mine was too. Funny, huh? Well, gotta go."

It was the last tape. I can hear it without a recorder. I played it for the first month or so, hunting for clues in Gary's voice, evidence of blame.

If his first answer was a lie, I ask myself, what was the truth? How could those soldiers inflict such torture on one another as to ask, Why are you here? It compares in its lunacy with my questions: What is time? What happened? Why? Why? Why?

What lie did Gary make up when he first walked on Asian soil, soil that I know was paper for him as much as the state of Illinois is for me? He was just eighteen. His voice was deep and young, his cheeks still thinly whiskered like a woman's leg. His body was so newly come to manhood that the muscles across his abdomen seemed stretched there like bands of sculptor's clay, having not yet accumulated the insulating layer of fat that would have blended them with the rest. He couldn't have known why he was there, I tell myself again and again.

I resist giving a name, clinical or descriptive, to what I am feeling right now. An article I read recommended the naming of feelings, but I doubt the author realized what she was saying. What I feel when I think of why he was there is the sensation of insects crawling on my skin, into my ears, my mouth, every opening of my body, insects that would make a crunching sound if stepped on. But the feeling does have a name. Shame. I am feeling shame.

I feel the urge to slump down in the seat, to hide from the sound of a sarcastic and blaming voice that plays on in my head, asking me, *telling* me why he was there. It's *my* voice, the ugly, disembodied one. I know it well:

> *He can't very well tell the soldiers about his parents, now can he? the voice asks. When he was fourteen, his father moved out of the house to live with a nurse he had met at the Walter Reed Bar and Lounge, didn't he?*

"Dad's shacked up, right?" Gary's changing, fourteen-year-old voice echoes.

"It wasn't that simple," I say to the hot air near Bloomington, Illinois. "Andrew was looking for what he couldn't find with me and . . . Wait just a minute!"

What am I doing, defending against rumors in my own mind?

In the car's humid interior, the silence is accusatory. I roll down the window. The air is hotter outside than in; a man and woman are walking by, their infant child curled in a pouch on the father's chest. I have no choice. I roll up the window. I go on with my defense, saying to some unknown judge, "This is just how *I* remember it, but. . . ."

In the first month or two after Andrew moves in with the nurse, Gary seems to straighten up. School is back in session after the Christmas vacation. He stays home more in the evenings. I receive fewer truancy calls from the school. "You okay, Mom?" he frequently asks. "Let's get dinner started," he says, falsely cheerful, as I sit like a corpse on the sofa, staring at the television news. Then one afternoon—a few weeks after Andrew joined us for Gary's fifteenth birthday—I come home from the museum. . . .

Gary's mother comes home from her day at the museum to find Gary incoherent, on mescaline, when he has just turned fifteen, doesn't she?

"Wha'th'fuck, Mom?"
I know that voice.
"Wha'th'fuck, Mom. Nothin' worry 'bout me, Mom."

And what does his mother do? She throws her hands in the air, doesn't she?

That's not true! I tried all kinds of things. Drugs are everywhere. And the schools . . . smoking lounges in the schools . . .

Then his loving parents reconcile after six months, to pull together again, don't they?

I call Andrew to tell him about finding Gary slobbering on the sofa. He comes right over. At first we see ourselves as aligned against the common enemy of our child: drugs. Then our reconciliation gets more complicated: "June says it can't work for her and me anyway. She says I have too much 'unfinished business.' " "What do you say?" I ask. "She's right," he says, accepting the nurse's diagnosis with a self-conscious shrug of his shoulders, a lowering of his eyes.

"For Gary's sake," the parents say. They get back together for Gary's sake, but Gary never knows the real reason his father came home, does he? No one ever sits down and tells him.

It never occurs to us to talk to Gary about it. We think we've learned some things, both of us. We want to try. I mean, Gary knows what's going on. He knows the nurse is out of the picture by then. He knows his father is home again.

"We thought that was enough, to be home," I say.

But what about the Air Force boss? The boss really kicks *him home, doesn't he?*

Andrew's boss, Jack Hunley, despises Andrew for playing in a country-western band. Country-western is bad enough—Jack likes music from the swing era—but in a bar! And he knows Andrew is living with a woman other than his wife. Jack is a former Air Force colonel and a Born Again. As Andrew puts it, "He's born again as both a Christian and a civil servant." Off the record, behind a closed door, the double-dipper boss tells him, "You might as well go full-time with your hick band, Masters. You come in late with that band as an excuse, you commit your moral indiscretions, I'll ride your ass till you wish you'd never been born." Andrew is struggling with the dissatisfactions of our marriage, and his infidelity and guilt, and his terrible boredom with that dismal but well-paying job, and it seems Gary won't understand or even need to know and . . .

Mother retreats to the home trenches, doesn't she? Concerned as she is for her son on drugs and concerned, as she puts it, "For my very life!"

The world was going up in smoke . . .

Gary's mother can hardly make her way to the museum through those crowds of protesting people, can she?

I was barely able to get off the bus when Johnson decided to bomb Tonkin and people were in the streets . . .

People who carry signs that read MOTHERS FOR PEACE? *Gary is a convenient escape, isn't he?*

There was so much Andrew and I didn't know . . .
WHY WAS HE THERE?

Isn't it noble?

"What a mother," I say, leaning my head on the steering wheel.

Isn't it noble, the voice goes on, *that Gary's mother stops going to the museum in order to watch over her son? Her son is almost never home, of course, by then dealing drugs, not using them . . .*

He didn't want to worry me, that's what he told me. He wasn't addicted. No heroin. No LSD. We still cared about each other. He didn't want me to worry about him getting hurt, so he stopped using . . .

But keeps dealing . . .

Yes, kept dealing, almost got arrested . . .

Which his mother knows . . .

I knew. I begged him to stop. I took him to a counselor. I tried to get Andrew to come too . . .

"Gary Andrew Masters!" I say it loud, shocked at the strength of my voice. "Why were you there?"

WHY WAS HE THERE?

Another voice begins. I strain to listen . . .

"Mrs. Masters, I have four hours till my flight to Philly."

On a Sunday afternoon Sergeant Peter L. Monroe calls us from Andrews Air Force Base. Only weeks after Gary is killed his first sergeant is on the way home from Vietnam. I pick him up in a cold, early-summer rain and bring him to the house. We talk over a hastily prepared supper of cold cuts and day-old chocolate cake.

"My husband feels Gary wasn't telling us certain things," I say. "He feels . . ."

Andrew chops the air with his hand, cutting me off. *"I'll* tell him what I feel, Roberta." He turns to the sergeant. "I think the protests over here must have disturbed him more than he let on."

I watch Sergeant Pete Monroe's face as he listens to us, his expression changing from painful distress when I mention "certain things" to a look of relief when Andrew mentions the protests.

"Actually," he says, "Gary was okay about the demonstrations, Mr. Masters. The rest of us were so fucking pissed—excuse me—and he wasn't. He said he just came to the War so he could grow up. This is how he said it: 'So I could grow up in peace and quiet!' We all laughed. We'd say that some nights, when it was, you know, bad. We'd say, 'How's this for peace and quiet, Masters?' But we knew what he meant. War over there, problems here, take your pick." Pete shakes his head and laughs sadly. Andrew and I offer weak, gray smiles.

I sigh, lean back in the seat.

He wanted to grow up. Was that Gary's answer? And was it the first answer, the lie, or the second answer, the truth? At least Sergeant Peter Monroe gave me something to hold on to. In February, when he first arrived in Vietnam, if Gary didn't say he was saving the world for his family, the family that was letting the home fires burn to ash, at least he was there because he wanted to grow up.

> *What about later? Does he whisper some other answer to a medic? At the hour of his death on May 20th does he whisper that he would not have even been there if only his mother had resisted. . . .*

If only I hadn't relented to his pressure. . . .

"Come on, *Mom,"* Gary says. We sit out on the screened porch, talking for hours, him in those slouchy clothes with so many pockets everywhere, his hair long and seldom washed. I get so disgusted with him, telling him to spend his time doing homework and reading instead of trying to talk me into signing a paper for him to join the army. And then he looks up, clear brown eyes, and smiles at me. "Come on, *Mom,"* he says.

If only . . . if only I hadn't signed a paper at the end of his junior year of high school giving the army permission to sign him up and haul him away. Would he have been there?

WHY WAS HE THERE?

These questions peel off my mind like layers of damaged skin. How many will I peel until I'm raw or just disappear?

Gary wanted to become a man. But becoming a man could not have looked very appealing to him, judging by his father's example. I've always felt that when Andrew saw Gary entering puberty he performed some panicky rite of passage, taking up with that nurse, blaming me for my inhibitions about life in the bedroom. Call it the Father-of-the-Son-Becoming-a-Man rite. Make it a memorial of sorts for the Once-Young Mother of the Boy. Father had stopped looking at Mother, and she became shrill of voice: "Just go."

JUST GO!

I hold my hands over my ears. I want to hide from this echo of my voice.

Gary is standing at the living-room window, his bags packed, a friend waiting at the curb to drive him to the airport. He wears khaki. His cloth hat is tucked precisely into his waistband; his jacket is called a blouse. These grooming secrets separate us. His long hair is now shorn, and the skin on the back of his neck is as soft as a child's—this much I know because I touch, quickly, before he pulls away. He is hesitating because we have yet to say good-bye, and because Andrew has gone on to work rather than face this moment.

"Just go," I say. "Your father will never deal with this, any of this. . . .

"Just go," I say again, softer this time, looking at him from behind bruiselike circles beneath my eyes and a ripple of pain that I feel cross my face and distort my mouth. We remember then, mother and son, all the days we have bumped against each other in that house, all the museums we have rattled around in, all the secret wishes, as he has grown older, to crawl back together to our cave. And instead of holding out my arms to him, and instead of him taking my bruised-looking face in his now angular man's hands, we stand facing each other. We stare,

mute, blinking our identical brown eyes. His deep voice hits a low note, then a high: "Well. See ya, Mom."

Why was he there? My God, what a question.

I roll down the window, squinting my swollen eyes into the late, slanting sun. Cooler air moves into the car. Like walking a dog on a leash, I let my mind outside.

The mounds of grass-covered earth have taken on a fuzzy, blanketlike appearance in the time I've been sitting here. I can't help but appreciate what must have been the reasoning of those prehistoric, worldly wise mound builders. "Gee, this flat valley gets boring," they must have said, waking to another day of life. So I guess they pulled blankets of earth over their dead, transforming the state of Illinois for themselves and everyone who has come afterward. The mounds are blankets under which their countless and blessed dead are resting. Sometimes maybe it's better not to count the losses.

Ten thousand Indian burial mounds. I would have found them by instinct, even without a guidebook.

It's almost sunset and I'm still locked in the car. Exhausted by voices.

Leaving the Dickson Mounds, I pick up speed. Hungry, thirsty, eager to move, I want out of the car. As soon as I find the Motel 6 in Bloomington, I jump out, stretch, hop back in to shut off the engine. "Whew."

I head straight for the restrooms in the restaurant next door. Then I wolf down the discount fish fry and salad just before the kitchen closes. I taste the food; I smell it; I feel it move into my body, taking up space. I feel anchored, still held by gravity, even if I'm not in the car. I walk to my room, reassured by the songs of truck tires on the highway and crickets in the grass. I take off my shoes and stand for a moment in the grass, touching ground.

Once in the room, wary of the voices echoing in my mind all afternoon, I avoid going to bed. I study Chicago, Illinois, and Superior, Wisconsin, on the maps, figuring tomorrow's route, dozing as the television flickers in black and white. Dick Cavett smiles ironically at his viewing audience as the credits scroll onto the screen, having just been informed by guest John Updike that sexual freedom, beyond any described in his early novels, will increase in the next decade.

I get up from the chair I've been sitting in. I stare back at Cavett, waiting for him to issue some kind of disclaimer: "Don't listen to Mr. Updike. He's talking about passion, and we all know what that can do." Something! But Cavett, shrugging off any personal responsibility to his viewers, just says good night. It's midnight.

I tuck my Trip-Tiks into my purse and step out of the clothes I've been in all day. I suds my bra and panties in the bathroom sink. More than a little bit troubled by Updike's prediction of sexual abandon, I am nonetheless *pleasantly* troubled.

I look at myself in the mirror: What if I were beginning now? Gary would never have been here at all if I were starting now. But there are reasons why he was there, in 'Nam. And here, in this world. And they all begin with me. Sometimes these threads of connection to Gary feel like a tangle to be avoided, other times so silky and fine . . .

I think about telling myself a story I've heard before. The good part of the story, that is. As the French say, all beginnings are good and beautiful. One thing leads to another, though. That's the thing about stories.

"Once upon a time," I say, sassy and sultry. The story hums like music, and my body, having a memory of its own, begins to dance away, away from the voices that came out of the mounds.

"Not long after West Virginia and Aunt Mae's Diner and the coal miner's son," I add, placing the fable more firmly in time. I fill the tub. I place one foot in the water, testing.

Is there someone to whom a person can go to apologize for her inappropriate responses to her life? To her grief? Maybe there are bereavement lessons. The Methodists I grew up with would not want to hear this story. Catholics at least have priests, but strings are attached there, too. Oh, well, no stopping now. I lower myself into the water.

"Once upon a time . . ."—and so the story goes.

At fifteen I am sometimes Robbie, sometimes Bobbie, but usually plain Roberta, Seductress of the Mirror. I spend long hours behind the bathroom door. Perched on the vanity, my feet in the sink, I talk to someone in the mirror. I suspect, at first, that he is John the Coal Miner's Son, but in time someone nameless becomes my prey. Frequently I whisper the phrase "Big Boy," something I saw on a Vargas calendar at a truck stop during the Aunt Mae's Diner trip. "Hi, Big Boy," the caption beneath the velvety-lavender woman read.

I look at my breasts, squeeze them to feel the involuntary but welcome squeeze in my abdomen. I try to comprehend their sudden eruption—startling, their fullness—bursting, their softness—velvet.

"Hi, Big Boy," I say to my mirror, avoiding as much as possible my freckled face, my mouth that puckers over large but not protruding front teeth, my eyes, dark and round and brown and fringed by pale lashes. No seductress ever looked like a friendly chipmunk. Whichever way I arrange my face, the effect is wrong. Cute or comic. Until one day, when I've pulled at my mouth so much that my lips are dry, I lick my lips: Comic and cute my tongue is not. "Here I am," the tongue-flicker tells the phantom. "You'd really like these," I whisper to the mirror. "Give it to me, Big Boy."

"That girl had such power!" I say. I sink lower in the Motel 6 tub. The water rises to my chin. "Was I really that girl?"

The summer after Aunt Mae's Diner I care for a neighbor's new baby. Encouraged by my mother, Virginia, I appear each morning at the Parkhurst's front door with the plea, "Can I help with the baby?" Mrs. Parkhurst allows me to bathe baby Sarah, change her diapers, and take her for rides in the carriage. The only thing I cannot do is feed her, for Sarah is nursing. When I bring Sarah in from a morning walk, Mrs. Parkhurst takes the baby from the carriage and thanks me for all my help. We change the diaper and Mrs. Parkhurst settles into the rocking chair in the nursery. The shades are always pulled by then—it is the baby's nap time. Pop. The engorged breast springs from the flap as Mrs. Parkhurst proffers milk, and the blissfully overwhelmed Sarah suckles. Mrs. Parkhurst nods her smiling dismissal to me.

In August of that summer, when mother and child have begun to adjust to their lives together, Virginia Patterson has coffee for Mrs. Parkhurst in the mornings. She decides on such a morning that lunch and shopping in town will be good for her young neighbor's morale. I can, of course, handle things at home.

So it is on an August afternoon, having just brought baby Sarah in from a carriage ride, having just taken a bottle from the refrigerator and wondered about the breast pump that has extracted all that milk, having just heated the bottle on the stove, that I sit down in the rocking chair. Sarah is pushing her tongue in and out through her lips; a look of pleasant anticipation widens her still-new blue-cast eyes. Seized by curiosity, I yank my blouse from the waistband of my skirt. I pull my brassiere above my breast on one side. It cuts me painfully under my arm, but I offer myself, blue-veined and unnaturally distended, to the infant's waiting mouth.

The infant howls. "Come on, Sarah," I whisper soothingly. "It's all right." But it is not all right. Sarah knows it; that's obvious from the way she rolls her head back and forth, a contorted expression of extreme distaste on her face. Rejected, I hurriedly rearrange my clothing. Sarah attaches her mouth to the rubber nipple and, with only an occasional irregular sigh, begins to drink not mine but her mother's milk. The baby rolls her eyes from my face (who can trust me again?) to the light at the window, scratching at my side with the fingers of one hand. Her tiny chest rises and falls in contentment; the sun makes silhouettes of leaves on the vanilla-colored shade at the window; the rocking chair sings a soft chant as its runners bump quietly over the rug. The baby sleeps. I rock. Then, eerily, I sense someone in the room and look up. Mr. Parkhurst stands in the doorway. He is planted on his feet, not leaning forward the way a person would be if he were just walking by a room. I watch him loosen his tie and unbutton his collar.

"I came home," he says stupidly. "I've got the flu or something." He flaps his arms at his sides, smiling lopsidedly as he pats his stomach. I notice that he actually looks kind of boyish when his hair is mussed this way, not slicked back and parted. I am no longer comfortable sitting in the rocking chair.

I carefully lay the baby in the crib and tiptoe into the hall. I hand Mr. Parkhurst the almost-empty bottle. "The baby will sleep for another hour or so," I tell Mr. Parkhurst.

He nods. "She'll be fine, Roberta. Thanks." And in spite of his sick belly, Mr. Parkhurst's chest rises and falls when he chances a weak and wily glance at my rumpled blouse.

The milk. The warm, moist air in the darkened room. It is all too much for the Seductress of the Mirror, bombarded by this onslaught of sensations. With the untucked flap of my blouse serving as a reminder, I run all the way home, past two brick houses, three maple trees, one last driveway, and home.

The house is silent when I walk in. No one is home. I pull the draperies, lock the doors. No one is home.

I go upstairs to the bathroom and start the water for my bath. I remove my skirt, my soggy little undies, my sweaty roll-up-sleeve blouse. I help myself out of the confining harness that keeps my big, bouncy baubles from the world. I parade myself through the dim, cool house: blushing brazenly before my father's armoire, shocking the historic andirons before the fireplace, scandalizing my mother's Big Red Apple of a cookie jar. The house is in the hands of a craven Shameless Hussy.

I lock the bathroom door. I check it again: locked. I pose before the mirror, my long arms in the air as water roars from the nearby Fountain of Evil. Afraid the tub will run over, I pull the drain plug; the water rushes out, the fountain continues its roar, pulsating its Eternal Wickedness as I lie back in the water, push my breasts together, and cry out in total bewilderment, "Give it to me, Big Boy Parkhurst. This is what you wanted, Big Boy, Sick Boy, Daddy of Sarah. Give it to me, Big Boy Parkhurst. Give it to me!"

Then, in my mother's house. Now, in the Motel 6. This body, the same body. "Give it to me."

I lie here in the water wanting to laugh, waiting for my teeth to stop grinding and my gums to harden up again. A sweet mystery, everything losing form for an instant. Probably the way the earth feels when there's a quake. But my laughter is short-lived, and like the earth's quaking, my brief escape from tension and fear has only revealed more. I'm considering the rest of the story and where it is leading me. Something warns me off, yet the child in me, the one who schemes to put off going to sleep alone in her room, insists on hearing more.

The Seductress of the Mirror has spent herself and turns off the water. There are voices; something is clattering against the open window above my head. My mother is throwing pebbles at the window. My mother has forgotten her keys, left them on the spice rack in the kitchen. Not only that, Mother Parkhurst has called home, learned of her husband's infirmity, and hurried home with the milk. They have walked from the bus stop together and are planning a quick glass of lemonade on the shady back porch of our house when Virginia discovers her dreadful mistake. They bang on the door, assuming I have come home. Unable to arouse the probably napping (but very aroused) girl, they go around to my bedroom window, tapping, tapping, tapping with pebbles at my chamber pane. But Hark! Sounds from nearby bathroom pour. 'Tis a bath—but much, much more.

I laugh, I weep for that girl. I step from the tub and towel off, alert to the dangers in continuing the story. I indulge this playful, sassy storyteller just a little longer . . .

I pull on my underpants, my harness, my sweaty blouse and wrinkled skirt. Rushing to the back door, holding it open, I say, "I'm sorry, Mother." Noticing that Mrs. Parkhurst is already hurrying past the corner of the house, I mumble, "I had the water running. I guess I didn't hear you."

Virginia places her shaking, white-gloved hand on the doorknob. She moves past me, opening draperies, raising shades, coming to pause at the credenza in the foyer where she pulls her gloves off one finger at a time, as if she is pulling the very idea of her dirty, sticky daughter off, off, off. She raises her arms above her head, looks quizzically at herself in the mirror as she removes the mother-of-pearl hat pin and lifts her dainty navy blue straw hat from her respectably dark auburn hair. Her dress is white rayon with navy blue piping on sleeves and collar, tailored in such a way as to reveal only a gradual swell in the region of the chest, a swell that rises considerably, then recedes, without ever having announced itself.

"Well, it's time I fixed dinner."

These are the words, Virginia Patterson's remarkable words to her daughter, Roberta, who has just taken on Mr. Parkhurst, John the Coal Miner's son, et al, in the bathtub beneath the Fountain of Evil. "Well." A word, brisk, broomlike, a sweeping word. It sweeps things, even people, under rugs. "Well," she says to me, my eyes begging for detailed explanations. "It's time I fixed dinner." Vintage Virginia. "Well," I say now, watching the water drain from the tub in this motel in the middle of America.

I wrap my head in a dry towel.

Once in bed, I check the clock, one-thirty, and then the telephone, willing either one to ring. But the alarm is set for six, and if the phone were to ring, the only person calling would be the desk clerk, and why would he call? I could call *him,* I suppose; I could tell him I'm having trouble sleeping and ask him to tell me a better bedtime story than the one I've told myself. Not part of his job description, he would probably grump.

I have told myself a story that didn't turn out quite right. Hearing another story wouldn't change the first one. That girl I was, the one who found her power, has lost it because . . . oh, because even though I've used it once in a while, I don't think I believe any longer that it's mine. I had no power to help Gary. I've had no power over Andrew's pain. I don't believe in magic any more. I don't believe in magic and I don't believe in passion; once they were one and the same. And anyone who knows fairy tales will tell you about magic, how if you don't believe in it, it goes away or turns into something else that's never quite as good.

I should call Andrew. What is the matter with me, letting the time get away like this? I promised to check in every few days. But if I think about it, his first question would be a logical one: "Where are you?" And for reasons I am too tired or unwilling to fathom, I know I would just snarl at him and say, "None of your business!" It *is* his business. He is the person with whom I've shared twenty years of my life. I think of his back, so thin as he bent at the table my last night home—what, two nights ago? And his eyes, under the light above the table. But no. I can't think about what I saw there. I can't do it. I can't call him. Not now. Not at one-thirty in the morning. Maybe not ever . . .

I turn out the light and lie back in the darkness, reviewing fairy-tale endings. "Ever after," the narrator always concludes. Ever after the wedding bells the girl is never heard from again. Neither is the prince, for that matter. If that's true, maybe my story is more of a fairy tale than I thought.

The dormitory room in the fall of 1950, after Andrew walked me back from the dance, was hardly the chamber of a castle in a magic kingdom. A more prosaic tale, this Roberta variant, more of a historical documentary than a romantic fantasy. A dialectic was moving as inevitably as the storyteller's voice spins out the plot: simple economics, the law of supply and demand. In the packed gymnasium, where girls more attractive than I stood unnoticed, it didn't seem necessary to run a market survey when the steel-guitar player came my way at intermission. Back in that dormitory room, where the radiator hissed at night and I woke up each morning with a layer of perspiration on my scalp beneath the rubber-tipped TipTop bobby pins of my pincurls, it didn't occur to me to weigh my options, either. Who ever heard of a fairy tale where the heroine is asked to consider the long-term implications?

There were so many implications in a freshman girl meeting a Senior Accounting Major at the first dance she attended as a college student. Why didn't they tell me, all those girls gathered in my room on the third floor of Agnes Howard Hall? Maybe they were squealing so loudly they didn't hear the bell (I was hearing things even then), tolling a death knell (in A-flat, if I recall) for The Historian in me. The Historian.

I cannot document that bell. Yet it canceled visits I had planned to Gettysburg, Manassas, Harpers Ferry. It signaled the end, before the beginning, of scholarly concentration with Dr. Glackin. *Dong, dong, dong,* the bell tolled. God help me. I did hear that bell. That's where the shame comes in: knowing and not responding, thinking further instructions would follow.

I don't cast the girls as wicked stepsisters in their Weejun penny loafers and roll-down anklets—no glass slippers in this down-to-earth tale. Dangling their shapeless legs off the sides of sagging twin beds and over the arms of chairs, they were asking the seemingly pertinent questions: "Did he try to kiss you, Roberta? Did you make out?" Their ears were just tuned to other sounds.

"Other bells," I say, flopping my head around on the pillow. I reach up and turn the light back on, resolving to let it burn all night long.

The girls heard other bells. Trite, white, and bright bells. *Bla-ang, blong.* Who could have heard the dignified tolling of the death knell in that din? Who wanted to hear the death knell when a Senior Accounting Major, free of obvious physical defects and able to breathe unassisted, walked me to my dormitory after the dance? The chime of Lohengrin in that room would have drowned out an air raid siren.

Wedding bells. Even if I hadn't heard them, my Sisters in Deafness would have pointed them out. I was an eardrum, a one-way receiver. The fairy tale ends, but the story just goes on.

THE END

"What a story," I say to the silent telephone and the all-night light.

4

In my third day of self-imposed solitary confinement it occurs to me that if I had called Andrew in the middle of the night from Bloomington, the exchange of words for words—snarly though they probably would have been—might have changed everything. I might even have had a night's sleep. As it is, I have slept only an hour or two, my stomach is queasy, and my mind is dull.

I have decided not to drive to Chicago, even though I am drawn to the city; its very name stirs visions of exactly what the Scenic Guide has described: Libraries! Museums! Galleries! But the visions are overshadowed by the only image I really see when I think of Chicago: stockyards. The association with stockyards goes right back to the fifth grade, to a teacher and a textbook both given to graphic descriptions. In the end, I get no closer to Chicago than the most remote ring of highway shown on the map.

I am worried because I am realizing that people whose opportunities for dialogue are even temporarily limited are capable of distorting, even altering reality in dangerous ways. That worries me, the idea of a lunatic fringe, the possibility that I may be part of it. In bypassing Chicago and heading north for Superior, I've already chosen what the Trip-Tiks call the Alternate Route.

Had someone presented me with new ideas I might have been persuaded to go to Chicago. With a passenger in the car, someone to talk to, I might have dwelt only a moment on the acres of soon-to-be slaughtered cattle Mr. Whugalter etched so vividly on my impressionable ten-year-old's mind. Instead, I talk to waitresses, gas station attendants, and motel desk clerks. I talk to myself.

I keep driving. I aim the car at Wisconsin, crossing the state line in a blur of green. I drive into the center of a mural drawn by children as the backdrop for a play. No doubt about it: Wisconsin was drawn with a set of basic eight crayons. Hills roll by in a shade of green I would know anywhere: GREEN. Barns are red with white trim. White farmhouses with pitched roofs and gables are hung with black shutters. Black cows graze on green hills; sometimes they are joined by herds of brown-with-white. And the clouds! Lofty cumulus that could have been drawn and filled in with white. No stringy cirrus, which would have required gray, but towering white cumulus cathedrals floating in a sky dependably, uniformly blue. I give the mural of Wisconsin a name I would have bestowed on the picture had I drawn it myself, a name as fundamental as its colors. I call it *Peace*. The way I see it, if *I* can find a moment of peace in a picture drawn with the basic eight crayon set, then the name belongs, no matter how ragged from overuse and abuse the word has recently become.

I stop for lunch at the McDonald's on the road outside of Madison. Carrying my tray to a table in the corner, I wonder suddenly if people who have not talked to other people for a while can somehow disintegrate, become extinct. I wonder about the causes of extinction. Maybe the dinosaurs failed to exchange enough information, vital messages regarding climatic trends and the movements of glaciers. And if they had the information, what did they do with it? What *could* they have done with it? Could they have adapted, or adapted more quickly?

I remember Daniel Stetson, the asthmatic curator at the Museum of Natural History, possibly the most cheerful pessimist I've ever known. Daniel, unlike me, did not take his history personally. He noted things. He told me once that the dinosaur's extinction was as inevitable for its time as acid rain is for ours. And this at a time when Rachel Carson was an obscure cult figure and pollution was not even a dirty word. Now, ten years later, I come up with my own theory of dinosaur extinction, a valid interpretation based on inadequate systems of communication and response, and where is Daniel? Probably gone to his grave, or unreceptive, in any case, to the revelation.

I almost unhinge my jaw to accommodate a bite of my Big Mac. This cultural adaptation isn't lost on me. Communication. Adaptation. *I* know what it takes to survive . . . I hope.

Considering the distance between this moment and my conversations with Daniel, I wonder whether time provides distance. Daniel and I experienced little sense of moral ambiguity or ethical discomfort, discussing as we were a prehistoric era. What could either of *us* have done? About dinosaurs? About glaciers? But the idea of exchanging information and formulating personal theories of history doesn't leave me. I feel accountable for something, for everything, in a vague sense that I can't think through. Something about seeing the patterns, knowing, and then acting and adapting. I wish Daniel were along to note exceptions to my theories.

I look up from devouring my Big Mac prey and sip Coke through a straw. My table is in the corner, near a real fern and a plastic philodendron. I can observe arrivals and departures. A group of girls sits down in a booth near me and my first reaction is shock: I have been too long in museums, or in the car. I have forgotten how white the teeth can be, how firm the thighs. The young people in McDonald's belong in that hand-drawn mural, with their blond, blue-eyed wholesomeness. "Peace," I whisper, lifting my hand with two spread fingers.

But the more I study them the more they resemble the cows grazing on the hills outside: contented, complacent. Once you've noticed complacency, you can taste it, smell it. It won't go away. Dangers encroach on these kids and they don't comprehend—even with Kent, Ohio, four hundred miles away, and the Kent State murders barely three months ago. What's distance, what's time? It's all happening at once. Over and over. Gary and 'Nam. Now and then. Happening for me. Probably for Andrew, though he won't tell me.

I know, at some level, how I would be perceived if I offered these kids advice. Yet I smile agreeably as they settle in. One girl sees my expression and, as if to accommodate me, gets up and asks if she can borrow the salt shaker from my table. "Yes!" I say. Then I start coughing because the Coke, and all the unspoken words, go down the wrong pipe.

I finish my coughing fit with a dismal thought: How can there be advice for children who do not see the connection between enemies who build slide-trigger booby traps into the sides of ravines and enemies whose bullets blow away flowers placed in the barrel of a rifle?

More dismal than that: How can there be protection for children whose parents pull the basic eight crayons from their hands and give them an M-16?

What I'm trying to say is that another mural will not be drawn. Preserve and restore! I want to say it, but I know I'd have to add that, uh, well, uh, I haven't done it too well myself.

Three boys join the girls in their booth. There is laughter, a great waving of hands and brushing back of hair. Maybe I'm getting old, thinking of them as boys when all three of them are probably past twenty.

One young man's shoulders—bare except for the straps of his tank top and the sweep of his long hair—are outlined in light, a holographic silhouette produced by the sunlight outdoors and the shadows inside, and probably, too, by my unreliable eyes. It takes my breath away, that velvet suppleness of childhood flesh stretched over angular neck and jaw and muscled shoulders. Skin, texture, that maybe only a mother would recognize.

Hunching over, I cross my arms. I cup my elbows in the palms of my hands. I look away, acknowledging my own dangers. "Bullets, booby traps, and crayons," I say as I stand up to go. No one seems to have heard.

The light-edged silhouette of the young man's head and shoulders suddenly reappears about twenty miles past Madison. Am I just remembering the image? Nothing remembered just pops up in front of you like that. Am I hallucinating? I can't be sure. An overlaid image on the black ribbon of highway, it seems to accompany me, or haunt me. I have drifted toward the silhouette again, into the passing lane. I pull back to the right. Now it's gone.

The glowing image, which appears again within an hour, this time at the edge of the road, is just more evidence of the problems I am having: seeing things, hearing things. I've been alone too long. PDS again. No matter what else is distracting me, I will call Andrew this evening from Superior.

Pilots have been shot down and are being held in isolation over in North Vietnam. I've read about the men kept in solitary confinement in

North Korean prison camps, how they began to see things, how they lost track of time. I have read, too, that the ones who survived tell about re-creating, in minute detail, the happiest or most intense times of their lives, replaying music or poetry memorized in childhood or, in their imagination, planning and designing and building a future dream: a house, a job, a lover, a painting, a piece of sculpture.

Creating a future wouldn't work for me. My future does not go beyond the green lines on the maps and Trip-Tiks. I know very well that's not a healthy sign, but at least I understand the past somewhat. At least I can come up with questions. So I go back as I drive along. I go back even as I go forward, and as long as I'm going back the glowing image of the young man's head and shoulders does not return. I work at this, as I call up the voice of the sultry, sassy storyteller. And the clouds, like dolphins swimming beside a lone shipwreck survivor, accompany me, play with me, divert me with these blessed moments of recollection as the time-wind blows us along.

Mornings on Branchview Court. Cleaning Time. I place *Mozart's Concerto for Flute in C Major and Other Favorites* on the Magnavox phonograph and the notes follow me through the house. I look out the kitchen window and see Gary in the backyard, sunlight chasing him as he darts from the grass to shadows in the woods. Gary, a whimsical note, untamed yet infinitely tender.

The Interim Hour, the time between Cleaning and Lunch, when my neighbors gather on the cul-de-sac sidewalk. I join them, bringing Gary's trike and my lawn chair and a pitcher of Snow-Crop lemonade. I am out of my element, talking to a circle of thin, slick-shaved, pedal pusher-clad calves and red-painted toenails. We're discussing Dishwashing as I leap from my chair to rescue a yellow flowerpot from Gary's clutches; I replace it on the Phinneys' blue porch-rail. Conspirators, this child and I, we understand each other. I shake my finger at him in an exaggerated gesture that he knows is a fake and I know is intended for my neighbors' edification.

When I return, the discussion moves to Husband Complaints. I jump in with a description of the clothing trail—jacket, tie, shoes, socks—that Andrew leaves when he comes in from work. It's then that Mary Sue Groves, petite little southern thing that she is, tells me that just seeing Andrew after a hard day's work, relaxed and easy in his blue cotton trousers with the elasticized waist and his skinny-strap undershirt, a cool Tom Collins in his hand, ought to make me forget all those silly little absentminded habits of his. "Bless their little pointed heads," she says by way of summary.

I add a footnote to the Husband Complaints: "Madame Pompadour said a man is a little boy with a splinter in his toe."

"Where did you read *that,* Roberta?" asks Martha Beardsley, B.A. in English, Agnes Scott College, class of fifty-one, who probably knows and won't admit it, but says instead, "I don't find much time to read anymore." Then, smiling at Mary Sue, she adds, "My life is so full right now, I can't say I miss it much."

Sunk deep into my lawn chair and a blue funk, I remember Martha coming over on a gray November morning and telling me that she does too read—at night. Interrupting ourselves to rescue chubby, constantly moving hands, we talk about reading. I tell her that I stay up half the night sometimes. Tired, knowing I have to clean the next day, I read, moved to tears sometimes by Churchill's prose and by the "whole inexorable march of time."

"I know. Me, too," she says, her face upturned as she leads her eighteen-month-old daughter out of my laundry pile and up the basement stairs.

And now this disclaimer.

Satisfyingly, I think of Martha Beardsley as the intellectual equivalent of Benedict Arnold. Less than satisfied, I think of myself as the Hester Prynne of Branchview Court: Outcast, scourge of my race and gender, I do not and probably never will clean the screw beneath the knob at the base of the toilet bowl which Mary Sue, as the discussion turns to Bathrooms, is now describing. "Tricky little devil," she says. "I take an old splayed-out toothbrush and I put just a dab of Bon Ami on it. . . ."

Yes, yes. We all wait receptively through long syllables and miles of drawl. Just a dye-ub a Bone Ahh'mih.

"And then I just scrub like heck around that knob."

I know now that for the rest of my life, as I swab away, Cloroxsoaked jockey shorts in hand, I can no longer philosophically ignore that yellow-brown ring around the knobs at the base of my toilet bowl. Then Mary Sue is stretching her dainty arms above her head, picking up her lawn chair and hurrying home. It's Lunchtime on Branchview Court. . . .

The silhouette has changed in the last couple of hours, has sprouted torso and legs, taken on the lifelike gestures of raising its arm and jerking its thumb. I screamed once, and it went away. I know it isn't a real hitchhiker, but it has a certain energy. I know my own draining energy is its source. I stop at a produce stand on a nearby access road. I buy a bag of peaches and a bag of plums, and drive away. The silhouetted image reappears. I must find a place to stop the car.

I drive to a turnout near a creek whose name I can't read as I go by. A few cars are parked here. It seems fishermen use this wide spot in the road as a parking place for unloading their gear, then walk down the bank to fish.

I get out of the car and take my bags of fruit along, realizing only at this minute that I may be having problems partly because I am hungry. I find a shady green place under a tree. I watch a man who is drinking a beer and flinging his line toward a round pool at the curve of the stream. He reaches up every now and then and pats his floppy hat. I shove a fat, blue-black plum into my mouth, and the juice drools down my chin. "Mmmm," I say, hunched against the trunk of the tree.

I go back to a rainy autumn, the fall of '54 or maybe '55, when it seems I will never stop eating. When I am not eating, I'm reading. Usually I combine both, hungry as I am. I swing between violent shifts of temperament, avoiding my neighbors for weeks at a time, leaving the house only for groceries, bringing in the bags and partially unloading them. Andrew has been telling me lately that we need another baby so Gary won't be an only child. I've ignored him, figuring it's another ploy to rouse my fading libido, but when I find Gary sitting forlornly at the front-room window, looking out at the other houses on the street, I am galvanized into cleaning, having neighbors and children over, exposing myself to their eyes. Otherwise I read.

Reading is not easy with a two-and-a-half-year-old child in the house. One problem is my habit of eating and reading at the same time—potato chips, apples, candy bars, preferably Milky Ways. Gary picks up my habits and takes his breakfast toast to his room in the mornings, apples for his afternoon naps. When Andrew finds the remains in his room and questions him, Gary gives him the straight facts: "Eat like Mommy."

Gary also snitches my chips. When I am especially involved in my pages, I look up and find his greasy face and round eyes gazing at me from the floor like a cheerful house mouse.

Not only does the boy want to eat, he wants to read. He brings me his pitiful volumes of Golden Books or Mother Goose rhymes. "Mommy read," he says. I read those books to him every night at bedtime and every morning after breakfast; I can't bring myself to subsist on such fare during the day as well. The solution to the problem evolves. I can't say when it occurs to me that the cure for all this subterfuge is simply to read aloud to Gary whatever I am reading myself, feed Gary whatever I am feeding myself.

It surprises me at first what a happy combination we are, sitting in lamplight on the sofa, stuffing ourselves with chips and crackers, apples and bananas. Occasionally we rise in unison to brush the crackling crumbs from beneath ourselves. But I realize that except for hearing a book or two of his own, the sound of my voice is all he really cares about. And I have to admit, I am happiest on those damp, dark days with his warm, small presence beside me. Car tires swish on the street sometimes; the wind brushes the maple branch against an upstairs window; and there is Gary, falling asleep beside me or rolling his trucks up and down the cushions of my durable thighs. We are nearing the end of Volume IV of *The History of the English-Speaking Peoples*. I consider switching to a light diet of historical fiction when this is over. I have gained another five pounds on Churchill.

In January, a cold, freezing rain has maintained a one-inch crust on the snow during the late-December/early-January thaw. The morning I finish *The Great Democracies* I look over at Gary and smile. I reread the final paragraph, which ends, "The future is unknowable but the past should give us hope. Nor should we now seek to define precisely the exact terms of ultimate union." I close the book, set it on the floor, and slap my thighs.

Gary looks up. "All done," he says.

He crawls into my lap, nuzzles his head to my neck. We are a couple of hermits, all right, but he doesn't seem to mind too much. I get up and carry him on my hip to the kitchen, standing between a couple of grocery bags—no perishables in them, just dry cereal, canned goods. We stand at the window and watch a cardinal feeding on a ragged ball of suet I put out in November. We discuss winter. We discuss the deciduous nature of some trees, the reclusive habits of certain hibernating creatures.

"Like bears and possums," I tell him.

"Yeah," he says, nuzzling near my ear.

Leaves and grass are rotting to mulch in the woods. I consider the early onset of decay and my twenty-second birthday, due to arrive on the eighteenth of the month. I think of Gary's third birthday, coming in March, at the beginning of spring. Can't I make his birthday something more than just a day spent under lamplight in a cave? He needs to understand that even if nature does have a rigid schedule of decomposition to keep, even if no one has consulted us about the schedule, he need never sink into despair. Schools run on schedules. And trains. People are always hopping trains they have almost missed. Tramps even hop trains they haven't planned to catch. I decide that someone should celebrate that spontaneity, that slap in the face of the inevitable. So I tell Gary that we are going to have a hobo party for his birthday.

"What hobo, Mommy?" he asks predictably, his hunger for words sometimes exceeding even mine.

"They're people with patches on their pants and all their belongings in a bandana tied on a stick. They eat dinner out of a tin can."

"Where do they live?"

"Oh, most anywhere," I say. "And they're always moving on to some place else. They hop trains to somewhere else."

Gary seems to think a hobo party would be fine as he lets himself down from my arms. I hear him wander upstairs to his bedroom.

For once I do not want to read. The sun is doing something to me. I am leaning on the counter by the sink and a triangle of sunlight is tracing its way across my hands. The sharp, clear focus of snow-dampened tree branches superimposed against the milky blue sky cannot be trusted—I know a breeze or the slightest shift in the equilibrium of this

January weather could jar the lens, throw it all into haze. Yet the grass is green in patches under the clothesline, and I know a good drying day when I see one. A load of wash can be ready by the time I coax Gary from his toys and stuff him into a snowsuit, hat, mittens, boots. . . . I look once more out the window, skeptical, but the sun seems to be holding its pose.

We go out through the side door in the garage, me tilting backward as I carry the oilcloth-lined basket of steaming laundry, Gary poking along underfoot. As we walk up the slope to the backyard, Gary lets out a whoop. I know what he means! All this oxygen has caught me off guard, too. He runs up ahead of me, waving his arms, stamping his boots in a remarkably accurate choreography of exactly what I am feeling.

I set the basket on the wet grass and watch Gary's dance as he leaps from snow to grass, grass to snow. As he dips his head down, his arms sweep upward; as his head comes up, his arms thrust down. I want to tell him what a fine companion he has been in some of my loneliest hours, and that the moment we now share will, I am certain, live forever in my memory.

I open my arms to him as I kneel by the basket, and his rubber boots carry him to me over the grass and snow. His hair, chestnut, the warmest color of brown, holds the clean air within and between every strand, and I breathe in the fresh scent of Gary and the air around him. I think of Andrew's remarks about the reading I do with Gary, want to tell Gary that I would read him more fairy tales, as other mothers surely do, but some hunger in me keeps demanding other things. I want to say to the bright blue back of his snowsuit as he dances away that I am empty, some part of me is empty. My God, he'll have gruesome dreams if I tell him there is a dark, empty hole inside of his mother, some place that will not fill up. The Freudians would have a field day with that one. As I reach my hands into the basket, the clothes still warm from the washer, I say a prayer that I will never be his only source of nourishment. I pinch the wood pins onto the corners of towels and sniff at the cold air, blinking my eyes at the brightness, unaccustomed to such light.

"Hey, Gar?" I call.

He peeks at me from a stand of birches. "Trees white. Like snow," he says.

"You're right, kiddo."

"We have fun, huh, Mommy?"

"Oh, yes, Gary. We sure do."

I pick up the empty basket and go around the corner toward the garage, searching my mind for a way to tell my son about hunger.

"Hey, Gar? Want to share some soup for lunch? How about a can of soup?"

"Yeah!" he sings, following me down the hill. "Alf-bet soup."

I laugh. I laugh so hard I am sure I will wet my pants. I have to sit on the step by the door to the garage. My nose runs; my eyes run. I sit on the step to the side door of the garage, laughing and crying because the house is a split-level and Gary already talks in multilevel language.

"Campbell's Alphabet Soup is our kind of lunch, you funny kid." I burst into giggles again.

He stands with his arms folded across his chest, smiling that amazed and somewhat uncertain smile of child watching adult come undone. I pull him close to my chest, soaking up his warmth. Tunelessly I sing to him, "Campbell's Kids, Campbell's Kids. God watch over us Campbell's Kids. . . ."

He pulls back, waiting for what his ear tells him will be the final line of the song. "Until we can grow up," I whisper.

Memories collide. Nothing is simple, nothing is sweet.

Gary's body arrives at Andrews Air Force Base, sealed in an aluminum coffin draped with a flag. Flags and solemn guards and tinny music from a band give order to the chaos of removing thirty-eight coffins from the belly of an airplane.

I am counting the coffins! I don't know how to mourn for him. At this moment I do not believe he is dead. Gary Andrew Masters is not particularly, specifically, individually dead. He can't be because his parents cannot breathe the same air that these other grieving parents are breathing. Andrew and I are a silent obscenity waiting to be spoken. We'll just go home and go on with our own griefless war when this ceremony is over.

At Arlington, during the burial service, Reverend Sherman Ellis reads from some sentimental piece that he never told me he was going to read: "Death is nothing. . . . Whatever we were to each other, we still are."

I am screaming. He goes on reading, in that goddam, resonant southern voice: "Call me by my old familiar name. Speak in the easy way you always have. Laugh as we have always laughed. . . ."

"No." Then I am whimpering, "No, please . . ."

"Play. Smile. Think of me. . . . Life means all that it ever meant. . . . There is absolute, unbroken continuity. . . ."

How could he do this to me? Sherman Ellis has known us for eighteen years. I would *never* choose such a thing to be read.

When the service ends, he says, "Time heals all wounds." I am carrying the folded triangle of an American flag under one arm, my other hand is slipped into the bend of Andrew's elbow, and Sherman Ellis has to go and say that. Maybe so, I think, giving it a chance. We hurry across the grass and onto the black path leading to the line of cars. Maybe so. But my father's death didn't feel this way. Harold Patterson was plucked right out of life by a heart attack. Somebody could have said the very same thing when we were leaving his services up in Potsdam, and we might have had some of these feelings, this sense of the impertinence of anyone or anything implying that time was moving—clocks ticking, cars racing past, rain falling—or worse, that nothing had changed! But look what went on after Daddy's funeral. We went back to the house; we told each other a dozen times how he'd collapsed behind the pharmacy counter at the drugstore and how his new automatic pill dispenser spewed Margaret Stewart's digitalis tablets all over him in a futile attempt at rescue. And for all the pain that brought, all the painful absurdity, we laughed. Andrew and Virginia and Gary and me and Aunt Caroline and . . . We laughed because Daddy would have found it hilarious, a story to be told around town if it had been his good fortune to survive the mishap. Time and retelling really *had* been the prescription for us.

Time isn't doing a thing for me as we walk away from Gary's grave. Time hasn't started, or stopped. I wanted to bury Gary by myself, cradle his broken body in my arms, weep, wail, moan, but I screamed instead. I screamed because we aren't anything like those other parents whose service we overheard. They'll go home and wait for the guests to depart and hold each other through the long night ahead. Not us. And we aren't like the parents on the television news, either, the ones who sit in matching recliners under a floor lamp, nod toward photographs of their shaved-headed baby-faced boy in a uniform, and tell the reporter their son has done his part, God's will, all of that. Not Andrew and me. We are less than respectable. You don't read sickly sweet comforting verses to us! Someone should have asked us to leave as soon as we drove up.

"You will go on," a voice whispers as we get into the funeral director's black limousine. Andrew slams the door and jerks his head around to see who it was. The voice and the person it belongs to have disappeared. He looks at me. A nerve twitches at the hollow of his cheek where the muttonchops meet his face. His skin is the color of dirty school paste. He smells sour. I look away.

I feel personally responsible for the emptiness we find in words of comfort coming from other people's mouths. I feel as if I may have caused a distortion in the waves of sound and meaning as they have reached Andrew's ears and mine. I wonder what going on means for us.

Just then he twists in his seat and rotates his shoulders so that they are no longer touching mine. As the car begins its slow return to the Beltway, he growls in that deep, raspy voice, "Gone too far already."

I am pounding my fists on the damp ground of the streambank somewhere in Wisconsin. "No more of this," I say.

I grind my teeth together, squeeze my eyes closed, hold back tears. There has to be a flaw in the character or the intellect of anyone who cannot find a way to short-circuit these physical symptoms. I should have bought and not just browsed in the self-help sections of the bookstores. I need Inner Reality, I need Cosmic Consciousness, I need Reality Therapy. Supposedly psychology has moved beyond Pavlov and Skinner, for God's sake. If ringing bells and salivating dogs, sugar pellets and maze-crazed rats can be overcome, then why not this hard-edged pain that came with the recollection of a blue snowsuit and an empty bushel basket, green hills with white crosses, and my husband's face in profile?

The man with the floppy hat is looking over at me. He walks up the bank and stands at the edge of his sunshine and my shade. "Can I help you?" he asks. "Is there something I can do?"

For the life of me I cannot think what to ask for. I try to get up.

My legs are so stiff I have to get on all fours and then rise, pushing off one knee with my hands. He steps into the shade and puts an arm at my elbow, to steady me. "Thanks," I say, my voice still muffled by tears. He stands back as I move slowly to the car. "Thank you," I say again as I get in the car.

5

The man with the floppy hat walks back to his fishing hole. I lean my head on the steering wheel, still sniffling.

I want to remember. I don't want a frontal lobotomy; I don't want my life erased. All I want is a rerouting of circuits, access to some sensible device that will stop this clutching sensation I feel in my chest when I think of my son as he grew, when I think of the fact of his dying. How will I ever take hold of this reality if month after month (year after year, I realize suddenly with dread) the clutching in my chest begins and a groaning sob squeezes its way through my larynx?

And what is this compulsion anyway, this need to relive, re-create, re-experience my life? This is new, a question I have not yet asked myself. I roll it around in my mind, looking for concealed hooks and triggers before I try to answer. I've said I want to remember Gary, but it's not Gary I'm remembering at all, not Gary's life but his transient passage through mine. I am puzzled but not yet panicked by the thought of my life passing before my eyes and Gary only along for the ride. I lean back against the seat.

Old selves. My memories are of old selves, strangers no more alive than Gary is. No more *dead* than Gary is, either. Something changes as the idea passes through like a flutter of ribbon. I don't know what's different, but nothing feels the same. Roberta Patterson is no more alive or dead than Gary. She lives in this same body. Gary lives as a memory in this same mind. How else can I remember him except in connection with me? Obvious, yet this is a different kind of comfort than I have felt before.

It does make me angry, though, this feeling of my body and my mind in some kind of tug-of-war beyond my control. I rub the palm of one hand against the finely webbed and freckled skin on the back of my other hand. Thin as tissue paper. Pulled taut, it seems it might tear. In thirty-nine years I have never heard anyone mention that endo and ecto are in some sort of conspiracy, trying to change places or merge. I can just hear the neighbors on Branchview Court. "Oh, didn't you know? Yes, Roberta Masters turned inside out this summer."

I straighten my shoulders and grip the steering wheel, cool and substantial beneath my thin-skinned hands. I suck in on my lower lip and breathe with the hiccupping rhythm of a child come safely home, all Band-Aided and settled in front of the television reruns.

"Okay," I say, pulling back onto the highway. So I'm not always glad to remember Roberta Patterson . . . or Roberta Patterson Masters, for that matter. Maybe some part of me does slink down in the seat when faced with the memory of my mumbling, fumbling, painfully dumb-smart self. It's my body and my mind, conspiring against me, probably entering the late stages of revolt and oblivion, but if that's what it takes to remember sweet Gary and still have some feeling that I'm running this show, then I'm going to remember my *self* while the time-wind is still blowing the clouds across the blue Wisconsin sky.

We give our little boy a hobo party in March and everybody comes, even a few early daffodils. Since our first year in the house Andrew and I have spent the winter months poring over seed catalogs, drawing landscape plans for flower gardens, then setting out plants in the spring or planting bulbs in the fall. He leans more toward shrubs, though the mountain laurels I planted in the woods have thrived. I watch out for sales on annuals like petunias and marigolds every spring. Last year I even collected seeds from the prettiest batch; the seedlings are sprouting in the basement, and we both have looked forward to March, knowing the time for planting can't be too far away. But Andrew is the expert on where the bulbs really are. No surprises for him, no tulips or daffodils that go unnoticed during the fall dividing. Or so he thought.

He takes the day off from work, cleans up the yard and keeps an eye on Gary while I decorate the cake. He comes in the kitchen and stands with his elbows out. "Gary's found a daffodil in bloom! Out in that bed by the south side of the house!" he says, pulling off his dirt-stained gloves. "I *find,* Mom!" Gary adds, smiling from behind Andrew, holding on to his father's leg. "Well, a birthday bloom!" I say, handing him the rubber scraper covered with icing for him to lick.

After lunch Andrew dresses up in a red-plaid flannel shirt, dungarees, and a straw hat, looking more like a scarecrow than a tramp. The neighbors bring their raggedly costumed children and stay to watch them drink Kool-Aid from tin cans Andrew has sanded smooth at the rims, to watch them eat slices cut from the boxcar cake I frosted in red and black with yellow letters: G&M Lines. But I seem to be the main attraction, for I'm playing ringtoss and tisket-a-tasket with the children, moving faster than any of them can remember me moving. Gary and I gathered sticks in the woods a week ago; I sewed up a dozen drawstring bags out of red bandana fabric. Andrew says he suspects I even went down to the U.S. Weather Service in the District and ordered the March wind to stop blowing.

"Will you look at this weather?" he says to Virginia and Harold Patterson, down from New York for the occasion, indicating with a wave of his hand the profusion of crocus in the grass, the swollen tree-buds, the sun.

At dinner that evening, Harold and Virginia lean back confidently in their chairs, satisfied that their daughter is doing everything right. Well, almost everything. When they watch me devour a huge slab of roast pork slathered in brandied fruit, three servings of mashed potatoes, and untold scoops of gravy, they do come forward again, eyes wide with concern. But on the whole their hopeful faces seem to say, gazing adoringly at Gary, I am some wife and mother.

Everyone comes but no one understands that Roberta the Reader is ready to hop a train to somewhere else. No one understands because Roberta the Mute doesn't tell them. Later, when Andrew is bouncing ecstatically over my breasts and belly, I do think of telling him about the ad I read in the *Washington Post:* "Volunteer docents needed at the Museum of Natural History." I'll be calling, I want to tell him, to arrange for an interview. Instead of telling him, I burst into tears as he leans over me, reaching for a Kleenex.

"What's wrong, Hon?" he rumbles, kissing my neck.

I say I'm not sure. He puts his arm under my head, pulls me next to him on the pillow. We watch a neighbor's headlights make a flashing sweep of silhouetted branches on the opposite wall. I am afraid to tell him, that's it. I will begin by telling him that there is something I'm afraid to tell him.

Just then he says, "You're worn out is all. Putting on such a great party. Gary loved it. Everybody loved it."

I am sorry that Andrew thinks it was such a great party. I want to tell him to quit being so pleased about the party.

"What're you doing next year, when he's four?" Andrew asks, yawning.

I know he is expressing sincere appreciation, admiration even, but I have a vision of strangling him and telling the jury at my trial that he threatened me with a life of birthday catering. I think of pulling off my nightgown, grabbing the feather duster from the hook above the dust pan in the broom closet, and running all night around the cul-de-sac sidewalk. Fat, white, and lumpy, I'll stand under tents of light from street lamps, waving my feather duster and screaming, "I'm a historian, yes, but I don't do birthday parties. There's been some mistake." I laugh and roll onto my side.

"Clowns," I say.

"What?" he asks.

"I'll hire clowns from now on."

I stop for gas and hurriedly check the maps for the interchange into Superior.

Suddenly I look up from my navigational study. I am smiling, I could almost say I am filled with joy. I have remembered Andrew! We read our catalogs; we planted our flowers. He was a father! He took the day off from work. He sanded tin cans. He was a devoted father to our little boy. Andrew was there. I will call him tonight and tell him what I have remembered.

I have not seen the hitchhiker all afternoon. I'll keep moving—lost in time and watching for road signs. This might work.

* * *

It's 1954. A full-scale replica of a triceratops stands in the park near the Museum of Natural History. The sculpture, cast in bronze and iron, endures climbing children and falling leaves with a slow-witted patience that I fully understand. With its small, dull eyes and the burdensome protection of its three horns and enormous scaly shields, it's a creature made dangerously slow by its natural defenses. Slow to the point of extinction. I can sit on a bench in the middle of October, leaves falling around me, the towerlike corners of the red-brick Smithsonian building across the street eerily piercing the sky, and I can relate to that dinosaur. I am safe. I am slow. I am nearing extinction.

But that is the way my mind works on bad days. Sometimes I am actually quite giddy as Gary and I board the 10:10 A.M. bus and ride into the capital. Before he starts school, I take him with me to the museums almost every week. Guards begin to recognize us; tour guides know us by name. We meet Daniel Stetson, when he is the curator at Natural History.

Standing in the bubbling blue light of the oceanographic section, in the shadow of the ceiling-mounted blue whale, Daniel finds us and offers his cheerful if somewhat asthmatic welcome. "Mrs. Masters!" he says. "Have you seen the new exhibit on African body adornment?" He escorts us to the third-floor exhibit, there to view life-size photographs of women with necks elongated by coils of copper, lips enlarged by disks of stone, abdomens and limbs made objects of decoration by sand- and cinder-implanted lacerations. A chart details the stages of nose-ring insertion.

"Primitive beauty," Daniel says with a somewhat apologetic glance at Gary, a philosophical shrug of his shoulders.

I am bent over a glass case that displays bits of bead, copper, and rope. "The eye of the beholder and all of that," I say.

"So true, Mrs. Masters. So true," Daniel chuckles, until stopped by a wheeze.

I am not sure what Gary's mind is doing with this information. He seems to tolerate the exposure to the bizarre and the banal for reasons of his own: a fondness for the triceratops and an interest in the delicate imprints of fossilized shellfish and ferns. He gets a sense of exhilaration when he sets foot on the cool marble floors, where he runs without tiring. He likes buying popcorn from street vendors at 16th and P, where we wait for the Arlington Heights bus, feeding the pigeons and ourselves. He also has no choice.

I find him rather trying the year before he starts school. He whines several times in the National Archives. On one particularly bad day he pitches a fit in the Library of Congress, calling the director of the tour a "stupid poopy." I feel like adorning him with lacerations that would knock the socks off those African body designers. I yank him by the arm, hard enough to pull it from its socket. I stand that kid up against the tall brass doors outside and administer stern warnings about the dark punishments awaiting the purveyors of Toilet Humor. But I'm cackling irreverently an instant later at the thought of the prissy man in the tour guide's blazer, his nostrils dilated in rage and distaste. By the time we descend the shaded marble steps and emerge once again beneath the unperturbed gaze of the sun, the sins of my child seem small, mine beyond measuring. I want to set him free—from me.

He sets himself free. A head taller than most of the children, calm and smiling in the midst of sobbers and screamers, he slips me a knowing grin as we part his first day of school.

"See ya, Mom," he says.

"See ya, Gar," I call, my voice catching on something in my throat.

I walk home and tell my empty kitchen, "Thank God!" And then, to my fulsome books I whisper, "God help me."

I am moving so slowly through time, but I am moving—barely.

Four years after deciding I want to be a docent at Natural History, I see a notice for volunteers on a kiosk at the Museum of History and Technology. This time I don't hesitate about arranging an interview and telling Andrew about my plans. He has no objections, just questions: "What is it about you and museums?" he asks. He doesn't care about museums; he doesn't worry about patterns and personal theories of history. He makes a promotion in the civil service every other year. He joins first a barbershop quartet and then a country-western band. Andrew is an accountant; he plays steel guitar. He also sings bass. Steel-guitar-playing accountants who sing bass are in demand in 1959—in more demand, anyway, than slow-witted dinosaurs upon whom children play. I am slow; I am nearing extinction. But I go to Lord & Taylor to buy a dress for the interview.

The gray wool flannel shirtwaist doesn't fit me. I know that when I buy it, know I am not built for its tailored lines. Looking at myself over my shoulder in the full-length mirror at home, I cringe at the melonlike bulge of my rump beneath the black patent-leather belt. Each time I move it seems as if something alive—a weasel, a ferret—is in there shifting from one place to another. Here a thigh bulge, there a tummy roll, a mound of flesh beneath my bra strap. Like dough rising, my body is already beyond my control. I concede the matter, leave it to the illusory business of the mirror. I have to be moving on.

Bundled against the chill in my black wool coat and black kid gloves, I drive to the corner of Bent Twig Road and Woodland Avenue, park the car in the vacant lot, and walk to the bus stop. The air—clear, cold, winter-morning blue—seems to swirl with me in gusts of excitement. Cigarette butts, the leavings of commuters, lie on the sidewalk, sullenly unmoved by my wholesome and purposeful radiance.

At exactly 10:59 A.M. I arrive in the basement hallway of the Museum of History and Technology for my 11:00 A.M. appointment. Penelope Welton is on the phone but waves me into her cluttered office. She is the assistant librarian, I discover, recruited temporarily for training volunteers. She tells me this with her hand cupped over the phone. Now she returns to the conversation. She is different than I had expected. No more than thirty-five, she's a bleached blonde with hair puffed around her face in a style that is up-to-the-minute: a bubble.

The phone call seems to be distressing for her. She is muttering only one-syllable replies. Not looking at me, she straightens a stack of papers on her desk, pulls at the center drawer, closes it. She is wearing a gray wool dress, too; I'm delighted. This one has a panel of pleats from neck to hem, a rounded white linen collar, and white linen cuffs at the wrists. I torture myself for a moment with the way the fabric moves independently as Penelope Welton sets the receiver down, gets up, and takes a pamphlet from a box on the floor. A size 10, I tell myself. Room to spare in a size 10. Anything is possible today. Anything. She hands me the pamphlet to read. I ignore this summary of museum policies and procedures already familiar to me. When she returns to the phone, the person has apparently hung up. She replaces the receiver and sits in silence.

I sneak glances at Penelope, stare at dry leaves clinging to cobwebs in the window well. Unable to endure the silence any longer, I squirm out of my coat and say, "You know, I don't look very professional. I've never had a job—any kind of job. Not even a volunteer job."

Penelope looks up, tapping the top of her fountain pen against the green blotter paper on her desk. "What did you say?"

I fold my coat across my lap. "I mean, I come to the District at least once a week." I cannot seem to shut myself up. "I've been to all the museums. I just don't appear . . ."

"You don't need to tell *me* about appearances, Mrs. Masters."

She opens the center desk drawer and slams a package of Pall Malls on the desktop. She lights one with a match from a matchbook imprinted with ARE YOU A FLOP AT THE BEACH? She rests her elbows on the desk; she puffs. She crushes the cigarette in an abalone-shell ashtray, stands up, turns her back, spins around again to face me. Her long fingers make the white collar of her dress flip up and down like wings on an insect, like leaves in a wind.

"My God, Mrs. Masters. Roberta, is it?"

I nod, pick up my glove from the floor, worried. What have I said?

"Don't think I don't know what you mean. Everyone seeing the outside, never looking in. That's what you mean, isn't it?"

She has seized upon my words, absolutely leaped in response to them. I want to say more about false impressions and mistaken identity. I want to cite quotations from somewhere, talk for hours, wave my arms in the air. But I can only nod my head, eyes fixed on the trembling intensity of Penelope Welton's face. I can only lower my head and raise it again in a mute, bovine way, slow old guernsey in the presence of a wild mare.

"Oh. Oh!" Penelope says, lighting another cigarette. "Don't think for a minute I don't know."

I try to offer more. "I read a lot is what I meant to say. I had planned to apply at Natural History, but then time got away from me.

. . . I saw the notice here at History and Technology. I figured, why not?"

"Of course. Yes." She has landed for the moment in her chair.

"I've been here many times. I know the permanent displays as well as my own living room. Maybe better!" I make an exhaling sound intended as a laugh—hmm-huh—but she just puffs on her cigarette.

"I always brought my son with me, but he's in school now so I have time . . ."

"A child?" Penelope rolls the glowing ash of her cigarette against the side of the shell, holding it between her thumb and index finger to put it out. "I have a son. With my mother, you know." She glances at the telephone. Her hand flutters near her face; she forces it to fold quietly with her other hand on the blotter. "I mean my mother is raising him."

"Oh," I say. I hold onto my purse, coat, and gloves, and cross my right leg over my left. Then I reverse my legs, and my coat sleeve slips down, hanging limp and linty over my ankle.

She says, "I'm sure you look at me and think I'm so, uh, put together. Everyone does. But let me tell you, Roberta, I am holding my life together with shoelaces. Shoelaces!"

I consider this phrase: Shoestring would have meant money problems. She is reaching for something else with her shoelace image—somehow shoelaces encompass more than money.

"You're a professional woman," I suggest. "You probably have degrees."

Penelope Welton nods, then rolls her eyes in contempt of the idea.

"You're so well trained for your position. A librarian. I can only learn as I go."

Quiet hands on a green blotter. A layered smoke haze in the air.

The room will surely implode in this vacuum of silence, and with its collapse the museum overhead will then fall in on us, relics and treasures tumbling down, all the destruction resulting from the fact that history and technology cannot begin to solve this problem.

I turn just enough to look at the marble walls in the outer office; I am checking for cracks shaped like lightning, listening for the first rumblings of disaster. A woman in flat-heeled shoes is filling the basket of a coffee pot that sits on a table. I turn back to discover that Penelope Welton's eyes have gone suddenly liquid, silvery, unstable, like mercury spilled from a broken thermometer.

"I'll tell you what I've been trained for, Roberta." She is almost whispering now, seems concerned about people walking by her office door. "I'm trained to throw tantrums. Yes. I'm trained to smash my life to pieces now and then so that someone—my mother, a man—can pick up the pieces. I want to just leave it on the floor!"

"Yeah. Leave us to our failures, that sort of thing?" I say. I congratulate myself: That was pretty clever.

"You *do* understand," Penelope says. "I hate the picker-uppers, don't you?"

"Well," I begin, our connection already weakening. "I don't know about the smashing. . . ." I cannot remember anyone offering to pick up after me. Maybe I belong in a different category.

"I destroy them. The men? I do terrible things to them eventually because I hate the picker-uppers. I left my first husband because someone else had more money, and after that . . ."

I know I shouldn't let her go on this way. It isn't right somehow. Yet I sit turned in on myself like the plate spinner in a seedy traveling circus, sending up one thought, then another, replaying my own words—Leave Us to Our Failures—as if the wisdom of the ages has just been uttered and I am the oracle through which it has been spoken. I stare myopically into the blinding light of Penelope's revelations as if lies are the only words I've ever heard—or spoken—and on hearing for the first time a truth, someone else's truth, imperfect and flawed but a truth just the same, I am elated. I am unable to absorb the distressing sorrow in Penelope's voice; I listen distractedly, the way I often listen to Gary's chatter, while above the room, on heat waves rising from the radiator near the window, Roberta the Purposeful is soaring on ever-widening currents of air. I would not stop Penelope's outpouring of pain if the last train to Paradise were pulling out of Union Station because this very moment is paradise enough.

"No matter what disguises I wear—my degrees, my job," Penelope is saying, "they smell it through my clothes." She pulls again at her collar, sensing my distance. "They seem to know there'll be pieces flying off if they wait around long enough."

She stands up, her eyes gone back to solid blue, her hands in check, folded at her waist. Moving around to the side of the desk, she says, "Women are never what we seem, Roberta. That's that."

"No," I say. I have to restrain a brief and inappropriate impulse toward toilet humor. Indoor plumbing, it will fool you every time! my unstifled mind shrieks. But then I say again, soberly, "No. I suppose not."

"Classes for volunteers will begin Monday," she says in a voice I will hear many times in the training classroom, in the offices and hallways of the museum, a voice with a finishing-school edge on the vowels. "I hope we'll see you then."

I attempt to drape my coat over my arm as I stuff the pamphlet into my purse. But a glove falls, and as I bend to pick it up I feel my coat slipping slowly to the floor. I wad the coat into a ball with my other hand, pick up the glove, and back out the door. She watches with the long-suffering yet determined fascination of a devout bird-watcher. She smiles.

"Thank you, Mrs. Welton," I say. "Thank you very much."

I propel myself past the desks in the outer office, rattling the frosted glass in the door as I leave. I find the stairway and grip the varnished banister until I reach the main floor of the museum. I drag myself to a bench and sit down, exhausted. Across the gleaming marble floor and at the center of the museum—partly in shadow, then moving toward light—a great brass pendulum sweeps hypnotically through an invisible curtain of time. As I watch, at the very instant I become aware of watching its motion, the pendulum silently topples one of the paper markers arranged on a circular pattern of floor tiles.

Only a coincidence, I tell myself. "Did you see that?" I say to an elderly woman at the other end of the bench. The woman peers suspiciously over her bifocals, then picks up her purse and walks away. Only a coincidence. Yet I feel I've been bumped, like a reluctant performer, from the wings out onto the stage. I've been recognized, I've been seen. I soar for days with the feeling.

Almost a year later, classes completed and several groups of schoolchildren and retirees to my credit, I am assigned to a busload of British dignitaries who have requested a tour. After leading them through a good sampling of the exhibits, I have decided to end on the main floor, since it allows them to depart through the 14th Street entrance and board their bus.

I explain the brass pendulum exhibit—its origins in Italy, how its sundial and pendulum concepts combine to produce visible evidence that a day has passed. Then, just for them, I draw on something I remember from Churchill. I talk about the interwoven destinies of the English-speaking peoples. "Whether we be British or American," I tell the group, "we live with the constant awareness of each other. Time passes yet loses its power to separate us when we consider the common origins of our cultural, technological, and philosophical heritage."

Obvious stuff, I complain to myself, but then someone in the group calls out, "Heah, heah!" Well, how charming. Warming to the task, I make allusion to some of de Tocqueville's less-than-flattering comments about Americans. "So restless they are that they clutch at everything yet hold nothing fast. Americans will build a house in which to spend old age, and sell it before the roof is on."

By the end of the tour I have moved on to lines from Shelley's "Mutability": "We are as clouds that veil the midnight moon. How restlessly they speed and gleam and quiver . . ."

I hope it's Shelley's poem, I think in a panic, searching their faces for amusement or contempt—the British do, after all, read their literature! But as I plunge into the last lines and turn to look toward the brass pendulum, a gray-haired man, his voice resonant, his eyes following mine, joins in. "Man's yesterday may ne'er be like his morrow," we recite in unison. "Nought may remain but Mutability."

I bid them good-bye, turn to go, then hear a sound that for just an instant is like a waterfall splashing on rocks. They are clapping. I turn to face them, embarrassed but pleased. Penelope is standing at the edge of the crowd. . . .

Returning my attention to the road, I am stung by the recollection of de Tocqueville's words: building a house to spend old age and selling it before the roof is on? Have Andrew and I done that? With Gary? With each other? Have we just thrown ourselves away? *I* want a tour guide, someone to show me the boundaries, give shape and perspective to this chaos of memory.

I haven't seen the hitchhiker, but I think I'm having mental lapses. I cannot account for parts of this afternoon. I must have been driving dangerously slow at times; I remember a farmer towing a hay baler passing me a while back. Somewhere I stopped for gas and checked the maps for the interchange into Superior. The wind has picked up; the fluffy cumulus clouds have turned to thunderheads, but I didn't notice them changing.

Now it's raining. Rain falls in dark, windy gusts that blow against the windshield, distorting my already dim view of road signs. The rain would have to start just when I'm ready to watch for the turnoff to Superior. If I hadn't been so involved in where I've been, I might have figured out where I was going! I could already be in a motel room by now. There's something to be learned from this, a larger pattern to be observed, something about time and change and the sacredness of the present moment. It hurts to think of it, though, with too many "present" moments already past, everything all out of synch on my timeline: the Seductress of the Mirror got mixed up with the Historian and then the Historian was detoured by the Great Mother and the Great Mother . . . well, she wasn't so great at all. And now the Grieving Mother can't even find her way through a rainstorm. *Whup-whap. Whup-whap. Whup-whap.* The windshield wipers sound needlessly sarcastic.

The interchange for Superior is a watery swirl of green and white signs. I put the wipers on fast speed and I still can't tell one sign from another. I keep driving. Before long I'm in Duluth, Minnesota.

The rain has settled into a steady downpour, but I'm too far off course now to consider going back. I check into a motel that is not on AAA's approved list. I have bypassed Chicago and missed Superior on the Alternate Route and now my plan, twice-removed, is to drive to the harbor in Duluth in the morning and see what I can see of Lake Superior, from a different point of view; then I'll go on to Fort Belmont in Jackson, Minnesota. So much for following directions. I'm lost. Why call Andrew? "Hi, Andrew," I'd say. "I'm lost. Please try to find me." I crawl into bed.

I dream about a woman who sits on the toilet seat in the bathroom of a house. She is bathing her child in the tub, but though she sees him and hears him, she can't touch him because of an invisible barrier of glass that isn't glass. The boy in the bathtub is swollen and bluish and floats on his back. His body keeps changing from toddler to schoolboy to youth, and his voice changes too, but in no relation to his body age. The only consistent part of the dream is that the boy says the same words to his mother. "Hi ya, Mom. See ya, Mom," his changing voices say. Sometimes he smiles and rolls his brown eyes to look at her. If she catches him looking at her, she screams but makes no sound. Every time she speaks to him, she has to turn around because she is distracted by a floating stack of open books—textbooks with bold print headings and colored maps, or thick, fine-print books—none of which she can decipher but which she can't seem to ignore, either. She turns around, raises her hand to wave at the swollen blue boy in the tub, then returns to her books.

6

In the morning I drive through the cold but diminishing rain to a warehouse parking lot at the edge of the Duluth harbor. A drawbridge hovers in the distance, a series of intersecting lines made dim by the gray mist. Closer in, an ore barge and some kind of cargo freighter are docked. Cranes and other hoisting devices stand idly by like gawking prehistoric fowl while men in yellow ponchos trudge from the deck to the pier and back again, laden with crates and boxes. The water lies motionless, gray as steel, pitted by raindrops. "What a view," I say.

Cold even in jeans and a sweatshirt, I roll down the window and stare at the orange hulls of the ships. They'd be rusty either decades old or only a year out of the shipyard. Age is just a matter of degree when it comes to corrosion, given water, oxygenated air, and a chink or two in the surface. I can taste the hull of that ship. Maybe it's just my own corroding body accelerating in its decline. I roll up the window.

I glance at the Minnesota Scenic Guide, half listening to the Farmer's Advisory on the radio. Both of them seem excessively optimistic. The Guide claims that Fort Belmont is a fortress built for families at the time of the early Norwegian immigration. Since when has anyone ever really devised a fortress for families? That idea sounds like the senility of someone who left home at a very early age and never came back. A sanctuary from the Indians, maybe. But not from each other. A fortress for families, indeed.

The radio says farmers can count on the weather lifting by mid-afternoon, but neither the rain nor my gray mood promise to lift easily. If I am going to escape the steel-trap sky in Duluth, I'm going to have to drive out from under it. I switch on the headlights, hit the high-beams button, and start the engine. Vietnam is being discussed on the radio. I turn it off just in time to miss the body counts, the Reading of the Numbers. Too many families. Not enough fortresses. Bleakness, gloom.

I navigate the besotted streets of Duluth, miss one turn, circle back, pull into a service station to read the Central States map. Minnesota 23, a thin red southwesterly line, intersects with Minnesota 71 and leads directly to Jackson. "Twenty-three to Seventy-one," I say. I repeat it several times until it seems that my mind, for all its resistance, might retain the information. It occurs to me that this is the same mind that my fifth-grade teacher, Mr. Whugalter, described to Harold and Virginia as "encyclopedic" and Penelope Welton once implied was "stable." I can only hope it remains functional for the five or six hours the Scenic Guide estimates will be necessary to reach Jackson. I settle in, going backward in time as I go ahead on the road.

The first year in the museum I find myself wondering why Penelope Welton has befriended someone so conventional as I am. One day at lunch, describing her steps for reforming her life, she tells me, "I've decided to cultivate friendships with stable people."

I instantly convert the word to STAPLE and decide that Penelope sees me as a sack of flour, say, or a bag of potatoes. How interesting is a potato? Yet the day she listens to my British tour, she catches me afterward on the stairs and says, "You were really something out there, Roberta."

"I get so carried away," I say. "I spout whatever comes into my head."

We walk down the hall together, she turns toward her office. "You were sparkling," she says, seemingly sincere. I try to believe her. A dull gleam, maybe, but sparkling?

The whole time I work with Penelope, nearly four years, I try to come up with a phrase that will reflect my impressions of her. Months after she has moved away, run off with a Canadian businessman, the answer comes to me. One evening during a bridge game I am taking a sip from the cordial of sherry I've been nursing since dinner. Joe and Maxine Malone are over; conversation is flowing. The image just comes to me:

Penelope is a glass of sherry! No, lighter than that, more golden. A pony of golden brandy rich and thick as syrup where light swims. A pony of brandy can shatter, but oh, how it shimmers. Who would ever *choose* to be a potato, I ask myself, holding my glass to the light.

Andrew speaks through clenched teeth. "For crissakes, Roberta. Can you bid or not?" He is the only one who takes this game seriously, and he's on his second scotch of the evening.

"Sorry," I say. "My mind wandered. I was thinking of my friend Penelope . . . two diamonds."

Two diamonds, I think suddenly. I have sixteen points, a four-card suit with honors, and I bid two diamonds? Isn't that the way it always goes? When you have the potatoes in hand, you go and try for the brandy. I look desperately at Joe. He rolls his big shoulders forward, bearlike. Patient and puzzled, he says, "Roberta, honey. I don't know why you're looking at me that way."

"No tabletalk," Maxine sings.

Instead of trying to figure out the play, I sit for a moment considering my new Bridge Philosophy: two suits, potatoes and brandy. My foot asleep, my hands sweating, I watch Joe lay down the column of cards. I count my losers. I look at Andrew, his brown hair, his pale brown eyes. He is hunched over, cupping his hands to light a cigarette as a breeze blows through the screened porch. A potato if ever there was one, I decide. Peel away the skin, cut slice after slice, and still the potato remains. Should I play the hand as dealt—and lose? Forget the brandy and just be a potato? Or should I lay my cards on the table—what a grand slam that would be!—and tell them all that I've always hated this goddam potatohead game anyway? In the next game I learn to play—I want to believe in an afterlife—there might be a shimmering pony of brandy and. . . . Suddenly I am afraid for Penelope, afraid for her because I think she's gotten the wrong idea about Andrew and me. She's out there somewhere in this deep, warm summer night, smashing things, pouring thick golden liquids down her long, white throat, and wishing for potatoes. Penelope has never seen Gary's face, a narrow face now at thirteen, the uneasy way he lowers his eyes when Andrew and I do battle, cursing and threatening over the band practices, the weekend nights when Andrew plays until two in the bar, the Mondays when he is late for work. I want to tell Penelope that in the split-level on Branchview Court we never really look at each other anymore, and I don't know what to do about it. I just know that potatoes don't shatter. They rot inside until the stench gives their secrets away.

"I pass," I say, pushing back from the table.

"You what?" Andrew whines. "You can't *pass.*"

"That's what I said, Andrew. I pass."

I lay my cards facedown on the table. I rise from my chair and go inside. I can hear them making arrangements for Joe to play the hand. "Now, Andrew, it's just fine," Maxine soothes. "Roberta can be dummy and Joe'll play the hand."

Roberta the Dummy eavesdrops from the kitchen. I scrape distractedly with my fingernail at the scum at the edge of the table. "What's wrong with Roberta?" I hear Maxine whisper to Andrew. He mutters something under his breath.

Maxine gets upset by discord. Maybe Joe has provided so much protection she hasn't found it necessary to wrestle with the larger issues of life. I've felt like The Grappler, some sumo wrestler, whenever I've talked to her about history, philosophy, death. Not that I comprehend; I just have this capacity for absorption. Soak it up, wring it out. Spongy old Roberta. I go to the sink, put my meaty fist around the scrubber, and squeeze.

The scum on the table is a revelation. How long has it been since I've cleaned it? If I were to really scour this table, the varnish, the maple finish, the whole veneer might come off. Yet scrape I do, listening to the voices drifting in from the porch.

Joe is telling about an old veteran who comes into the Walter Reed Bar and Lounge. Joe is in the band with Andrew; they know a lot of the same people.

A pause. Andrew hates this chatter during bridge. He's deciding whether or not to answer. "Harry?" he finally says. "Jeez. Poor guy."

Slip-slap. The cards are falling fast.

"He's sixty-nine years old," Joe adds. "How can he claim he got arthritis in the trenches in World War One? The government's paying him booze benefits!"

I rummage beneath the sink, find a mesh-covered sponge, squirt it with Windex.

"Rheumatoid arthritis, Joe. Bad stuff," Andrew says.

Andrew's a hypochondriac! He's been reading those *Reader's Digest* articles, "Joe's and Jane's Organs" or whatever they're called. He rubs his alleged watery knee—I see him through the window as I'm rinsing the sponge.

"Down two," Andrew announces.

Later they all tromp in from the porch, cheerfully ignoring my sulk. I serve key lime pie for dessert; I eat a piece in the kitchen before I bring it out. Andrew and Joe practice the third verse of "Your Cheatin' Heart," and Maxine keeps me entertained with the finer points of hanging wallpaper around doorjambs and windowsills: "Leave a little edge for yourself. You can always trim later." Andrew pours himself another scotch and mimics the drunks at the Walter Reed Bar and Lounge. It's funny for a while, his rubbery-faced expressions, his slurred speech.

"In comes Sarge from World War Two, and then Harry. They tell each other lies. Sarge? He's still wearing a crewcut like in the war. Same one army give him in forty-one. Veins busted out all over his face; belly's like a beach ball. They drink at the Walter Reed Bar and Lounge, the WRBL."

"It sounds like a radio station," Maxine warbles.

"Parents and spouses. Somebody in for diabetic coma and gangrenous limbs. Cancerous lungs, brain tumors, kids in car wrecks."

I want him to stop. He rearranges his facial muscles, tests his tongue against his teeth. He is no longer *pretending* to be drunk. "Cardiac arrest and cerebral hemorrhage, though. They're the ones really bring 'em in. The shockers."

Has he really learned all this in *Reader's Digest*?

"'Member last week? Lady came in? Husband would kill her if he knew. 'He's an officer!' she says." Andrew's voice is falsetto; he pats his hair, pulls at his shirt collar. "She said, 'It was here or the hospital chapel, but here I am!' Kid was in a head-on collision. Bringing home a twenty-year-old infant is what she was doing. A vegetable. Gonna care for it for the rest of its life—or hers."

Just then I hear the back door rattle. Eerily, Andrew looks at me, both of us with the same shuddering awareness. Gary has just come in. Thirteen years old and unwilling to stay home in the evenings, has he been out running head-on into *his* life?

I go to the kitchen, just in time to see his eyes red as fire, his pupils round as moons.

"Hi ya, Mom," he says, leaning for a moment on the well-scraped table and turning toward the stairs.

"Gary," I whisper, touching the sleeve of his shirt as he pulls away. I breathe for the first time the sweetish scent that clings to him, knowing marijuana without being told what it is. I stand in the kitchen, immobile. The only thought running through my mind is the message I would give to Penelope if I could find her. Do you see this, Penelope? It ain't all sun-warmed earth and hoed-down dirt clods. Clouds do come passin' over the potato patch every now and again.

I stumble back to the living room, drunk not with liquor but fear.

"Gary's home," I say, not sure what my voice is revealing.

Andrew looks at me and pours yet another scotch. I consider going to bed. Joe gives Maxine signals that it's time to leave, shifting his big frame uncomfortably on the sofa. Andrew ignores us and hurries on with his tale.

"It's a good gig," he says. "The nurses from the hospital make it all worthwhile. Right, Joe? Little white caps and uniforms? You forget all the morbid stuff when they come in after the swing shift."

I sit like a zombie, seeing Gary's eyes, remembering that marijuana smell. Andrew drones on, weighing the pluses and minuses of hospital personnel going to a bar so close to the hospital, the risk of encounters with their patients' family members.

One comment grabs my attention: "Remember the guy asking June when his wife was gonna die?"

June? Does he always end up on a first-name basis with women he meets in the bar? Who are these people, I wonder all of a sudden. Have I just not listened before to this shadowy cast of characters?

"They got him settled down, though. June said, 'He's just distraught.' " Falsetto again.

Joe sets his glass on the coffee table. Maxine picks up the dessert dishes.

"Those nurses. Looking for somebody to notice them. Big bright eyes darting around the room. One of the nurses came walking up to me at the break. I got off the stage and was goin' toward the head—'scuse me, ladies, the restroom—and she says to me, she says. . . . What'd she say to me, Joe?"

Joe looks down at his feet, leans his elbows on his knees. "I think she said you were staring at her from the stage, Andrew."

"Oh. Yeah . . ." Andrew says, suddenly quite sober. He glances quickly at me.

I have certainly sobered up, or waked up, or been shaken up. Whatever form of neural anesthesia I've been under has definitely worn off tonight. Gary is smoking dope and Andrew is looking at women from the stage? I must be a catatonic waking from a trance.

He looked at *me* from the stage and look where we ended up! In the world beyond Branchview Court there are women—SHOCK—who might actually find his rumbling low voice attractive, find his muttonchop, potato-eye face wry and gentle. There are women—I am weak in the knees—who would not even hiss in his ear, "Goodness, Andrew, stop it!" when his mouth goes exploring their bodies. "There's a sexual revolution out there," he yelled at me two months ago, the night he stomped from the bedroom. "And you're locked in a goddam museum." Women!

We walk the Malones to their car, and I look up at the night sky. The sky is not dark at all but pierced by the light of hundreds of stars that I would swear have only this evening—yes, I tell myself—only this evening begun to gleam. I close my eyes; I go inside.

Now I am Roberta the Rememberer. I'm hurtling down a two-lane highway in the middle of Minnesota, doing the only two things I can do. I'm laughing and crying. If only I could reach back in time—not very far back in time, either—and shake those shoulders, make that empty head flop back and forth. Oh, Roberta, I want to shout, you Brain-Dead Dummy! But I can't do that. Instead I stop at a truck stop and devour breakfast, the Lumberjack Pancake Special, sitting at the counter between two large men in white T-shirts, one of whom says as he is leaving, "You know, Red, I like a woman with a good appetite." I smile at him and say thank you.

The sun comes out not long afterward. The horizon expands.

Grassy fields and farmland brighten into deep greens and sun-flecked gold. Yet there it is: gloom. The radio reports mayhem in the city streets and carnage in southeast Asia. It all goes on. America loses her sons one way or another. Powerless, the passive victim of her own mistakes, America is going to pieces, and so am I. *Going* to pieces? I've *been* in pieces since the potatoes.

I have a brief fantasy of myself as some kind of savior figure. I imagine the whole thing. Speeches, a statue in my honor, but I get stuck on the idea of the statue. What would it look like, what would it be named? The Statue of Trivia, draped not in the elegant Grecian manner but in a very American-woman way, surely wears a chenille housecoat and fuzzy slippers. She is waving good-bye. Towed on a rented flatbed. Viewed at diners, gas stations, motel parking lots. Telling America what it needs to know. But the only thing that comes to mind when I think about Trivia in her housecoat is the smell of bacon grease in an empty kitchen at 9 A.M. Isn't that what comes next, after the good-bye wave? The longing? Wanting more? There has to be more.

I stretch the Savior of America fantasy as far as it can go, to an interview with Dick Cavett, but the luster is gone. I tell him that my bones are rusty, the color of an old barge. I can see him, bent forward at the edge of his chair. He quips that he has nothing against rust, just that in his experience rust has usually respected the laws of nature, attacking metal, basically. No, the Savior of America feels compelled to explain, rust is working on the laws of corrosion in my case, and working on my bones. Cavett consults his notes, probably wondering who on his staff could have booked such a guest. Better than bruises, I awkwardly assure him. Bruises change color like the flowers on a grave, but rust just gets rustier, a preferable, less traumatic form of deterioration. . . . My watery brown eyes stare back at me from the rearview mirror. Cavett fades out, disappointed that the Savior of America does not have her act together, though she has indeed taken it on the road. I try to smile the way talk-show guests often do, with a toss of my head. All the fillings in my teeth show, and the broken capillaries on my nostrils are especially obnoxious from such a view.

These spaces of inattention are frightening when I return my mind to the road. Now a green-and-white mileage sign appears, but it's gone before I can read it. I check my watch: one-thirty. Jackson can't be too far away.

Before I can reach for the map strips, another road sign appears in the distance, but it is black-and-white, the local variety, probably for farm roads. I squint, once again annoyed with my eyes, afraid to believe what I see. It does seem that one of the words is MONTEVIDEO, which is the capital of Uruguay and just goes to show you what a blind old bat I really am. Then I focus and the words jump out at me in black-and-white:

OLIVIA	5
COSMOS	9
MONTEVIDEO	15

Olivia Cosmos Montevideo. It reads like a name. My own name wilts by comparison. Roberta Patterson Masters sounds plain, safe, and undecided; Olivia Cosmos Montevideo sounds exotic, dangerous, and downright emphatic. A woman with a name like that could never have lived on Branchview Court! I can't imagine such a neighbor. Her gestures would topple trees; her words would humiliate husbands. I cannot contain the image.

"What a woman!" I say as I drive into Jackson, immediately spying the fort as I drive past the town park and eat at a local fried-chicken drive-in. Warmed up, I take a pair of shorts and a short-sleeved shirt into the restroom to change clothes. As I peel off my sweatshirt and jeans, I realize this heat is more like a cold sweat.

Fort Belmont is an unqualified acoustical success. The steps creak as part of the surveillance system; my labored breathing echoes off the vines and tree leaves as I climb wooden steps that wind their way up the hillside in three transversing tiers. Anyone would know I was coming. But where are the people who belong to the cars in the parking lot? Are they hiding out? Is this an ambush?

I reach the gate in the middle of a tall fence, rough-hewn posts painted Park Service brown. "Closed!" yammers a carving hung on a rope. OPERATING HOURS 10–12 AND 1–4 another sign contradicts. I glance at my watch—almost three—and pull the leather thong on the gate. The fortress for families opens.

I have the strangest feeling that I shouldn't have come here, should have stayed in the car, kept moving, but just then a woman about my age comes over to greet me. "I want to welcome you on behalf of our local historical society," she says. "I'm Ann Jensen. I'll be your guide today."

She didn't need any introduction. I'd know her in a minute: a well-meaning, middle-class matron who believes in history. I don't need to read Ann Jensen's name tag to know her.

In a shack posing as a lookout tower is Jennifer, the woman's already name-tagged prepubescent daughter. Sweetly, so sweetly it tears at my heart, the blond girl takes my crumpled dollar bill. Her bony shoulders are straight with the seriousness of her task, her flat, little-girl chest covered by the delicate pink cotton of her summer T-shirt. I feel the clutch of something close to panic. I have the feeling that I should run with this little girl before it's too late. I don't know what I would say to her. As the mother/guide assembles people for a tour, I get the impression that if I could just take the girl and sit with her under a tree somewhere, she would know what I know now, be saved from all the sorrow I've caused or been through. I guess the Savior of America wants to take over here. I walk quickly to catch up with the tour.

A staircase of varnished pine rises at the center of the fort. Glass cases line the walls. Journals open to yellowing pages where ornate scrawls attempt to tell the stories of the early settling families' travails and triumphs. Sepia photographs try to capture moments in the lives of hard-faced men and women squinting into the sun as they stand in front of earthen dwellings or wood-frame walls. The Indian adversaries are remembered with scalps and headdresses and photographs out of which darker faces no less savage or struggle-ridden stare. The tour guide in me acknowledges that the displays are well done. But something is missing here, I keep thinking. Something is not being said.

As we walk upstairs I want to share with the group my vision of the Indian women waving good-bye—to their sons, the braves—and turning back to their flour grinding and fire tending. You see the connections of course, I want to say.

Ann Jensen recounts rape and pillage, house burnings and winter starvation, numerous acts of courage and endurance. But I keep stopping her to ask who raped whom, who starved when, trying to define the participants in this struggle for a homeland, a place for families. She's telling history the way I've always told it, with the tour guide's remarkable detachment. But I'm hearing it through Jennifer Jensen's ears, and I know it is madness. History can't say everything. It doesn't know how.

Somewhere in the back of my mind I realize that Ann Jensen is the woman I thought I was. No wonder I felt I knew her! But this very minute something has happened, *is* happening, to me. I try to listen to the lengthy descriptions of maneuvers the Norwegians used in keeping the Indians so long from the fortress, but I can't help myself. I keep asking questions.

"For *how* long?" I ask.

"Two years," Ann Jensen answers, patient but losing her enthusiasm.

"But what about inside the fortress?" I persist. "Inside!" The war inside.

Ann walks over and places a warm hand on my plump, clammy arm. She smells like flowers. I breathe her in, wondering what I must smell like. "If you can save some of your questions until after the tour, I'll be glad to discuss them with you. I do have the others to think about."

The "others" are all looking at me with expressions ranging from distaste to horror, and I don't see why. I have my sunglasses pushed up on my head just the way they do. Didn't hear *you* asking any of the big questions, I want to jeer. I smile down at Jennifer as we're descending the pale pine staircase. "You'd think this was school," I say. Jennifer's laugh rings out in one clear note, which she immediately swallows behind her cupped hand without even a word or a glance from her mother Ann. Too late.

At the Sod House Museum we stand in the shade of a diseased silver maple whose leaves curl like old hands. I think better of asking about the nature of that blight when Ann Jensen places her manicured hand on the sandy wall of the sod house. She advises us that the building is a replica. "For instance," she says, "this house has windows, but windows were actually rare. If these houses had windows at all, the panels were usually quite small and made of mica."

"No wonder they went mad," I say. "I've read that a lot of the pioneer women went mad out here."

"Uh-huh," Ann says quickly.

"No windows and all that wind howling outside," I say. "Those women were searching for something simple. A place. A home. And no real-estate agents to help them find it!"

"Right," Ann says, keeping a close eye on me as she continues her defense of the historical society's efforts to produce "as close a facsimile as possible" of those early dwellings. She stands back from the doorway, her hair gold in the sun, and points out that flowers bloomed on the roofs of houses made from prairie grasses. Then she nods for the group to go inside. I hesitate a moment and press my cheek against the rough wall, fascinated with the idea of living within the growing earth.

Inside, the air is musty, cool. Ann is holding up a rush broom. "An example of the implements used by the hardy women of this period," she says. "In this domestics department of the prairie are baskets—dried-out creations of woven straw that carried grain, water, wood kindling, and babies."

I notice a cross-stitched sampler hanging on the wall above a table. The cloth has gone yellow, a water stain zigzagging a brown line in its corner, but the threads of red, green, yellow, and blue still brightly and hopefully speak their prayer: "God Bless this House" . . . please?

"The sod houses were usually temporary shelters which the settlers were probably glad to abandon when more permanent structures were built," Ann tells us. I watch the precision of her mouth and tongue forming words, the calm of her hands and fingers pressing a basket to her chest. "But there is considerable evidence to suggest that some families lived six months or longer in homes like this. Timber had to be cleared or shipped in, and the gardens had to be planted. Consider the hazards of these homes as well as their novelty, for the settlers sometimes paid for this built-in air conditioning with their lives. The sod dried out in the summer. . . ."

I imagine the walls going from damp, deep brown to lighter tan in the heat of a searing prairie sun.

"Great fires are known to have swept across the plains, whipped by violent winds, leaving the inhabitants no means of escape." Ann sets the basket on the bed. "It was a difficult life." She pauses and nods to the spinning wheel near the door. "Yet life did go on in the most routine ways. You'll notice the spinning wheel, the woven coverlet on the bed."

The sustaining yet never-ending dailiness of life. I know it. I feel it. Children's supple little bodies to scrub, their chestnut-brown hair to wash and brush out dry. A garden to plant and hoe, vegetables to put up for winter. On the best of days, and maybe even on the worst, pink and yellow blossoms to pluck from the roof and place in a cup at the center of the table, or on a grave.

Even here in this replica, this imitation of what has been, I feel a sense of time suspended. The tidy house seems to be waiting, not for a visiting tourist but for a woman far back in time who has dashed out to pump water, intending to be right back. I lean my elbow on the thick windowsill, peering out through rippled glass at the world in its mid-afternoon rotation, thinking of all the things that never change and the never-ending changes, seeing all of it: colors gone white as an overexposed photograph, shifting variations of green in the sun, shadings of dark blue in the shadows.

The rest of the group follows Ann outside to view a miniature replica of a waterwheel and pump house. I watch them watch water gush from a wheel and tiny drops spin off like beads in the sun. I turn back to the darkened room and kneel at the edge of the bed. I'm startled by the intimacy of the clay floor touching my legs. The bed is stiff as a board. I lift the coverlet and find just that—a board. The brochure claimed that a rush mattress was on the bed. . . . But I let that go. It doesn't matter that the bed is not a bed. The sod house and the rush broom and the history of the woman who might have lived here are as real as . . . as real as the kitchen and the husband and the grave I left only days ago. The sadness of it all takes hold of me, tears at my chest, doubles me over, sets me back on my heels. "Women!" I cry. "Women," I say again, my hand to my mouth.

Jennifer has seen me. Apparently bored with the waterwheel talk she's heard before, she has returned to the doorway of the house. She steps inside. I wave her away, but she just moves closer, standing quietly beside me.

Women! Sweeping floors and embroidering samplers and teaching their sons—and daughters—about history. They swept and sewed and sent their sons to wars. Wars with Sioux sons. Oh, dear God. Wars with VC sons and all the other mothers' sons who ever lived. I feel such rage, and then comes memory—Mothers for Peace marching through this darkened place. It's too late for me now. Too late for Gary. "It's too late," I cry. But I turn to look at Jennifer, whose hand is now resting on my shoulder; I feel the pain recede. I know. At least I know. I know it's too late, if nothing else.

Ann Jensen reappears. She sees Jennifer; she sees my face. She comes to bend over me, sweet flower scent, warm hand on my shoulder, whispering. "What *is* it. What can I do?"

I can't talk. Mute, I can't control my voice any more than I can control my mind. Next thing, Jennifer's hand is pulled away and she is backing out the door. Members of the group crane their necks to see inside. I look up and see in the window a woman's face, distorted by ripples in the glass and by her efforts to see. This audience gives it all a touch of melodrama, the trappings of the stage. Gather round, the barker calls. The Native Woman will now grieve for you . . . for *all* of you!

"Let's move on, now," I hear Ann clucking to her flock of gawkers. "We haven't yet seen the tools and farming implements."

"You haven't seen anything yet," I mumble.

I sit on the floor, moaning, my chest heaving, my head in my hands. I am so sorry. I am sorry to have been born a woman and sorry for everything that came with it. "Born a woman," I whisper to the dank air in this earthen cave. Born: Woman. Née: Woman. They could have given me any name. Roberta Patterson Masters doesn't worsen the condition by naming it. The sins, the stains, the sorrows remain. Sins of trivia. Stains of sons' blood. Sorrows and losses beyond counting or naming. It's a shame. Being a woman is a damned shame.

But what about that road-sign woman? I breathe the fresh air brought in by a breeze and struggle to remember the words I saw on the sign. Olivia Cosmos Montevideo. Now there is a name. There is a woman. I am present at The Creation. I create her. I give her life, this Olivia Cosmos Montevideo. Tall? This woman is tall. And naked as a jaybird. Breasts like overripe gourds just lifted from the ground. Mud clinging to her in smears and globs. Rippling, stretch-marked belly. I give her the grimiest thatch of pubic hair my imagination can conceive.

This woman is rising from the slime. Olivia Cosmos Montevideo is rising from the primal slime, and she looks back only occasionally to check on the creature behind her, to be sure it can keep up. Two-legged and as filthy as she is, it's a man. The woman with the road-sign name cackles. She throws her tangled red hair over her shoulder, slapping her bulging thighs as she lifts her legs from the muck. She stops to laugh again as if she knows something funnier than any joke the universe has come up with yet. And I know why she is laughing. I can't quite laugh with her, but I know why she laughs. She has seen it all. Olivia Cosmos Montevideo knows. She's always known. She knows that everything is a curse and a blessing. For just a split second, I know it too. And then it's gone.

As suddenly as it came, this afterflash of the life of the human race goes back to flat hard time and puts me back in my place—on my knees, on the floor, at four in the afternoon. Where did it come from? How can such a vision leave like bats flying out of a cave at dusk? I want more. Later I'm going to think about this, why I call up time and history this way. Was it my early interest? Historical novels, old maps in our neighbor's attic? New England was rich with history, in houses, graveyards, barns. Yet history wasn't just my interest as a girl; it's been an obsession. I want to think about this later, about a room filling up with history. I want to know why.

I leave the sod house and head for the gate. Ann Jensen and her daughter, Jennifer, are ending the tour. They come over and pull the thong for me. "I'm sorry," I say. "My son, my husband, I . . ."

"Oh, yes," Ann says.

"Bye," Jennifer whispers.

"Take care, now," Ann says, walking with me to the first step.

I turn to look at her. We stand for a moment, silent. I nod and start down the steps.

Driving away from Fort Belmont, too shaken to even question my trembling hands or flowing tears, I get the intrusive sensation that a secret place inside of me has been forced into the light, dim as the light in that sodhouse was. And then I see him: Mr. Whugalter, his flat, mashed-clay nose, his pale blue eyes.

Absurd and banal, I protest, but there he is. Grade 5, 1942. *He* is the one who gave me history, such as it was. This is a case of mind molestation! Yet for a moment I defend him, knowing his intentions were honorable when he used my paper to recall his place on the outline he wrote every day on the board, when he depended on me, only me, leaving chalky fingerprints on pages that read:

A) Battle of Manassas.
  1) Bull Run.
    1a) . . .

"Your notes are always accurate and easy to read, Roberta," he would say to me seriously. He always looked seriously into my plain brown eyes. I don't think I've ever stopped searching for that seriousness he seemed to see in me. Maybe the seriousness was only a charade played out in artificial light for that one shining year, but I can't defend him against the charges. I know it's true: He gave me history, and I took it.

The seriousness couldn't have lasted more than a year, I realize suddenly. Puberty set in right after that, all those hormones surging through my bloodstream, a violation of everything serious I can think of at this moment. No one ever really looked seriously into my plain brown eyes again. They never got past the breasts that swelled on my chest, but then neither did I, neither did I!

History? Hormones? Serious, yellow-chalk moments with Mr. Whugalter, tucked away all these years in dark private spaces?

"And now I'm a woman?" I ask.

Cause-and-effect logic does not explain this journey.

As I pull into the motel parking lot in Sioux Falls, South Dakota, the vision of Olivia Cosmos Montevideo returns. She is out of the slime by now, standing on solid ground and shrieking like a banshee. Woman. It's been a long time since anyone has looked seriously at her, either. But she's laughing. She has seen it all. Even war. Even mothers.

I sleep the dreamless sleep of the dead. I awake, not relieved that my dreams have left me but uneasy about the form they may assume when they return. My head, my entire body echoes with the emptiness of having lost something that would be indistinguishable even if I were to keep poking through the rubble of memory. Worst of all, my mourning for Gary seems further away, outside me. With a perverse nostalgia I want to reach for the sorrow, draw the intensity back, if only for its familiarity. More than grief and dreams seems lost. Just where am I, I want to know in the morning as I climb wearily into the car. And who am I if not my old, remembered self?

7

Mid-morning, at the junction of Interstate 90 and South Dakota 83 from Pierre. A young man stands at the edge of the highway, his long curly hair blowing like weeds in the hot dry wind. He holds his thumb out to me. I greet the reality of this hitchhiker and the certainty of my picking him up as a fait accompli: It had to happen.

I pull off immediately, but he has to run a ways to catch up to the car. I watch him in the rearview mirror. He's wearing those multipocketed shorts that Gary liked to wear. I used to call them his "cargos," and he picked up the term, too. "Hey, Mom," he would shout from upstairs. "Where're my cargos?" For a time I found rocks and baseball cards and long-ignored notices from school in the pockets; later, seeds and a small brass pipe. Finally, the last two years he was home, I quit emptying his pockets for the laundry. I didn't want to know what he carried. That was when he told me everything, as if he knew when I stopped sorting through his possessions our lines of communication might snap. He told me everything I didn't want to know, but now I'm glad he did.

"Where ya headed?" the young man shouts.

"West," I call, feeling the hot, invasive wind push through the car.

He shrugs off his backpack and tosses it in the backseat. We pull onto the highway and the young man unabashedly turns his face toward me, sizes me up.

"We always know each other," Gary said, the day he told me everything. "Like when you took me to the shrink down in the District. I wasn't doing stuff then. But I still looked that way, you know? Like those people came up as soon as I got out of the car."

But I know why he looked "that way." It wasn't tread sandals or filthy jeans or shoulder-length hair, or even the obvious clue that day we went to the counselor in the District: a shirt made from the covering of a bale of Colombian pot that a young woman had given him, claiming to have sewn the shirt herself. Gary looked like part of the underground of searching souls because of his eyes. They had a trapped look, more of a *presentiment* of entrapment, a reflection of the trap his parents writhed around in every day. I know this now. I did not know then, when I needed to know.

"I'm Jeff," the hitchhiker says.

"I'm Roberta," I say, making my assessment of him as the car settles into its endlessly straight lane. "How old are you?" His eyes have no hooded look, just a fringe of thick blond lashes and brows. This is the face of a lifeguard I worshipped in the Catskills in some other far-off time, a time-warped reincarnation.

"Twenty," he says, easily meeting my eyes, not trapped at all as far as I can see. "How old are you, Roberta?"

I return my eyes to the road. "Old enough to be your mother," I say.

"My mother's forty-three."

"Oh. Well, I'm old enough to be *somebody's* mother."

"Whose mother are you?" he asks, sincerely interested, it seems, in the art of conversation. I have been wanting someone to talk to, but I did not expect this. I am hating Jeff's mother, whoever she is, because Gary once shared conversation with me this way; he spoke in intelligent sentences that connected with mine. Look where that led.

"Does your mother know you're wandering around on the highway this way?" Who am I to ask that question? Look where I allowed my son to wander.

"Yeah, she knows. More or less."

I know I can get hold of myself if we can just switch the subject. But what else is there to talk about except family? I interview him. I move him toward college, find out he was going to Dartmouth until he dropped out. But we go back again to family. I discover that his mother is somewhat shakily married to his father, a Boston businessman. "He's corporate," Jeff says. "Establishment. They've had trouble over the war."

"Trouble?" I ask, my ears pricking up at the thought of this perfect woman's perfect son needing to escape his father.

"My mother protests and my father objects and, like, gets uncomfortable."

I know what's coming, but I ask anyway. "How does she protest?"

"Well, I mean she's really been doing it for years. When I was little she went away for a week and went to Washington, D.C. That's the first one I remember. She came home and told me about Martin Luther King. She was, like, on fire with this thing."

"Civil rights," I say.

"Yeah," he says.

When he was "little" means 1963; he means the early marches. When Gary was little I was telling him about dinosaurs! I feel there's not enough air in this car. I roll down the window. The wind creates static electricity in my hair. My hair is getting in my eyes; I'm having to let go of the steering wheel to brush the strands from my face. I roll up the window.

"She didn't leave you by yourself, did she?"

"She went to a lot of local marches. But yeah, she left us."

This is some new kind of status for children: My mother marched. A new kind of shame: My mother *didn't* march. It occurs to me that I could run the car off the road, just take it bouncing and bumping in the wind toward the horizon.

"My grandmother stayed with my sisters and me lots of times. Then Mom went to Washington again in sixty-seven with Another Mother for Peace. She took us with her then."

He knows the difference between me and his mother. He is making an assessment, judging by clothing, jewelry, hairstyle. There are so many outward signals these days. I guess it wasn't just Gary and his friends; it's everyone. Always that question: Are you with us? It hangs in the air when people meet. Whatever *with* means. Jeff leans back against the seat. I know he has his answer; I can feel the space between us widen out.

"You have a family?" he asks, unable or unwilling to let me disappear into my shell.

"I have a son," I say. Attempting to avoid further questions, I add, "But he's gone now. It's just my husband and I."

"Where is he? Your husband."

The wind is dry and hot in the world outside. And Jeff is relentless with these questions. I don't know if he means to be, but I want to ask for a time-out. Hey, I've just barely begun to get the idea, I want to tell him. I feel the sobs begin in my chest. I'm wailing. My voice sounds like a Vietnamese woman I saw on television. She was standing over a funeral pyre; she seemed so far away. I pull over to the shoulder of the road.

"Did I say something wrong?" he asks, his voice gentle. His eyes follow a car that roars past us, then return again to me.

I try to distract him with the Trip-Tiks. "You might not want to ride with me," I say. "I stop a lot at historical sites. Badlands, next stop," I say, blowing my nose and handing him the folded out section in the maps where the monument is marked. I aim my shaking finger at the green line stamped with a red arrow pointing west.

"It's okay, Roberta," he says, handing the Trip-Tiks back. "I'll ride with you that far."

I cannot get control of myself. I go on sobbing, looking at him as long as he's not looking at me. His square hands spread out on his knees, he waits for me to stop crying before he asks any more questions, but I know he is thinking them up as we sit here. He looks out the window on his side, then looks straight ahead, then puts his arm on the back of the seat and turns to face me.

"You want me to drive for a while?" he asks.

"No!" I shriek. "No," I say, my voice lower. "You're not insured."

Absurd, considering the last few days of my trip and the miracle that I've survived this "insured" driving of my own. I am terrified at the thought of letting anyone else touch the steering wheel.

Until this moment I was thinking that I'd grown stronger, that the shifting feeling I had yesterday in Minnesota was a sign of something better ahead. Now I realize that I'm in a new stage, just as if I had a disease. I think I know what this is. I think it's mental illness. A few days ago I couldn't trust my perceptions, hearing things, seeing things. Now I can't trust my mind, my ability to reason—I tell this boy that he can't drive my car because he's not insured? And look at me. . . . I glance in the rearview mirror at my wreck of a face. I am more than a little bit loony.

"So, does your son go to college?" Jeff asks.

I can't assign evil motives to him. He's operating on a reliable assumption: Ask a mother about her child and she's going to feel better.

"What's your full name?" I ask.

"What? Oh. My full name? Geoffrey Alston Mills, the Third. Family name. You know, Geoffrey with G-e-o."

"My son, Gary Andrew Masters, the One and Only, is dead," I say, my breath catching on every word. "He died in the war. May."

"Oh, my God," he says. His face goes gray. It seems that the news shakes his body. It shakes mine as I sob. "I'm sorry," he says. He puts his hand on my shoulder. The wind is blowing outside; a gust thumps the car. He pulls his hand away and pounds his fists on his thighs, rocking forward and back. "Goddam military-industrial complex," he spews. "Fucking warmongers. Goddam murderers, all of them."

"Wait a minute," I say, unable to add anything else.

I am thankful that he is sharing this sorrow with me, but there's nothing personal here. The rhetoric of the protest is too familiar. I've been hearing it on television. I heard it in the streets outside the museum. I am removed from his words; for just an instant, I find a breathing space.

"Wait just a minute," I say.

I know I've been a liar. But this is dogma, too, as profane and empty in its way as the lies I've told as history. Like the whispering commentator at a televised tennis match, I am removed. Jeff and I are at Love-All in the match, this game to win my mind. We volley.

Pock. Jeff: "When did they draft him?"

Pock-pock. Me: He wasn't drafted."

Pock. Jeff: "You mean he signed *up?*"

Score still even. Love-all.

Pock. Me: "Yes."

Pock-pock. Jeff: "Was he going to get drafted? Couldn't he get a deferment? College? Four-F? Canada, even?"

Pock. Me: "He didn't try. I signed the papers. He was seventeen." *Pock. Pock. Pock.*

Game.

* * *

Jeff is silent for an hour or more. I drive with a zombie's staring concentration. I am empty and evil and will blow in the wind forever and ever and . . . Jeff wakes up. He starts in again. "I don't see how you can live with yourself, Roberta. I'm so damn sorry your son died. I just don't see how this could have happened."

"I don't either, Jeff." I smile at him, wickedly insane. "See how it happened, I mean. Or live with myself. Either one, Jeff. Take your pick. I don't see how."

"There's got to be . . ." he says, ". . . something you can do."

He's torn between rage and compassion, so he's going to do something. He asks me to stop the car. He gets out his backpack and sits on the roadside. I assume he's jumping off here. He's trying to light a cigarette, the smashed little marijuana kind. I lean over to close the passenger door.

"Wait!" he calls, his voice hitting a high note that pierces my heart, the voice of a boy at twelve. If I'm drugged by voices, I can't just leave him on the roadside smoking *his* dope. I wait for him. He gets back in the car. My God, I think. Did his perfect mother teach him not to smoke dope in the car?

He lies back, very laid back, and goes to sleep. He has done something. What can *I* do? My stomach knots up in my empty body and squeezes strong acid into my throat. I burn.

I stop at Wall, South Dakota. Every vehicle seems to stop. There was Sioux Falls, and then Pierre, and now there's Wall. There has been nothing for so long, nothing but the wind, and suddenly this tawdry tourist trap that's been promised by billboards for a hundred miles materializes. I stop without any critical intelligence functioning, without any pretense of trying to separate myself from anyone else traveling along this road. Wall, South Dakota, is the gateway to the Black Hills, the Badlands. Of course I stop. I look out into the distant horizon and see the jagged peaks jutting out of the prairie flatlands like a great subterranean hacksaw. I wouldn't dare keep going.

I'm looking out my window at the mountains when I hear Jeff

stir in the seat beside me. I turn just as he reaches for my purse and opens his door. "Hey!" I yell.

He opens the rear door, grabs his backpack, and runs toward the gas station at the far edge of the buildings. I bump out of the car, my legs so stiff I know I can't move fast enough to catch him. I throw my voice, instead, like a line with a lure and a hook.

"What would your mother say?" I scream.

He stops running in order to reach into the purse and extract what I know to be almost one hundred dollars in cash from my wallet. He stuffs the bills in one of his many pockets. My driver's license, I realize. He might run off with my driver's license! I run, I run right into the wind.

"Shame on you," I say as I catch up to him.

He backs away, shaking out the contents of my purse as he checks for loose cash.

I talk fast: "I know you, Jeff. I understand you. You're stoned and you want to stay stoned because you don't want to grow up to be like your father, and you're not sure how else to be."

He looks up at me quickly.

"What would your mother say?" I ask him again.

"Fuck you, Roberta! You bitch. My mother would tell you to quit fucking around with my head!"

He slams the purse to the ground and takes off for the gas station. A family piling out of their Winnebago has seen the whole thing. The man starts after Jeff.

"Don't bother. No," I say, waving the man back.

My knees burn from the pavement as I kneel, and my hair blows stringy into my mouth as I grab my wallet—credit cards still there, travelers' checks. I scrape the debris of used tissues and lipstick and maps from the asphalt and into my purse. "My son. Family problems," I lie, ignoring the facts but telling the truth. I watch Jeff disappear into the restroom. Don't go. Don't leave me. . . .

The man reaches down and takes my elbow, helping me up. "Kids, huh? What're you gonna do—lock 'em up? My kid's got hair past his shoulders, and his clothes, for cryin' out loud. . . ."

Please stop talking, I want to say, knowing at the same time that he has conferred on me some sort of blessing with his understanding.

"Yes," I say to this unlikely priest, pulling my arm away as quickly as I can without seeming ungrateful. "Thank you," I say. "Thank you."

I get back in the car.

It is mental illness, utter madness, to think we know what is best for our children. Always too late. Parents always find out too late.

I spend a sleepless night in Rapid City, South Dakota. As if to compensate for years of sleepwalking, I thrash around in the motel bed, helpless with rage over the encounter with Jeff. How dare he bring his perfect mother into this, I weep. Has he ever tried to wake a sleepwalker? Roberta Patterson Masters has been trying to wake up all along . . . hasn't she? Bumping into shadowy forms that turned out to be walls, furniture, people, trees, I've been *trying* to open my eyes. Who's to say what I've seen? . . . or haven't seen?

He stole my purse; he took my money; he believes in a cause. "Like hell," I sob, pounding on the pillow. "He's probably an escaped inmate!" He might have gotten away with my driver's license; he will never know the damage he might have done.

I listen to the wind blow all night long, wondering if there are self-help books for reformed sleepwalkers. Maybe there's an organization . . . but no, I stop myself. There I am again, waiting for help. I decide, instead, to name myself as the charter member of the newest thing in American psychology: Sleepwalkers International. I can see myself stumbling to a table in a gymnasium and signing up. I turn to a crowd of tottering, bleary-eyed people with knots on their heads, bruises on their knees. "I was asleep and now I'm waking up," I say. "O-yez, o-yez," the people whisper.

I doze off briefly toward dawn and dream that I find, in the mailbox on Branchview Court, a letter rejecting my application for Sleepwalkers International. "No," I'm saying. "You can't reject me. I *founded* this organization . . ." I wake up as if startled by a loud noise.

"Just a dream," I mutter as I shuffle to the bathroom and sit down on the toilet. But I have to wonder if I know anymore the difference between reality and the torments of dreams. The warm stream of urine leaving my body and splashing into the bowl gives me the first substantial clue I've had all night.

8

In Wyoming I think of giving in, shattering my empty shell to bits and merging with the incessant wind. As if this were a game of Truth or Dare, the wind gusts become stronger. I look at mountains far in the distance, the sides of a huge channel where the wind gathers velocity and power. I'm afraid to live and afraid to die—not much daring in that, but it's the truth.

I come to a town and miss its name on the road sign. I stop for gas. The service-station attendant insists on checking the oil. "This car don't sound too good, ma'am," he says, wrinkling his forehead.

"Okay, fine, whatever," I tell him.

I get out to stretch my legs and walk around. The wind comes with me, past storefronts and a brick department store. At the end of the block I stop to look at the display window of a sporting goods store. Orange caps with earflaps. Fluorescent vests. Rods, reels, knives, and rifles. A tumbleweed—a real tumbleweed—comes whipping around the corner after me. *Whump, whump, whump.* It startles me so that I dash inside the store.

I am a woman alone. I'm being attacked by tumbleweeds! I wonder if I need to protect myself from the likes of Jeff the hitchhiker as well. I compare my concern with self-defense to Jeff's need to *do* something. He "turned on," but he was trying to turn into himself, away from me. I suspect I cannot turn into myself. I believe that I have actually lost myself on the highway. Voices of neighbors on Branchview Court set up a refrain: "It's true! It's true! Roberta Masters just lost herself on that trip she took." I won't listen to any more of *that.*

Angry now, I head for the hunting and fishing section, a tangled forest of poles in upright containers and rifles in locked glass cabinets. Moose heads and deer heads form a watchful semicircle of glass eyes from the upper portions of the walls. Then I catch the smell. Oiled steel and leather and wood. I know this smell. Gary told me about the smell of oiled metal, how it was everywhere when he got to the war. I can smell the death these hunters are after. I think I've been tracking it for six days. My throat is closing up, the room is closing in. What on earth am I doing here?

A man appears behind the counter, offers his expertise.

"I need a gun. Someone stole my purse yesterday. I got it back, but. . . ."

"Yes, ma'am. If you had a hunting license, I could sell you a rifle, ma'am. . . ."

The man is clean-shaven and short-haired. He is questioning me with his respectful eyes. Respectful in the old way, I can tell. I can hear my great-grandfather Patterson telling my tormenting male cousins, "Just you remember, lads. Every girl could be a mother someday, and you know how blessed mothers are." I want to tell this cowboy-gentleman-hunter, in the new way: YOU KNOW WHAT LUNATICS MOTHERS ARE! GIVE ME A GODDAM GUN, QUICK! I look back out the glass doors and see a woman in a headscarf leaning into the wind.

"But frankly," he is warning me, "unless you're planning a stay here, you couldn't get a handgun until you got it registered, and with this being Friday, this late in the morning, the earliest we'd get the registration would be next week sometime."

I haven't given a thought to guns being legal or illegal. I might get arrested for having an unregistered gun in the car? Hah! I should be arrested for letting Gary have a registered U.S. Government Issue rifle in his hands, in his precious hands.

In the insane way of lost mothers, I am overjoyed as I leave the sports store empty-handed. I don't need a gun! I don't have to do a thing. Awake or asleep, I just have to wait. Sooner or later the Madness will take me. If I let it. If I choose. . . .

But must I wait in this wind? In the car again, driving toward Cheyenne, I am so irritable I could spit at a snake. My eyes are already scratchy from lack of sleep. I'm sick and tired of my hair whipping in my face every time I get out of the car. I watch those weeds and bushes and occasional trees out there, slapped around by blasts of air coming through this wind tunnel. Rooted there without a choice, waiting, waiting for the wind to stop, and it's never going to stop. But not me. I'm waiting too, but I have a choice. I can wait where the goddam wind doesn't blow.

I am reading roads signs in a way I have not read them this whole trip. My eyes are performing beyond their capacity through the sheer force of my desire. I read every road sign until I see one that tells about something other than wind:

I–25 SOUTH

DENVER

That's for me.

I go south. I drive toward the mountains I've read about all my life. I drive into the Rockies and the wind stops blowing. I know wind blows in the Rockies. Sure it does. But it's not blowing now. I check into a motel on the outskirts of Denver. Outside my window the mountains look close enough to touch. Although I wake up almost hourly, listening the way a madwoman listens, eyes wide and head atilt, I never hear the wind blow all night long.

Southern Colorado, northern New Mexico. It's not all that different from South Dakota and Wyoming. The distances between towns are so long I feel like I've dropped off the earth. Isolated, desolate. But there are mountains. At least things go up and down.

I drive along on I-25, on a collision course with Mexico, Central America, and other points south, having no idea what the AAA Alternate Route would have been. Some formula I came up with. Keep Moving and Follow Directions? I haven't followed directions since I bypassed Chicago, and I probably missed turns I didn't know about before that. As for staying in motion, I am suspicious of that part of the formula as well. I can wait for the Madness standing still. Besides, I have an overall sense of slowing down, a feeling that goes beyond malaise and fatigue and disorientation. Everything around me is slowing down. Even the car.

This wagon used to be a sparkling blue. It's a murky color now, like a muddied-up river, what with bugs, dust, and rain spots. It hesitates when I try to accelerate on the steep inclines of mountain passes. I lag behind loaded semis. On one cut through a sheer cliff in a place called Raton Pass, I thought the car was going to stop altogether, but then it seemed to revive.

I suspect my mind may be causing the physical slowdown of my body and my car. According to a talk-show guest on the radio this morning, mind energy is physical energy. No wonder this car has trouble with forward motion—talk about energy depletion! My mind is disintegrating, sending out confused and garbled messages to my body: Keep moving, but don't ask *me* to come along. Follow directions, but don't ask *me* what they mean.

I know I'm moving because the roadside still blurs somewhat as I go by, but I have definitely lost momentum. I have begun to drift.

The car has been pinging on the upward grades ever since I left Colorado, somewhere along the state line. I watch the gas gauge: FULL. I see a red light on the instrument panel: OIL. I keep driving. Road signs talk about Taos and Santa Fe. Seventy-five miles to Santa Fe. Stay at La Fonda Hotel in Santa Fe, 15 miles. Just as the Santa Fe exits appear, the noise reaches a raucous metallic crescendo. I can't even hear the radio over this clanking din. I drive slowly into a gas station at the Nambé Mills exit. White steam and gray smoke billow out from under the hood; the odor of burned rubber casts a pall in the air. I am deathly calm. I take the time to set the emergency brake before I get out. What do I care?

The service-station attendant makes a great show of flinging open the hood as I open the door and walk from the car. Jumping back, grabbing a rag to remove the cap from the boiled-out radiator, he and a cluster of local patrons who have gathered to watch inform me that my engine is probably ruined. They have softly stretched out accents, probably Hispanic.

"Whole cooling system's ruined," he yells, thrusting his head toward the edge of the pavement, where I stand contemplating my mortality. He pronounces it "sees-tum."

"Oil's almost gone!" another disbelieving, almost grieving voice calls from beneath the hood.

The attendant advises me, "Lady, you gotta take *care* of a car if you expect . . ."

"It's my husband's fault," I snap, tuning them all out in a hurry, cutting short any lecture on car maintenance. "He never mentioned the oil. Besides, I had it changed up in . . ." I don't know the name of the town in Wyoming. "Up in Noname, Wyoming."

They give me a blank look.

I blame Andrew for the car breaking down? What a curious thing, I think, walking toward the station. Actually, I think he did mention something about changing the oil, when I pulled out of the driveway and jerked to the stop sign at Branchview and Woodland. I suspect there is a lot I haven't heard Andrew saying. But that was so long ago. All things being relative, that was so very long ago.

I am staring at the remarkable blue of this sky, breathing in air that is bracing and fresh, even with the settling exhaust fumes and smoke. I sign one of the traveler's checks Jeff the hitchhiker didn't take. For a moment my mind returns to him, Geoffrey Alston Mills, the Third. I skim back to the sports store in Wyoming and the gun I might have bought. I let the thoughts go when the attendant calls to me.

"Tow it to town for you, lady?"

"Tow it!" I command him, adding belatedly a majestic sweep of my arm.

My only means of transportation is being dragged like a corpse behind me. Can't I even muster the distress appropriate to the occasion? I wonder if I am suffering from some form of altitude sickness. The city-limits sign said Santa Fe is six thousand and some feet above sea level. This is thin air. I feel giddy.

Why keep moving, anyway? Rolling red hills are sprinkled by dark bushes that hug the earth. In the distance mountains rise. The air is tingling, even in the heat of summer. And the sky, the sky, I tell the truck driver too many times.

"They must sell a lot of sunglasses out here. So bright. Blue, isn't it? I mean really blue. *Blue*-blue."

Blah-blah. He hasn't listened to a word of it, leaned against the door the way he is, elbow poked out the window. He takes the car to a garage next to a salvage lot where he seems to know the people. I sign some papers; the mechanic hands me a card and tells me to call tomorrow. I give the hood of my old blue car a solid farewell whap and climb back into the truck.

"Where to, lady?" the driver asks, his first words of the afternoon.

"Is there a hotel called the Fonda?" I ask, trying to remember the billboards on the highway. I think longingly of bed and bath and food. Forget the money. I'll charge it.

"La Fonda," the driver says.

"*La* Fonda," I say.

I feel dizzy as I get out of the truck and stand on the sidewalk in front of the La Fonda Hotel. Rounded adobe buildings cast cooling shadows on the intersection. Shelby and San Francisco streets, I note, still trying to navigate. Instead of going inside, I walk up the street a ways, toward what must be the town square, with a bandstand in the middle and grass all around. A sign says the Plaza was built in the 1700s, but everything here feels new. New to me!

"The Plaza," I say aloud. I like that. It sounds more festive than the *town squares* of those dour founding fathers in New England. And it's a close race as to which date would be the oldest if I compared the bronze plaques marking many of them. I keep having the feeling that I'm not really here, but then something happens, I touch the letters on the plaque, a breeze moves the sleeve of my shirt, and I know that yes, I *am* here. Odd.

I window shop the stores that encircle the Plaza. I stop before the gallery window of one.

A ceramic sculpture not more than a foot high has caught my eye. I squint past the sunlight reflected on the window; I frame my hands against the glass to see inside. It's a child figure, sitting tailor style, his round head bent slightly forward, in his lap an open book almost too large for his hands to hold. I see myself in the window glass as my hand flies to my mouth, ready to stifle whatever wail, whimper, or moan is about to escape. That little boy . . .

"Ah, Gary," I whisper. But then I resist the familiar despair, the shame that wants to crawl all over me. That little boy, I tell my reflected image, despite all the misinformation he received, did spend a lot of happy hours with his mother and her big books. No war can take those moments away from us! The thought is a resolution: Be it resolved . . . and it *is* resolved. The woman in the window's reflection hoists up the strap of her shoulder bag without a whimper. I am the woman in the reflection, and I walk right into the gallery.

"I want that little boy," I say to the clerk. "The piece in the window."

"Yes," he says.

I follow close behind as he walks toward the displays. "The boy child," I say. I feel a chill, suck in my breath, as he lifts the foot-high sculpture from its shelf and dust motes scatter in an arc of bright sunlight. *"The Boy Child with Book,"* I say slowly, reverently, and with authority.

"Yes," the clerk says. Who is he to quibble with an art collector? He wraps it in several layers of brown paper while I pull out my plastic credit card.

I carry the sculpture from the shop, clutched to my chest, warm and solid as a kitten. Maybe life is just a sad series of suitable and less-than-suitable substitutions, I think gloomily. I keep expecting the comforting sensation of the statue to be gone, but it still feels good held close.

As I walk from the shop I see Indian women sitting on the sidewalk in front of an adobe building—the Palace of the Governors, I read on the wall plaque. They have jewelry and pots laid out on blankets before them. They wear dark purple or scarlet velvet blouses over long bright cotton skirts. Some work their fingers over objects they are creating out of leather or wood; others sit quietly and look far away when I try to catch their eyes. Small children kneel beside the women. I glance up at the huge clock atop a verdigris lamppost, its glass face a blaze of sun, unreadable from this angle. What time is it getting to be?

I rush back to the La Fonda, hoping I'm not too late to get a room.

I enter the hotel through doors painted blue. A shop in this tunnel-like entrance displays bright fabrics in the window. Woven, high-fashion creations drape casually on antique chests; exquisite stuffed toys for children float on puffy cotton clouds. Suzette's is a little treasure chest of color and texture within the earthen walls of the hotel. New Mexico is only tan on the outside, I realize. Tan is the agreed-upon color. I can just hear a decorator on a morning talk show with this: "I mean, look, honey. You've got this sky. . . ." But who needs greenery when inside each building, behind every window these colors just burst, bright as a sun-drenched prism? My heart races at the sight of the colors, the textures, as if my miserable mind can't stop my body from enjoying the show.

I pass through more tall blue doors and into the cool hush of the lobby. I stand a moment, letting my eyes adjust, probably looking somewhat bewildered. From behind the desk to my left a clerk offers assistance.

"Yes," I tell him. "I want a room."

I imagine myself a rich eccentric who never makes reservations. The clerk tells me I'm getting his last available room. "A fortunate cancellation," he tells me conspiratorially. "In the old section, too."

"How nice," I say knowingly, as if I've always known.

I hesitate as I sign the register, worried that I may be asked to provide some sort of identification, something more than a driver's license. My name, it's true, is Roberta Masters, but that's not the whole story. And they want an address. All right, then. Here's the whole squalid tale: "Roberta Masters," I write. "In Transit."

The clerk is either too young or prematurely jaded to ask questions. And why would he ask questions? People move around. I stop arguing with myself about my lack of credentials, but it is a bleak summary of my existence on that page. Roberta Masters. In Transit. What sort of a statement is that, and am I *really* here? Maybe things vaporize in the desert. I tuck my purse and the wrapped-up statue securely under my arm as a precaution.

The clerk signals a bellboy and then leans out over the desk to check for luggage. My suitcase is still in the car. It never occurred to me to take it out. At this very moment it is probably being ransacked by thieves as the blue carcass is stripped and prepared for the boneyard.

"In the car?" he asks.

"No luggage," I say.

He cancels the message with a sidewise wave of his upraised palm.

Roberta Masters. In Transit Without Her Luggage.

As I walk to my room I hear a song or maybe the echo of songs I've been hearing on the car radio. It plays in my mind; if not Janis Joplin's voice, then her type of voice, straining her vocal cords to be heard, sailing off into madness with her pain: "Freedom's just another word for/nothin' left to lose. . . ."

Humming the tune, I sit down on the bed, its headboard a cluster of carved, handpainted flowers. I unwrap the statue and set it on the end table next to the telephone, trailing my fingers over the roundness of the boy's head. I feel as if hands have been working on me since I got into this town. Everything I've seen has been the work of someone's hands. The mud walls. The sculptures and paintings and weavings and beads and pots and now these carved flowers. Hands and fingers just working away. Is everyone in town a craftsman or artist? I don't know about this place, this strangely handmade place, so far away from who I am and yet comforting somehow . . .

I reach over and dial home, waiting for Andrew to answer, not sure what I will say. The ringing goes on. There is no answer. I call the desk and ask for the time. Six-fifteen. Mountain Standard is two hours earlier than Eastern. That makes it eight-fifteen in Washington. He *must* be home from work. I dial again. He does not answer the phone. I call the operator and she dials. Andrew is not at home. He is not available. I have been gone for seven days and never even tried to call him; I must not panic if one evening he doesn't answer the phone.

The idea of him not being there has set off a chain reaction: He's had a wreck out on the highway while looking for me, he's asleep, he's over at the neighbors, he's gone back to the band and is practicing at Joe's house, he's seeing a nurse, he never stopped seeing the nurse named June, he's living with her. . . . But those little explosions don't even count. The big bang in this chain reaction, the most powerful punch in this explosion of unreality feels like living in a split-level house. You're upstairs and something drops downstairs in the kitchen, or you think it's the kitchen. Upstairs, where you are, you know you've just dropped the book you were reading or the basket of laundry you were carrying, but you don't know for sure what has happened down below. What was that, who was down there when you were last there? It takes time to call out and maybe you won't be heard, so you have to go downstairs to find out that Andrew dropped the big frying skillet or Gary dropped the bean pot. That's how this is. I can't get at the *real* reaction, the one that has jolted me so that I am suddenly standing at the window in my hotel room, looking at the sunset over rooftops of a city that I must surely have dreamed. Some kind of patient excavation will be required to trace the epicenter of this explosion: I NEED ANDREW. He is not available now and he was not available when I was home, but I need him bad. I HAVE LOST GARY AND LEFT ANDREW AND I AM ALL ALONE. I lie down, turn on my side. I feel the design of the woven spread being imprinted on my face. I ought to pull back the covers. I should have stopped for shampoo and toothpaste at the newsstand, should have called room service for dinner, should have gone into one of those shops and bought some clothes, not a statue! What am I going to do when Andrew starts getting all the bills for this trip and decides to close out the checking account and write me out of his will? I HAVE LOST GARY. I reach for the statue and curl myself around it. I think of the Indian women I saw on the sidewalk, some of them very old, their hair blue-black but their brown eyes clouded with a whitish cast. What if I grow old in Santa Fe? I will have no grandchild to bring with me as I do my vending on the sidewalk. What will I sell if I have no beads or silver or pottery that I have made with my hands? Who will hold my hand and walk with me into the future? Whatever will become of me, I think, sunk in gloom and fatigue. No use worrying about my old age now. Maybe I'll wear bright cotton skirts and velvet blouses and dance for my supper in the blinding sun. Maybe I'll just dance until I drop. I HAVE LOST GARY AND I NEED ANDREW AND I AM ALONE. WHERE AM I? WHERE ARE THE PIECES? Lost somewhere on the highway, probably, but all I know for certain is that I'm staying in Santa Fe for a while. I have no momentum. No means of leaving and even less desire to do so. I have stopped.

II

WORDS

She heard a voice saying, "Your innocent children were given to you to keep. Now you must search for them until the end of the world." And to this day her voice can be heard, often at night, starting about eight o'clock, crying, "Alas, my children!"

—"The Weeping Woman Forever Without Rest" from *The Hungry Mother: Myths and Legends of the Aztecs* by John Bierhorst

1

I wake early, six-thirty, but when I call Andrew in Virginia he doesn't answer. It's already eight-thirty back there. Andrew has left for work, and I've forgotten his Pentagon phone number. All of that seems so unreal to me, anyway: the Pentagon, the War, the doorbell of our house on Branchview Court, and Gary, our son. Actually, I still *have* a son. His brown eyes, his soldier haircut. I can remember him and see him, but I cannot remember Andrew's Pentagon phone number. This is selective recall.

By seven I am out prowling the hotel corridors, the little boy sculpture clutched to my chest, hoping to find the newsstand and dress-shop again—and food. Showered but not shampooed, I have brushed my wet hair back from my face and stepped into the familiar stench of the clothes I've traveled and now slept in. Only the tap-slip-tap of my sandals on the tiles breaks this eerie, early-morning calm. I can't shake the feeling that things might vaporize or disappear out here.

At the mezzanine I lean out over the rail to see the quiet rectangle of the lobby. A dining room gleams like a capiz-shell box in a curio shop, bathed in sunlight streaming from skylights above my head. I don't remember the glass walls of that dining room from yesterday! I cannot place myself. I wonder if I am in some other part of the hotel, or in another hotel altogether.

I hurry down the stairs to examine the alternating panels of clear and frosted panes framed in turquoise painted wood. Red and blue flowers, brown burros, birds of yellow with eyes of green—all painted onto the glass. Hand-painted glass! The perfect foil for the massive calm of these walls, the hard, dark sheen of the tile floors. A white radiance seems to splash through the glass walls of the dining room and into the just-waking lobby. I've never reacted to sights as if they were numinous visions! This place excites me. I haven't forgotten that I need to buy shampoo and toothpaste, but I am excited.

An older man is now at the desk, the telephone receiver propped between his shoulder and his ear, routing slips of paper to guests' boxes with his palely efficient clerk's hands. A row of carved benches on the other side of the lobby sits unoccupied except for an Indian man who seems to have dozed off. Life is signaling to them from the dining room, I think, mystified. Don't they notice the tinkle of crystal, the hum of voices, the dance of the light?

A dark-haired woman in an elegant dress of turquoise and black gracefully rises from a chair behind the cash register to assure me that I am "just in time for breakfast." I haven't been just in time for anything on this trip. Is this a sign? Picking up a menu and smiling at me, she tips her head atop her swanlike neck and says, "Just one, then? For breakfast?"

Melodious words, rapturous questions! I answer both. "Yes, yes," I say, wanting to be responsive and polite, wanting to create for this resplendent woman, whose filligree earrings shiver a little melody on the sides of her neck as she walks, as pleasant a morning as I am experiencing. I bounce along behind her, smiling at the few diners who are up this early, grateful for her assistance in finding my way. I've been navigating without my Trip-Tiks for two days.

And then I'm seated, admiring the crisp white linens, squinting to read the menu, basking in the rosy effulgence of a cranberry-colored glass lit from within by a shaft of sunlight. Wonderful place, I keep thinking. The waitress brings a hot plate of beans and eggs and tortillas and other things hot. *"Huh-way-vohs Ran-chair-ohs,"* is what I think she said I ordered. A shyly smiling busboy even brings me Kleenex when I start blowing my nose between bites of this New Mexican breakfast. I think about the letter I'm going to send to my mother. I'll begin with where I am and may or may not get around to how or why I've come.

After another shower and a much-needed shampoo, I sit for a while in my room and read the *Santa Fe New Mexican* I bought at the newsstand.

I'll need to stay somewhere besides a hotel, I think, flipping through the classified ads. Until the car's ready. Until I know what I'm doing. Who knows how long *that* will take?

Houses. Apartments. Rooms. The columns blur. My head hurts with the effort of thinking so far ahead. I drop the newspaper to the floor, get up and wrap my reading-boy sculpture in a towel and place it in a paper bag. I take the bundle with me.

At Suzette's I buy an apple-green cotton dress. When the clerk finds a size to fit me the dress looks more like a tent, but I am actually beginning to feel somewhat "overhauled." I stuff my traveling clothes into a trash container in the lobby, glancing around as I do it. No one has seen. Compared to my old blue car, I'm the survivor.

I ask about rentals at the desk. The clerk refers me to a real-estate office on the concourse. Offices open off a short hallway upstairs in the other wing of the hotel. One sign on a shingle above the door indicates a land company; the other shingle reads ROMERO & WATKINS, REAL ESTATE. I walk in.

It's almost eleven o'clock, but the real-estate office is deserted. Two men in the land-company office stand pointing toward a cluster of colored pins stuck into a topographical map that covers one wall. They're talking about oil wells, but maybe they can help. They turn when I call out a greeting.

One man, white-haired and wearing cowboy boots, waves. The other, tall and probably thirty years old, comes over. He has a straight black ponytail and strands of hair falling loose around his face.

"I'm Alex Romero," he says, shaking my plump hand with what I notice is an elegant, sun-browned one. His fingers are long, thin, and tapered. . . . "What can I do for you-uh?"

I know from what little talk I heard while getting the car towed that an extra, interrogatory syllable seems to be a common inflection in this Hispanic accent. But now I notice only that the quiet extra syllable seems to bring the questioner closer to the person he is addressing. The hearer wants to answer, pour out her personal secrets to the questioner. I hear the simple question of this Alex Romero and I'm making connections with Maurice Chevalier—the tenor of his voice, his accent—which causes me to remember Leslie Caron and an actor named Horst or Borsch making love on a boat dock in *Fanny*. The scene burns at the front of my empty head. There is no explaining such things. I know that much. And I have been in solitary confinement for a long time; my ability to interact appropriately with others may have diminished considerably. Now Alex Romero is guiding me toward his side of the suite.

"We'll go into *my* office," he is saying to the other man, calling over his shoulder. Then he says, exaggerating his accent, "Travis is jealous, man. We get the lovely ladies. He talks to smelly *rancheros* all day." He grins, waiting.

"Sh*ee*t, man," the voice whines from the other room.

Empty flattery, but wreck that I am I'm saying prayers of gratitude for my clean and odorless apple-green dress. They should have seen me yesterday. Alex Romero would have been the one whining.

This is today. We sit in upholstered chairs on wheels, behind a partition near the window. He puts his arms behind his head and stretches. He seems to have an adenoid problem; his jaw is always a little slack, taking in air. But in this cramped office there is precious little space *or* air. We are already knee-to-knee and we're going to be knee-to-crotch if the wheels start to roll. On the car radio I heard a talk show host talking about sex in the workplace. I half ignored it; Daniel Stetson was the only man in my workplace. I stare out the window until the light burns a white rectangle into my eyes. I know I ought to talk. He leans forward, his arms resting on his thighs.

"You're here to invest in some property? Mrs. . . ."

My name! Why does even the simplest thing have to be so difficult? I blink blindly into the rectangle. Roberta Masters in Transit Without Her Luggage does not say it all, and someone needs to tell this overcrowding man a thing or two. My name? I straighten up in my chair. I speak as slowly as I can, so I won't stutter, so it might sound as if I've said this name before.

"Olivia . . . Cosmos . . . Montevideo," I say.

He leans back. That got him. But what am I going to do for an encore? My hands shake.

"Olivia," he says, letting the last syllable linger on his breath: ahh. The name is beautiful, spoken that way. I revel in the sound of it right along with him, then snap myself back.

"Yes, that's right," I say, not trusting my voice, seeing myself as one who knows but has never had the sense to speak.

"Olivia," he says again, giving a more guttural thrust to the middle syllable, so that I envision the word phonetically. *O-hleev-ee-ahh.*

I am dazed, blinded, lost outside of time. I laugh the laugh that usually turns to tears, but it only gurgles in my throat. "Okay, well," I laugh, "now that you know my name!"

He watches me laugh. Maybe he does not believe my name any more than I do, though nothing in his expression would indicate such doubts. He looks as dazed as I feel! My chair thumps awkwardly into the partition and we both sort of come-to.

"Do you live in Santa Fe, Olivia?"

"No. I just got here," I say.

"So you'll be staying?" he asks. I swear there's a note of hopefulness in his voice.

"Well, maybe," I say. "An apartment to start with. Until I get things settled back where I used to live."

That's news to me! Since when was I planning an apartment? I was going to rent *something* for a while until Andrew and I could figure out what's next. And what's this "used to live" stuff? I pray he doesn't ask me where.

"I want a job," my voice is saying.

I *do?* This is Roberta calling. My dim voice goes unnoticed in the confusion.

"You have a license then?" Alex Romero asks.

"Oh, yes," I say, wondering for one wild moment how I can *lose* my driver's license, with its old name, its old sorrows. Stolen, I think, practicing the lie. A hitchhiker stole my purse, didn't he? Suddenly I laugh with relief. He means a *real-estate* license! They must have run an ad for a real-estate agent's position.

"A license!" I say. "Oh. Yes. No. I don't have a New Mexico license. I would have to take a test. Each state is different."

Where am I getting this information? What is going on here?

"So," he says, folding his hands behind his head. "You need an apartment and a job."

He's right! A succinct rendering of complex data.

"Right. I want an apartment and a job," I say. "In that order," I add, impressed by my power to set priorities.

"In Santa Fe, we like to have lunch, Olivia. Lunch is the most important part of the day," Alex Romero says. He takes a wrinkled classified section from the desktop and ushers me out the door, stopping to introduce me to the secretary who has just come up the stairs. Patrina Lueras smiles: Does she know my name is a fake?

"We'll have lunch," he says as we walk outside. "And then we'll find you a place."

Over lunch and margaritas at the Bull Ring, an appropriately named circular gathering place where Alex seems to know everyone by name, I find I can tell him very little about myself. He's asking valid client or potential-employee questions—employment, marital status, education, source of income, children, pets—but with every answer I am stopped in mid-sentence by the need to fabricate a new history to match my name, or to avoid the old history when my memories start rolling back.

"I'm married, but . . ." When our son was killed in May, it seemed we had nothing left of our marriage. *Son. Killed.* I cannot say those words out loud again. "We're separated."

"I went to college, but . . ." For so long I was raising a child and living in museums. "I've never really had a job."

"I had one child but . . ." When I finally realized he might grow up and set me free, he had gone to the jungle and died, and I'll never be free, never be free . . .

"I have no pets," I am able to tell him with certainty.

Alex Romero leaves my unfinished sentences, like the spicy enchiladas I leave on my plate, undisturbed. Instead he allows me to guide the conversation with my questions about his real-estate business. He narrates the dubious history of Romero & Watkins, Real Estate, by sharing his own history.

"I met Joe, my partner, at Berkeley in sixty-two. I was a sophomore, Joe was a senior. I was there on minority money, you know? First-generation American. Indian blood from my family in Mexico. I'm good at taking tests. Some people made sure I went to college."

"You had a scholarship?"

"Well, yeah. I played football in high school."

"Oh," I say. "An athletic scholarship, then. My goodness."

"Well, no. I studied pretty hard for a couple of years." He stops talking as the waiter clears the plates, seems to drift away from his discussion of schoolwork. "We went to rallies for the migrant workers. We talked about the draft and the Cuban Crisis. Joe and me, we went to hear Joan Baez. She sang in bars then."

I'm thinking of the *later* Baez of the war protests; I'm hearing her voice. I thought the voices had stopped, and now Joan Baez is singing. I am hearing her high, haunting voice, singing lyrics I didn't know I knew: "Come away, Melinda / come in and close the door / you're just remembering yesterday / before they-y-y had the war. . . ." And a lower, angrier Baez voice with a thrumming guitar behind it, saying it another way: "With God on their si-i-ide." My throat is closing up.

"Did you go to Vietnam?" I ask.

He knows I'm kind of crumbling into pieces over here but he doesn't know why, so he keeps on talking.

"I was deferred, Olivia," he says softly. "I could always take tests. I made good grades, I cut up frogs. I majored in biology."

"Oh," I say. I am trying to concentrate, but nothing is adding up. Pieces of his story don't fit. He's as evasive as I am, I realize. A football scholarship but he never played football? And why Berkeley? Why not one of the New Mexico schools if he was on some native-son type of scholarship? Whatever. I respect his privacy. And I know about history, too, how the dates and the facts don't even begin to get it said.

"My father's family had an old *rancho* near El Paso." He lapses into his accent, giving me the full dramatic effect, but I think he's also detaching himself from that uncomfortable college identity—he's not as detached as I am, of course. I have a new name. . . . "My grandmother, she had lived on the *rancho* and the oil companies wanted it. They offered to buy or lease. She was living with us by then. She leased it. Then she died and left it to my father." He pauses to sip water. "Oil was discovered on the *rancho,* Olivia. Lots of oil!" He rubs his hands together and hunches forward over the table. "*Mucho dinero*. My papa, he sold it for a lot of money. He was rich."

A man stops by the table to greet Alex. "Don't believe a word of it," he says to me, winking, massaging Alex's shoulder. They laugh. He walks on by.

"Papa gave me my share right then. My father, he's always

thought he will die all of a sudden. You know? He always makes his decisions based on a possible heart attack or car wreck."

"Not such a bad idea," I tell Alex. Why didn't I ever think that way, make decisions as if my days might be numbered? It seems I've always thought I'd learn how to do this better, get a chance to go back and tidy up. Now it sounds like a great idea, leaving all of a sudden. Poof! Leaving it all undone! I want to tell Alex you don't even need to have a heart attack or a car wreck to leave your messy life behind, but I would be lying. Mine has followed me here.

"My mama, she cried on the extension phone when he called me in Berkeley to tell me. 'Don't give it to him, Max. He's crazy. He'll lose it all,' my mama said."

"Did you?" I can't resist asking.

Alex looks surprised by my question. "No," he says. "Almost, though. If not for Joe, I would have. Joe had a trust of his own. He wanted us to invest together. He wanted me to change my major to business and join him at Boalt Hall—the law school out there."

Surely, I am thinking, surely he doesn't tell this to everyone he takes apartment hunting. Maybe he has a different story for each client. "Did you?" I ask again.

"What?" Alex asks, distracted.

"Major in business. Go to law school," I say.

"I dropped out my senior year. Hey, I *flunked* out, man. My head was messed up. I bought a VW bus. Then I bought my truck with bucket seats. I came back home to Santa Fe after somebody turned me on to a shrink who did LSD. So then I marched around for a while."

Is that how protesters are, heads messed up and whacked out on LSD? I ought to join them. "How do you become a protester?" I ask.

"You get fucking mad," he says, pulling his hair loose from its rubber band. His voice rising, his accent returning thicker than ever, he says, "Hey, man. The reporters, they like me for TV. I'm mestizo. I go either way—Indian, Mexican. I don' like establishment, I don' like war, I don' like Wounded Knee. *Grahh!"* He raises his arms and leans at me across the table.

People are listening; several men and a cocktail waitress who know him applaud. *"Sí,"* he says, waving to them, his white teeth gleaming. *"Gracias,"* he says. I pick up my sculpture bundle and we leave the Bull Ring. I wonder if I have the energy to get fucking mad.

On the way to the car I am wondering what sort of a business these two must run, the wealthy lawyer from the East and the angry protester from New Mexico. I ask him, "Whatever happened to get you into real estate? Aren't you angry anymore?"

He nods. "You ask good questions, Olivia," he says, a bemused smile spreading across his face. "Joe and me decided to be partners last year. He finished law school and had a practice with his brother, back East in Rhode Island, but he didn't fit there anymore. He drove out here and looked me up. I wasn't doing much of anything." He opens the door.

Maybe protesters aren't always angry at what they're protesting, I think as I get in, uncomfortable with the thought.

"But there was plenty of good grass in those days at Berkeley, Olivia. It was a good time."

"Marijuana," I say, tasting and smelling the word. I remember Geoffrey Alston Mills the Third, sitting on the roadside. I remember Gary, slinking around, his eyes glassy. And Andrew slinking around, too. Now *that* makes me mad. He could be slinking around now. Maybe *I'm* slinking around. A black mood descends on me as I think of Andrew and the specter of endless explanations and details that will be necessary when I go home from my "march"—or if I don't go home. Where *is* home? Then I remember Alex's words: an apartment and a job. I feel better. One thing at a time.

"You'll meet Joe," Alex says as he gets in the car. He says it with such assurance. He acts as if it's a foregone conclusion that I will stay in Santa Fe and be a real-estate agent with Romero & Watkins. What a job interview this has turned into, I think, remembering my only other job interview, with Penelope Welton, at History and Technology. At least I was myself back then. Now I'm pretending to be someone else. Maybe I'm not anyone at all.

I am discouraged by the sterile new apartments and appalled by the shabby older ones, with their questionable wiring and plumbing. Some mentioned in the classified section of the newspaper are too costly even to consider. Finally, we turn up a one-way street where the chipped adobe walls of buildings butt right out to the edge of the road. Sometimes the walls enclose a courtyard; sometimes a sidewalk gives a narrow margin of safety between the cars and pedestrians. I let out a groan. "Not another one of these run-down neighborhoods!" I say.

Alex laughs. "Olivia, you gringo. This is Canyon Road. Top-dollar real estate."

"No," I say.

He points to an old building where a narrow alleyway is barely accommodating a silver Mercedes sedan as it pulls in.

I hold up my hands in surrender. "Okay. I'm a gringo." I should have remembered. New Mexico hides its treasures behind tan walls. I look more closely at carved-wood signs hung on wrought iron holders, or tiles set into plaster that quietly announce artists or weavers by name, or the names of shops and galleries. Iron bars protect some of the windows—there are treasures inside.

He turns up a steep road. Camino del Monte Sol. I'm intrigued by the name. "What does it mean?" I ask.

"Mountain of the Sun. Actually, Way of the Sun Mountain."

Mountain of the Sun. It captures my imagination. I think of our steep climb as the ascent to a southwestern Mount Olympus where the gods might smile warmly on me. Or better yet, a Mountain of the Sun where the gods might neither smile nor frown but maybe just ignore me and let me catch my breath. Let the gods go to the Bahamas for a vacation. No more bolts of lightning; I'll spend some time in Santa Fe. I negotiate the celestial deal with consummate skill as we drive to the apartment on Camino del Monte Sol, a rehearsal for the real thing: I know I will rent the place. I can feel it in my rusty bones.

"And *your* name, Montevideo . . ."

"What about it?" I ask. Is he suspicious? Has he found me out?

"Mountain view," he says, looking over at me. "In view of the mountain. You didn't know?"

"Oh. Of course," I say. "Yes, quite a coincidence." He drops the discussion of my name as he pulls to the side of the road and parks by an adobe wall.

"I remember this one now, Olivia. I didn't mean to bring you here." He sits disconsolately, the classifieds still in his hand. *"Hijo.* There have been problems . . ." he says, his voice rising as he gets out of the car and thinks about the problems.

"Oh, look!" I declare, ignoring his ominous tone. "An arched little gateway in the wall."

"La entrada," he says. "But Olivia, I have to tell you, there is litigation pending on this place. Multiunit in a single-unit area. Rich people who live around here, they don't like this place."

What does Alex know? *"Entrada,"* I repeat, pushing my hand against the milky blue painted gate. It opens—like magic. A broken latch! Fortuitous. A sign of welcome meant for me. I step into a brick courtyard where grass grows up through the cracked masonry and gray-green bushes crowd a small garden area.

"What are these weeds called?"

"No, no, Olivia." He smiles patiently, the botanist in him taking over. "This is *chamiza.* Not a weed. Honey comes from the yellow blossoms. My grandma used to make the honey for me." He touches one blossom, rubbing the dusty golden pollen between his long fingers. "Well, it's honey if you get to it before the bees do. Otherwise it smells. Like dog shit," he whispers. "Ahh, the honey smells so bad if the bees pollinate the flowers first. But it's not a weed, Olivia. A beautiful bush to grow in the courtyard. *Chamiza.*"

"Cha-mee-sah," I call over my shoulder.

I peek past the faded FURNISHED/FOR RENT/FOR SALE sign in the window of a corner apartment in the U-shaped building. I can see a lamp, a chair, a sofa. Off from the sparsely furnished living room there's an eating area, table and chairs; French doors open out to what looks like a patio in back. A Garden Apartment, I label it, relying for the time being on my Easterner terminology. Two other units across the courtyard are empty, and in need of repair, judging from the ladder that stands in one.

"This will be my place," I say.

Alex is knocking on the door of another apartment. "I remember this woman, Olivia," he whispers to me as I come to stand beside him. "Strange woman. I tried to buy this place when I first came back to town. She was the only tenant." He curls his lip; he growls at the memory of the woman.

I smile, drunk with delight. I spread my arms wide and turn to look again at the courtyard, the adobe walls, the milky blue trim on the doors and windows.

"No one home. We can't see it," he says quickly. "But just as well."

"This is where I will live! I've found my place." I grab his arm and spin him around, losing my own balance in the process. As I stumble, he catches me. His expression seems to say, Take it easy. His expression seems to say that I don't look like a person who ought to be making decisions.

"Hijo," he grumbles as he holds open the gate and walks with me to the car.

"What's *ee-ho?"* I ask.

"Hijo means what am I going to do with you, Olivia-uh?" He starts the engine, a grin on his face. "You are so excitable, Olivia."

I shiver at his words, at the thought of living in the old hacienda-turned-apartment on the Mountain of the Sun. A house full of someone else's ghosts and history? Ahh. What a haunting it would be. What a relief.

"It must be your red hair that makes you so *loca."* He taps his finger against my temple.

I don't have to ask about loco; I know that universal symbol for crazy. I wonder what he knows about madness, but I don't ask. It's another Spanish word for my new vocabulary, and I am hungry for words. I reach up and touch the side of my head where he has tapped me with his finger. It throbs like any other human temple throbs, but it seems as if magic is there. Olivia, the goddess of Camino del Monte Sol, knows about magic after all.

We return to the hotel the back way—up Cerro Gordo Street. "It means fat hill, or large hill," Alex tells me. He makes a quick phone call to the property manager handling the rental. We say good-bye in the lobby. I shake his hand as he continues to offer warnings. We walk toward the Shelby Street entrance.

"Olivia," he says, somber with concern. "I don't know. . . ."

Is he uncertain about me or the apartment?

"It's okay," I assure him. "I like it!" I back toward the lobby until I collide with a man coming the other way. Alex walks toward me again.

"They don't want apartments," he says slowly, emphasizing

each word. I enjoy his slow pronunciation; I realize he's saying "a-par-ments."

"They're trying to get the zoning commission to rule against the landlord. He's a man from the East. He never comes to the hearings. He never answers the letters. I know this one. Bad things will happen."

"Not a chance," I laugh, waving to him as we part. "Besides, I'm only renting. Let me know when I can move in."

"Sí," he says, and walks to the stairs.

Bad things do happen as soon as Alex leaves. It has nothing to do with the apartment. The intoxicating magic drains from me like light from a window at dusk. Hunched over, staring at the floor, I have to sit down on the first bench I come to in the lobby. I am empty, nothing left. I'm convinced now that I really have been loco for several days, probably since Wall, South Dakota, and have mistaken this high-altitude elation for magic. Andrew wasn't home when I called. What am I going to do?

Then my hands slap the bench on either side of me, grope to my lap, slam against my forehead: I have left my sculpture in Alex's car! Oh, God, I've lost it. The Boy Child with Book is lost, I think, as I jump to my feet and run for the stairs. He is coming in the door as I reach the concourse.

"It's okay, Olivia. Here's your package," he says, handing me the solid towel-wrapped bundle in the paper bag. I cannot restrain myself; I rip it from his hands, hold it to my chest. I feel the swell of tears rise in my throat.

He puts his hand on my shoulder, then lowers it to my elbow when he feels me sag against him.

"You're happy about the apartment-uh?"

I cannot answer. I nod.

He leads me to the stairs.

"You want to celebrate about your new place, Olivia? I'll cook for you. We'll drink some wine."

I am putting one foot and then the other on the cool, dark tiles of the steps. I am on the sidewalk outside. People are going by; their sandal-shod feet slow to let me pass.

2

I wait in the car while Alex Romero stops for groceries at Foodtown. I watch a young woman push her blond, curly-headed daughter to their car in the parking lot. Their cart is loaded with Pampers and Kraft Macaroni & Cheese Dinners. I turn and smile, painfully sympathetic, for though I wasn't acquainted with disposable diapers, I do know those macaroni dinners. Ever try Chef Boyardee Spaghetti? I'm tempted to ask her. But I don't. My throat closes up, a squeezing sensation that comes at the sight of that baby's plump fist holding a box of animal crackers, golden down shining on her tan little shoulders under the straps of her cotton sunsuit. I see Gary's tiny shoulders as he splashed in the bathtub, probably nine months old. For a split second I would swear I hear his baby voice chattering. "Won't this ever stop?" I whisper. I turn with relief to see Alex come bounding out of the store.

"Fruit for your feast, Olivia!" he calls.

We load the groceries into the trunk. He has a watermelon the size of a minor boulder; long loaves of French bread protrude from one bag, and inside are cantaloupes and apples and honeydews and peaches.

"Are you expecting a crowd? Look, if you're having a party . . ." I say as we pull onto Paseo de Peralta.

"Just for us," he says.

My practical objections to his generosity soon melt in the orange blaze coming from the western sky. A few turns later we come to a road called Arroyo Hondo.

"Oh, those mountains over there," I say, breaking the silence, taking in the vast expanse of sweeping flatness and shadowy blue-violet peaks.

"Jemez," he tells me.

"Hay-muz," I say.

"And those!" I say, leaning forward to view the gold-tinged, snow-flecked peaks out his window to the east.

"Sangre de Cristo," he says, feeding me his Spanish words, an appetizer, some sort of preparation. I feel safe hiding away in this magical new landscape.

We plunk down the bags on a rickety round table in his kitchen. I can't imagine eating anything prepared in this kitchen. The cabinets are a ghastly pink, trimmed in green yarn braid that had to have been attached with Elmer's Glue at the height of the crafts movement in the sixties. The stove is a gruesome turquoise color where it isn't scratched or rusted or brown with grease.

I follow him on a quick tour of the house, which he seems to feel obligated to give. A greenhouse opens off the dining room, revealing great round clay pots with plants thriving, as if in the hands of a master gardener.

"Yours?" I ask.

"They came with the house," he says. "I take care of them."

The long wall connecting the L-shaped dining room and living room has a massive carved door at the center, then one long narrow window on the living-room side. The sun burns its way into the house from there, the western exposure. The rounded contours of a corner fireplace dominate the living room, and on either side are built-in adobe benches covered by bright red cushions.

"I like those benches," I tell him as we pass quickly by.

"Those are *bancos,*" he says.

"Bahn-cohs," I say.

"These bricks on the entry wall are harder than regular adobe. They're pavers. No plaster on them—to show off, be authentic, I guess. Whoever built this addition was worried somebody might think he used cinderblock underneath."

"We all need to feel authentic," I say.

He looks at me and nods. *"Sí,"* he says.

He is careful with me. There are little things he does that tell me he knows how frightened I am. When we pass by his bedroom, sheets and blankets knotted in a heap at the center of his bed, we do not go in. He stops at the doorway to point out the beams in the ceiling, the pine branches laid in rows between them. *"Vigas,* the beams. *Latillas,* the branches," he says, moving on.

"Vee-gas. Lah-Tee-yahs," I echo.

In the bathroom down the hall, an exquisite pedestal sink of blue and white porcelain coexists with brass fixtures beclouded by hard-water stains and a window covered by cardboard.

"What happened to the window?" I ask.

"Can't have glass on every window," he says, grinning at me. "It's against my religion. The evil spirits need a place to get out."

I ponder that, in the trusting way I used to ponder my father's tall tales, not knowing whether to believe him but ready to laugh with him or hear another tale. I wonder what he defines as evil spirits. We walk back to the kitchen. "Do you have a lot of evil spirits in your house, Alex?"

He hovers over the grocery bags like a wizard. "So many devils, Olivia." He tosses me an orange, a honeydew melon, a fuzzy kiwi. "They have to be fed. Tonight we feed the evil spirits!"

Counting on his lighthearted voice to keep *my* spirits up, I offer a smile.

Alex works over his pot of chili, making frequent tastings, adding sauce, spices, more tomatoes. I work the fruit. I grow weary, slicing for twenty minutes on his worn linoleum counter and hardly making a dent in the produce supply. As we arrange the tray I suggest a creamy sauce for the fruit, and we trade recipes like a couple of rumpled housewives, his interest sincere and intense. He has to watch as I blend mayonnaise and sour cream, powdered sugar and lemon juice. Nothing will do but to rearrange the whole tray to accommodate my tiny bowl of sauce at the center. My back hurts but the kitchen is warm, the air full of moisture and spice. I have a moment of knowing that this is the place for me to be right now, that this is good. I remember my desolation at the hotel. I might have gone on up to my room; I might have missed this. I am thankful.

With the chili simmering to his satisfaction, Alex turns on the stereo: a Brandenburg concerto.

I'm surprised. I expected popular music, folk music, even Mexican music. Maybe he's lost himself, too. At Berkeley. His own generation, his culture? No, my relentlessly suspicious mind suggests, he's playing classical because he assumes that I, a gringo woman, older than he, will like it. MAYBE HE JUST LIKES THE GODDAM MUSIC! another exasperated part of me shrieks. I press my fingers against my temples.

He pours the wine, Chianti, into crystal wine glasses. I take a sip and hold the glass up to the sunlight, treating my eyes to the red-orange glow. He lights candles in ceramic holders sitting on the windowsills, returns with cheese and crackers. I sit on the couch and tuck my legs up under me. He brings the fruit tray.

"I will smoke the peace pipe while the chili cooks," he announces, opening a compartment of the coffee table and bringing out a small black pipe. He opens a leather drawstring pouch and begins stuffing a pinch of the greenish brown herb into the bowl. I watch the ritual, my mood turning sour.

The Brandenburg ends and a flawed recording of Liebestod from *Tristan and Isolde* begins. Oh, brother. I get up and turn off the music. I scowl at him for playing his seduction tape for me, but still working with his pipe, he doesn't notice. If he wants to honor my new home on the Mountain of the Sun he should play Dvořák's *New World Symphony*! I try to get hold of myself, wondering what on earth I am doing in Santa Fe, New Mexico. I rummage through his disorderly box of tapes and records and find Beethoven's *Eroica.*

"I read that Beethoven dedicated the *Eroica* to Napoléon Bonaparte," I say, hoping to distract him with this tale of disillusionment. "He wrote it in great exultation. He tore the dedication into shreds when he heard all the evil the emperor had done."

Alex stands up, walks over to the stereo, and pushes a cassette into the tape deck. "*Sí.* He tore up the dedication, Olivia. But not the symphony." He places his hand on my shoulder.

Beethoven did not tear up the symphony: Alex must know the depth of this insight into the lowly origins of art, into the unlikely inspirations for most of humanity's highest accomplishments. Does he know, too, the evil that comes from the best of intentions? I remember the sod house museum, I remember all museums and all mothers and sons. I try to smile. I lift my glass to meet his. The crystal strikes a fine, light note. The first tinkling bars ring out through the speakers.

"To the symphony," he says, triumphant as the music.

"To the symphony," I say.

We carry our glasses and our knowing smiles back to the sofa. He returns to his pipe.

"That's illegal," I say, knowing I sound foolishly prim. "I have no use for marijuana."

Alex lights the pipe and the smell crawls through the air. Gary's room smelled this way; I hate the thought of it. I stand up, sit down, feel such a flood of feeling that I want to weep, to kill, to curse, which I finally do: "I am *not* a goddam gringo lady," I say in a shaking voice, "who has come here to get stoned and screwed."

He looks at me like someone in a tour group, all ears and eager to listen. That makes me angrier yet.

"I am a decent person who is temporarily lost. . . ." I swallow hard. Tears are simply not an acceptable solution to this problem anymore. "Who will find her way with or without your help, Alex. So just put away your peace pipe and let's get on with this, this powwow!" I eat a grape. I feel old, ancient, mistakenly arrived in my life.

He continues smoking, drawing in on the pipe, his long black hair fallen forward, concealing his face. He sets his pipe down and leans against the cushions. "Hashish. Strong stuff. The best. Pure," he says, talking to himself, more the way an Italian chef makes a taste test. I'm surprised he doesn't put his fingertips to his lips and kiss them. Now he's smiling. I see that glassy look. I see Arlington and Andrew and Andrew and Gary and Gary and Andrew. It's all the same.

"Olivia?" Alex says. "I'm smoking because I want to. You won't smoke unless you want to. I felt so much sadness coming from you today-uh? Why? Tell me what has hurt you."

I dip an already discolored peach slice into the sauce, eat it, consider its fermented sweetness a puzzle my tastebuds can't explain, that razor-thin line between ripening and decay. I sag against the sofa. I am utterly lost.

"All day," Alex says, "you have looked very sad."

"I have my problems," I say. My chin quivers. I don't like being in this position of just needing someone, anyone. I'm ashamed of this feeling, but it's not self-pity. I do not feel the way I felt on the road, those spasms of sobs that rocked my body like the wind rocked the car. Something is different here. I'm shy. I'm just plain shy, the way a child is shy when she's gone beyond holding in the secrets or the hurts. I'm ready to pour it all out.

But instead of waiting for my flood of sorrow he hands me a wedge of cantaloupe. And instead of crying I bite into the fruit with my sharp teeth.

"My problem is that I do get hungry," I say. A laugh kind of rolls up my throat behind the cantaloupe. I hold it all in with my fingertips.

He relights the pipe and hands it to me.

"I don't smoke," I say.

"Ever tried it?" he asks.

"My son did drugs. I didn't."

I stare at the smoldering mess in the bowl of the pipe, remembering the psychiatrist down in the District, the first time I took Gary. I told him Gary had been such a good little boy; he said passive children often reveal their problems later. I told him we had to get Gary off drugs; he told me I ought to smoke a joint and decide for myself whether the dope was at fault or if the circumstances of the marriage I had been describing to him were a possible cause. He said the drug use was a "symptom." I thought he was a quack. I cried; the counselor handed me a box of tissues. Gary cried; I handed him the tissues. Andrew was at the Pentagon. He didn't cry. "That S.O.B.," I say.

Alex looks at me.

"My husband! Not my son," I explain.

I put the pipe to my mouth. He leans over and puts a match to the stuff as I breathe in. "Hold it in your lungs for a long time," he says in his soft, slowed-down speech.

I cough, sputter, feel as if my throat will burn from inside. Like creosote in a chimney, the smoke will burn the greasy residue from inside my throat until I have no voice, no words, only the smoldering mess of ashes that was once my voice. The cellos of Beethoven thump beneath a chorus of violins. I try again, hold in my breath, exhale. Burning, burning.

"Bueno," Alex says proudly, his voice conveying the satisfaction of a master to his pupil. "Good, good," he says.

He goes back to his pouch, refilling the bowl with another pinch. When the match flame touches the greenish stuff, there is a loud pop.

"What was that?" I ask.

"A seed. The seeds pop."

"Is that right?" I say. "The seeds pop, the weed burns."

"Sí," he says.

We smoke more. I eat another wedge of cantaloupe. He hands me a cracker topped with Brie cheese. I eat that too. I smile, expecting to feel dizzy, not feeling dizzy at all. We sit.

Alex stands up, pipe in hand, and motions for me to join him. "I haven't shown you the studio. Come," he says.

"Oh, we'll see the studio," I say, pleased that he has remembered the studio but a little surprised that it takes us so long to get around the coffee table and walk toward that western wall where the sky has gone pink though the long, narrow window.

He opens the great carved door. Errk! It swings open. I touch my fingers to the carved surface of the door. I study its floral and geometric patterns, all of them evolving eventually into circular designs set in squares, which of course eventually results in the large rectangle that is the door. I run my fingers into each dusty crevice of the door, loving its geometry.

"Careful on the stairs," he says.

He is showing me the way up the stairs. I could have found the way. But I will follow him, this kind young man who flunked out of school, or maybe never went to school, but has inherited enough money to own such a house and has, at this very moment or at some similar moment very much like this moment, a chili pot simmering on his turquoise stove, just for me.

A magical staircase it is, all rough and earthen and set with jewels. Pieces of colored glass can look like jewels, indeed be jewels, at particular moments in time, at particular places in space, if they are set just right into the tower of a staircase and are seen through the eyes of a redheaded *loca.* Madness and magic—they can change glass to jewels and jewels to glass, until the glow just becomes a moment, and the colors of the moment are ruby and sapphire and emerald. The magic staircase is lit by the sun.

The blue glass beckons. I stop to stare into the deep-blue, six-inch square of glass, feeling compelled to tell Alex, who has gone on ahead, obviously unaware, that I can see the stars, the universe, in the bubbles of the glass. It will take a long time to tell him what I have seen—the patterns, the light, the tiny explosions of fire in that deep-blue glass—but if he waits there, two steps above me, I will get to him, I will get it said.

"I saw the stars in the sapphires," I say. "You know, the big picture."

"Sí, sí," he says, enlightened now.

I climb toward him, smiling, knowing I am smiling, knowing I have smoked the evil weed. Only a symptom it was. I'm glad that Gary might have felt this way, known so much, dulled his sorrows, heightened his joys.

"Good ol' Gar," I say when Alex turns to look at me.

We reach the top of the stairs and enter a wide, open room, windows on all sides, magenta sunlight washing across from the Jemez to the Sangre de Cristo. Turning from the window, I express the idea brilliantly to Alex, impressing it upon him by squeezing his wrists and looking very carefully into his Spanish-Mexican-Indian eyes: "A solar flower unfolds before you, one perfect petal in the garden of the universe!"

"Ah," he says, turning me around to look south across the valley. "Albuquerque is that way."

"And those mountains?" I say.

He grins, silly. *"Las Sandías,"* he says.

"What's so funny about that?" I ask.

"The watermelons," he says, laughing with a high-pitched sound that sounds like *eye-yee.*

The mountains do sit like an elongated mound of melons out there in the desert, and here we are having a feast. I cackle like a witch and slap him on the back. He laughs again. He is staggering, but that is because I almost slapped him down the stairwell. We lurch toward a sofa; we will lurch until we reach the fluffy red pillows on the sofa and then—POOF—we will laugh ourselves silly.

He lights the pipe again and we smoke. He is downstairs for a long time after that. I lie on the red sofa as the sky loses all traces of blue. I get up and walk to each glassed-in point of the compass, watching clouds form and disappear in the purple south sky, watching searchlight-like beams of white light occasionally burst open on the western horizon nearest the descending fireball, watching the mountains to the east go suddenly deeper blue; and then, looking north, my eyes somehow unprepared for the sight, I watch more stars than I would ever have believed could crowd the celestial ceiling blink into being. Each time I look away, then return my gaze, another tiny aperture slides open and blinks another star into place.

"Blink, blink, blink," I whisper, a participant in the night's arrival.

Alex has brought up the fruit platter. I know he is there, but I can't begin to acknowledge him, it would take so long. And then he leaves again, and returns, and yet another time, bringing bowls, plates, flatware, linens, and more wine in the crystal glasses—or is it plates and bowls and. . . .

He hands my glass to me.

"We'll eat up here," he tells me. "I'll bring the chili now. *Hijo,* the bread's in the oven. I have to remember the bread," he mutters. He's preoccupied. Such a busy time, getting a meal ready all at once. So seldom that meals or friends or thoughts ever come together at one time. I feel a wave of admiration for all the food providers and party givers and idea processors of the world, giving out all that enormous energy to synthesize our moments for us. I should do something to help. I spread tablecloth over desktop—there, I have helped.

I crawl onto the red fluffy couch, tuck my legs up under me, then unfold myself again with the sole (HO-HO! I think uproariously) purpose of removing my shoes. Ah, one shoe off—my "soles" are killing me. I'm seeing all the stairs we've climbed today. Or was it just this one staircase? No matter. I have found my place. And now I have climbed Alex's magic staircase so I can see the stars. The other shoe . . .

"Olivia," Alex says. He clears his throat. He is kneeling in front of me, his hands helping my foot from its shoe. His hands are rubbing my foot. "Olivia," he is saying to me, calling me by my name. I try out his. "Alex," I say. "Alex." I burst into snorts of nervous laughter, thinking of the comedian I saw years ago who, back to the audience, arms working up and down at his sides, called out, "Marsha. John. Marsha, Marsha, Marsha. John, John, John." I didn't laugh much back then, but I am laughing now. And Alex is laughing with me, unoffended, as if he gets the joke. Maybe I *told* him the joke just now.

A long moment ago he was rubbing my feet, but now he is gone again and my skin, beginning with my feet and moving up my legs, wants him to return and let me tingle again that way. I stretch out my legs in front of me, and when he comes back from lighting the candles on the desktop dining table, I draw in my breath at the sight of him, his hair all loose and wild, his eyes tracing my thoughts with glints of black obsidian light.

Why? I ask him with my hands held out to form a question. Why me? Why us? What about my body, I never much liked my body. . . . He sits beside me and takes my hands in his hands. He brings our hands together at my neck and holds my face, pulls my hair back from my face, pulls at my hair from somewhere at the back of my head. "I think it's your hair, Olivia. It's your hair. *Rojo,* red."

"Ro-ho," I try to say.

His hands. The buttons of my apple-green dress. One button, two buttons, three buttons, four. All of my buttons, undone.

"Olivia," he breathes, finding my mouth with his.

It takes so long to kiss this man. How long can I hold my breath and still keep his hot breath on my face? It takes me so long, but I remember how to breathe through my nose. I moan. He moans, pressing his heavy body against me, pulling me to him, reaching over me for a pillow and placing it gently beneath my head. "Olivia," he groans in the candlelit darkness.

The darkness. The star-filled sky is dark now; a breeze comes through an open window and brushes against us. The candles flicker in the rustling air. Something from Pasternak flickers, too—". . . and in the open window, a candle burned, a candle burned . . ."—am I reciting this for Alex, am I only thinking it? Pasternak, burning with poetry, gone now. I arch my back for Alex as he sets my breasts free. He watches as I reach down to cup my breasts and rub the hardness of my nipples against the palms of my hands. He struggles to loosen his turquoise-and-silver belt buckle, rip open the pearlized snaps of his shirt. I lie here, staring down at my breasts and squeezing them.

One flash of protest blinks at me, some useless defensiveness that tries to claim I'm not myself, don't know myself this way. But I do know myself. I know. I know he is standing above me, his hair long and straight and black. I know he is watching as I work at my body with my hands because inside is a pulling that prevents me from lying still or looking up, and it commands my full attention now.

He is lying across me, probing my mouth with his tongue. Hot and wet, his mouth finds my breasts and then, sucking, he sucks as Gary, only Gary, sucked, and the pulling in my belly is as painful as Gary's sucking made it painful. I want to tell Alex about the sucking and the pulling and how good the pain is, but my mouth is open as if propped by an invisible wedge set between my jaws. Instead I reach my hand down to touch his face, to thank him without words, but when my hand touches his face he grasps my two fingers, my two fingers, and he sucks on *them*. Oh. He has surprised me. He moans and sucks my fingers like an infant sucking his own, but these are my fingers and I am groaning with the heat of his mouth and the roughness of his tongue moving against my fingertips.

"Alex!" I scream.

But still he seems not to hurry, though he's heard my cry. He turns me over, squeezing, kneading my body. His mouth finds my ear, his hands find my breasts, I feel him push into me, throbbing. Ahh. I reach with my hand to find his mouth again. Too slowly I try to find his mouth, so I bring my fingers to my mouth and when I suck, the pulling in my belly goes into such a wrenching, throbbing ache that I know, infant-mother-woman that I am, I know what has to be done. I know I have to do it.

Sucking my fingers, moving my rough tongue quickly along my fingertips, panting through my nostrils, groaning, screaming in my throat, I reach with my other hand for my belly, and at that moment Alex's hand lets go of one of my breasts, leaving it swollen, scratching against the sofa, and our hands begin a slow-motion journey down my big round belly and I get there first, grabbing my stiff, wet hair, rubbing my finger next to the moist, hard center of all the pulling. And we pull together, he with a handful of flesh from the inside of my thigh, me with my hand, my fingers, rubbing it, controlling it, keeping it there. I suck my two fingers, I guide with my hand, I do what I've always known to do. Alex, throbbing, filling me, filling me up, pushes into me now, keeping me there. He throbs, I feel him pounding. We pull, push, throb, and it is a very long time before we stop.

We lie so quietly now, propped against the pillows. There is no sobbing; my eyes simply run with these tears. And we whisper. As if we have signed a pact, these secrets we must tell require quiet, the utmost discretion and security.

"This may have been a terrible mistake," I begin.

"No, no," he says, stroking my hair back from my face.

"I left my husband last week. His name is Andrew. Our little boy was killed in the war."

"Your little boy?" he asks, still whispering.

He is picturing a toddler, I'm sure, or a ten-year-old, who somehow wandered out of his yard and into the war. I leave the misunderstanding, don't attempt to clarify. It's all the same to me.

"In May," I whisper. "Gary died in May." I describe the ravine, the booby trap, the night patrols.

"Olivia. Your son," he whispers. "Your sadness is hurting me." He is on his elbow, leaning over me, his long hair brushing my shoulders as he shakes his head back and forth.

I look at his long face in the candlelight. His brows are black and feathered as they leave the space between his eyes and fly off above his eyes. His eyes are so dark and fringed by lashes that they make his sad expression seem extravagant. Tangled and ragged along the sides of his face, his hair is silky at the center where the part is. I touch his hair there, at the center. When I die, I will see this face: the hair, parted; the brows, flying; the eyes, damp. But I can't die now . . . yet. His compassion feels excessive, almost unnecessary. It makes me angry.

"You're a protester. You don't know my sadness," I hiss.

"I can *try* to know your sadness. I can imagine my mama losing *me.*"

What an odd thing to say. What an odd, sweet thing to say. His childlike sweetness goes through me like a needle through cloth, piercing me but stitching me up. I bring his head to my shoulder. I weep now; I'm back to pumping the tears.

"This is what the protests were about—*are* about," Alex says.

"You don't know what the protests are about," I say, my whispering voice becoming a hissing weapon. I regret my authoritative stance as the guru of gloom.

"No. I *didn't* know. Not exactly." He straightens up, apparently wanting to look at me more closely. "That's why I quit doing it," he whispers. "There was this one march in Chicago—I looked at all these people, I couldn't remember why we were there." He buries his face in my neck, still whispering. "Just for a second, you know? I forgot why everyone was yelling and why the cops were out. That kept happening. . . ."

"Now you know," I say. Now we both know, I think, desperate but wise. This story he's told me about protesting has come out of him in pieces, as if it's a confession he's never made aloud. I say nothing more, knowing how hard it is to tell the truth.

"I'll learn from you, Olivia," he whispers.

I sniffle and rearrange him, cradling him in my arms. I moan as I rock slowly, his big shoulders in my lap. When he peels himself gently back from me our chests are clammy, his face and hair are damp. He is smiling.

"You're hungry now-uh?"

I stop rocking.

He reads me with some dark, divining instinct. Beneath the globs of dead, scaly skin that hang on my bones, he seems to hear my heart pounding and my blood flowing. I am ashamed of this. I am ashamed that even as my tears have flowed, even as I have whispered Gary's name and Andrew's, I have been distracted by the spicy smell of the chili, the yeasty aroma of the bread still warm in its foil wrapper. I suspect I am ashamed of being alive. What can he possibly learn from me?

He crawls away from me and makes a cape of what I now realize is a red bedspread covering a daybed; we throw it over ourselves and shuffle slowly to the table/desktop where our food is waiting. He turns on the desk lamp, looks at me with that wizard's gleam. He pops a slippery slice of kiwi into my mouth. I reel it in with my long frog's tongue . . . *gulp*. We slide two chairs together and I ladle out a bowl of chili. I aim the spoon between the long straight curtains of his hair, right into his mouth.

"Ha, ha. Olivia, we are so hungry," he growls, ripping the French bread out of the foil, tearing a piece and handing it to me.

We eat.

3

I get back to the hotel about noon, driving a car Alex has loaned me. I park the car and walk into the lobby. The older, daytime clerk tells me I have messages. I am surprised that he recognizes me. Maybe it's because I am always carrying this same bundle and have worn the same green dress for two days. An eccentric who never changes her clothes or washes them? I doubt he's thinking that. "Thanks very much," I tell him.

He may have seen Alex and me yesterday, I think, absurdly paranoid. But what he can't possibly know is that we cleaned house all morning. Upstairs in the studio, then down in the kitchen, we cleaned. I had to do it. Alex was understanding, probably even grateful. How many of his lovers clean his house? Like workers from a janitorial service, speaking infrequently to request a mop, a sponge, a trash bag, we grunted with the grim satisfactions of scrubbing, sweeping, and sweating. I took two showers in Alex's bathroom; evil spirits floated out with the steam through his cardboard-covered window. I'm in the Big Ten now. Adultery is No. 7, as I recall.

I go up to my room and return the calls on the message sheets.

The mechanic at the boneyard garage where my car was left off says they can actually fix it.

"Are you sure?" I ask. "Really?"

"Seven hundred," he says.

"Well, then. Go ahead and fix it, I guess."

I ask about my suitcase.

"In the car," he says.

"In the car?" I ask. "Really?"

"We have it at the office here."

"Thank you!" I say as we hang up, my enthusiasm more forced than sincere. My suitcase? My old blue car? I'm not so sure I want them back.

I look at the other message sheet. The property manager for the apartments on Camino del Monte Sol has called. It shows that Alex is doing his job; I *told* him I wanted the apartment. But I'm not so sure about that, either.

Afraid to go back and afraid to go forward, I dial the number.

"It's vacant, Mrs. Montevideo. You can move in any time."

"Today?" I ask, almost panicked. This is probably not a good idea, I want to warn her.

"Right now, if you want. Just come by to sign for the key, pay your deposit, and you'll be all set."

Right *now?* I ask myself as I hang up the phone. I have the strange sensation of being offended, as if this woman has somehow broken the rules of propriety by renting the place so easily to someone like me. She ought to know better.

And so *soon?* I ask my sculpture bundle as I pick it up and slip my purse strap over my shoulder. I haven't even talked to Andrew yet. I head out the door, down the hall, through the mezzanine, to the lobby. I check out.

As long as I was staying at the hotel, and house hunting with Alex, the idea of moving in implied a certain complexity of lifting boxes and arranging things, an event to take place at some remote point in the future. Now, all I do is drive Alex's car to the boneyard garage, pick up my suitcase, and sign some papers for them to fix the blue car. I go to the property manager's office and get the key. Then I drive up Camino del Monte Sol, park out front, and carry my newly retrieved suitcase to the gate. This is my moving day? Who am I kidding? Isn't anyone going to stop me?

I peek in at the courtyard. A woman in a baggy cotton smock, loose trousers, and leather sandals stands in the sunshine with her back to me. She is hanging batiks on a makeshift clothesline; I feel excluded by the cryptic patterns on the dark fabrics. Alex told me this woman was an artist. I've never studied art! All I know is history. I turn, ready to run for the hotel, but I bump the gate with my suitcase. The broken latch clicks, and the gate opens on its own. The woman jerks around, dropping one of the wrinkled pieces of damp cloth. After Alex's description of her I hadn't known what to expect, but I am greeted by the rather open and friendly face of a woman in her sixties.

"I'm sorry to startle you," I say. "I should have knocked."

"I jump at anything," she says. "Bad nerves. I've been like this since I went through the change."

Boldly, I thrust out my hand to this woman who has been through "the change." I wonder what sort of change *I've* been through. "Olivia," I say quickly. "Olivia Montevideo. I'm moving in today. Apartment three."

The woman reaches her hand out to me. "Leona McCleary," she says, stopping first to wipe her dye-stained hands on her trousers, not in apology, it seems, but in acknowledgment that I have taken my chances in reaching out my hand.

We shake.

"This is no swinging-singles complex, I'll tell you," Leona McCleary says, looking me over.

"I *chose* to live here," I say, surprisingly firm. "I didn't want that type of thing." No moonlit romps of nymphs and satyrs for me? Oh no, not me.

"Well, good, Olivia. Thank God we don't have to be animals *all* our lives," she says.

"I know what you mean," I say, ducking my head under the clothesline to reach my apartment.

I unwrap my statue of the Boy Child with Book and place it on the counter between the kitchen and the dining room. I can see him from the living room, content as can be, his little round head bent, the book open in his lap. As I carry my suitcase to the bedroom, I glance back from the hallway, almost tripping on the uneven brick floor, the rumpled throw rugs. I come close to sprawling on my face trying to check on that statue.

I set the suitcase on the bed, a huge bed that takes up most of the room. I can't sleep on this bed! I'd get lost. I open the suitcase but put nothing away. I'll sleep on the sofa tonight.

Toward evening Leona McCleary brings homemade rolls and spinach salad for my moving-day supper. I tell her just a little about Gary and even less about Andrew as we eat at the plastic table on my patio.

Her reaction is both a relief and a puzzle to me. She listens, then watches me, studying me as if I'm a subject she's painting. After a few minutes she moves on to her brief history: "I was married for a very short time. Then I taught art at the Indian School in Albuquerque. Thirty years, teaching art. You know what?" she asks me.

I realize the question is not rhetorical. "No," I say belatedly. "What?"

"Sex gets in *everyone's* way."

"Oh," I say, wondering why she's chosen to tell me this.

"Got in my way. I got married instead of going back East to art school. Got in my sisters' way. They're stuck out on ranches. Got in the way of those young Indian people. You should have heard it. One of the girls got pregnant. Wonderful artist. Fifteen years old. She did those clean, geometric designs—animals and clouds and so on. The headmaster asked her why she let Benny Jaramillo take her out by the sand hills and do that to her. Do you know what she said?"

I interrupt, saying "What?" Our words bump into each other. "Sorry," I say. "The headmaster asked her?"

"The headmaster asked her why she let Benny do that and she said, 'He ask me.' " Leona stiffens her arms on the table, flings her face skyward. "That's it! 'He ask me.' "

How well I know.

Dumbfounded, I sit here at twilight, staring at a round plastic table on a brick patio in Santa Fe, New Mexico, relating like mad to Benny Jaramillo's young lover. There's not a word I can add to that story.

Finally, Leona gets up and comes to stand beside me, hand on my shoulder. "Your son's death is a fresh wound," she says. "You won't know much for a while."

For how long a while, I want to ask.

We carry plates back to the kitchen.

"I may want to borrow your phone," I tell her. "Mine won't get hooked up till tomorrow."

"You *can* call out," she says, holding up the receiver of my wall phone for me to hear the dial tone.

"Oh!" I say. "Well, then. I need to call my husband."

No incoming calls, and me able to call out. No change there; that's pretty much how it's been for the past week. I wonder if that's how I want it. Maybe I want no calls coming in so that I can still disappear if I choose. Poof.

"Your husband has to do this for himself. So do you," Leona is saying.

Is she telling me I did the right thing, leaving? Is she saying I shouldn't call Andrew at all? I can't tell what she means.

"Not that we can't need men. I did need Tobias, but not for long," she says, discussing her first and only husband. "But most women can't make distinctions after they've needed that first man," she says. "Like animals after that, some instinctual need. . . ."

After the first man? After the first man came the first baby, the only baby. . . . "I'm not sure I know. . . ."

She moves on to something about walking to a café for breakfast. The name of the café she refers to begins with an M. I can't retain much else. I'm still worrying about needing that first man.

"I'll let you get rested now," Leona says slowly, as if talking to an invalid. "And remember what I said about breakfast. I try to start down the hill by about eight or so."

"Thanks. I'll join you one of these days."

After Leona McCleary leaves, I sit for an hour on the sprung, stained cushion of a cactus wood chair, one of the many questionable items filling in as "furniture" in this "furnished" apartment. The wood recalls the head of a hairless cat I once saw in a science textbook of Gary's under the heading of MUTATIONS. All wrinkles and grooves, this wood has the texture of sun-dried bone. I'm sitting in the skeleton of a once-living organism. Not content with the ghosts already in the room, I'm inviting in my own. Insane, but there it is. I have to do it. I will call Andrew.

I rehearse this call, knowing before the phone rings exactly what Andrew will say.

On our money you're renting an apartment? I'll sell real estate when I get a license.

Just like that, you'll walk out on twenty years of marriage? It didn't happen "just like that." And I'm not walking out, I'm just. . . .

You're changing your name to what? A professional alias, really. Bill collectors have them. I saw it on a road sign in Minnesota.

Do you expect me to take this lying down? Think what I have taken lying down.

I'm coming out there on the first plane from Washington. Just try to find me without an address.

What was that name again? Olivia Cosmos Montevideo.

And where are you living? On the Mountain of the Sun.

How can I ever tell him?

In spite of the expected responses, he surprises me. For one, he picks up the telephone on the first ring.

"Andrew!" I say. "Oh! You're there. It's me, Roberta," I whisper.

In the static on the long-distance wires, people are talking. Maybe Leona's television is on, or maybe Andrew's.

"Andrew?"

"I'm here," he finally says.

Is his face as hot as mine, are his hands as cold?

"Where the hell *are* you, Roberta? Virginia's called three nights in a row. The neighbors are beating the goddam door down. I almost reported you missing just to get everybody off my back."

"Oh, no. I didn't mean. . . ."

"This is a hell of a thing you've done, Roberta."

How could I have ignored, been in ignorance of, the effects of my disappearing for more than a week? Unable to even grunt in acknowledgment, I gesture with my hand at the army blanket covering the window. I bring my hand to my forehead.

"Well?" he asks, impatient. Then, "Oh, my God. You all right, Hon?" he adds sheepishly, as an afterthought.

"I'm in Santa Fe, New Mexico," I state in disbelief. "Santa Fe!" I say again, convincing myself.

I want to tell him that I'm the female Che Guevara of that sexual revolution he always talked about. The Romero y Montevideo Incidente. I want to share with him my suspicion that he's not the only reason I'm running away. With too much to say, I say nothing for a few long seconds.

"I'm okay, Andrew," I finally say. "I'm all right. There were some bad times, of course." Duluth, Minnesota, in the rain. Wall, South Dakota, with Jeff. The sporting goods store in Noname, Wyoming, and the gun I never bought. And all that wind. Bad times. "I don't think I can come back for a while. That's why I rented this apartment, such as it is. I . . ." Somehow the story of my trip gets told. Most of it, anyway. And he does try to listen, but then the words come blasting out of him, more or less the way I had expected: our money, change your name, just like that, not taking this lying down, coming right out there. I'm ready for those responses; in fact, I can't even blame him for saying it all. But then, out of nowhere, other words. "I went to the cemetery this morning. I missed that kid, Roberta. I needed you. . . ." His gravelly voice cracks.

He cannot do this to me.

I get up from the chair. I pace around on the cold brick floor, wave my hand in the air. I pull the receiver away from my ear. "Oh," I nod, bobbing my head toward the mouthpiece. "The cemetery?" Still, I hold the mouthpiece away from me. I must stop for just an instant to think. My eyes are burning. My bones are turning brittle. Something is clawing at my skin. I think maybe my body is breaking.

Because the matching cactus wood lamp next to the chair is turned on, I sit down in a lighted space. And probably because of the blazing one-hundred-watt bulb I put in the lamp earlier in order to see both the living and dining rooms and walk without tripping, I am able to hold one lucid thought in my mind.

That one-word thought is NEED. Like a burrowing insect, like the tick we found once in Gary's scalp, this word has turned with its hindquarters in the air and is drilling itself into feeling, into memory, into flesh.

Stalling for time, I put the receiver to my ear again. He's saying my name, but it sounds like the wrong name now. "Roberta?" he's saying.

"Yes," I say, rubbing my eyes with the heel of my hand. "I know it must have been difficult."

There. I put the receiver in my lap. Elbows resting on the chair arms, fingers pressing my temples, I desperately inspect this word: Andrew NEEDS me. My intestines groan, draw up like knots in a rope. I NEED Andrew. But only yesterday Alex had it all summed up: I needed an apartment and a job. Yet here is more; I need more. A home, a child, a man.

A man? This man?

Words echo. I find myself wishing I could stuff the words back in my head and let them out in a different sequence. A child, a man, a home. Maybe even a man, a home, a child. This room, though furnished, is empty, and the echo stays. A man, a man.

The words won't fit into logical patterns. I select quickly from the thousands of words Leona McCleary left circling in the room. That *first* man. I have to think. I pick up the receiver and hear my name again.

"Roberta, I'm not going to sit here talking to myself."

"I'm here, I'm here," I say, my voice bouncing off the bare walls and back into the light. If he can just hold on a little longer I might be able to talk.

I sift through memory, groping with the brazen dignity of an alley cat checking out trash cans.

The vivid recollection of a classroom at West Virginia Wesleyan promises no quick solutions. This is not the precise definition of NEED that I am seeking. The vision is fraught with trouble as soon as it appears: A damp, early-spring morning in 1951. Second floor, Hopkins Hall. Tall, rippled-glass, double-sash windows. Outside the misty windows, new-green tree limbs are suspended forever by my memory in their mid-air pose. An English professor . . . yes. Now it's clearer. A woman whom rumor follows in trails of vapor the way cologne drifts upward from my wrist—Roberta Patterson's wrist. Affairs with her students was one ripe accusation, a husband with a wandering eye, another . . . yes. Roberta Patterson has just started her period after a month of terror when she thought she was pregnant. She is thinking about those winter nights after her weekend waitressing job, in Andrew's car, parked by snowbanks behind Maggie's Cafe and her saying yes, yes. Roberta is wondering if her professor could be so wild and outrageous. . . . No, not her professor. Roberta is the only one. The professor is explicating the text of Byron's *Don Juan* while students scribble notes in the margins of tissue-thin pages in their clothbound copies of the *Norton Anthology of English Literature, Volume II.* From the Romantics, from Byron, the big daddy of them all, comes not a clarification, not a definition, but a puzzle with no readily apparent solution: "In her first passion woman loves her lover." Roberta Patterson's eyes widen on hearing that explosive word read aloud: *Passion!* Someone else has felt it, too? "In all the others all she loves is love/It grows a habit. . . ."

A habit? Is my memory for verse deceiving me? It *has* been a very long time.

"I know, Andrew," I say to the telephone. "I'm thinking."

A habit? Not only marriage, but love, a habit?

Layers of meaning. A bespectacled boy at the front of the room to point them out. The woman professor finds him a tiresome but necessary part of her daily routine. "Yes," she often says to him. "Yes. It's all there for us, isn't it?"

A habit? A garment to put on after taking blind vows? The repetition of unthinking, long-unexamined actions? Love and NEED are habits? If it was all there for Roberta Patterson at that moment, she did not see it. Roberta Patterson Masters never caught on in twenty years. What are a few more minutes now? I have to try.

Andrew is talking but I have to think.

Byron wrote: "It grows a habit she can ne'er get over/And fits her loosely like an easy glove."

The habit of passion has *never* fit me loosely. The habit of passion made me swell that summer of 1951—so ironic after the narrow escapes of the spring. This habit gave me Gary, and now I've lost him. In fact, until last night with Alex, I thought I had broken the habit of passion.

Rage. That's my only habit. Rage and lies. Too late to share, too late to listen, my boiling blood pressure tells me. Unable to take hold of this writhing tangle of thoughts and feelings, I return my attention to the telephone receiver.

"The things I remembered, standing there!" he is saying. "If I hadn't remembered, it wouldn't. . . ."

Something in me leaps hopefully in response to his remembering. I know what he felt. "Did you remember yourself more than Gary, and feel guilty?" I ask.

There's a pause. "Yeah," he says. "I remembered things that had nothing to do with him."

I can't tell him right now, but he *has* helped me by telling me that he remembered himself. I think of being on the road and remembering *my* life, and Gary only along for the ride. . . .

"Sometimes I try not to remember anything," I say. "I try not to feel anything, either. But then I feel worse."

"That's exactly right, Roberta," Andrew says. "It's like picking your poison."

"I know," I say, terrified suddenly by knowing he feels what *I* feel.

I don't want Andrew to talk about Gary, yet what was my lament when I was home if not my whining NEED to share my grief? And I hate him for saying I am "exactly" right, for taking comfort from my words. I always hoped he would listen to me, but now I wonder, *should* he? If we were to combine our feelings, would we explode, erupt like a volcano in a flaming, oozing gush? Maybe we've escaped a natural disaster. Maybe my running away was the right thing to do. I feel myself pulling back from him, this time not to blame him but to save him, us, from . . . what?

"You were right about something else, Roberta," he is saying.

"What?" I snap, a turtle forced out of her shell.

"Dan Weston's been hitting Patti."

He turns casually to neighborhood gossip? He's referring to the family who moved into the Beardsley's old house two years ago. I was always telling Andrew that something about them was not quite right.

"He hit her?" I ask.

"She came over Thursday afternoon looking for you," Andrew says.

"Afternoon?"

There's a pause. "I had taken off work," he says. "Thinking you might call."

"Oh . . ." I try to say thank you, but the words get swallowed in regret.

"Anyway, she had been crying. She had the boy with her."

"David."

"Yeah. She's afraid of Dan. He's been hitting her for a few years, apparently. Once in a while, you know, and then nothing would happen. Things would get better. Then he hit David recently. Had she ever told you about this?"

"No. She just seemed too, I don't know, submissive, agreeable. Poor Patti. He's a football coach, the big ape! What did you do?"

"I didn't do anything. I offered to let them stay here. . . ."

"Well, Andrew," I put in quickly. "That was nice."

"But she'd just come over to tell me they were leaving him, leaving Dan."

Another woman leaving? Does Andrew think I classify him in the category with Dan Weston, the wife-beater? I don't. Yet these Home Wars just keep burning, women and children, refugees on the road. What a solution.

"Has she left?"

"She's gone. She said she wasn't telling me where—for my protection, so I wouldn't know."

"I'm so sorry. I'm sorry I left. . . ."

"I know," he says. "I know you had to. . . ."

"I did. I had to."

"So, anyway, Dan's a lunatic and Patti's gone. That's the latest around here."

We're both looking for Gary, I decide. I'm sure when Andrew offered to let them stay at our house he was hoping desperately they would. Seeing a little boy like David, probably nine or ten, crawl into Gary's bed? I would've begged them to stay. Andrew is obviously operating on that same Principle of Substitution I've recognized in myself. In the middle of South Dakota I picked up Geoffrey Alston Mills, the Third, didn't I? I bought the statue of the Boy Child with Book. And then there's Alex, a not-very-simple substitute indeed.

Andrew and I are feeling the same things; we're grasping at everything and everyone who can get us closer to Gary or closer to what it felt like when Gary was with us. I want to share these insights with Andrew, but I leave the Principle of Substitution alone for now. Why am I so frightened by this? Guilt about Alex, maybe? I guess. Such a low motive, such a limp reason for keeping this distance. . . . "Can you send my clothes?" I ask.

I change the subject to clothes? I am showing an incredible lack of sensitivity for Andrew's feelings. I think my capacity for human concern must have shriveled while I was on the road. Worse than that is the thought that maybe I have been this way all along!

"You're really staying out there, aren't you?" he asks, controlling his voice, keeping it flat.

This is not the voice of a man whose wife is staying an extra week at their cottage on the lake. He deserves an answer. On the question of whether I'm staying, his guess is as good as mine. I give him the most reliable information I can. "For now," I say.

The wires chatter again; or more accurately, I realize, the electronic chatter becomes noticeable again in the silence.

"Besides, the car's being serviced," I add. He is listening for false notes. Well, what I'm saying is partially true. If you call $700 a service call.

Wondering now why I earlier resisted telling him my address—Why hide? He's grabbed me through the telephone, anyway!—I recite my Camino del Monte Sol address for Andrew to copy down. But the notion of living even a small part of my life in Santa Fe, New Mexico, seems no more real spoken aloud.

"Call your mom, Roberta. She's a good woman, but I don't want to talk to her every night."

"I wrote her a letter. But okay. Yeah, I'll call her."

More static on the wires.

"You okay, Roberta?"

"Are you?"

"I think so."

"G'night, Andrew. We'll talk."

"Yeah. We'll talk soon."

I sit in the chair for a long time. I fall asleep sitting up. I try unsuccessfully to remember one minute what I have been thinking the minute before. Finally, I write another letter to Virginia and go to bed, curled at the very edge of the bare mattress, next to my unpacked suitcase.

The dream begins as a news report, the familiar body bags and helicopters. Then it shifts, like a special documentary segment, and I am in the dream. This is something new, I think in the dream. I am watching the documentary, but I am there, too, waiting to be interviewed by a reporter who never quite gets around to me. It's not a war zone anymore, but a place closely resembling Bishop's Lodge, a resort hotel Alex showed me at the edge of town. Buildings are set into a hill, much like the local resort, but these buildings are redwood or park-service brown, not adobe. Lush vegetation covers the hillside, a tropical green, and blooming flowers, a flowing stream, pine needles on pathways despite an absence of coniferous trees.

The documentary has already been filmed, it seems, yet cameras, cables, technicians clutter the foreground. The dream seems to be switching constantly from documentary on-screen to documentary in-progress. Voices accompany the on-screen broadcast—a physician and a reporter having their own interview, but a therapist or an attendant in a white coat, clipboard in hand, mouth moving, stands in front of the main building. In my dream mind I am trying desperately to read the sign out front; I seem to think I have eyeglasses in my purse, but I never actually find them. The overlaid physician's voice is speaking: "We have no cure for these women," he is saying with unassailable authority. "That's what I want to make clear from the beginning. They have come for treatment, not cure."

Now the camera pans across the grounds and onto a wide porch where middle-aged women—all of them redheaded and with hair piled in top knots—are gathered in small groups. I watch the camera zoom in for close-ups of faces. All of these women have brown eyes. The voice drones on, explaining that the phenomenon seems to occur mostly in women nearing forty, up through sixty, sometimes beyond.

Cut to the white-coat and a reporter with a microphone. "This state of diffuse erotic stimulation is induced by sexual involvement with men ten, twenty years younger than themselves. What appears at first to be a rejuvenating sort of euphoria reverts at some point to insatiable arousal." The word nymphomania hangs in the air, unspoken, as the camera just happens to linger on an ample bosom, a round behind. Whenever I'm watching the on-screen documentary I am looking around, somehow looking for Andrew.

I am trying to get the reporter's attention. Now that I know the subject of this film, I want to be interviewed. Maybe they will interview one of the women on the porch. I keep losing track of what it is I'm going to tell him. I feel paralyzed, bound up, locked in.

Now the reporter with the microphone, his voice unsuccessfully concealing titillation, asks for a list of symptoms. "Take, for instance, Mrs. X," the doctor's voice is saying. No, that's not the doctor's voice, that's Andrew's voice. Oh, my God, I'm thinking: Andrew's voice. Meanwhile, I am somewhere trying to find the reporter, but I am also watching the on-screen interview. The camera has now moved inside the building, to a screening room of sorts. A film projector is being loaded; images begin to move on the screen. A nude woman with breasts just like mine is displayed on a hospital bed. The overlaid physician's voice has disappeared, and the doctor and the interviewer are now apparently speaking to one another in the room.

"You'll notice her hands moving constantly over her body—we asked her to tone it down as much as possible so as not to offend your viewers. You see the rather glazed look in the eyes. . . ."

I heard that catch, that higher inflection in his voice when he spoke the word "eyes." And now that disembodied woman's voice—a voice that I realize has been laughing at times during the dream—has stopped laughing. The voice is spitting out words: "Those sons of *bitches! Goddam pigs.*"

Cut to the therapist outside, the roving bands of red-headed wild women. "It's uh—heh, heh—the equivalent of a permanent erection in a male. You can see the difficulties this could present. Many of these women have jobs. Some of them live in respectable tract homes. One of our patients has described the extreme isolation she feels among her contemporaries due to this compulsive need to push her fingers against her lips, to rub. . . ."

The on-screen film has been edited for the next frame, which brings the viewer into a doctor's office. The physician is describing the treatments used at the resort/sanitarium. He holds up a device resembling an athletic supporter.

The voice of Gloria Steinem—yes, I am sure as I listen to the voice editorializing in the dream—Steinem now calls down her final judgment. "Assholes!" the voice yells.

"We recommend cold compresses, sleepy-time teas, aerobic exercise, knitting projects, in some cases telephone calls from children, grandchildren, concerned spouses, even elderly parents ready for the grave if we think it will help. We have to weigh carefully the impact of guilt and remorse, however. Tremendous guilt factor working here."

The announcer's voice comes in, energetic with relief, eager to summarize. "But nothing seems to work, and so they gather here in this tranquil, wooded setting to discover that they are not, it is obvious, alone in their problem."

I pull myself out of the dream, knowing the laughter I hear is my own because I can feel my abdomen going up and down, but when I am fully awake I find that I am also rubbing my fists in my eyes, weeping.

Exhausted, I remember Alex's question, Why are you so sad? I think if he were here right now, I'd probably tell him, "Maybe I'm just mad. Sad mad. Loco mad. Angry mad. Mad, mad, mad."

I sleep until noon.

The telephone man wakes me, banging on the door. He wants permission to check the hookup on the back wall of my apartment. I lead him to the doors off the dining room and out to the patio.

The sunshine blinds me for a moment. My head is throbbing. I feel sluggish, drugged by sleep. I sit down on the plastic lawn chair as he tinkers with the wires and cable.

He goes inside. I can hear him. He is placing new phones in the bedroom and on the wall of the kitchen, that one with a long cord. He is opening up the lines. He is reconnecting me.

"Calls can come in and you can call out. That's all you need, ma'am."

I know he tried, but I NEED more than my wires fixed. He's waiting for me to open my eyes. Finally, I squint at him. "Unh," I grunt. "Thanks."

"If you could just sign here," he says, placing his clipboard gently on the rickety plastic table and, after I sign, leaving through the back gate.

Gradually, as if I am a magnet and the sunlight metallic, the dry heat finds me and soaks into my chest. I feel something going on in my chest, some sort of elegant compassion—this heat, this comfort, this place. Hot and healing, soaking in.

4

The next morning I get in the car and drive. On Cerillos Road, south of town, I discover some ordinary stores: a Safeway, a PayLess. They're brown plaster, but they feel like back East. The windows of the Safeway store are painted with messages I can decipher: GROUND ROUND $1.29 #. SPECIAL ON BROCCOLI 29¢ BUNCH. This is life as I've known it. I use my last two traveler's checks. I buy food. I buy bubble bath and Bon Ami. I buy dishrags.

On the way back to the apartment I stop at some shops in town. In one I buy orange sheets and pillow cases, in another a yellow-and-orange bedspread—king-size, handwoven, as bright as the sun. I charge it all to my credit card. I leave the shop, steaming with a sudden fantasy of my red hair spilling over the spread and Alex Romero groaning over my body. Then Alex is gone and Andrew is in the picture, not groaning—he doesn't groan—but full of admiration. I notice that not only my body but my mind are different when I am having these thoughts. Like Novocain numbs not only the nerve and tooth but also the lip and cheek, so these unbidden thoughts shoot into my mind and even the bruises, even the memories ease, rest, lie back and say *ahh*.

I am bent over the trunk of the car, moving the grocery bags around to fit the bedspread in, when I jerk upward suddenly and bump my head on the trunk lid. I have not taken a single birth-control pill since I started on this trip! What have I *done,* I think, slamming the trunk lid. I stumble around to the door and get in. I could be pregnant with a stranger's child! My hopped-up brain cells seize on the idea: a baby, a baby, they babble. My mind is numb all right, but a small voice of reason just keeps saying no. No baby. No Gary. No substitutes.

* * *

No, I tell myself, back at the apartment. I just finished three days before I left for the trip. Eight days spent driving. My first day in Santa Fe was with Alex. Twelve days total. Too early in my cycle. People are supposed to ovulate in the very middle. *Sure,* says the cynical voice in my head. *You have all the luck. You won't be pregnant. Not you.* My middle would be fifteen days; this is just too close. Ready to end the argument, as if thinking about it could have caused me to start, I rush to the bathroom, checking. I've already been here! I was nineteen years old, and now here I am twenty years later, again! No luck. What did I expect? This is only the thirteenth, *maybe* the fourteenth day.

The phone's ringing. I zip up my slacks and hurry down the hall to grab the kitchen phone.

"Olivia?" Alex is saying.

"Oh," I say, strange with him now. "How did you know my number?"

"My friend at the phone company told me. Small town, Olivia. Hey, how about lunch today? At the Shed. You can meet Joe," he says.

"The Shed? Joe?" I ask.

"My partner, Joe Watkins," he reminds me. "We can give you the real-estate regulations to study. Before long you'll get your new license and go to work. How does that sound, Olivia?"

"Lunch?" I ask him. License? I ask myself. What a harebrained idea, thinking I could just settle right in and change my name and get an apartment and start a job!

"*Sí.* And you can come with us afterwards, if you want. We have an appointment to list a house."

"I could go, I guess." Nothing on *my* calendar. I don't even have a calendar. If I had a calendar I would be counting the days: fourteen down, sixteen to go.

"We'll meet Joe at one."

"At one," I say.

"It's only ten-thirty, Olivia. I could come over . . . now."

The bright orange-and-yellow bedspread, still in its package, appears in my mind . . . then the fantasy hits a wall, THUD!, at the thought of my unused birth-control pills.

"What has happened, Olivia-uh? What's wrong?"

Too much wrong to tell him all the things that are wrong. I pick one: "I haven't taken any birth-control pills. I had them with me on the trip. They were in my suitcase, but I haven't been taking them."

"Sí," he says, making a soft sound, low in his throat.

"I'm not saying I *am,* Alex. Pregnant. It's just that I won't know for a few weeks. I'm not even due till the first week of August. This is all such a terrible mistake. . . ." Ignoring all his reassuring words—"No, Olivia. We won't worry. We can do other things till then. It will be okay, Olivia"—I just keep talking. "And I'm not a real-estate agent, and my name's not Olivia, and . . ."

He is gently interrupting me. "I know these things, but you are still Olivia and I still want you to work for us. I want to see you."

"You do? You know?"

"Sí," he says.

"Oh," I say. "You know."

"You told me."

"The other night, I guess?"

"Sí," he says. "The night at my house. You told me about your boy and your husband. You used to be Roberta."

The phone cord twists in my hands as he speaks my old name and I remember his kind face bent over me. I walk to the French doors and look out at the patio, stretching the tether, this thread of connection. I walk back to the kitchen and I say, "Thank you, Alex."

"De nada."

"Day nah-thah?"

"It means you're welcome, it was nothing, it cost me nothing. In fact, it was my *pleasure,"* he groans, a kind of push from his chest to his throat: "Umhh."

I give in to this healing potion, this tonic of pleasure he pours over me with his voice. *"De nada,"* I say. "For me, too."

"Other things, Olivia. Until you find out, we can do other things."

The man is making such sounds. Where is he? In a public phone booth? In that tiny office at the hotel? Do people in Santa Fe listen to his conversations and applaud when he hangs up the phone, like at the Bull Ring when he told me those stories?

I am so aroused, so confused, so comforted by him. I'm going to either laugh or cry if I don't get off the phone. "What about lunch?" I ask quickly.

"Ahh! You'll go, then?"

"You need to tell me the directions to the Shed, the restaurant," I say, trying to hold in the hysteria that's ready to burst.

I write the directions on the back of a grocery bag. We laugh when I can't spell the street names. "See you at one," I say.

I put orange sheets on the bed and orange cases on the pillows. I unwrap the bedspread and wave it like a magician's cape across the bed. I walk outside to the patio and stand in the clear light of the mid-morning sun. If I were a plant, even the seeds would be steaming.

I scan the diners at the Shed—all these women in their long cotton skirts or denim jeans and bright blouses. I look down at my kettlecloth skirt, my sleeveless blue blouse. I did wash my hair and pin it in a top-knot. I did put on mascara and lipstick. In one of the adjoining rooms I see a man, in his early thirties and dressed in a gray Western suit, get up from his table. The silver tips of his string tie and his polished cowboy boots flash in the sunshine from the window. Just then he raises his hand in greeting, enough to catch my attention yet not cause a distraction for the other diners. "Are you Olivia?" he asks as he reaches me.

"Yes," I say. "Are you Joe? Are you waiting for Alex Romero?"

"I'm *always* waiting for Alex. I gave up on him years ago!" When he laughs, pale creases fold into the suntanned skin around his eyes. We shake hands. His handshake is just firm enough to be sincere yet not seem pushy.

Alex comes in the door, faded Levi's, canvas shirt, hair flying. So tall and . . . windy. Alex is careful to introduce Joe and me, though he knows we've met. Then he turns to Joe. "Hey, José," he says. *"Qué pasa?"* They share complicated handshakes, laughing, saying "Hey, Buddy." You'd think they hadn't seen each other in weeks. What a pair they are. Joe with gleaming, blond good looks, identifying him almost immediately with an image of wealth, old money. His wavy hair is thick, sandy-brown, his eyebrows at their upper edges a velvet, downy blond, almost white. He glistens, he gleams. We start toward the table Joe has already staked for us. I look over at Alex. Maybe it's his breathing through his mouth, I don't know. He doesn't wheeze or drool, it's just that his mouth is open, and he's smiling at people he knows or doesn't know, and he takes up a lot of air and space in these cramped little rooms full of painted chairs and white-clothed tables. He's like wind, and in a rush he has arrived.

"Olivia," Alex says as he sits down and leans over to me. "What a great day-uh? You're moved in! You're going to work for us!"

"Uh-huh," I say. I find myself smiling. There's no denying his magic. I walk in here feeling like hell and Alex just breathes the life back into me.

As we order, Joe tells the waiter that we will need a quick lunch. "We need to be out by two," he says. And then to Alex, "The appointment's at two-thirty."

Alex nods.

We eat salty corn chips and a pleasingly spicy tomato sauce—*salsa*—as we wait for our meal.

Joe pulls a thick notebook from his briefcase. "As Alex has probably told you, Olivia, there's nothing really complicated about becoming a real-estate agent."

"I don't know about that," I say. Maybe I can discourage them from this idea. One thing for sure, I don't even *want* to pretend I've ever done this before—as if they'd believe it, anyway; as if they would care. "It seems pretty complicated to me."

"You just have to learn the regs and pass the test," Joe says. "I'm not talking about succeeding as an agent. Only what it takes to start."

"Oh," I say. "To start." Now there's a distinction. "So that's what you did, Alex? You studied for the test?"

He nods. "I took the agent exam. Then we took the broker's exam; it's more complicated."

"This first one will take you a few weeks to get ready for,

Olivia," Joe says. "I think the next tests are August first and fifteenth in Albuquerque. Anyway, the first and third Saturdays. The only thing you really can't do without a license is sign contracts to list property or sell it."

"You'll come along with us sometimes, like today," Alex adds.

"Of course," Joe says. "And you can meet clients, show property, go to sales seminars. . . ." He leans toward me and grins ironically. "You know, hype sessions." He rolls his eyes.

Alex puts on a ridiculous expression, his head tilted, his mouth contorted. He actually looks as if he might be retarded. "Smile!" he says. "People will wonder what you're thinking!"

"There you go," Joe says. "Some of those seminars . . ." he begins. He gives up trying to be serious and businesslike. Laughing, shoving Alex in the shoulder, he braces himself for Alex's return punch. Alex laughs, shoves him back. Punch, shove, punch. They're like teenage boys—*rich* teenage boys!

Alex returns his attention now to me, leaning both arms on the table in case Joe has another jab. "And *other* things will come up. All you have to do is ask," Alex says, then smiles, his face beginning to perspire in the heat of this little shove-fest. It's a quick series of things he does next: looks down, leans forward, then turns his head to look again at me.

Other things. He knows what is happening to me—the blood is pumping into my face. I must be a red tomato. Has Joe noticed? I avoid looking at Joe as I take the notebook from his hands. I set it on my lap.

"We're going to list a house today, Olivia," Alex says, and turns toward Joe.

"She's been leaving me messages for two days, but I've been up in Taos," Joe says, pulling a small sheet of paper from his shirt pocket. "Eva Kettlar," he reads. "She calls me this morning: 'My house for sale. I have your card. I call you first.' Definitely a foreign accent. In Santa Fe, Olivia, foreign is anything but Hispanic or Texan. Right, Alex?"

"Sí," Alex says, grinning.

"This one sounded European, German. So I tell her I can come out today, but she's still irritable—she's thinking it over. 'Vahhhl . . . I have fine olt house. You not in ven I call your office. You are bizz-ee, bizz-ee.' " His imitation, the voice and the accent, are convincing.

"She'll love Joe. The perfect Nazi youth," Alex says, stiffening his back and arms to attention. "I'm coming along to make it interesting."

They laugh wickedly. The conversation moves on. Lunch gets served.

Everything is play to these people. They seem to play with their own racial stereotypes—Joe the blue blood, and Alex . . . Alex the hot-blood. They seem to get energy from playing with their differences. Alex went to Berkeley instead of New Mexico; Joe moved to Santa Fe from Rhode Island. It's as if either of them would wither away if exposed to too much similarity, too much of the expected. And I think they are playing with this real-estate business too. Not that they aren't making money with it, just that if I were to predict what they will both be doing, say, five years from now, I doubt they will still be Romero & Watkins, Real Estate.

They're even able to play with the not very playful possibilities of human evil this Kettlar woman brings to mind. War, hatred, death is what she brings to *my* mind. When Alex called Joe the perfect Nazi youth I felt myself cringe just hearing the word: *Nazi*. The woman may turn out to be utterly sweet and innocent, but do I really need this? Something is warning me off from a visit to the home of this woman. Maybe I need to listen better when a warning like this goes off in my mind. Maybe it's time, after all the warnings I've ignored.

Besides, I could just go home and start reading the big book of regulations still sitting on my lap and presently cutting off the circulation in my legs. But as we get up to leave and Joe announces that we can all ride with him, I tag along, at first—a kid, the neighborhood misfit, the one who's always saying, "Can I play too?"

I expect a Mercedes or a Jaguar, but Joe has a pickup truck. Not just any pickup truck but a big wide one, with scratches on the loading bed and a wide tool box mounted behind the cab. My grandfather Patterson, a farmer, classified his trucks by the ton; he would have called this one a three-quarter-ton at least.

Maybe Joe's a builder and not an artist. Everyone else I've met has some kind of art or handwork though. Alex keeps all those plants going in his greenhouse room, his handwork.

"Are you in the construction business?" I ask, climbing in beside Joe as Alex gets in next to me.

"You'd think so, with this monster. No, but I'm always hauling something. I do some cabinetry at my house and I work on the cabin."

"We own a cabin at Tres Ritos, Olivia. Nice place. Near a stream."

"I'm getting married in December. Keely's finishing her M.A. at Brown. You'll meet her. She says she won't marry me if I don't build shelves for my pottery collection, so I'm doing a lot of cabinets lately."

"Damn weird, this woman he's marrying," Alex says.

"Yeah! Why can't I keep my goddam pottery collection all over the floor of the bedroom and living room?" Joe asks and slaps his hand against the knob of the truck's floor-mounted gearshift.

"And the kitchen, too," Alex adds.

"Yeah!" Joe says. He backs out of the parking space and drives toward the street. We all laugh, but the mystery of this place settles on me again. Art. Artists. Collectors of others' art. I picture a house where round earthen pots cover all the floors and only narrow walkways allow one's passage through. I would like such a house, but I'm out of my league. . . . "Oh, there's my car!" I say on impulse.

They turn to look at me, Joe from my left, Alex from my right. Joe stops the truck.

"Well, the car I'm borrowing from Alex," I add. "I just realized I can't go with you! I have to get my apartment settled!"

Alex looks at me as he opens the door and steps down from the truck. "Okay, Olivia," he says skeptically.

I slide out. "Thanks for lunch. I'll go with you next time."

They wave as they pull away.

My heart pounding as if I've escaped some inexplicably dreadful fate, I set the thick notebook in the trunk of the car. I'm too restless to go back to the apartment. I need to walk and be outside. I get a city map from the glove box and walk the streets that feed into the Plaza. Map in hand, scouting the places where I might be spending some time, I mark an X on one corner of the Plaza, for the Museum of New Mexico, an art museum it seems. I mark X at another corner, for the Palace of the Governors, a museum that records the early Spanish settlement in Santa Fe; it's the place where the Indians are selling their wares on blankets, just as they were that first evening I arrived. And down a side street, by now a little warm and sleepy, I discover the city library.

I walk inside, intending to spend the rest of the afternoon in this cool, shady place surrounded by thick adobe walls. I find a book about New Mexico history and sit down at a wood table with carved legs. The leather-seated chair creaks satisfyingly when I move, that sort of mind-body dialogue I've always enjoyed when reading, sounds that keep me in touch with this world while I'm off in another.

One map shows the vast lands where Indian tribes originally lived; another shows reservations, where they ended up. Places for families? Sons who went to war? I just glance through the book, unable to concentrate. I cannot read this history. I can only feel it, and it does not feel good.

Sad, disoriented, I close the book. This feeling isn't only about the lunacy and sorrows of human history, though that would be enough. It's about my mind. My mind has been damaged by the Vietnam War, by Gary's death, by traveling out here, by changing my name. I know too much, but not enough. My mind has been burned out from the inside. I am without a mindset, a framework, a way of knowing things. I have lost my mind.

I go to the librarian's desk. I fill out the paperwork for my library card, momentarily hopeful that the idea of belonging somewhere, and having a card to prove it, will help. I kind of dance around in the stacks, ready to select all the books I'll check out. It will be okay, I tell myself. But I pick out just three books and return to the librarian's desk.

She smiles approvingly at me as I check out. "You're studying the old stories?"

"Oh, uh-huh," I say, not sure what she means. History is an old story, all right.

"Los cuentos," she says.

"Lohs kane-tohs," I say. I fear I've sunk into a dark place where the only words in my vocabulary are history words, where no new words will ever stick in my mind. Bad enough if the words were the likes of

genocide and Nazi and Agent Orange. But they aren't and it isn't fair and I rush to my car from the library with three books and only these words, these watchwords, warning words: It will happen again, it will happen again, everything will happen again. If we're careless—I might be pregnant. If we don't keep watch—I can't even read road signs. If we don't learn something new . . . my God, I think as I rush to the car, maybe I can't learn fast enough.

It's almost sunset by the time I shower and go to sit on the patio in my bathrobe.

Alex will be here. Believing it is an act of faith: Alex will be here. He must surely have been annoyed with my disappearing act, but he's got to be here.

I hear his engine, his knock on the door. He calls my name through the screen. After a long moment, I get up, step inside the open French doors, call for him to come in. He comes in the door, not seeing me at first.

"How was your appointment?" I ask him.

"Pretty weird," he says, coming into the living room, handing me an already-open bottle of wine—the Chianti we started the other night. "What made you change your mind, Olivia-uh?"

"The Nazis, I guess. I doubt I'll ever be a real-estate agent."

"*Sí*. Joe and me, we feel that way a lot. Not about Nazis. I mean, we don't feel like real-estate agents."

"Oh," I say, mildly surprised to hear him say it.

We sit on the stools by the kitchen counter. "So you listed the house?" I ask.

He nods his head. "But when we got there, two agents from other companies were leaving. Who knows what she's doing." He imitates her accent: "I call fife agencies. Only tree show up. Bat otds.' " The sound of it chills me.

"What's her name again? Maybe she really was a Nazi," I say. "You know. Maybe."

"Eva Kettlar? Oh yeah, a Nazi for sure!" he says, joking now. "The house was too clean. She has a house full of cats and it doesn't smell. She has her cats on a rigid schedule. She said she feeds them on three eight-hour shifts." He straightens his back and arms again as if marching. I listen intently, forcing myself not to overreact. He must wonder why this is so interesting to me, but he goes on talking. "She has an old brother whose name is Adolf. I saw him, he was outside in the rose garden. He had on an undershirt and baggy old trousers. There's a big lock on his bedroom door."

"Maybe she locks him up at night," I say. Knowing I have no lock on *my* bedroom door, I get up and pour Alex a glass of wine in one of the plastic glasses that came with the apartment. I pour one for me. "Is she . . . evil, this Eva Kettlar?" I ask as I hand him his glass.

"Evil," he growls, pulling me next to him as he sits on the stool. "Evil," he whispers, standing up and pulling me to him, his face in my neck.

We are backing into the dining room wall, I am loosening his hair from its ponytail. But then I stop and look at him. "I went to the library and I couldn't read the history books," I say, my voice shaky but still in control. We walk toward the living room, sipping our wine. "It's serious, Alex."

"The history books?" he asks.

"I couldn't read them. I think something has happened to my mind," I say.

He stands there watching me for such a long moment. "What," I say, so self-conscious that I poke at my hair, pull my robe closed at the neck.

"*Bueno*. Good. This is good." He stands there thinking a moment longer. "Not that you lost your mind, Olivia. But that I feel so important to you, you know-uh?" He walks toward the front door, walks back toward me. "See, I think I can help you. This has not happened before to me. I mean, I think I can tell you the other things, but not like I thought before. That too, but some other things. . . ." He starts for the door, then turns to me. "Wait for me. I'll come back."

He leaves. I hold on to the strand of hope he has spun—all of this, a holding on. I sip my wine. I walk my bare feet across the brick floors. One room, then the next. Out to the patio, back in the house. I hear him, his truck engine, his door, his knock on my screendoor, his voice calling my name. I don't know what he means by "other things," but he's back now and he's carrying a suede bag, kind of a rucksack with a flap across the top that's tied by a rawhide lace, and I don't know what's in there but it is dark now, outside, and I take him by the hand and walk with him down the hall to my bedroom, where the orange-and-yellow bedspread seems to glow in the light from the hallway. I slip off my robe. I do. I just slip off my robe and lie down. I raise my arms to touch the headboard. I ask him. I say: "Alex. Show me the other things." He kneels beside me. He pulls the pins from my hair.

Alex wakes and gets dressed before dawn. As I'm rising out of a misty sleep, he sits on the side of the bed, pulling on his boots. He tells me that he needs to return home for his solitary morning ritual: walking on the mesa, watching the way the clouds form, tending to his plants.

We smoked from a pipe. He read me a story, several stories. We made love, in the night, without making love the way we made love before. Now I reach up to touch his long black hair and bring him to me. "She was an old crone, right? Hmm?" I ask him in my sleep-muffled voice.

"Sí," he whispers, covering me with the orange-and-yellow spread. "Go back to sleep now."

"She waited for the Sun God?"

He read from a book about the Spider Woman stories. At first I thought it was a comic book. Maybe I dreamed all this, I think, becoming wider awake. But the Woman of Hard Substances returns to my mind, formed and strangely whole, as if she were a memory of mine and not a story at all.

Every day she takes these offerings called *pahos* to the Sun God from those few who are brave and good enough to survive the journey to her kiva beneath the waters of the river. She lives in the kiva, a hole in the ground, lined with turquoise and coral and shells. There is an iridescent shell ladder for climbing down. Her face is craggy. "Like the rocky face of the Colorado River," Alex said, or read.

Every evening when the Sun God returns, the old woman gives him the *pahos* left by the brave travelers. As she makes her offerings, suddenly she turns into a beautiful maiden dressed in white deerskin clothing and moccasins! Or in the story's words, "Each day, she runs the course of her life. . . ."

I know why her face is cracked; sorrow does it to you, and madness. But why must she go through this every day? Isn't once enough?

"Wait, Alex," I call half-heartedly. I want him to stay and tell me the stories once more, when I can listen, when I'm not distracted. . . .

But I know why that old woman runs the course of her life every day. The stories are the reason; they're the offerings. The stories have to be told, again and again.

As I roll onto my side and my breasts move, I remember how we acted out the stories. "Ohh," I whisper, opening my eyes wide, lying back. The stories are in my body now, a different kind of insemination, a different kind of conception.

I hear Alex softly close the door. I hear his truck start up. "Strong medicine," I murmur, sinking into sleep.

5

I sleep only a short time before my own morning rituals, mundane but necessary, call to me: toilet, shower, shampoo, and food. Hungry—juice and a slice of toast at seven only whet my appetite—I decide to get dressed and join Leona for breakfast. In the courtyard I notice she has set out geraniums in big clay pots beneath her window. The morning sun, slanting in through the arch above the gate, has found the dewy blossoms, red and pink against the soft round shapes of the pots. I wonder if the pots were there before, if SPD, or whatever I called it on the trip, is still going on. I'm probably missing things I need to notice. Important things. Warnings, maybe, though I surely felt a warning yesterday. I'll call an eye doctor before too long.

"Good morning, Leona. Yoo-hoo!" I call through the screendoor.

"Well, Olivia," she says quietly. "Good. We'll have breakfast." She goes inside to get a sweater, then she locks her door. I think of going back and locking mine, but why?

The air is cool as we start down the hill. We pass a white-haired couple wearing expensive-looking sweaters that match. She speaks to them briefly and introduces me. Maybe they've been together a long, long time, I think as we walk on. Maybe they had tragic losses in their lives and survived them all intact, still together.

Leona says, "Apparently, they broke up both marriages to be together."

"Oh," I say. So much for the long, long marriage. Maybe their passion was that great. At this point, though, I'd believe either story. Long marriage? Great passion? Either story.

I stop to admire a lone sunflower growing outside a neighbor's adobe wall. I watch as the breeze ruffles the petals of the sunflower's round face.

"She's a writer," Leona continues. "He was a physician and left his wife and four children for her. She left her husband, but he was a drunk anyway. She had three children still at home. Now it's the two of them."

So there you have it. "They're lucky it all worked out," I say. Thinking aloud and talking on an empty stomach, I add, "I don't think I want to be alone all my life."

"You're already alone, Olivia," Leona says. "We *all* live alone in this life."

I turn to look at her. She isn't sarcastic or scolding, just direct. "Well, Leona," I say. "You know what I mean."

"Up in Los Alamos they have a machine that splits atoms. Do you know they've discovered there are even vast subatomic distances between the electrons spinning around nuclei?"

What is she after here? Is she telling me I'm lonely in my atomic structures as well as in my neighborhood, my marriage, my whole life? What am I supposed to do with this information?

"In fact, Olivia, we could drive up there today. We could have a picnic on the way back."

"No, Leona. I don't think so. Thanks. No." I saw a sign somewhere advertising Los Alamos as the Atomic City. I don't know what those scientists have been doing up there for thirty years, but I am feeling nauseated, like maybe I could get radiation sickness just thinking about it!

"You know what I mean," I say again. I'm not even sure I know what I mean. I was never alone in my life until last week on the road . . . or was I? And when have I been alone in Santa Fe? Not much, I realize, thinking of Leona bringing my moving-day supper, lunch with Alex and Joe, and, of course, two nights with Alex. Am I afraid to be alone, I wonder suddenly. Do I invite people into my life, or have these things just happened?

"Oh. What's that thing on that garage?" I ask, suddenly distracted by the three- or four-foot metal structure on a rooftop. At first it seems to be an exotic antenna with projections jutting out from a vertical post. Then, as I look more closely, I realize it's a primitive representation of a human figure, a stickman such as a child would draw, with a circle for a head.

"That's Gustave Baumann's studio," Leona says. "A woodcut artist. He did puppets, too. I guess that's one of his designs."

Of course. More handwork.

"Wonderful," I say. "Strange." I'm a kid on a scavenger hunt, finding scraps of information at the homes of strangers. The problem is, I have no itemized list to direct me in my search.

"You'll hear more about him when Fiesta comes in September. He's an old man now, but they say he helped design the first Old Man Gloom, Zozobra."

We walk on down the hill. I am about to ask about Old Man Gloom when we round the corner at Canyon Road and a small tile sign appears: MUÑOZ CAFÉ. In a walled-in patio at the front, people are sipping coffee and reading newspapers in the sunshine. A beach umbrella imprinted with the name of a Mexican beer is open at a table in the corner, but no one sits there in its shade. As we open the door with its full-length panel of glass, a bell that arcs lazily on a metal strip is roused to life. It jingles our arrival.

"Leona! *Buenos dias!* Good morning!" The voice seems to rise from the steam at a stove behind the counter. "You brought a guest!"

The man hurries to greet us and show us to a table near the storefront window.

"My new neighbor, Olivia Montevideo," Leona says.

"Santiago Muñoz," the man responds. "Welcome to my place. You are my guest today, but just this once! Eat up. Right, Leona?"

She nods, getting settled in her chair.

"Coffee?"

"Fine," I say, hesitating before sitting down. "Um, how did you say your name again?"

"Sant-yah-go Moon-yos," he says slowly, giving me more accent than he had used in his original pronunciation.

"Sant-yah-go, your café smells *muy bueno,*" I tell him as I sniff the air.

He beams at me. *"Gracias,"* he says.

"It's that green chili. He keeps it simmering all day just to make people hungry!" Leona says, and grins at him.

He hits his forehead with the palm of one hand and presses his chest with the other, in mock horror at the charge. I sit down. He leaves us to get the coffee.

Santiago Muñoz has apparently built his business by catering to the whims of regulars like Leona. On her orders we drink only fresh-squeezed orange juice. We order his bran-and-berry hotcakes, and she expects and gets unsulfured molasses to accompany them. She tells me she has tried to give him "plenty of information" on fiber, bulk, and organic foods. Plenty, I'll bet, considering her direct methods. But Santiago must have listened well, for she greets him with a charming smile, and I realize as I look around that several of her pen-and-ink drawings hang on the walls of his establishment. I suspect it's an arrangement that, though mutually beneficial, has to represent Leona bestowing the status of acceptance on Santiago, rather than the other way around.

Leona's is definitely the larger view. For whatever reason, not much for the inbetween, she's either concerned with the tiniest domestic details or she's asking the big questions. I wouldn't choose her kind of conversation as the accompaniment to my first cup of coffee every morning. Her discussions about our animal nature and needing the first man were one thing, but this morning, as we are finishing our heavy, bluish hotcakes, she is suddenly dive-bombing the issues, *my* issues. But why?

"I know the loss of your son has been devastating for you," she says, watching me through her wire-rim glasses, her face kind of dough-like and soft with concern.

I'm hunched protectively over my orange juice.

"But what is it going to mean in your life?" she persists.

"Mean?" I repeat. What does *she* mean?

She waits for a response, neither restating nor embroidering the words. Like the designs in her drawings, her questions are a series of fine, quick strokes. Lines. Only occasional shadings. Either the eyes see—in this case, my ears hear—or they don't.

I fumble around for words. "I don't think I've found much meaning, Leona. I mean, that's the problem, isn't it? When Gary. . . ." The only phrases that come to mind are the euphemisms my mother uses; I lapse into Virginia's language of escape. "When Gary passed away, I couldn't find *any* meaning, anywhere. I ask myself what it means and I don't know. . . ."

I feel like throwing up.

Silence.

Another question.

"What are you going to learn from the disintegration of your marriage?"

Devastation and disintegration? No wonder I use Virginia's words. They're an antidote for Leona's vocabulary. I don't know whether to punch her or beg for her wisdom. She's just intelligent enough in her questions and solicitous enough about my welfare to make me want to go where she seems to be leading. But these questions!

"Andrew and I are just separated right now, Leona," I say, an evasive maneuver that produces only an arch of her eyebrow. An ironic curve of her mouth squeezes the lumps of her cheeks into a smile. Watching me, her eyes smile too—not unkindly. I try to change the subject.

"These pancakes have blue-corn flour, don't they?" I ask.

She nods.

"I've read about blue corn. They had it in an exhibit once at Natural History."

I am coming to think that the true indication of superior wisdom has to be silence. I clam up, stuffing the last of the hotcakes into my mouth, drifting away from Leona. I stare at an oversized horizontal poster hanging on the wall opposite our table. A voluptuous Mexican maiden lies on a marble slab. Her breasts, which conveniently escape the bodice of her skimpy white dress, spread out round and flat on her chest. A young man kneels at her side in his leathery warrior's loincloth. In the background two or three mountain ranges in garish oranges, reds, and purples are painted to look as large as the figures in the foreground. A sensational thing, really. For me, anyway, it sizzles: Alex kneeling beside the bed, the stories. . . .

Santiago is standing by the table, offering more coffee, more orange juice, more hotcakes.

"That big painting—or poster, I should say." I point to the wall.

He turns toward the poster. My face feels hot. I swear Leona knows what I'm thinking. "What's the story behind that?" I ask.

Leona turns to look.

"Ahh, *dolores,* a very sad story," Santiago says, setting the coffeepot on the table. "A Mexican legend, Olivia. The warrior, he left his beautiful princess to wait too long for him while he fought in the war battles. He returned to find her dead, of loneliness and sorrow. *Dolores,*" Santiago says, his voice going low.

The dress is a burial dress, the marble slab a final resting place. The artist captured the suppleness of youth in their glistening skin, their full mouths. And the maidens of legend are apparently always freshly dead—the young woman's stiffened nipples are poised like thorns, piercing the young man's heart as he looks at her. Is this Alex and me, or is this *Andrew* and me? Maybe it's better that the maiden be dead of loneliness than caught in a torrid affair with some geographically convenient lover. Maybe the warrior has murdered her! Maybe I won't tamper with the story. She's dead either way. "It's very dramatic," I say.

Santiago, arms crossed on his chest, nods in agreement. He turns to us, picks up the coffeepot again, fills our cups, and goes on to another table. Leona continues to study the poster.

"The warrior's face is full of grief and shock," I say to her. "That much is convincing. The intensity of the lovers . . ."

Leona turns to look at me. I blush.

"Probably a pretty good artist painting when he was horny," I say with a laugh.

She raises one eyebrow and her eyes smile again. She seems to agree with my critical assessment.

"Olivia," she says, getting up from the table. "That man who's been coming to see you probably has no mind."

"Leona!" I say. She has seen him. How could she not?

"Consider it," she says, leaving a tip, walking to the register. "He could be some idiot savant, flashes of brilliance with no depth to support them, integrate them."

"No, Leona," I say, as we walk up the hill. "No, I think you've got it wrong."

"I hope so," she says.

Leona's just remembering the consequences of some long-lost, ill-spent passions of her own. And I await the consequences of mine, an echoing thought reminds me. Leona of the uncomfortable questions and penetrating silences. Leona of the dye-stained fingernails and impeccably glistening rolls. As we walk back up the hill I decide that to my limited experience of life she is eccentric, but I have to admit it's probably a good thing that my days in Santa Fe, at least some of them, might begin with a walk down the hill and what I equate with the discipline of a cold shower: breakfast with Leona. She has certainly got me awake today. My eyes are wide open.

For a moment I feel the sweet realization that my life is continuing, the very existence of these complications being evidence of things moving on. Then the thick, dark sorrow of regret falls over me like cloud-shadow in this blindingly bright sky. I should have kept on driving when the car broke down on the edge of Sante Fe. I should have stayed in the car.

At the library later in the afternoon I speak to the same woman I talked to yesterday, the one who said I was studying the "old stories." I tell her about the figure I saw on the rooftop when I was walking with Leona. I sketch the figure for her. She directs me to a book on Zuni symbols.

Koshare. Ko-sha-ree. A symbol of joy and delight, the book says. Gustave Baumann, the German artist, must have designed, cast, and mounted his clownlike symbol for himself.

I sit with the book of designs a while longer. I pick out two more books. The librarian smiles at me as I check out. Driving up the hill, I glance again at the playful figure on the roof of Baumann's studio. Maybe that's The Big Magic: the creation of joy and delight. Maybe that's what the artists do. They play, and when the work of their hands and mind is finished it's an object of joy and delight. I sigh.

Only when I get home and settle on the sofa to read do I realize what the librarian was saying about old stories. Here I thought I was checking out history books, and all but one of the books I've checked out are collections of tales and legends! I have only one history book with the old reliable Dates and Places arrangement. I wonder how that happened. I wonder what that "means," as Leona would say.

I find a version of the Woman of Hard Substances story Alex told me last night. This one goes into more detail about the pahos. These offerings are sticks with feathers attached to them: "feathers from the inside of an eagle's thigh." Such an intimate, breathtaking image. According to the books, all the animals have sacred significance for the Indians, but the eagle is a symbol of awesome power. Sinking one's fingers into those downy feathers, pulling them one at a time, attaching them to an offering stick, a paho . . . It must be a powerful ritual: the skin on the back of my neck prickles just reading about it.

I sit back with my eyes closed. Then I stack the books on the floor by the sofa. I walk out to the car and take the real-estate notebook from the trunk. I read real-estate regulations for a while, but then I go back to the stories. Then real estate. Stories. Real estate. Stories. No telling what answers I'll give when I take the state exam, if I take the state exam, if I stay here, if, if, if.

It's almost midnight when I finally get up from the sofa, my legs stiff as broomsticks, my feet crunching the corn chips I have spilled around me. My eyes are bloodshot when I glance in the bathroom mirror. I need glasses. People with eyes like mine need glasses.

I walk to the bedroom, crawl to the very center of the huge bed, and lie on my back. My strained eyes sting but they're open. I am reviewing the day: Muñoz Café and Santiago's warrior-and-the-princess story; the *koshare* figure on Baumann's house. I am thinking about Leona and her questions: Gary's death—devastation? Andrew and me—disintegration? Alex—mindlessness? These aren't questions; they're her equations!

But I'm remembering, too, some of the things that I have read this evening. I am remembering that before the close of escrow there must be a walk-through inspection in the presence of the buyer, the seller, and their agents. I am remembering that the heroes in Indian legends are often portrayed as twins—one so wise that he breathes life into the humans and provides what they need at just the times they need it, and another who is a trickster, a fool called "Coyote," whose lustful or thieving urges give him life. Sometimes the hero is both in one person.

Maybe I'm learning something from my reading—even if it isn't history.

6

Saturday morning. This is becoming familiar, calling Andrew and getting no answer. I know he's out mowing the grass, but I just keep trying. Then I call Information to check for my new listing. "A Thursday installation will not appear until Monday," the operator says. Finally I sit at the round plastic table on the patio and write in a lined tablet I bought at PayLess.

"Dear Andrew," I write. "I think we should set up definite times when we can call each other. Saturday or Sunday mornings would work for me." When I am by myself for any length of time, I seem to think of myself as Roberta. I am Roberta. I compile lists of things to tell Andrew when we talk. Today I don't want to wait until we talk, so I go on with the letter. I write about my plans to study for a real-estate exam. I tell him about Leona and breakfast at the Muñoz Café. I notice the way I am censoring this letter, omitting the poster and Santiago's story of the warrior and the princess, and my forgotten birth-control pills. "I'm reading a lot of folklore and stories," I write, failing to mention that I have the services of my own storyteller, Alex. I shiver with guilty pleasure.

The phone rings. I dash to the kitchen. Andrew, I decide, has somehow gotten my number from the same friend Alex knows at the phone company!

"Yes?" I say eagerly.

"Olivia," Alex says. "We can spend the day together!"

"Don't you work on weekends, Alex?" I ask, noticing that whenever he calls, I go through an initial feeling of reluctance that feels almost like dread. It's as if someone else, some temporarily unfamiliar persona, requires transition time to come to life.

"Patrina's in all day," he says. "She doesn't go to the business school on Saturdays."

The secretary takes up the slack? No wonder they wanted to hire a new agent—someone has to work. "Oh."

Alex is quiet for a moment. "No news yet?"

He means my period. News means *breaking* the news, breaking up the foggy curtain that hides whatever comes next. Maybe I'd rather not know. "No news," I say. This is day seventeen. Thirteen to go.

"Should you see a doctor?" he asks.

"What for? It's too soon."

"I guess. But you will need to be healthy if you are going to have a baby."

"Alex! I *am* healthy. And a doctor can't tell anything for at least a month."

"Sí," he says.

I think he *wants* me to be pregnant. Maybe he wants something accidental to happen and change his life so he won't have to make it happen. He doesn't yet know what I've had to learn, that nothing accidental is all that simple. It occurs to me that maybe people have an accident allotment and once they've gone over their limit, look out. I may already have exceeded my limit. I'm startled when Alex speaks again.

"What, Alex? I'm sorry. What did you say?"

"Would you like to have lunch with my parents?" he asks. "We could go for a drive after that and talk."

"Your *parents?"*

"Sí."

"Alex!"

"Olivia, I've told my parents about you. They said I should bring you by. They eat their dinner meal at noon."

"You told me your brothers and sisters go over there every weekend. I can't do this."

"On Sundays, *sí*. Mama makes a big dinner on Sundays. Today it will be just us."

Resigned to the fact of meeting Alex's parents, submitting by now to my irresistible curiosity—what in the world makes him tick?—I say, "Okay, I'll go."

"I'll be by about eleven-thirty."

We hang up.

I hadn't thought about Alex having a mother I'd have to meet. I've been reading about the *doñas,* old women who accompanied unmarried daughters of the rich on every step they took outside the family hacienda, protecting their purity. Is this a custom in the older woman–younger man culture, a courtship ritual requiring that after one week of hedonistic pleasure the parents must meet their son's lover?

I quickly lick the seal on my censored letter to Andrew, press down the flap until I'm sure it's stuck. Then I take it to the mailbox outside the gate, and I raise the red flag.

We enter the Romero house by way of a walled-in courtyard dwarfed by a sprawling cottonwood tree. Alex tells me it is the same house they moved into twenty-five years ago when they moved to Santa Fe.

His mother, Aurora, answers the door dressed in a beige-and-black striped dress with a white collar and a black bow tie. She is slender and refined. His father, Max, is tall and thin, his hair as dark as Alex's hair, except for a touch of gray at the temples and forehead. Just as we're ready to be seated, Aurora remembers her pie.

"Alejandro," she says. "Would you go to the freezer? Choose a pie."

"Come with me, Olivia," he says.

"Oh. Okay," I mutter. I've been helping Aurora place perfect fried chicken, creamy mashed potatoes, and fresh green beans on the table. Nothing is as I expected—especially Alex's mother.

I am whispering to Alex as we walk out through the courtyard to a freezer in the garage: "This is my problem, I know. The stereotype was in my head. But I was expecting tamales and a fat peasant woman!"

He laughs as he opens the lid of the long, horizontal freezer.

"I feel terrible, expecting such things, but it's partly your fault, Alex. You do that dumb-Mexican routine. You call her your 'mama.' I about fell over when she answered the door."

"You like her-uh?"

We bend over the open freezer. Alex lifts an apple pie that his mother has wrapped with white freezer paper and marked with black grease pencil: APPLE. OCT 16 '69. Suddenly, it's so familiar, this frosty Tomb of the Homemade Pies. Gloria Phinney was the Queen of Freeze on Branchview Court, specializing in lasagna and broccoli-bake casserole. . . . She *was?* She still is. I've been gone only two weeks. Who am I? Roberta or Olivia? Do I carry parts of myself around in cold storage? What will happen when it all melts? The freezer triggered this time warp. . . .

"Olivia?"

"Very much, Alex. I like your mother very much." I take the pie from his hands, feeling the cold move into my fingers. "But I know she's worried. I'll be forty in January. You just turned thirty. In the kitchen she told me you're her wayward son. . . ."

He laughs again. As we leave the garage, he bends over me and nibbles my neck. I am still blushing when we walk in the door.

Aurora unwraps the pie and slips it quickly into the oven. We all sit down.

After dinner, while coffee perks and the pie cools, Alex watches golf on television with his father. Aurora wants to show me something in the bedroom. We start down the hall. "You said you'll be fixing up your apartment?"

"Trying to. It needs a lot of work," I say.

She stops as we enter the dim room. "Alex told me about your son," she says, putting her hand on her chest. She closes her eyes and lowers her head. Maybe I'm imagining things, but it seems for an instant that she has taken the heaviness all away from me. A short rest. Handing a suitcase to Andrew while we're walking into the airport, taking it back a few moments later. Oh, what a strange feeling. I can't afford to question it.

"Thank you," I say. We look at each other. I am so comfortable standing here. I was tense through dinner, figuring they didn't know about Gary and me. I might slip and say something that sounded maudlin. But she has kindly waited to bring it up. I've been feeling I have to do or say something whenever Gary's death is mentioned, especially with Leona. Not so here.

Aurora straightens her shoulders. "I will tell you about my collection. My *santos* and *retablos.* I have them in every room, but most I keep in here," she says. "They are decoration for the house, but also, oh, something extra for the spirit."

An entire wall is hung with the collection of flat boards painted with images I can only assume are Catholic patron saints. I think I recognize Saint Francis, Saint Christopher. "You must have collected these for years," I say.

I am impressed by the size of her collection. I also feel something, a comforting sort of presence, all their gentle eyes looking out. She nods as if she knows I am feeling this. She lifts one dark and smudgy rectangle from the wall and hands it to me.

"You've heard of Saint Francis?" she says.

"Yes. The animals," I say. A tiny bird perches on his shoulder, the head of a burro is barely visible at his side. The eyes have an intense staring look, sharp in the fuzzy blur of the rest of the figure.

"It's the oldest. It belonged to my mother. The paints were made from berries and roots and leaves."

"My neighbor's an artist. She told me the name of the waxy varnish they used to seal their dyes with. They still use it, I think."

"Gesso," Aurora says.

"That's it. Gesso," I say. "And when they're painted on boards they're called *ree-tah-blose?"*

"Yes. That's right. Your pronunciation is very good."

"Gracias," I say.

Aurora laughs. I'm not sure why. Maybe she likes words, too. She puts Saint Francis back on the wall. We go on talking about the protection of the *santos* and the history of the *retablos,* but we really aren't talking with words. We are taking readings of other sorts, patting a wrist, breathing in each other's cologne and bath oil scents, brushing against each other where the fleshy part of our upper arms, beneath the fabric of our sleeves, feels like a cushion between us, and laughing again, seemingly at nothing. It's a mystery, but we've met now.

She stops to open a dresser drawer and takes something out. Her back is to me, I can't see what she is doing, but then she turns and hands me a small *retablo*.

"Oh, no, I never . . ." I begin, worried that my admiration has implied a request for this gift.

She puts her hand on my arm. "This is Saint Christopher, Olivia. You are living in danger; you will need him."

I can't even say thank you. I can only put my arm around her shoulders.

Later she brings apple pie to the living room on a silver tray. Max gets up and switches off the television. He returns to the recliner chair, taps the bowl of his pipe against an ashtray on a stand. So much like Alex, the same long face. Alex has told me his father is past seventy, but his hair is so black.

"Alex tells me you lived on a farm before you came to town, Max. What was it like?" After I ask the question, I realize I could have asked about his more recent life; he did move twenty-five years ago. But going back seems to be fine with him.

"It was near Mora. I'd say forty miles northeast of Santa Fe. Alex can tell you-uh?" He grins at Alex.

"He's teasing, Olivia," Aurora says from the straight-backed dining room chair where she sits. "Once, Alex was going to move back to the farm. He didn't like school, he missed the goats. He was going to walk back, and we didn't find him till he was at the edge of town." Aurora looks at Alex as if she thinks he might be planning to run away again. She clucks her tongue. "Such a little boy to do such a thing."

Alex says, "I clocked it once. It's almost exactly forty miles."

He looks at his mother in the tolerant way I would look at Virginia if she launched into one of her favorite Roberta the Terrible stories. This is a family story, a familiar trinket brought out when acquaintances appear certain to become friends. I feel sorrow creeping over me like the relapse of some insidious illness: I will never do this with Gary. Gary ran away and no one had the sense to pursue him to the edge of town. No one even tried. I feel my throat closing up, ready to pump tears. I take a couple of deep breaths. I have to start them talking again. I have to listen to their stories. I've heard enough of mine.

"You raised goats on the farm, right?" I ask Max, realizing he has been watching me.

"Sí," Max says, tilting his head and then taking his eyes away from me, giving me a break.

Aurora brings coffee for me, holds up a tray with a sugar bowl and creamer, raises her eyebrows in a silent question. I wave my hand *no* over the cup. Max pauses to spoon several scoops of sugar into his.

"We raised goats. But the goats weren't the reason we left the farm."

"Oh," I say, wondering what he means.

"It was in the fall of the year when I said to Aurora, 'We need to go away,' you know-uh? Autumn is such a sad time of year," he says softly. "Everything is dying."

Aurora goes to the kitchen; Alex watches her go; I watch Alex watch his mother.

"I got up at dawn that morning," Max is saying. "Up in the high country, it gets so cold. I went myself to milk the goats. I didn't wake the older boys."

"We have two other sons and two daughters," Aurora explains as she returns.

"Ah," I say, nodding, feeling better as I eat my pie.

"Olivia, the sky looked smudgy. Pink and rosy, but like somebody had got up before me and rubbed ashes all across it. I didn't like the looks of that sky. And the ground. Frost can look furry—like an old man's chin?" He rubs his own and smiles wistfully. "The wind was blowing so cold and gusty at dawn. I wasn't an old man then, but somehow I smelled death. My mother had lived with us; she had died in the summer. I might have a heart attack, a car crash, I thought. The children might be hurt. I went back in the house to see if the children were breathing. I checked on each one. They were asleep." He has hardly touched his slice of pie. He leans back in his recliner, picks up his pipe, taps it on the side of the ashtray, *chock, chock.*

"I guess I was *loco* that day, Olivia. Crazy, you know? I stood out there and looked at the clouds. Right then I saw Doña Sebastiana riding across the sky." He hesitates. "You know her? Doña Sebastiana?"

I look over at Alex.

"A representation of death. Like the Grim Reaper," he says.

I nod my head, pull my shoulders forward.

"To this day, I think I saw her," Max says. "In the clouds. Blowing. She had on her fancy black cape, her skeleton was rattling on her horse. I could see the sockets of her eyes."

Max shakes his head and lights his pipe. It's as if someone has tapped him on the shoulder and reminded him that old men's stories do not interest younger people. But I am enchanted by the softening rise in his voice when he drifts up against his feelings. I am experiencing something close to compulsion in my need to hear his voice.

"Please go on. I do know what you're saying," I tell him, urge him. "Sometimes death shouldn't seem so close, but it's there. Like a shadow," I say.

"*Sí,* Olivia. That's right!" He looks at me for a moment and then continues. "Oh, so I went out to the barn to milk the goats. I pulled on the teats. Have you ever seen steam come off the warm milk?"

"No. I was raised in town," I answer quickly, ignoring summers on my grandfather Patterson's farm, not wanting Max to lose the current of emotion that seems to be flowing in him.

"The steam just rises off the milk. You squeeze and it shoots into the bucket. You can't help thinking about the life in the animal's body. . . . Life, you know? *Hijo.* I was a farmer all my life. Well, two years I went to the university in Albuquerque. But I was a farmer. My father raised sheep. My people had lived the same life, cattle and sheep in Mexico. Before that in the Basque, in Spain.

"But that morning—ay, Olivia—that morning I kept thinking of little Alex. He was only four or five then, uh? He had cried when we slaughtered the kids. I told his mama, 'Keep him in!' But that boy—an imp—he came out and saw the baby goats' necks being slit and blood spurting out. It does, you know? Like a faucet."

I nod. I look at Alex and Aurora, sitting together on the sofa as the afternoon sun comes in. They are listening, living the course of their lives again today.

"I didn't leave the farm because of the hard work. You see Alex? I was big like that boy." He grins, leaning toward me. "Stronger than he is. He's lazy-uh?" He grins. "No, Olivia, it was something else that morning. Like I was to make a choice. *Sí.* I had explained to the boy that the kids had to be killed or they would drink all the milk we needed to sell in town. But I thought, 'I don't have to do it. Maybe Doña Sebastiana is trying to tell me something.' I turned around and called out at the wind and the clouds. *'Vámonos!'* I said." He smiles, a little embarrassed, as Aurora shifts, gets up from the sofa, and goes to the kitchen. "We moved to town that winter, Olivia."

So they sold the farm in Mora, I think, piecing together Alex's family chronology. Maybe it was Aurora's family who had the goat farm and Max's family who had the *rancho* and had lived in Mexico. And the oil company bought the *rancho* near El Paso much later, when Alex was at Berkeley. Oh, whatever the history, Max retired from his state job as an agricultural inspector. He smokes cherry-scented tobacco in his pipe, puts on a white dress-shirt every morning, a tie and slippers. And their son did not slit the necks of goats. A father made a choice for his son, depriving him of one life, the life Alex seems to grieve for, but his father made a choice nonetheless. I sit for a moment, contemplating the fearsome power of parenthood.

"It doesn't seem to matter where we are that time of year, in the autumn," he says, looking over at Aurora.

Sitting again in the straight-backed chair, Aurora waves her hands, places them stiffly on her knees. "Just look at the sun," she says.

I turn, catch Alex's eye as he turns to look toward the living-room window. He points a finger at his watch.

"Sí," Max says slowly, drawing the word through that higher range of feeling. "But autumn makes me sadder every year. Everything is dying. And I can see it coming. In August? Next month? I will see it in the clouds."

"The sky is such an aqua blue this time of year, almost turquoise in the summer," Aurora says, as if to lift us all from the clutches of Max's sadness. "We grow our chiles now—has Alex told you? We string them in the fall. *Ristras*. And we rake leaves and can the garden vegetables in the autumn. We do our outside work then, because it's warm here—not hot or cold."

"I can hardly look outside that time of year," Max says, relighting his pipe, which has gone out. I know he's serious, but I sense him half clowning, too, the way he glances at Aurora.

Aurora stands up and walks over to Max's chair. "You know, Alejandro, Papa is sad because he doesn't keep busy—without goats or a job to tell him, 'Max! Go out of your house!' Poor Papa."

Max leans back against the cushion of his recliner, admiring his wife, taking in the whole of her—her body, her spirit. I feel the connection between them. This familiarity, these things they have said so many times before, have become a testament to their need of one another and their graceful acceptance of the need. I want to get this, hold on to it.

"I stay so busy," Aurora says, touching her white collar. "I sew for the grandchildren. I go to church. This man! He sits and tells me he's so sad."

"No, no!" Max laughs gently. "We're *both* very sad. Mama, too, Alex. You should hear her when she talks about the ones who are gone. So many friends, her sister last year. But she's a good woman. She thinks nothing will die if she's busy. . . ." He waves his veined and bony hands, fluttering his fingers, spilling flakes of tobacco from his pipe. "Ah, but it's a relief for us when summer ends and the leaves fall and winter finally comes. The snow comes, *la manta blanca*. A white blanket. Like the Anglo saying, the shoe drops? No more waiting. Then I feel better." He smiles at me.

"Then you say it's too cold!" Aurora says.

Max laughs. "I know. But then I'm no longer sad, Mama. I'm just cold!" He winks at me.

I want to hold them both and keep death away from them for one more season, one more year.

Alex stands up to leave.

Is it really three o'clock? The sun has moved in the sky; the bright glare has gone from the living-room window sooner than it should have, it seems to me. Is this the descent toward autumn Max talked about? But it's only July.

We stand at the door. I take Max's hand.

"Olivia," he says. "You'll come back again-uh? I'll let you talk."

"Oh, Max," I say, laughing. "I liked your stories. I did." No way to tell him what I've learned when I am not even sure myself. *"Los cuentos,"* I say. Old stories—different from history.

"Ah! *Sí,*" he says. He nods to Alex and puffs his pipe. Alex embraces his father, kisses each cheek the way I've seen European men do in films. *"Papá,"* he says.

Aurora has draped a sweater over her shoulders, and pulls it together now with her fingers as she watches Alex and Max embrace. As if she's in pain, a muscle twitches beneath her eye, the cords in her neck stand out and recede again. No wonder. I remember watching Andrew with Gary, when things were good between them. Aurora is the one living in a danger zone. She loves them. *This* is life at the edge. I go to stand beside her. Our upper arms touch.

Max makes a sweeping wave with the hand that holds the pipe, then walks back toward his recliner. Alex holds his mother.

"I'll get fat, Mama. Two pieces of pie." He pats his slight bulge of belly.

"You need exercise," she says, straightening her back, giving her head an efficient little tilt. She looks at me.

"Gracias," I say, holding up the small piece of painted wood, Saint Christopher, and placing it carefully into my purse.

Aurora takes my hands. "I am glad you could come. Alex, bring Olivia back."

"Sí," he says.

The door closes. Our feet make dry leaves crackle and twigs snap as we walk through the courtyard and out to the street.

"My father really got going, didn't he?" Alex says, starting up his truck.

"He knows about Gary, doesn't he? Your mother knew."

"I told them," Alex says. He looks over at me. "Olivia?"

"I feel as if your father was trying to tell me something about death. His stories . . ."

"You asked about the farm, that's all. He got started on the goats."

"Could be," I say, unconvinced. I am thinking about Doña Sebastiana and how she told Max to move his family to town. I am thinking about Aurora's lovely gift of the *retablo*. They were teaching me. Maybe I need to walk on the mesa and watch the clouds at sunrise, as Alex does, as his father did before him.

We pull onto the highway.

"We'll go to Four Corners today, Olivia. Have you ever heard of this place?"

"Four corners . . . a place?" I ask. Rectangles and squares have them: four right angles.

"It's where the four states meet. Utah, Arizona, New Mexico, and Colorado."

"Oh," I say. "Sure. Wherever."

I'm only along for the ride anyway, but couldn't he show me this on a map? Why drive to the border? Driving to Four Corners would seem an outing more suited to surveyors and cartographers who want to check each other's work. Does each state hire linesmen, like in baseball and football stadiums, employees who run out there every day with the lime spreader? Or is it chalk dust?

"You'll see some of the northwest part of the state. Indian country."

I pour coffee from the thermos Alex brought. I hand the cup to him. He takes a sip and hands it back. We ride some time in silence.

Soon the rounded mud Navajo dwellings I have read about—hogans—seem to multiply, as we head west. Flocks of sheep graze on open land. Pickup trucks dot the highway.

"They don't actually live in the hogans, do they?"

"Sure, it's their way," Alex says.

"What about in the winter, the snowstorms?"

"The helicopters drop food. The Indians must stay here. This is sacred ground. Their ancestors lived here."

"What about the animals?"

"Helicopters drop food to the animals, too," Alex says.

Different from my nightmares. *Helping* helicopters.

I keep imagining the land underwater. Flat, stratified layers of earth create the mesas, aptly named tabletop remains of what must once have been the very surface of the earth . . . or the bottom of the sea. Every time the clouds move across the sun, the mesas change color, from ochre and lavender in the light to charcoal and slate in the shadows.

"You saw Santa Clara, near town. Black Mesa is their sacred place. Almost every mesa is more than a landmark to the Indians. They do all kinds of rituals out here."

We drive on.

Mesas take on pinkish hues, miles roll by, the sun moves.

We pass a road sign.

SHIPROCK	15
FOUR CORNERS	50

"Do you know, when I was growing up we could go to Canada and Vermont and back to Potsdam in the time it's taking us to get to the Colorado state line?"

Alex has nothing to say regarding the sizes of states and their artificially imposed boundaries. Miles are still miles, whatever shapes we lay over them. Yet we are driving to Four Corners.

I see the wind outside, rather than hearing or feeling it. Cumulus and cirrus clouds rush across the sky as if late for an appointment; the contrail of a jet disperses almost as soon as it appears. The mesas and the flatlands around them hold firm, but sagebrush along the shoulder of the highway is whipped side to side.

"Alex! Look at that rock."

To the left of the highway a promontory arises. No, it hasn't arisen, actually. A shape distinct from all the rest, a stone formation, it has been visible for miles. Now it looms at the center of my vision.

"That's Shiprock, Olivia."

"The road sign! I should have known."

Alex doesn't look at the rock; he watches me. His dark hair is silhouetted by the backlight of sun; his eyes move from my face to the road and back again to my face. As if he's seen me dead and now resurrected, he seems to witness my excitement. I feel self-conscious but not enough to stop my reactions to this, this ROCK.

No doubt about the nautical connection in this grand design. The broad middle section of the stone formation takes on the contours of a ship's hull. The narrowing prow to the front points north. The ship seems to glide with the clouds that course across the sky behind it, changing at split-second intervals from gray to purple to blue. I keep reminding myself that the raw materials this ship is constructed from are just homely browns and tans and umbers, soil and stone. But it keeps on changing!

"Oh! Gary would have loved this," I say. I twist around in the seat, look out the back window, peer through Alex's window. "This would have captured his imagination—a ship rising out of the desert! Can you believe this?" I can feel tears standing in my eyes when I look at Alex and smile. Something gleams in his eyes too. I go on in a rush of words, the tears receding in deference to the finer, richer flood of memory and joy. "He would have gone home and sculpted this rock out of clay, and papier-mâché, and then he'd have sketched it on paper for months. . . ."

I lower myself onto the seat again, staring out the back window as we speed ahead on the highway. "Alex?" I say, an inviting, suggestive tone in my voice.

He runs his hand back through his hair. "I cannot take you there, Olivia. That is sacred ground."

I move next to him, put my hand on his thigh. "Alex."

"These dudes do scalps, man. They could have a lot of fun with a redheaded white lady."

I feel the muscles in his leg contract as he shifts gears. He is bringing the truck to the side of the road. "Alex," I say. *"You're* here. We'll be safe."

"They won't be fooled by me! *Hijo.* The civil rights people would die. You think if you've seen one brownface, you've seen them all? Olivia, where have you been?"

I wave his words away like flies, with quick flips of my wrist. "Asleep. Brain-dead. I've told you that."

He stops the truck, looks over at me.

"So teach me, Alex. Teach me about Shiprock."

"I'll drive over to that barbed-wire fence. We'll be less than a mile if we go to the fence."

After crossing the highway and bouncing along a rutted path, we both spy a wire gate less than a hundred yards away. That is, Alex sees the gate and looks away, glancing quickly at me and grunting, knowing I've seen it too.

Forgive me, I say to those unknown spirits who inhabit the stone ship. Forgive me, but a mile is too far away; I need to get closer. I jump from the truck and yank open the gate, tramping down underbrush to allow it to swing wide. I wave him through, listening for war whoops and hoofbeats in the wind that whips my hair and cuts through my T-shirt. I hug my arms to my chest as I run to the truck and climb back in. "Whoo!" I say to Alex. I pull my sweater from behind the seat and slip it on.

The wind is a solid thing. Constant, yet invisible. Hot, yet strangely chilling. It thumps in my eardrums, fills my lungs even as I push it out with my panting exhalations. The air remains in the strands of my hair and inside my T-shirt, penetrates to my skin as I place both hands on the dashboard and stare, transfixed, at Shiprock as we bounce forward on what is surely a horse trail and not a road.

Approaching the eastern edge of the rock gives me the stiff-necked feeling of trying to view an oversized painting from the front of the crowd in a gallery. I keep pulling my head back, thinking it won't seem so close, so tall. But in this case the canvas is the height of a multistory building. Alex reminds me of the harassed docent with an inattentive group of schoolchildren: He's speaking quickly, hoping to bring the tour to a speedy conclusion.

"Okay, Olivia," he says, stopping the truck. "This is Shiprock. The Indians believe their people first came to this land in a ship when everything was covered by water. Actually, the ship had wings and landed them here."

"I've read that the Indians remember these things, in an ancestral memory way. . . ."

"Whatever," Alex says.

"Sure!" I say. "A Noah's Ark kind of thing. And there *is* the Bering Strait theory. . . ."

"They believe. . . ."

"I kept thinking it looked like it had been underwater!"

"They believe there could be another great flood, and they will escape in this ship. No one can mess with this rock, Olivia. No one should even remove a pebble from this land."

Alex gets out of the truck. He looks behind him, all around, as if he might actually see something in all that empty space. He even glances up to the top of the ship, as if checking for sentries behind its double masts. His hair tangles in the wind as he paces.

"Alex," I call as I join him outside. "From the back you look . . . authentic! I think you're an Indian chieftain. A great wise chief. Do you have a story about that?" I laugh and my teeth chatter.

He brushes up against me. We watch each other and this ship made of rock. I touch his belt buckle, I wrap my leg around his. He kisses me, pushing against me, but then pulls back.

"Alex," I say. "No make-believe?"

"No, Olivia. This place feels bad for us."

He paces some more, looking all around. "Up in Colorado there's another sacred place. You would really get into this one, Olivia-uh? It's called the Sleeping Ute Mountain. We might see it today if we leave now."

I make no move to leave.

"The Sleeping Ute is hills shaped like a sleeping brave on his back with his hands crossed on his chest. There's even a narrow hill of rock and sand that looks like a feather extending from the top of his head. Huge. Maybe a mile long in all."

"It really looks that way?" I ask. I sit on the hood of the truck. I am shivering in this hot wind. I put my hands between my legs to hold myself still.

"The Utes say the sleeping brave is going to wake up one of these days and when he does . . ." He draws his finger horizontally across his throat.

"Get the white man?" I ask.

"You guessed it."

Dry-docked flying ships and sleeping braves and holes that lead to underworld kivas. Only the desert can hold such secrets. Always more than meets the eye. I mull it over, almost ready to leave. Then the thought occurs to me that the sleeping warrior formation was there long before it ever had a legend to go with it, before Indians ever knew about the white man. An obvious deduction in geological and cultural terms, I know, but I give Alex this information anyway.

"So?" he says. He leans against the bumper, his hands tucked under his armpits.

"So? Don't you see? They've revised the legends just the way we've revised our religions." I am jerking now as I try to talk. "I'll bet only the Indians will board that ship when the great flood comes. I'll bet that's how they tell it. Just like the chosen few who'll reach the pearly gates."

I look up at the sheer cliff of layered rock, wondering where my discourse on comparative religions will take me. Will an image appear there in front of me to clear up my confusion? "Or else they've just done with their legends what they do with their sand paintings: edit them for mass marketing."

Alex waits, comes over and leans against my leg.

"Have you heard any variants of these legends?" I sniff.

"We'll find you some more books, Olivia."

He is patient with me. He could climb in the truck and rev the engine, threaten to leave me at the mercy of Hopis on their way to the big *sipapu* in Arizona. As it is, I keep flinging my questions against the wall, into the rock, hoping, I suppose, to imbed in the hull of this ancient vessel of stone some fossilized reminder that I, too, have been here. What's the use?

"Why must I do this, Alex?"

"Hey," he says, turning to look at me. "That's your way. You like to go back."

Far enough back, I think. It has to be far enough back. "That's just it, Alex," I say, dreading the way my mind is drifting. "I can't go back." I jump down from the truck. "I can't start over!" I stiffen my arms at my sides. Irreverently as a two-year-old, I kick an unsuspecting pebble from its resting place. Immediately sorry, I formulate a charge: Disturbing the Peace. But I'll never have any peace; I *know* my punishment for this violation of sacred space. Won't this misery ever stop?

Not sure if Alex will even hear me, I walk over toward him, whispering into the wind. "I held that baby."

Alex seems to have stopped breathing. His skin is sallow. Beneath his eyes are dark smudges. Lines I've never noticed before now carve into the flesh beneath his nostrils and the corners of his mouth. His lips, his tongue, when he opens his mouth to speak, are the blue-black color of a bruise. I will make an old man of him with my caterwauling pain. Suddenly I realize what he's been doing. He's been trying to take this pain from me.

But some other part of me wants him to suffer. This protester? He likes my pain so much, lances the wound, opens me up again? I'll make a death mask of his face; I'll rip off the mask as soon as it has hardened, grind it into the sand with my heel, smash it against the hull of the stone ship in commemoration of this dead day. That's what I'll do.

Watching a muscle tic working at the inner corner of his eye, I say, "You talk about gods? A tiny, blond god."

He is holding my gaze; he is staring back at me.

"That baby's shoulders were gold, plump as a peach, downy. My God, Alex! Swirls of hair like thumbprints of spun gold. In the hospital room? I was nursing him? I pulled him off my breast and held him up in the sunshine. First front, then back. Gold." I bring my fist to my mouth, biting my knuckle; a sound comes from my throat.

"*Bebé dorado.* Golden baby," Alex says. He shakes his head, reaches for me.

"Don't look at me!" I shriek.

A strand of hair blows into my mouth, sticks against my teeth, as if a snake has whipped its tail. Medusa's head, Medusa's mad scene, I think, rejecting on one level my capacity for exaggeration, accepting on another the monstrosity of what I seem to be saying, aloud, to another human being. "Don't look at me, Alex. I killed the dorado bambino. I killed that baby."

"Bebé dorado," he says, correcting me again, looking closely at me.

"Whatever!" I shout. I turn him around by the arms, causing him to face the ship's empty hull. I shake, but I don't know what I'm shaking from: nerves, cold, laughter? I'm laughing: "It sounds like something condensed in *Reader's Digest* from *True!* 'I Killed the Dorado Bambino.' "

My throat feels thick, as if I've been running.

"I fed him poison. I told him that men just went off to war. 'Look,' I said. 'See the wars that went before?' We went to museums! My God, Alex, I took him to museums!" I whimper. I bring my arm up to wipe my leaking eyes and dripping nose on the sleeve of my sweater. I notice that Alex is bent down on one knee.

"Andrew *said* it was my fault. I fought him. I mean, he was building bombs, Alex. Bombs!" I draw in my breath, steady my voice. "But I held that baby up to the sun. What if I'm pregnant again? What if I kill another baby, another son? Worse yet, a daughter? What could I teach a daughter? I can't be! I just can't." I press my fists against my forehead. I look up. Alex is watching me again. "Turn around!" I say.

He stands up, shuffles his feet, and then shoves his hands in the pockets of his jeans, causing his shoulders to seem abnormally wide as his back tapers down to the vulnerable narrowness of his pelvis. I see the bones of his pelvis now, abandoned at the foot of a great mesa, not bleached-white-and-clean Georgia O'Keeffe bones, but bloodstained, picked-at-by-birds bones. My heart goes out to him; I hate him.

I sniffle. I wonder if I'm crying. But the sound I make is more like the shriek of some high-flying bird of prey. A hawk, maybe. A big-winged condor, vulture family. The shadow of Shiprock has moved closer to us. Alex is at the edge of the shadow. He keeps his back to me, just as I asked him to do. He probably knows if he looks at me I'll freeze his face.

I lean forward, my eyes fixed on him. "You know what's gotten me through?" I ask.

Alex doesn't move, but I can sense his body shifting, *preparing* to move. Maybe Shiprock has chosen this moment to dislodge itself from its moorings. Maybe the clouds are blowing so fast that Alex and I and his truck and the whole rotting planet are a train waiting in a station while another one streaks by—clickety-clack, the ground beneath us vibrating. But the illusion of movement will end, I know, just as soon as the capricious time-wind shifts direction. There we will be, the same as before, no movement at all, everything happening again.

"I've been thinking I'd go crazy. I mean really *loca.* I figured I would have gone crazy by now." I hear the disappointment in my voice.

The sky is listening. I hear the wind.

"It's not going to happen," I sob, pounding my fist on the hood.

Alex moves now. He lifts me up and helps me into the truck. He pours a cup of coffee from the thermos and puts it in my hand. He gets in the truck on his side.

"No loca," I say. *"No loca en la credenza."*

The corners of his mouth turn up ever so slightly, though he still looks somber. *"Cabeza,"* he says. "*Esta es no loca en la cabeza.* And no, you're not crazy," he says.

"Cah-bay-suh," I repeat.

He is turning the truck toward the highway. "We're going back," he says. "We'll go to Four Corners another time."

Save those right angles, those balanced geometrical configurations, for another time.

As we drive away, though I don't look back, I wonder if maybe the shadow of Shiprock is moving toward us and, like a dark hand, reaching for our departing backs. To keep away the shadow, hoping Saint Christopher is still in there, I pick up my purse and squeeze it: I hold my breath until the truck hits the smooth pavement of the highway.

Settled in the truck, one sock-foot propped on the dashboard, I feel a rush of affection for Alex, a need to reassure him of the mental stability beneath my gloomy, changeable exterior. I glance at him, my forehead resting on my upraised knee. "I know I'll have some good days, too," I say. "One of these days."

"I know," he says. "You look at death in a . . ." He is choosing his words too carefully; it disturbs me to realize this. "In a different way. But you're not crazy."

"I make sense on my good days," I say.

"You try to take all the blame. Fate has a hand in it too-uh?"

"Things happen. Accidents happen," I say, more to myself. I hear him talking as if from a long way off.

"Do you know the Day of the Dead? All Saints Day? My grandma always baked bread for Diá de los Muertos," he begins.

I want to listen, I want to hear the sound of his voice as he tells me ways of his people that are, it seems to me, only fond memories for him. His family has changed, and he loves this childhood he left behind, or lost. I try to listen to his other way of looking at death.

"As far back as I can remember, we had the candy skulls and skeleton dolls. And the kids had picnics on graves. Well. . . . My mama, she didn't like that. But as long as my grandma lived, we celebrated that holiday."

He touches my shoulder, pats his slender hand against the steering wheel, smiles and sighs, spreading before me, on a blanket of words, this comfort that actually belongs only to him. But I listen. I listen so attentively that he thinks I understand. I listen because for me his words, his voice, his breath are the only life I feel in myself, in the hurtling mass of steel that encases us, in the shifting, wind-whipped desert. In all of the universe at this moment, there is only Alex and the sound of his voice.

Just as the light seems to be abandoning the sky, leaving dark purple shadows on clouds, Alex's voice slows down. He seems to be summing up. I try harder to focus on his words as sounds possessed of meaning, trying to think what I'll say if spoken responses from me are going to be necessary to keep his voice from stopping.

"To me, Olivia, you have to see Doña Sebastiana as a party crasher. Nobody *invites* her, man. She comes."

"Who?" I ask, knowing my lapse of attention gives me away. I play his words back: Doña Sebastiana. Okay. The Grim Reaper. The symbol of death Max talked about. "Ahh," I say as if in recognition. The sky is dark, the clouds puffs of phosphorescent cotton that hold on to the light. "Um-hum," I say. My teeth are grinding, getting ready to chatter.

Alex is trying too hard. He seems young, naive, yet wiser than I'll ever be. He's right in comparing death to a rude and uninvited guest. In no one's book of Exit Etiquette are RSVP's ever mentioned—a come-as-you-are affair if ever there was one. Guests can't pause at the threshhold to ask the skeletal hostess, "Hey, *señora.* What's the occasion?" Life! The occasion that prompts death's arrival is life! Does Alex know that? I am not the one to tell him.

City light and starlight, equally anonymous and remote, hold the night sky in a twinkling, perforated vise. Nothing moves. In the eerie light of the instruments on the dashboard, I look over at Alex as he weaves through the Saturday evening traffic at the interchange near Albuquerque. Soon we're on the road to Santa Fe.

Alex says, "Gary wouldn't blame you for what happened to him."

His voice sounds so hoarse I'm not sure I've heard him correctly. I lean toward him, raise my hand questioningly. "What did you say?"

"I was just thinking: If Gary thought of you when he died, I don't think it was to blame you."

I turn to the window on my side of the truck, see my face, a yellow-green witch's mask in the light. I feel his tenderness, his concern, but why? What is he doing, trying to give me some answer? I haven't asked him a question! I must look like a problem waiting for a solution.

"I don't know what to say, Alex."

He ignores my nonresponse. "When I was a boy, I asked my grandma, 'What happens to the goats when they die?' She told me she didn't know, but when she was a little girl in Mexico, the Mexican Revolution was going on. She lived near the El Paso border, Olivia. The *rancho* was near this place."

I nod.

"It was a disorganized war," he says. "Skirmishes were going on everywhere, sometimes near her house. The women and children, doing the wash in the river, they just ran for the house if the soldiers and *banditos* got into it nearby."

Alex keeps looking at me, sly storyteller that he is, making sure I'm caught before he moves his narrative along. He has put in those women and children doing laundry at the river at just the right time. I was working on a timeline for the revolution, back in my history books again.

"One time, my grandma said, she was playing alone in the sand by the river. She dug holes in the mud and found roots at the edge of the river. Suddenly popping noises began!" Alex is so loud. He jerks the steering wheel when he says this, then takes control again. My head bumps against the window.

"Alex!" I say.

He goes right on with the story. "My grandma was scared, but she was curious, too. She thought the sounds were coming from the sky. She looked up to see.

"My grandma was so old when she told me the story, Olivia. It wasn't long before she died. I was four, five. I remember I couldn't imagine her as a little girl. But her eyes got so bright! She looked so young and so old when she said it: *'Pájaros de patine!'* I looked at her. I didn't know what silver birds would look like, but her eyes were so bright I figured maybe they looked like my grandma's eyes. She said she saw the tiny birds all around her and she thought it was magic.

"Her aunties and her mother came screaming out of the house. They dragged her inside. They shook her shoulders. My grandmother shook me, Olivia; she put her old bony hands on my shoulders and she shook me. They told her she must run away when the bullets were flying."

Is that it? A morality tale Alex the Peace Marcher has provided me for future reference? When the bullets fly, run like hell? A little bit late with your advice, Alex, I think, noticing what a small space my spirit seems to occupy. It seems I could just accept the gift of his story, but no. . . .

"As a little girl she had cried—and my grandmother, she cried in telling me. She told her aunties that the silver flying things could not have hurt her; they were so magical and shiny, more beautiful than anything. . . ." Alex's voice quivers and stops.

More beautiful than anything his grandmother could ever convey to her little grandson Alejandro, she probably thought. But the old woman must have succeeded magnificently. Look at his face in the night, look at his eyes glisten.

"I've never forgotten that, Olivia," Alex says, his voice still husky with feeling.

His father Max can pare feeling right down to the bone and his voice rises like music to accompany it. I can imagine the struggles Max has gone through to achieve that harmony. I see Alex's struggle now. How I admire that harmony, how far I feel from it.

"I can't help thinking," he says, "that when death comes, we see the *pájaros de patine,* the silver birds."

"The bright light," I say sadly, wishing to believe.

"*Sí*. Doña Sebastiana scares us to death. But death? *Hijo,* I don't know."

I hear his voice rise, feel a surge of joy, a desire to rise with him, but this long day has weighted me down. No escape, no refuge, no comfort.

"I should never have changed my name!"

"What?" Alex asks.

"What's the use?" I say, losing control of my voice. "Roberta's a perversion of a man's name. Robert—Roberta. And Olivia's a euphemism."

"What?" he asks again.

"I've been hearing it all day while we were driving. Can't you hear it? Olivia—Oblivion. Olivia—Oblivion."

"Stop."

"A euphemistic way of saying 'oblivion.' Olivia—Oblivion."

We're in town, on Paseo de Peralta. Why would he be stopping at the side of the road? Fool! There's traffic. Even if everything is closed, drunks are always walking on the roadside. He grabs my shoulders. I feel his fingers squeeze through skin and muscle down to bone. "Can you stop this?" He shakes me, hard.

I lower my head, sobbing. "Can't stop."

"Then I'll stay with you tonight at your place. But I will slap you if you say that again. Do you *hear* me, Olivia?"

"Yes."

"*Slap* you!" His eyes are black as beads. "Do you believe me?"

"Yes."

I believe him. I know now. I cannot vaporize out here on the desert.

7

I've been lying here watching the light come in my room. Alex has gone home. I went to sleep last night with him sitting on the side of the bed. He just sat. No more stories. No more lovemaking.

I've known that silhouette, the shape of someone being there, before. My father, Harold, sitting beside me and my measles, when I was five, answering the endless questions I remember devising to keep him there. "What about *after* the dinosaurs?" My mother, Virginia, in the doorway. Their voices, their laughter. Andrew, bedside on Branchview Court, Gary and I lying there, victims of an intestinal flu that attacked Andrew the next day and caused us to change positions. But on that day, Andrew, sitting, handing us the magical cures he and I had brought with us from our own families and blended together in an agreed-upon sequence for ourselves: Ice chips, first, in a cup. Then flat Seven-Up. And, as the day went on, the sure sign of our recovery, sugar-sprinkled toast in a bowl of milk, a texture and taste that in health would have induced vomiting, yet there, with my tiny boy beside me and my husband sitting on the bed, a healing potion. Gary, looking at us with the pleasure and power of his patient status, saying, "Mommy and me frow up!" Snuggling his head delightedly into the pillow beside me. Andrew and I exchanging wry smiles, at some level agreeing with Gary, wanting the sickness to go on a little longer, too, if that meant this gathering, offering, accepting, caring. Just an instant of feeling stronger, but with a mildly anxious hope that we might have forgotten "well" and so could remain comfortably "sick."

I see the parallel. I even ask myself the question: Have I forgotten "well"? But how can I compare twenty-four-hour flu and a loss like

Andrew and I have had? They can't be compared, can they? This is more like polio, a lengthier incapacitation than flu. . . . Stop! Just as Alex did it for me last night, I cut short for myself this pity-practice session. "Stop!" I say, dialing our number on Branchview Court. Andrew doesn't mow on Sundays.

"Oh, I'm glad you called, Roberta. I tried to call you, but an operator said Thursday . . ."

" 'Thursday installations will not appear until Monday.' " I give it my Lily Tomlin nasal imitation. We laugh, lazy with Sunday rhythm.

"How can so much happen in two weeks?" Andrew asks.

Oh, Irony, hold thy tongue. Two weeks? Eighteen down, twelve to go.

"I don't get this," he says.

"What?" I ask.

"I don't know. Starting to feel better. When you were home, I was a mess, I know it. I guess that's why I'm not *too* pissed off at you for leaving. I oughta be."

"Andrew, I know." He really *hasn't* sounded angry in these phone calls. . . .

"Now you go out there, I hear about this group, and only two weeks have gone by."

"A group?" I ask.

"A group of parents who've lost their children. I saw it in the paper that day I took off work—when I thought you might call."

I don't want to ask, but what does LOST mean? I am concerned that Andrew might get discouraged in a group of parents who have a chance to FIND their children. Geoffrey Alston Mills's mother could find him—she could put out an All Points Bulletin. I'd help. I'd call in. I saw him in South Dakota two weeks ago, I'd say.

"What does the group call itself?" I ask.

"I don't think it has a name. They said they run an ad once a month in the *Washington Post.*"

"What did the ad say?"

"Parents of lost children? Call this number? I don't remember. I hadn't paid that much attention, then I thought of it Wednesday, at work. Well, not at work. I was jogging. . . ."

"Jogging?" I shriek. "You've never jogged!"

"I know. I run and then walk." He laughs but doesn't seem amused. He sounds embarrassed.

"So you thought of the ad while you were jogging," I say, interested, feeling that Andrew might be someone I don't know at all, feeling an odd sort of attraction, as to a stranger.

"Yeah, you know how they run over the bridge and by Lady Bird Grove and then back to the Pentagon on their lunch hour? I was running. I've done it two or three times. I did it a couple of times before you left. I never said anything to you about it."

"You weren't talking," I say.

"No, I wasn't," he says. "I get so tired my mind goes blank. I can feel all the cigarettes I smoked when I played in the band. I mean I *feel* them, like black goo in my lungs. That day, I thought I was actually going to die I was so tired. I was hanging on to the signpost at the Fourteenth Street bridge, gasping, and this ad popped into my head. I dug out the newspaper in the trash can at home."

"And you called." I wonder, like a jealous child, why *I* never saw such an ad. But given my eyes and all I've missed, I shouldn't be surprised.

"Yeah, I went to the Thursday meeting and liked it, so then I went to the Saturday morning meeting, too. Yesterday. They meet on Saturdays, so more people can come."

"So how'd you feel? Did you talk? Did you tell them . . . ?"

"I told about Gary. I said you were . . . gone for a while."

"Is this, like, a singles group?" I ask, my eyes narrowing.

"Roberta," he says, warning me off. "Some of the marriages have broken up since the kids, you know, died."

"Oh."

"The stories weren't only about the war, either. One couple's boy walked head-on into a bus down in the District. He was on an acid trip. He seemed to think he could just push it back with his hands."

"Oh, no," I say, knowing their horror, knowing that a doorbell—maybe a telephone—had to have rung for them, as it did for us. I can feel my mind widening out, covering the parents in Andrew's group with my knowing. "Oh, yes," I whisper.

I can't talk for a moment. Maybe Andrew can't either.

"Did your clothes come?" he asks.

"Hmm? Oh. No. Not yet."

"I sent them Monday."

"Thanks."

My throat is closing, swelling the tissues, the muscles, with tears.

"They still smelled like you. When I put them in the box. I missed you."

"Um-hum. Me too. You, I mean."

"You okay, Roberta?"

It requires a broad definition, being okay. It means running till you're almost dead and then hanging on to signposts and gasping for air.

"I think I am, Andrew. I think I'm okay, you know, for now."

"Thanks for calling."

"Maybe we can do this. Call on Sundays."

"Okay. Yeah. G'bye, Roberta."

I go outside to see if my newspaper delivery has started. Sure enough, a thick Sunday edition of the *New Mexican,* thinner than the weekday *Washington Post,* lies near my feet in the courtyard. I pick it up and start inside.

"Olivia?" Leona calls. She pokes her head out the screendoor. "How about a cup of coffee?"

For just an instant I think she wants me to make coffee, then I realize she's inviting me over. I suddenly wish I had a pot already made, to offer her.

"I'm not dressed, Leona," I say, spreading my robe out around me.

"So?"

I notice she's dressed, looking as if she's been up for hours in her slacks and a long cotton smock. But those sneakers, the color of concrete. Is she painting? What *has* she been doing in those shoes?

"I'm throwing pots this morning," she says.

I picture noisy acts of destruction until my mind moves on to a second definition of *throw.* "You do pottery?" I ask. She nods as we go inside.

We bring our coffee cups to the small, second bedroom she has converted to a studio. She sits down at her wheel. "So. You're doing pottery now," I say.

"I've lost interest in batiks," she says.

A shelf holds clay in clear plastic bags—brown, red-brown, gray-white. But two bags contain a greenish gray clay. I ask about those.

"That's molded clay. The Japanese wait decades for some of that green slime. This isn't anything so exotic."

"You do all these things. Batik. Oils. Pen-and-ink. And now pottery." I wave my arm in a wide circle to include what I know of Leona's work. "How do you decide which art form you're going to work in?"

"The weather? What's going on in my head? That's really not a question one asks oneself."

"Oh," I say. "Why not?"

Bent over her potter's wheel, everything surrounding her an involvement of dust, earth, powdery glazes, and paints, Leona doesn't answer. She pushes the pedal and leans her tiny body into the shaping and supporting of some reddish clay at the center. Her hands press the clay—away, into, against. Leaning on the doorjamb, lost in the whirling of the wheel, I'm startled as Leona stops, straightens, and looks over at me, wiping her hands on a cloth already caked with clay. "That's how it works," she says.

"Oh," I say, wishing she had shown me more. Maybe this is the closest I'll ever come to art, just looking over the artist's shoulder as she works. But maybe not. "Do you think I could do this?" I ask.

"I'm not sure," she says, squinting at me from behind her mud-spattered glasses. "I might try to teach you."

From Leona, those are encouraging words. "I might try to learn," I say.

I shudder at the thought of her impatience and my inherent clumsiness, but the dank clay smell lingers importantly in my nostrils as we move toward the kitchen and the rich, sweet scent of her baking. We sit on her shady patio where magenta impatiens bloom in carved wooden boxes attached along the wall.

As I am leaving, Leona hands me a plate of coffee-cake slices covered with wax paper. I notice for the first time that I never leave her place without something she has given me; she never comes to my apartment without something she has brought for me. I wonder if I will ever be that way, have something to bring, to give, to offer. I thank her and turn to go.

"Wait!" she says.

I stand here, covered plate in hand, looking self-consciously around her living room while she goes to her studio. From a box near the screendoor, small, rounded ceramic pieces poke out like baby birds or chicks, their olive-brown glaze catching the light. Unframed paintings sit on the floor, leaning casually against the sofa and a chair. So alive, these works of Leona's hands! This could be 1955 on Branchview Court; these could be her children watching television; she's gone to get her donation to the March of Dimes, and I'm the block captain come on behalf of afflicted children to pick it up. . . . She returns with a paper bag. She holds it open. I halfway expect to see a slotted card with silvery dimes peeking out from the slots. I'm surprised, looking in, to find a gray slab of clay, six inches thick. When I reach my hand in the bag, the clay feels cool, damp, and dense.

"Mush it around for a while at home," Leona says. "See what you come up with."

All afternoon I read. Real-estate regulations mostly, but later one of the books from the library, a book of Indian "creation" stories. I don't know whether to laugh or cry at one Crow story which explains that Old Man Coyote and two ducks did all the creation work when there was only the Great Water. Old Man Coyote was getting concerned after he had created the women, because he noticed there was a dying off of passion after the initial taking of wives. Then he noticed that wife stealing was going on. He himself had lost and reclaimed one particular wife three times and decided she was the best wife he had. "Under the blanket she is hot—she has learned things," he says. When his younger Coyote brother asks him how he can say such a thing when the others laugh at him for this, he says, "Under our buffalo robe, I am laughing for my own reasons."

The clear, simple syntax of the stories I've been devouring seems to have infiltrated my mind—a pleasant invasion, a lot like the voice Alex took on the night he taught me the other things. I imagine a ritual dance, the Dance of the Returning Wife. Andrew did the Dance of the Returning Husband when *he* came home after living with the nurse. He held his eyes low, bowed his head often, turned his body sideways. "Oh, Andrew, Old Coyote Man," I say, shuffling around the room. Old Coyote Man who jogs, will you ever take *me* back? Will we ever laugh again under our buffalo robe?

Stories! The Indian stories begin to mix in my mind with Leona's tale of the pregnant Indian girl, and Santiago's story of the Mexican warrior and the princess, and Alex's stories, and Max's, and Aurora's. . . . I am remembering even the words of people at Gary's funeral and the voices of strangers I met on the road. What was it that fisherman at the roadside in Wisconsin said: "Is there anything I can do to help?" Strong words. Soon I'm pacing the floor, filled with energy.

I look at the Boy Child with Book, sitting quietly on the shelf between the kitchen and the dining room; Aurora's *retablo,* Saint Christopher, hangs on the wall above him. Something is happening inside of me, a bubbling energy—intense, euphoric. I keep thinking about the slab of clay in the bag, wondering what will happen when my hands touch it again. And then I'm in the kitchen, taking it from the bag, standing over the table, pounding on the cold, stiff clay, poking at it, pulling at it. One minute it is stiff and resistant, the next it's soft, warming to my hands. One minute it's a ball, next a ball with holes all over it, and next a collection of mouths. Lips actually. Full soft lips, thin pursed lips, some wide-open mouths, others barely parted. Lips, no teeth in them at all. All of them telling me stories.

I know where I got this; I know it's nothing new. It's a variation, I argue, defensive as the discouraging voice begins in my mind. I saw a picture of the Hopi Storyteller Woman. So I'm not that woman, okay? So I don't have the children climbing on me. But I can do this. This is my first piece—all the people talking, helping me with their words. This is my first piece. I pick it up. It is gray and heavy. I hold it up, in my hands, my hands. I raise it up, above my head.

III

OFFERINGS

And the tower spoke to Psyche saying, "As you cross the sluggish river, a dead man, raising his rotten arms, will pray you take him into your boat. But you must not be moved by pity, for it is not lawful. . . . Yet you must not go empty-handed through the gloom."

—"The Tale of Amor and Psyche" from *The Metamorphosis* by Apulcius

1

The optometrist, Dr. Salazar, has taken me in on the luck of a Monday morning cancellation. "Can you be here by ten?" his receptionist asked me when I called at nine. I arrived at nine-thirty. The harried receptionist was pleased. We were off to a good start. Now the silver-haired doctor's hands are touching my face as he aligns me with his masklike machine. His face is close to mine as he asks me to peer through clicking lenses and tell him what I see. Now the diagnosis, preceded by one click of the tongue and a shake of the head: "Tsk. Mrs. Montevideo, you are severely near-sighted," he tells me. "It's a wonder you were able to drive safely across the country."

Who said I drove safely?

"I don't usually do this, but I want you to wear these glasses when you are driving." He places a pair of glasses with reddish brown frames on my nose and tucks them behind my ears. So fatherly and gentle his touch—I want him to do it again. "These are loaners. They are not your prescription, but very close. It will be two weeks before your own glasses are back from the lab. We'll run the glaucoma and other tests then." He shrugs his shoulders; he smiles at me. "We're so rushed today."

"Thank you," I say, already staring at the elaborate details of the painting on the wall across the room. I get up from my chair and go to another room to order frames. I select green plastic ones with great round lens openings.

When Dr. Salazar sees me leaving, he excuses himself from his patient. He walks over to hold the door for me, then reminds me once again. "Mrs. Montevideo, you *need* these glasses. Always wear them when you are driving."

I think he's afraid he'll meet me on the highway!

"Oh, I will!" I say.

He doesn't need to worry about me wearing these glasses, though. The fir trees outside the window by the reception area have hundreds of needles. The cottonwoods by the river have leaves, shimmering little individual leaves. Road signs clearly mark my way to the La Fonda parking lot. I see the shingle for Romero & Watkins, Real Estate, as soon as I walk in the Shelby Street entrance. I remember now. I used to see this way.

Not long after I walk in the office, Patrina, the secretary, arrives. She has come directly from her classes at the business college; she takes her lunch from its paper bag. "I'm starved," she tells me, placing items wrapped in waxed paper on the desktop.

I am reviewing the book of real-estate regulations. She is taking phone calls and typing. We chatter constantly in between. As she finishes her last bite of sandwich, she says she feels she knows me because Alex has told her so much about me.

"Oh, no," I groan.

She laughs. "No, Olivia. He says nice things. You are so smart. You are so beautiful."

"Oh, my," I mutter, feeling myself blush.

She is slender, in her late twenties, possibly early thirties. The whites of her eyes are so white, like a child's. I watch her brown eyes. They sparkle behind long lashes bent by the Maybelline eyelash curler she applies to them while gazing into a hand mirror. She quickly blots a fresh coat of red lipstick, then returns the mirror, the lipstick, and the eyelash curler to her purse.

"Joe says I can take the licensing test down in Albuquerque the first Saturday in August," I tell her. "But I'm wondering how much more I'll have to read. I may not be ready."

"How much have you read?" she asks, shaking into the wastebasket crumbs from the waxed paper that wrapped her sandwich. She smooths the wrinkled paper on the desktop, folds it, and replaces it in the brown paper bag.

"I'm finishing this first book of regulations," I tell her, holding up the cumbersome volume Joe gave me last week.

"Oh. That's all there is!" she says.

"Really? That's all? What a relief."

"You see? So smart, so quick!"

If Alex has told her so much about me, I can't help wondering how she sees Alex, through her bright, clear eyes. "Um, Patrina. How long have you known Alex?"

"Oh, a few years. We were living up in Wagon Mound. One of Alex's brothers was living up there. He told me Alex was going to have a business and he needed a secretary."

"He's so good about helping people," I say.

"Sí, he has been good to Ramon and me. Ramon was working for a rancher and the man died. His wife had to sell. Ramon lost his job. We were so grateful to Alex." She looks at me quickly, then whispers, "Sometimes it gets him in trouble." She clicks her tongue in a gentle scolding sound, smiles and shakes her head. "That girl last year. Her brother was dying. Aye, yi, yi." She says it as if she assumes I know.

"Oh," I say. "He helped her?"

"I'm not sure. I think he got hurt in the process."

Is he prone to this rescuing of sad women, I want to ask. And does he save them all the same way, I wonder nervously. I am somewhere between jealousy and understanding. I never asked him, not once, if there was someone else. Do you ask the fireman who pulls you from a burning building if you're his only rescue that month, that year? He has brought me back to life. I can think only of his kindnesses: bringing my bundled-up statue to me at the hotel when I thought I had lost it, telling me story after story after story. . . . But do I protest too much? Is he just a Latin lover with a bag of tricks and lies, or is he a medicine man who has saved me from. . . . I don't even want to think what I would be doing now without him. "I don't really know him that well, Patrina."

"You are lovers," she says, quietly matter-of-fact.

"Yes," I say, wondering if she means that lovers are just naturally strangers. Not such a far-out concept, actually.

"It is so hard to be lovers . . ." she says.

We sit in silence with the idea of lovers.

"What about you, Patrina? What about your family?" I ask.

"I was the *ilegítima.* A child born out of wedlock," Patrina tells me. "My mother was sixteen. It was the shame of her family, living in the little village in Mexico. That's what I mean, about being lovers, you know?"

"Oh, I didn't mean . . ." I didn't mean what? I expected the edited-for–*Good Housekeeping* version of her life? I asked about her family and she's telling me. I lean forward in my chair. I need to know about lovers. I might need to know about the *ilegítimas.* I listen hard.

"My mother's brothers came banging on the door when they heard it was her time. They warned her they would kill the baby if it was a girl. My mother, she was just a girl herself. She didn't know what to do. She got out of bed when she heard them in the house, and threw the baby—me!—out the window into the rain."

"Patrina, that's so terrible," I say.

"No. It was *good.* The brothers were drunk. They ran in the room. My mother rolled on the bed and screamed. They thought she was not delivered."

"Oh, I see." For just a moment, in hearing this story, I have a flashing insight, something about the occasional benevolence of harsh solutions, but I lose it in the revelations that follow.

"They named me Soila, a term of shame. But I chose a new name when I was seven. On the holy days we went to mass at a church in the bigger town. A little girl there, she wore a velvet cape embroidered with glass beads and sequins. Her mother and father called her Patrina. She smiled at me. I was going to be Patrina after that."

"Yes," I say.

The young mother finally married the boy who was Soila-Patrina's father. Other children were born. But, unable to withstand the constant harassment from his violent in-laws, the father had disappeared before his first daughter could fix him in her memory. "I have this thought of him, though. I used to trail along behind him in the bean field."

"Thoughts that should have been memories," I sigh. I shake my head regretfully.

But Patrina beams a bright smile at me, as if to cheer me. "I do remember his voice. He sang to me," she says.

Does it really make any difference what raw materials we use in creating stories—*or* history? Everything is just fission and fusion, and distance and changes, and hearsay. . . .

"The Church wouldn't let the village abandon me, but no one, not even my mother, could protect me from her family. My grandfather would sit out in the yard in his old wood chair, padded all around by pillows. He would hand out candy. He gave sweet things to my brothers and sisters and my cousins. But when I would squeeze into the circle and stick out my dirty little hand, he would say, *'Vámonos, Soila. Bastarda!'* "

Patrina goes on, answering a call, filing a contract, nibbling on a cookie from her lunch.

"The neighbors gave me candy when no one was looking. They had *pity.*" Her voice deepens, guttural, as she says the word. A dark expression crosses her face. Apparently, she views this pity as a necessary temporary fix but nothing she would have cared to extend indefinitely—I think I see what she means. "My mother told me I was so special. I was a special girl and the world was my *familia.* She told me that so often and she cried when she told me, so I don't think she really believed it. But you know, Olivia, *I* believed it!" Patrina laughs, delighted, I gather, by such a fortunate error in interpretation.

The secrets and the sharing of them continue like beads strung on a long, durable strand. It takes me forever to tell her all the misery about Gary.

"He died," she says at one point, as though she must say it to believe it. "He died in the war."

"Yes," I say. "In the war."

"Aye," Patrina says. *"Madre de Dios,"* she says, her eyes damp and wide.

We are interrupted by phone calls and clients. A man, his wife, and their young daughter come in, and I make an appointment to show them a house tomorrow at noon. It feels so natural, talking to them. I feel excited for a moment, knowing just what they feel and what they need. Maybe selling real estate wouldn't be too bad; I can help find places for families.

After they leave I return to my narrative, slamming my fist on the desk as I tell about Andrew's indiscretions, his silence, our marriage. Travis from the land office in the other half of the suite comes over to see what's going on, but by then I'm speaking in a softer voice. I'm telling Patrina that Andrew seems to be changing now. "We're talking on the phone, at least," I say.

I grin at Travis. "Yes," Patrina tells him. "We're just talking."

Once he leaves, smiling and shaking his head, I am waving my arms in the air. The road sign, the sod-house vision of Olivia Cosmos Montevideo, and how I might have bought a gun in Wyoming: this part of the story seems to require dramatic gestures, too.

Patrina is a responsive listener, but she's the one teaching me about history—and perspective. Now, as I am winding down, she is asking me questions. "I didn't want to grow up, Olivia. Did you ever feel that way?"

"Not exactly," I say, rolling my chair back from the desk, stretching my legs in front of me. "I think for me it was just the reverse. I grew and then I wanted to go back and be ten, forever."

She nods her head. "My uncles were so terrible. I already knew I didn't want to get older!" she says. "It seemed to make them angrier, the older I got."

Patrina's trembling and reluctant departure from childhood was greeted with renewed hostility. Drinking on hot nights, sitting on the patio of her mother's small house while Patrina perched quietly on the doorstep, the uncles would return to the night of her birth.

"They said ugly things. And they never called me Patrina. My mother did, but never around her brothers. They said 'Soila' was coming to the age of womanhood. I was going to stain the family name and bring more shame. Mama would tell me, 'Soila! Go for the tamales on the stove. Bring the wine from the shelf.' But I knew what to do!" Patrina brings her slender hands together in front of her face, then breaks them, like a curtain parting.

I wait, breathless, experiencing every moment of her story.

"I would run for the backdoor. Run so fast! I thought I ran faster than the wind. I would go to the house of my grandfather. I would crawl under the bed in the back room." And though her grandfather never acknowledged her with candy, Patrina is able to generously observe, he always ran off his drunken sons.

I am leaning across her desk, my hand on her arm. Her dark eyes take on a sparkle as she thinks back on her girlhood: "I saw a lot of shoes from under that bed!" We both laugh.

"Won't I ever accept things, Patrina?" I ask, feeling that acceptance must be something bred into her lovely Hispanic soul. "You don't seem bitter."

"But Olivia," she graciously points out, "these things that hurt you are so new. Give yourself time."

"I don't know," I say, walking to the rectangular window, looking at flat rooftops and blue sky. "Maybe sorrows don't ever go away. You keep on remembering, just like we've been doing."

"But we have to remember, Olivia. That's all there is."

"Well, there's really only one option and that is . . ."

The phone rings. Patrina answers, holding up her hand for me to keep the thought. She hangs up.

"One option and that is you have to decide . . . I can't remember!"

"Oh, Olivia," Patrina laughs. "You can't forget our only option!"

"Maybe I'll think of it again."

I think of how she and her husband Ramon are building their lives together. Hoping to change the subject and fool my memory, I ask, "You and Ramon have no children yet, right?"

She hesitates. I want to take back my question, but it's too late.

"When Ramon and I ran away to the North . . ." Patrina smiles. "Alex says you love to learn Spanish. *Esta es el Norte,* Olivia."

"Gracias," I say. *"El nor-tay."*

"Sí," Patrina says. "*El Norte.* Well, the people in my village thought I was pregnant. I was only sixteen. Ramon had no money—why would I want to just run away with him? Like mother like daughter! That's what they *really* said, but my mother would never tell me this. But it was not that way for Ramon and me. We were afraid to be lovers, at first. We got married in El Paso, and then I heard right away about the ways to prevent. The pill, you know? Ramon got a job on the ranch up north, near Wagon Mound. That rich Anglo lady, she hired me as a maid. She taught me English. Very nice. So sad when her husband died. . . ."

I wait, unable to help, while Patrina walks all the way around the question of children and then confronts it: "We had a beautiful baby daughter. Yolanda." The name is like music; her brown eyes fill up as she says it. "She died when she was one year. It was the spinal meningitis, Olivia."

"Ahh, Patrina."

We try to talk about night classes at the business college, and day classes, too. And the rich Anglo woman who was so kind. I try to recall that one option; I said that a person really has only one option, but I can't remember it to save my soul.

We hug each other, rocking back and forth. I hand her the box of tissues and take one for myself. We're still sniffling, some sorrows being always new, when Joe and Alex walk in. They take one look at us and ask no questions. But by now our mood has changed. We are feeling the power of having shared such secrets. It's as if we speak a secret language. We could call it the Secret Language of Women Who Have Changed Their Names! Our power is like a presence in the room. I can feel it. Alex and Joe seem to feel it, too.

Glancing furtively at me while Joe and Patrina are talking, Alex seems to be testing his magic, wondering if I still draw in my breath when he looks at me that way—I do. He's also worried, knowing I've been crying. But the two of them go on with their discussions, picking up messages, paperwork. I tell them about the family I'll be showing property to tomorrow. They are gone in five minutes. It is six o'clock.

Patrina and I look at each other and laugh. Dabbing at our eyes and picking up our belongings, we walk from the office and lock up. Long shadows are already forming in the parking lot behind the hotel.

"Good night, Olivia," Patrina calls as she gets in her car.

"Good night, Patrina. *Mañana!*" I call.

She waves as she backs out.

I put on my new glasses. The old blue car is filthy; I will hose it off when I get back to the apartment. I observe the separate petals of pink hollyhocks fluttering against an adobe wall as I drive home.

* * *

It's after two when I get to the office on Tuesday, having taken the young family to see the house. Alex and Patrina are eager to hear about my first clients. "Actually," I say, "they took *me,* since I couldn't find it on the map."

"You got lost?" Alex asks as I begin my description.

"Well, no. I told them right off I didn't know where it was. They helped me find the place, and they liked the house, and the woman, Sally, is a flutist, and I told her about the chamber music festival they're planning, and she said she had read about that and . . ."

"Wait," Patrina says. "You say they liked the house?"

"Yes, they want to buy it. I told them I'd call to make an appointment to sign all the papers and make an offer. I figured you could help, Alex. They'll be here all week. We can set up a time."

He nods.

"Olivia. Your first time out. This is wonderful!" Patrina says.

Joe walks in as Patrina and Alex are shaking my hand and giving me hugs.

"A sale, hey?" Joe says, laughing with surprise as he shakes my hand. "Was this from that list of referrals we gave you?"

"No, it's the people who came in yesterday when I was here in the office," I say, hoisting myself onto a desktop, swinging my legs in front of me. "I figure I'll go back and walk around that neighborhood. I remember realtors coming by now and then back where I used to live. Canvassing, isn't it called? The couple next door were out cleaning their garage when we were leaving. Their house is so tiny, in that little alley area. They're thinking they might move to something bigger when their baby comes. I left them one of your cards, Alex. I don't have any yet. . . ." I look at the three of them. No one is responding.

"We don't do canvassing," Joe says at last. He looks at Alex questioningly.

Alex shrugs his shoulders. "Why not?" Alex says. He rolls a chair over and sits down. "She's already made a sale," he says proudly.

"Okay," Joe says. "Olivia? We're going to show you the black book."

The Black Book? I am immediately resistant. It has the sound of faithless lovers, poorly kept secrets, obscene jokes.

Joe unlocks a cabinet behind the desk. He does indeed bring out a black binder.

"Just about everything in Santa Fe is for sale, Olivia. For the right price. To the right person."

I get down from the desk and walk over to look. "Ahh! Oh!" I say, flipping the pages. I am amazed at the properties listed, the names of the owners, the prices.

"Privileged information," he says. "But we don't do canvassing, okay?"

"Um-hum," I say. Since when is he such a go-by-the-rules guy? This is about money and I don't like it. Before I can even stop myself I've slung out my hip and poked out my elbow, pretty close to sullen. "Your book doesn't list those little families, Joe. Like the ones I met today? No one puts *them* in any black book. They need someone they can call." I hear the echo of my words; I sound like a mother hen but I like the sound of it.

"In Santa Fe, we just don't do this, Olivia. Some agencies do. The best ones do not."

"You do lunch! What's the difference?" I ask. I turn away, flipping my arm, whiplike, in the air.

Joe's face looks blank. Alex smiles, tips back in his chair and says nothing. Patrina busies herself at the file cabinet. Joe begins to pace. I may lose my job.

"You're right," he says at last, his golden skin flushed pink, a just-ripe apricot. "Tell you what . . ."

He unfolds a map of Santa Fe and the surrounding communities and spreads it across one of the desks. He picks up a large marking pen, the one they use for writing sales on the wall-mounted grease board. He draws blood-red lines around various sections of the city map, making graphically clear where I must never wander. He posts the map on the wall with thumbtacks. We shake on it, careful with each other, somber.

As they leave, Alex puts his hand on Joe's shoulder. In his Dumb Mexican voice he says, *"Hijo,* José! That woman tol' you-uh?"

I breathe easier when I hear the rumble of Joe's laughter.

* * *

Leona and I have just returned from breakfast on Wednesday morning.

"Come on in," I tell her. "I want to show you what I made with the clay."

She looks a bit dubiously at the ball of clay I take from the counter between the kitchen and the dining room. I hold it in my hand.

"I call it the Storyteller Ball," I say, grinning proudly at the name I have come up with this very second. "Variation on a theme," I add.

Suddenly interested, she takes it from my hands and carries it out to the patio. She holds it up and runs her fingers across the now-drying lips. "This is an interesting piece, Olivia. You are not literal. Very creative."

"Really?" I ask. I bring her a cup of reheated coffee and she sits down.

"Do you think I could bake this ball in the kiln?"

She smiles and leans toward me. "This ball cannot be *fired,* Olivia. You have much to learn about preparing the clay."

"Oh," I say, feeling like a balloon that is slowly deflating.

"Here is what you must do." She holds up her fingers for me to see. "First, you can bring this ball to my house and we will fold it back into the clay. Then . . ." She hesitates, seeing my disappointment. She puts her hand down. "Nah. That's not true. You can bake your ball out here in the sun. Just leave it out here for a week."

"Great! I will," I say. "And . . ."

"And I don't believe in this, really—putting people on a wheel when they haven't even learned the clay—but you probably need to learn about centering anyway. That's it, isn't it? You want to do the wheel."

"Yes!" I say, trying to restrain myself from begging the way a schoolgirl whines at her teacher: Pleeeeeze?

When we get to her apartment and she sets me up on the potting wheel, I quickly realize how inadequate I am. The wheel takes me around. When my foot is moderate on the pedal, my hands are sliding around on the clay. Then, just when I get my hands placed and my thumb begins to press, *varroom!* I goose the pedal instead of the spot at the center of the slippery clay. This goes on for a few minutes until Leona asks me to stop.

"This is strange," I tell her.

"You were breathing very deeply. That's important, the breathing."

I hadn't noticed my breathing, but now I remember feeling that I should take in air, almost float above the clay, and feeling that I was not at all successful at this floating.

"I seem to make progress and then I slip back," I say as I stare at the dusty disk.

"Yes," Leona says.

"I feel so good and then it wobbles worse."

Leona climbs onto the stool at her work table. Her back is to me now. I sit at the wheel. I'm dizzy as the wheel takes me around. My shoulders ache. I have yet to make a pot.

"Think," she says from her perch. "What is in you that creates imbalance? Think of that thing. Think what will balance it. Then let it go."

The lip of my pot gets thin as paper and tears.

"Begin again," she says, still not turning around.

I pick up the clay and mash it around. *Thwack!* I hit it against the wheel, taking out air bubbles. She calls this wedging. I make it round.

I drizzle murky water from a scrap of sponge onto the ball as I place it on the wheel.

I take a deep breath and position myself over this wad of resistance.

I place my fingers with equal points of pressure along the clay, push the pedal, lean over the wheel. I think of Gary and I think of the day the soldiers came to our house. I think of M-16s. The wheel keeps turning. The clay is rising between my fingers. I think of Andrew in his group, my new friends, my new green-framed glasses. The base of the pot is keeping its thickness, the sides of the pot are rounded and smooth. I reach for the piece of sponge with one hand and let the water drip down lightly. I return my fingers to the pot. I can't think of anything to think about. The clay begins the familiar wobbling and my thumb goes through the base to the surface of the wheel. I lift my foot off the pedal and lean back, winded as if from running.

"You felt it," she says.

"Oh! It seemed so effortless when it was working!"

She has stepped down from her stool and put her hand on my shoulder. My lesson is over. I go home to contemplate the lessons of real estate and art: To walk at the edges of the red zones. To keep memory, delight, and balance. To breathe.

2

The upper curve of the sun floats at the horizon as Alex and I leave town on Friday morning, headed for a mystery destination. "Wait and see," he keeps saying.

Clouds, as if on cue, put on a show, a pastel theater-in-the-round that spins me around in my seat. They're everywhere, a great arched canopy stretched out in thin smoky bands, and then, as we get on the road toward Albuquerque and the light expands, they're scattered suddenly, spilling like gold and silver cottonballs above the Sandias.

This sky could never become routine. Summer afternoons in Potsdam used to stop me in my tracks with green depths of grass and leaves and petunia-scented air that refused to go unnoticed after a rain—afternoons that slowed me down, insisted I sit on the porch a little longer, to read or daydream. But a morning like this! It makes my blood race through me, makes me take in deep gulps of air. Saying, "Oh, my!" and "Oh, my!" I seem to be trying to inflate my lungs, prepare for flight, take off and join the sky show.

"I can see why you walk on the mesa," I tell Alex. "I'm going to start walking up the hill before breakfast. Up by the museum," I say.

He looks over at me, brooding and quiet. "Olivia," he says, putting his hand at the back of my neck. "Where are we going-uh?"

He's driving; he knows where we're *going*. He just doesn't know where WE are going. Neither of us do. I could move over next to him, let him stroke the back of my neck and pull out the pins from my hair, let the steamy substance of our edgy uncertainty run us off the road into a gully—*arroyo*—and into the bed of the truck, where we could wrap ourselves around each other and hear only the sounds of our blood pounding. He knows I'm thinking this; I can tell the way he watches me from the corner of his eye, lowers his eyes, raises them again to turn and look at me. But he moves his hand back to the steering wheel, and I stay here next to the door. Nothing is that simple, least of all a brilliant round sun that rises every morning and sets every night, or a pearlescent, microscopic ovum that could be retracing, at this moment, the shadow left by that other pearl that once implanted itself in the blood-rich walls of my body. Twenty-three down; seven to go. We're waiting for the question to be answered. We're waiting for the problem to be solved. We're waiting for the other questions and other problems the answers will bring, but—Oh, my!—the sun keeps rising.

"You were crying at the office," Alex says as I hand him coffee from the thermos. "What was wrong?"

"We were crying about Patrina's baby who died. Yolanda. And about, you know, everything."

He makes a sad, groaning sound. *"Madre de Dios,"* he says.

"I was crying for someone else. That's progress," I say. Clearly from the look on his face, I'm still a problem needing a solution.

"Is *this* where we're going?" I ask, as we leave the highway and drive into the sleepy village of Algodones. I look for movement, my eyes scanning like a radar dish the deserted main street. A man in a plaid wool shirt is sweeping the parking lot of a tavern. Further on, a woman enters the side door of an adobe church, her head covered with a white handkerchief. The dusty windows of a locked-up store make even the morning sun look flat, cold, discouraged.

"You love it already-uh?"

"I can't wait to see it in the spring. I'll spend my golden years here," I say, suppressing a grin.

He laughs. "Olivia," he says, squeezing my leg. "I think this can be a good day for us."

"Wonderful, I'm sure." I lean back against the seat. "Just so we're back by noon. To take care of my sale," I say, feeling the pleasure once again at the thought of signing papers that will put a family into their home.

"We'll be back in time," he says. "I have a friend here in Algodones."

"Does your friend want visitors before eight o'clock . . ."—I check the dashboard clock—". . . seven o'clock in the morning?"

"He's expecting us. I called him yesterday."

"Well?" I ask, arms opened out, head poked forward in anticipation. "You've made me wait this long . . ."

"His name is Eddie Braceros. He's my analyst, I guess you could say. I think of him as a healer."

"A doctor? In Algodones?" I place my hand on his forehead. "Are you sick, Alex?"

"Do I look sick?"

"No. Well, actually, now that you mention it. . . ." I lift my glasses and peer at him more closely.

He grins. "Wait and see."

We bump down an ungraded road, past a vacant space where tumbleweeds and tall grasses grow. Off across the fields sit squat adobe houses shaded by cottonwoods. Alex slows and stops in front of a shabby house trailer at the dead end. He leans back from the steering wheel and puts his hand on my shoulder. "This is it."

An analyst? I'm puzzled and apprehensive as we get out of the truck. Walking to the trailer, I find myself chattering to Alex. "Trailers like this used to be in Potsdam after World War II. They had a country-cottage appeal at first. You know, in those tree-shaded courts, with little fences and squares of grass in front of each one, window boxes spilling with ivy and petunias. Even the ceramic flamingos and plastic daisies were sort of charming."

He nods, patient but uninterested.

"Then the veterans found jobs and moved to new houses they bought on VA loans. A different element took over—transient workers at the paper mill, students from the college, welfare cases." I run my hand across the varnished, blond wood trim on this trailer. "The wood fell off or was painted colors like mint green or robin's-egg blue."

Alex stares at me. I'm talking like a tour guide without a museum.

"My friend in grade school lived in a trailer park," I say. "That's how I know."

This trailer could have found its way to New Mexico from a

trailer park in Potsdam, a long, twenty-five year process of migration, just like mine. The effects of the journey are evident to even the most casual observer: scrapes and contusions, bruises and dents. What a trip. The thought of it makes Alex and me strangers, too many miles behind us, too many blind spots ahead. I wish I had called Andrew last night, to tell him about my sale. . . .

At last, Eddie Braceros appears at the door, his bloodshot, translucent green eyes squinting at the morning sun. My first reaction is to figure he's a drug addict or an alcoholic. Blond, bearded, and barechested, the man welcomes us to his "pad" as he and Alex exchange hugs and handshakes.

Eddie's hair is fluffy in the way of a sheepdog's matted coat, though it does recede a little—a first clue to his age. He's as old as I am—older. Once inside, I notice the lines of fatigue near his eyes, the sag of flesh at his chest and abdomen, which he finally covers up with a tan Coors shirt, left unbuttoned. Dressed now, he searches for his glasses, explaining to me that without his glasses he is legally blind.

"I haven't seen those glasses in over a month," he says. "I've been getting by with a pair I found on top of the cash register at the café where I eat." He continues lifting magazines, blankets, pillows, even a couch, in search of his glasses. Just as I'm ready to tell him about *my* bad eyes and my loaner glasses from Dr. Salazar, he turns to Alex and with a great rolling of R's tells the story of finding his temporary glasses. " 'Whose are thees, Rosita?' I asked her. 'I don't know, Meester Braceros,' she says, 'are they yours?' *'Sí,* Rosita. Now they are mine.' "

"Sí," Alex says. "Rosita." He nods his head appreciatively. Alex is standing with his hands behind him, leaning on the doorknob, as if he sees that position as one he might expect to keep for some time.

"Well, I've lost those glasses, too," Eddie says. "But here, come, sit down."

We make our way onto floor pillows while Eddie closes the disintegrating blue fiberglass curtains on the east window. As the curtains come together, Eddie flings them apart again, having discovered the original lost pair of glasses on the windowsill. "Ah-ha!" he exclaims, as if the glasses have been trying to get away all the time.

Next he conducts a brief but futile search for a special incense he had wanted to share with Alex, gives that up, and picks up some weeds tied with twine.

"Sage," he says.

He lights it at the top like a torch and carries the smoke-trailing bundle through the trailer, waving it over our heads as he completes the circuit. The smoke, on my empty stomach, makes me momentarily nauseated as it rises into the shadowy clutter of the trailer, but I actually like the smell. He sets the sage in a clay pot on the table in the kitchen area and blows out the thin ash of leaves; they drift carelessly floorward.

"The Indians believe sage purifies the sacred chamber," Eddie says. Inhaling, he presses his palms together, fingertips toward his chin. He lowers his head. "I believe it, too," he adds, looking up at me.

I glance at my watch. Twenty minutes have passed since we arrived. I am so tense I can feel my jaw bones fusing near my ears. This friend Alex said was expecting us sits down at last in the "sacred chamber."

"Olivia," he says, smiling, revealing narrow, grayish teeth. "The Capricorn woman has her work cut out for her." Eddie Braceros might take a while getting around to his guests, but he focuses—how he focuses—when he gives someone his full attention. "Alex told me your birthday. I worked up your chart. Do you mind?"

"Oh, you do astrology. No. I don't mind, no," I say, minding a lot, actually, but too off balance to say so. "Alex said you were an analyst."

"In one of my lives. Yeah. You could have called me that. Business suits and file cabinets." He looks at Alex and they laugh over the image.

Eddie focuses again on me. "So many ways of knowing," he says. He runs his fingers across, pats his fingers on, his matted hair. Then he seems to have trouble again with the glasses. He pulls them off, huffs each lens, rubs with his shirt. The man's gestures are making me crazy. "Astrology is good. It's something to work around in."

The glasses are returned to their perch on his nose. He blinks, watching me. "Alex is in his Saturn return. You're ruled by Saturn. I can see a certain inevitability there."

Alex nods his head, seemingly illuminated by this gibberish that's been on radio and television talk shows for the last five years at least. Alex pulls the rubber band from his ponytail. He leans over and massages the back of my neck, as if this gentle hint will make clear to me our Saturnine connection. It does not.

Eddie breathes deeply, the way I breathed in the sunrise this morning. But I don't have that good feeling now. I'm thinking of a traveling revival my usually sedate parents took me to when I was ten. I'm thinking of black, Southern Baptist, gospel-singing churches I saw on television at the height of the civil rights movement. In both instances, I am realizing now, I longed to be made of the fiber and feeling that would have caused me to jump to my feet, flail my arms, shout, "Praise the Lord!" I have the sense that I really am made of that same material, yet I never jump to my feet, or flail my arms, or shout. I wonder what it would be like to agree with Eddie that Alex and I are on a predetermined collision course with the planet Saturn. Would I leap to my feet and shout? "A-men, Bro-thuh *Ed!*" What's the use? In this worn-out house trailer in this tiny New Mexico town, nodding the head and loosening the hair would be signs of understanding, and I do neither. Alex told me stories, but even that's no help here. This is something different; it's about reasons.

"Do you believe that people meet for a reason?" I ask.

"Could be," Eddie says. "At least if we look for the reason, we can usually find it."

This is a circular dance Eddie is doing; he never stops in the middle, though. Meanwhile, the sun, behind the blue fiberglass curtains on that eastern-facing window, keeps turning up the heat.

"You're an earth sign. You resist being carried off," he says.

That *would* explain the feeling of almost floating, almost letting go . . . the man is following my thoughts!

"I don't know astrology, Eddie," I say. "Do you have any other ways of knowing in your little black bag?"

He slips right past my defenses. "I understand your resistance. Capricorn women don't trust strangers. And you have a very sensitive nature to protect."

Maybe so, but I've sure been trusting strangers since Gary died. And for some reason, even with his eerie mindreading or maybe because of it, I do trust Eddie. It's a decision. I decide that I will trust him.

"Yes," I say, giving in to his careful scrutiny. "I protect myself."

We sit cross-legged on the big pillows. I have the sofa behind me; I lean back against it, glad for the support.

Eddie stares into my eyes as if taking a reading on the very stability of my molecular mass: Will she come apart or won't she? Apparently satisfied that I will not, he says, "Your son is dead. You've left your husband."

"That's right," I say. Just like that, without any hesitation, I say it. Whose analyst *is* this, anyway?

"And you've changed your name."

"Yes. I have."

I feel my face getting flushed and hot. Even with the curtains drawn, the sun beats on the window, the sage smoke hangs in the air. This is a firetrap.

"It was an impulsive thing," I say. "I don't know why I did it. That first time. With Alex. I mean when I told Alex my *name*." My concern for propriety goes unacknowledged; neither chuckles from Alex nor insinuations from Eddie. I relax further.

"I thought you were a goddess when I met you, Olivia," Alex says.

"What?" I ask.

I sneak a glance at Eddie, who has assumed a yoga position—not on his head yet, just elevating his legs while reclining and rolling onto his shoulders. One more way of knowing, I guess.

"I thought of it that day I met you," Alex says. "I thought of Cortés and the invasion of Mexico. The Aztecs had a myth about a blond god. I thought about a redheaded goddess!" He pulls in air through his teeth, shakes his head. "Man, I don't know why, Olivia. I think of you that way."

"My God, Alex!" I say. "Look at what that 'god' did to those people!" The Sequeiros painting I saw in one of the library books has flashed across my mind. Cortés is lasciviously fondling his Indian consort, Malinche, her earth-brown body, with his white hands, while she snickers ironically for the viewer—snickering at the destruction of her people, their culture, their civilization. The artist put it all on the woman, all her fault. It occurs to me that the Garden of Eden experience got this same interpretation. Women, mothers . . .

I restrain myself from elaborating on the rape of Mexico. What would Eddie read into my recollection of the painting, I wonder, knowing as I watch him lower his legs that he's been "listening." He returns to the lotus position, back straight, thumbs and index fingers opposing one another. He takes in air through his nostrils.

"That first night, and later . . ." Alex reaches across to touch my knee. "Eddie knows," he says, as if to give me reassurance. Eddie's green eyes are following the action. "I thought of you as a goddess."

A goddess. Not that I'm not flattered. Already I'm sitting straighter. Freckles float from my face, bulges leave my body, flaws are erased from my character. I'm amused, too. Trying to stifle laughter, actually. Such a giant step in the big Mother May I game, the fantasy life of the male. From Andrew's French peasant girl to Alex's redheaded mythical goddess? I'm moving up in the world. . . . I wish.

Before Alex can say any more, Eddie speaks: "You don't see yourself as Alex sees you, Olivia." He speaks as if just returned from a trance, though I suspect he hasn't gone far. Only inside of my head! "Does that disturb you?" he asks.

"Well," I say.

"You may be feeling that all of your power is evil. You think that even as a goddess you are Malinche, the traitoress."

Holy shit, I think, astounded. He must have my brain bugged.

Traitoress. We all listen to the clumsy word as it stumbles around in our minds. There's something appropriately scummy about the word, an unwholesomeness that makes my skin shrink up. Traitoress to her children, her people. The artist intended that interpretation, the book said. How would an artist paint Alex and me? And then there's the question of Andrew. . . . I cringe. But Eddie's right. I do have the feeling that I can't do anything for Alex, that I've kind of invaded his life—even if I was invited in. Now I see a vision of Montezuma kneeling to welcome Cortés, the blond invader/god who would destroy him. . . . Arghh! I've read too many books! "Alex keeps helping me," I say. "I don't do much in return."

Eddie shrugs. "Maybe. Depends on what he needs."

"I've learned about the war from you, Olivia. I needed to think about the ones who had no deferment, no college. . . ." Unable to continue, Alex looks down at the floor, shakes his head.

"You mean you feel guilty about protesting?" I ask.

"No, not that. I wanted the killing to stop. I . . ."

"You hadn't thought about the ones who had already died, their families," Eddie says, seemingly restating for Alex a conversation they've already had.

"Sí," Alex says.

"Oh, Alex," I say, laying my hand on his shoulder.

Eddie lifts his arms and stretches until his arms are pressed against his ears, then slowly lowers his arms to his sides. As his arms come down, it feels different in here. It's as if he has cut a vertical column through the air in this trailer. "So," he says. "What do we have so far?"

Alex and I treat the question as rhetorical. We look at Eddie with the slow comprehension of remedial students.

"We have a war. We have a goddess," Eddie says. "They sound like distractions."

"Distractions?" I ask, surprised.

"Alex is turning thirty and wondering what to do with his life. You've left your husband and changed your name. You meet each other," Eddie says. " 'Is it you?' "

"What?" I ask.

"That's what Montezuma said to Cortés: 'Is it you?' We're always *looking* for someone, or hoping someone is waiting for *us*. Aren't we?"

Eddie reaches over and places his hand on my arm. "Alex has some doubts about his antiwar stuff," Eddie says carefully. "Your son has died in the war."

We all hit the ground with a thud. No more of the astrological and divine. As if I've breathed in the fumes of some harmful chemical, my muscles begin to ache. I know he's a kind man, this Eddie Braceros. I know he means no harm. But talking about the story of Montezuma, Cortés, and Malinche was easy. Doesn't he know how this hurts?

"Sometimes we *need* a distraction. Sometimes we take a detour," I say.

"Yeah," Eddie says, looking away. "I've taken a few myself."

"What do you do when you take a detour?" I ask.

He looks at me, as if he's almost surprised to see me here. "Hm? Oh. Lots of things. Sometimes you figure how to get back.

Sometimes you take off on a new road. And, uh, sometimes you stay on the detour."

Suddenly Alex looks up. *"I've* felt like I was on a detour ever since my grandmother died. Since we moved from Mora!"

I turn to look at Alex. Eddie nods his head, considering. He continues in the lotus position.

"Why would I feel like that? My brothers and sisters liked being in town." He turns to me. "You saw my parents, Olivia. They left it behind."

"They seem content," I say.

I want to say more to Alex about his detour. I think I've got something I can tell him about grieving for your childhood until you have your own children or . . . but I can't say that! He'll think I'm wanting him to marry me if I don't start my period. Besides, Eddie will tell him something.

But Eddie just goes on with his what-we-have-so-far list. "So," he says. "Things are left behind. There are detours. We find distractions."

I left Andrew behind and my mother in Potsdam and . . .

Eddie looks at me. "Olivia, what about your other name?"

I am almost getting used to him walking into my thoughts. "You mean Roberta."

He nods his head.

"I don't know."

"When you changed your name, how did you feel? Did you feel any different when you said the new name?"

"Yes."

"In what way?"

"Free. When someone says 'Roberta'—like my mother calls, or my husband—I feel like I'm carrying around a suitcase." The room feels warm and soupy now. Alex has set me up for this. Out of a combination of curiosity and concern, he decided that I needed to talk. He needed it, too, of course. But set up or not, I'm comfortable now, buoyed by the sensation of buried thoughts tumbling from my mouth as spoken words. "I feel I'm someone else when I'm Olivia," I say.

"Do you want to always feel that way?"

I look at Alex, back at Eddie. I reach up, pat my hair, poke a loose hairpin into place. "Always?"

"The other person—Roberta—is difficult for you to deal with right now. She's left behind."

"Well . . . yes."

"What's she like?"

"Dumb," I say quickly. "Real dumb."

"A kind of innocent fool," Eddie says.

"NO!" I don't mean to yell. When I speak again, my voice is softer but I can hear it shaking. "No. She is *not* innocent. She is *dumb.*" I rise to my knees, spread my damp palms on my thighs.

"So you're angry with her, ashamed of her somehow?"

I feel a quiver, a pull, something very akin to a sexual feeling. My reaction to his emotional probing is to be aroused? Leona would have something to say about this: animals, habits, can't make distinctions. . . . But I must make distinctions! Now! He is asking if I'm ashamed of Roberta. Where does this sensual feeling fit in? Has my body been closed up? Maybe what I feel is my body opening, to Roberta, to . . . Oh, my God, what am I thinking? Maybe this is when the Madness gets you, just when you think you're strong enough, confident enough. . . .

"I don't want to talk about all this."

"You don't have to talk, Olivia," Eddie says. He takes my clammy hand from my leg. He holds my hand in his. His hands are warm as they close around mine. I want to lie down in his warm hands, curl up and sleep like a kitten. I want to say everything, but I don't seem to have any words. I take my hand away, extracting it gently from his grasp.

"Who is Roberta?" Eddie asks, getting up on his knees like I am.

I'm silent, more accurately mute.

"Who is Roberta?" he asks again.

"She's dumb."

"But *who* is she?" he asks.

My face is falling forward onto my knees. My chest has surely caved in. Eddie and Alex are holding my shoulders, as if I am vomiting, or maybe giving birth. "She's Gary's mother," I whisper.

"And who is *Olivia?*" Eddie asks.

"What?" I ask, sniffling, lifting my head to look at Eddie. His face is red with the heat of this room; his green eyes are filled with light.

"Who is Olivia?" he asks again.

"The same."

"The same?" he asks, putting his warm hand on my forehead.

"Olivia is . . ." What's going to happen to me if I answer this question? This feels like death must feel, an abandonment, a drifting away.

I hear something. I hold my breath and tilt my head, listening. *Clink.* I glance at Eddie and Alex. They're both looking at me; they've heard nothing. Is this the Madness? Am I hearing things? No. I'm okay now. I'm back last year, July '69, and Gary's at Basic Training in Georgia, and black-and-white television images are flashing. The moon lander is docking with the mother ship, Columbia. *Clink.* Probably an animated simulation I watched. Maybe the real thing. *Clink.* Thousands of miles from earth, moving at blinding speeds, beaming in on fragile signals, finding each other. And the only sound was that same sound. *Clink.*

"Gary's mother," I say. I look at Eddie and say it again: "Olivia is Gary's mother."

I'm not sure how long we sit. Alex watches me. I look around for Kleenex to blow my nose, and he gives me his handkerchief. I pat his arm with one hand as I pat my nose with the hankie.

Finally I stand up, and Alex follows my lead.

Eddie inhales his purified, overheated house-trailer air, and it seems to bring him effortlessly to a standing position. He exhales loudly through his nostrils. "You're not dumb, Olivia . . . neither is Roberta."

Alex puts his arm around my shoulders.

"I don't know what to do with all this, Eddie," I say. "If you told me all your ways of knowing, I still wouldn't know."

"You'll know," he says. "You *already* know." He holds his arms open and I lean my head on his shoulder as he hugs me. He turns to Alex. "It's good, Man. I know what you mean. Mora, and coming to town, and the War," he says, using a shorthand of familiarity that I can follow but can't quite share. I haven't been here as long. "Call me in the winter, Man. We'll do a ritual."

"Okay, Eddie," Alex says. They clasp hands, grip arms. Alex adds something warm and round in Spanish, rolling his R's. Eddie responds in Spanish.

We walk out to the truck, and Eddie goes back inside.

At last, after what seem to me hours of silence, Alex says, "You want to know about him-uh?"

"Yes. That thing he said about his own detours. He looked sad. Well, maybe not sad, just far away."

"Sí," Alex says. "Eddie, he was an early hippie. He'd already been living in a Taos commune when I met him in sixty-four, when I quit Berkeley. I told you—my head was messed up."

It's a familiar transformation that Alex sketches for me, the story of a talented professional man caught up in the changes of the sixties. As Eddie said, business suits and file cabinets at forty. Now he's gone to bushman and incense at fifty. But his distinction, in Alex's view, is that he came upon the changes sooner than most.

"He has helped you."

"Sí," Alex says. "I'm never sure how he does it. He's never the same way. Today he seemed more . . . traditional. Like he didn't want to scare you."

"Was he ever married?" I ask.

"Before, he was. You know, before he dropped out. Why'd you ask that?"

"I don't know, Alex," I say, hesitating. "Oh, I do too. I was thinking of Andrew. You know, what I've left behind. He hasn't moved into a commune, but he's changing." Everything's changing. Andrew, in his group of parents. Andrew, jogging. Would I know him if I went back to find what's left behind? Would he know me?

We come upon a slow-moving truckload of Navajos, children and women crowded in back, the driver and two men wearing jeans jackets in front. Alex shifts down, and looks over at me just as I'm ready to speak. Our words ricochet off each other.

"Isn't Braceros a Spanish name?" I ask.

"He changed his name!" Alex says at the same time.

"He doesn't look Hispanic," I add.

Alex laughs as he leans out to check the sideview mirror and flicks on the turn signal. "*Braceros* means workers, Olivia." He passes the

Navajos and swings back into the right lane. "Eddie was Of the People. Socialist. Power to the People . . ."

I look at him. He glances at me, returns his eyes to the road. "Olivia," he says quietly, as if making the connection for the first time. "He *did,"* he whispers. "He made it up. He changed his name, just like you! I never thought to tell you that."

"No wonder he knew how I felt! He changed his name!"

Everything's changing.

By nine-thirty Alex is fixing a quick breakfast for us at his house. Here it is summer and he builds a fire, but it actually feels good in the cool house. The fire has begun to crackle, tiny ribbons of piñon smoke escaping into the room as the chimney struggles to catch its breath. The kettle whistles, ready for tea. Suddenly I jump up from the sofa.

"What am I thinking, Alex? My clients! I haven't even taken a shower yet this morning! I have to go home and shower and change clothes before noon!"

He walks me into the bathroom with the cardboard-covered window. He moves aside to point out his wooly bathrobe on the hook behind the door. He pulls a towel from the cabinet beneath the sink and folds it over his arm. He bows. "At your service."

I can hardly ignore the reflection I see in the mirror as I pull my sweatshirt over my head. My hair is snarled all over the place. Freckles and streaks of mascara smear my chalk-white face. My breasts are heavy with their useless weight. I look at Alex. "Why do you do this?" I ask.

He looks away, as though I have somehow found fault with him.

"No, I don't mean it that way. But I know there must be women in your life, right?"

"Why do you come to *me?"* he asks, tossing the question right back.

Helpless without Eddie to guide us through this maze of feeling, to tell us what we have here, we just stare at each other. I step into the shower, turn on the water, and peer at him quizzically from behind the curtain.

"Why, Olivia?" he asks again, as he closes the door and returns to the kitchen.

"Distraction? Detour? No," I mutter to myself. "More than that. But what?" Nothing is clear.

I dry off and wrap myself in his bathrobe. I brush my hair and plop my bare feet along the hallway to the living room. I am still pondering the question as he brings toast, and tea in rough clay mugs.

"Why do you come to me?" he asks again, taking out his pouch of marijuana or hashish or whatever it is, stuffing his pipe. He has *his* way of preparing for the answers, but what about me?

I watch him as we sit on the floor, our backs against the sofa. I hold up one foot to the fire's already dying heat, trying to concoct a palatable answer that will give him knowledge, not injury. But the poison seeps in. Sweet as this tea is, sweet as the smoke smells, I am brewing bitter thoughts.

"Back where I come from . . ." I begin.

I look at him and smile. *Back where I come from* sounds like I might be getting ready to tell a story, like I might have some ancestors, a history, a life. Maybe this bitter story is better than a bitter life; maybe that's why the story got started. . . .

"Back in Potsdam," I continue, "there's a Welsh legend. My father's people were Welsh—my mother keeps track. Anyway, Alex, this isn't going to sound very good, but we are figuring out why we come to each other."

I sigh. I hold the mug in both hands, considering. "My aunt told me and she heard it from my great-grandmother, so it's all hearsay anyway." What *isn't* hearsay, I think, grumbling historian that I am. And is Alex even listening? He does look up when I stop talking.

"So, when someone died in a Welsh family, the whole community mourned for him. Small towns, you know—villages. They laid out the corpse overnight. Outside, by the front door, they put out all the foods he had liked when he was alive. If it were you, Alex, they would put out a pot of chili."

He smiles, glassy-eyed. I'm *glad* he's getting stoned.

"They believed that someone in the community came around in the night and ate the food!" I pause, wondering what he's thinking.

"The food was rotten by then because the wake had gone on for days. They'd been saving the food for this night, this occasion, to save the person from his sins before burying him. When I heard the story, I could not understand why they didn't just keep the food in the refrigerator. My aunt looked at me kind of strange when I asked her. She said I had missed the point. By setting out spoiled food, they were allowing the dead man's SINS to be eaten."

Just as I am realizing what an awful thing this is to say—just as I am picturing myself as a not very attractive version of that princess on the marble slab in the poster, all my past mistakes rotting on my body and dear Alex charged with the task of salvaging my rotten soul—he nods his head.

"Sí," he says. "Like *pan de los muertos."* He pulls at the loose sash that holds his robe around me. I push his hand away, watching his face in this mixture of sunlight and firelight.

"Listen to me, Alex! This is not the *pan* your people bake. This is not the bread of the dead. I'm talking about the rotten things, Alex. I'm talking about a Sin-Eater. Do you hear me?"

He has no mind. Leona said I ought to consider whether he's some kind of idiot savant. He is fumbling with his clothing. He is opening the robe again.

"Alex. I come to you because you are my Sin-Eater!"

I have given him a death sentence, chained him in a dungeon at the very least. Why doesn't he push me away in disgust, curl his lip in distaste, call a cab to take me away? Now he's stopped smiling. Maybe the marijuana is wearing off. I consider handing him the peace pipe, to drug him into forgetfulness.

"I can handle that!" he says suddenly. He kisses my neck, my eyes, as I struggle to see his face.

At last I pull away and prop myself on one elbow. "You can handle it?" I ask.

"You *taste* so good, Olivia," he says, grinning like a fool.

He puts soft, nibbling kisses on my face, my neck. He pulls my upper lip into his mouth and sucks on it, then my lower lip, my chin.

I laugh. From my belly, up through my chest, into the air. I laugh. I laugh. Oh, I could just laugh this morning away!

"Get up, Alex," I say, still smiling and warm all over. "We're going to my house."

"Olivia, stay here," he groans.

"No, Alex. Get up. Come on," I say, lugging him to his feet.

We're driving up Camino del Monte Sol, him at the wheel half stoned, me naked beneath his bathrobe. We shift around in our seats, both of us enjoying the suspense, the goodness of me leading him. We could slip into my bed when we get there. But I think I understand what this is about.

"Come in, Alex. I have something for you," I say, knowing only in this instant of saying the words just what I am going to do.

Out of consideration for Leona's sensibilities we park out back and come in through my patio. I pick up the Storyteller Ball as we walk past the round plastic table. The clay is warm from its solar baking.

We enter the kitchen. Alex's long torso dwarfs the countertop as he leans on his elbows, adjusting himself on a stool. Behind him I carry the heavy clay piece in the palms of both hands. I hold in my breath, let it out. "This is for you, Alex," I say, holding it out from me with hesitant, childlike pride.

Alex turns on the stool to look at me. Then he sees the clay ball.

"It's my first piece. The Storyteller Ball. It's for you," I say.

"Olivia," he says, still slow to react.

He takes the ball from me and looks down at the clay for a long time, rotating it in his hands. He sets it on the counter and pulls me to him. We are perfectly still.

In the mid-morning quiet, I feel the process begin inside my body. It is not a tightening spasm but a softening, as butter, on a warm sunny table.

I leave Alex sitting there on the stool in the kitchen, knowing he'd be more comfortable in a chair but knowing also that he's content where he is. I collect my underwear from the bedroom drawers, pull a green skirt and a white blouse from the closet and hang them on the door hook in the bathroom. I close the door and let Alex's robe drop to the floor. My body seems slender. Well, less lumpy than it was. Has all the walking changed its contours? My familiar pouch of a belly has diminished in size. I hadn't noticed until just this minute. Why didn't I see it this morning, in Alex's mirror? I glance in the mirror again, quickly, as if at a new acquaintance.

I reach into the box beneath the sink; I do the things I always do. A thin streak of blood has escaped along the inside of my thigh. As I run the white washcloth under the faucet, wring it out in my hands, and take it along my leg, I realize the blood is not a scarlet, fiery red but a rich, reddish brown. Like clay. A new substance.

3

ROBERTA MASTERS
C/O OLIVIA COSMOS MONTEVIDEO

So Andrew has addressed the box of clothing that arrives a week later. Friday afternoon, the day before I am to take the state real-estate exam, the box that's been almost three weeks in getting to New Mexico is here! It's the size of a washing machine and looks as if it got wrecked on the way, with one corner collapsed like an accordion and several punctures on the sides.

With my leg I shove it into the living room and tear into the corrugated cardboard. Kettlecloth skirts. Sleeveless Banlon tops. Cotton broadcloth shirtwaist dresses in powder blue, lemon yellow, and beige. I know these clothes by their stretched-out buttonholes, torn hems, and small faded stains that had become invisible in their familiarity. I pull them from the depths of this hole like skins shed long ago and now discovered in a cave. A delivery truck brings a box full of musty memories—the Return of the Shed Skins! There are more clothes still lying in the box.

I sit on the floor, folding what's out and considering what's still in there. It does make me wary. If I've learned anything it's to be watchful, to keep an eye out for signs of trouble. Alex keeps watch, walking on the mesa. And Leona decides, in her own strange way, whatever art forms she will work in on a given day. But I'm beginning to suspect that they look for signs of something *other* than trouble. Could I actually discover something good for me, that playfulness I can't seem to grasp? I get up on my knees and dig again into the sagging box.

The top layer of summer clothes hides dark winter garments I had somehow not expected Andrew to send. I feel panicky: Does he know more than I do? Is he predicting that my absence will last more than one season? Whatever Andrew's motivations for including them, the wool sweaters scratch at my arms on this warm afternoon as I pull them, along with linty wool pants and skirts, from the box. I press one dark-green sweater to my face, trying to find the smell of *me* that Andrew said he had noticed when packing this box. The camphor residue from mothballs assails my nostrils first, but the scent of Arpège is in there, identifiable, a faint sweetness buried in the yarn. I was wearing Arpège when Andrew and I met at West Virginia Wesleyan, when Gary was born, when I worked at the museum. I even wore it to Gary's service at Arlington. I close my eyes. Almost choking, I take the sweater away from my face and toss it onto the pile already on the floor.

Out comes the black wool coat I've had for years. This is good, I tell myself. It will protect me when the snow comes to Santa Fe. I wore this coat in November when Gary was home on leave, between basic training and infantry school. Was he really alive then? Six, eight months ago, did I really walk around in these clothes, a mother whose son was alive?

Unlikely as it seems, Mother Whose Son Was Once Alive has to acknowledge that something else is true. As much as I grieve for *Gary,* I know that *I* was less alive back then than I am right now. My chest constricts in familiar anguish: The gods have erred! The sequence is wrong: It's parents then children, life then death! Not children then parents, death then life! But now every piece I've ever read on nature and its cycles pops into place and I am thinking of flowers/seeds/flowers; rain/rivers/rain. . . . The comfort is intellectual and the constriction in my chest does not go away, but the expansion in my mind remains. A bigger picture, a larger compassion, the possibility of seeing something more. New as the sensation is to me, I feel hopeful. Confused as ever, bruised as ever, but hopeful.

I lean over the box, pulling out more sweaters, blouses, an old chenille bathrobe, and then I stop short—sharply alert, sniffing the air the way animals do. The very air in my apartment is changing.

I go to the phone and dial the number for our house on Branchview Court. "Andrew?" I say, pulling the long cord around the corner from the kitchen and back into the living room. "The box finally came. I got my clothes."

As if this box were a dollhouse and I a small child, I sit down beside it. But now the walls of the dollhouse are disappearing and I, looking in, can finally see. I see him alone, as he has been since I drove away three weeks ago. I watch as he walks, alone, in that split-level house, walks by Gary's room, and now, *into* Gary's room. . . .

"Good. It took long enough," he is saying.

How could I not have seen this? What's the use of having glasses if I can't see *this?* But maybe it's okay. Maybe just seeing whenever you can will do.

"Remember that year you spent all Christmas morning setting up the train for Gary?"

It's so real, I have to swallow to not cry out. I am opening a gift from Gary that contains a ceramic Santa, its head so small as to be mongoloid. I am thanking Gary for this gift, burying my laughter in the velvety soft curve of his neck as tears spring from my eyes and soak into the cowboys on the collar of his flannel pajamas.

"Yeah. Your dad and I played with the train all afternoon." He laughs.

I can see Andrew laughing. We're getting ready for bed in that house on Branchview Court. I am doing my mimic routines—Gary's antics, the neighbors, people in my museum tours. I can see the two of us at the table in the kitchen, drawing up our flower-bed plans. If the air had colors I would see the blue of our sorrow and the yellow-and-rose of our laughter rising in misty ribbons of vapor. I breathe in, I breathe out, until my tears block the flow and I have to reach for a tissue.

I want to tell Andrew that I know more now than I did before I opened this cardboard box. I don't know what will ever happen to us, either of us, but I want to tell him what I've seen. Yet my revelations spill out like so many apples from a bushel basket: "I got the car fixed. I made a sale! Can you believe it? And I got some glasses. I'm learning to make pots on the wheel. . . ."

What a pitiful sort of narration this is—no detail, no suspense.

How can I share this with him, this day-to-day, minute-to-minute suspense of just being able to open my eyes? I have begun to see differently, I've begun to see *Andrew,* and I can't find the words to tell him! How can he know what's going on if I give him such sketchy information?

I sit down in the cactus wood chair, resigned to the fact that I'll have to write a letter, or trust myself to some kind of mindwave communication. I glance around the room and play back the echo of his voice just one more time.

Suddenly he says, "I ran three miles today, without stopping!"

He doesn't explain all that to me, either, but I know it's important. Maybe we don't need any more suspense and elaboration. Maybe He Who Puts One Foot in Front of the Other understands what I'm saying in my cryptic way. Maybe the Indian storytellers have the right idea: first this, then that, then the other.

I go for it. I say, "I can see your face now. I couldn't see your face for all this time."

"Sometimes," he says, "I can see Gary's. Sometimes I can't."

"I know," I say.

"But I remember your face, Roberta."

"Thanks."

I'm curled up in bed by eight o'clock, noticing that the apartment has a different sound to it with so many clothes tucked into drawers and hanging in the closet. I go to sleep with the thought that tomorrow I will take the New Mexico licensing test for real estate, and that it doesn't really matter if I know what's going to happen next. I'm learning to make pots on a wheel. I made a sale. I picked up my glasses with the green frames.

Saturday morning. August first. Albuquerque. I finish my real-estate-license exam in two hours. As I am leaving the Kiva, a round classroom building on the University of New Mexico campus, a woman joins me. We compare notes on the test, and as we reach the Johnson Gymnasium parking lot we stop a moment before going to our cars. "What would be the best place to go today? I'm brand new to town," I say.

She ponders for a moment. "It all depends. I like the pueblos," she says. "One in particular. If you're lucky, one of the Indian women will take you into her home and bake bread. I don't really understand why they do that. It seems such an invasion of privacy, when they claim to *want* their privacy."

I nod, but I'm wondering what I would have done at this point in my life if I hadn't been able to invade other people's privacy, peek into their lives. "Maybe if they share easy things like bread, they can keep their big secrets."

She gives me a knowing look. "Ah. You've heard about the sandpaintings, have you?"

I nod again, using Leona's silence-is-wisdom technique. I know only that the sandpaintings they sell are not the exact replicas of those used in the medicine ceremonies. Maybe I know enough, maybe not.

"If they gave us the whole design, we wouldn't know how to use the magic anyway, would we?" She laughs.

"True," I say, making a chuckle sound, wishing I could know her better.

"The pueblo is south of town, near Los Lunas. It's called Isleta." She walks toward her car.

"Ees-lay-tah."

"Hey, you're good for a newcomer! Have a good time," she calls.

Highway signs point the way to the Isleta Pueblo, and immediately other signs appear, handpainted and tacked to trees: FRIED BREAD FOR SALE. I turn in at an adobe house shaded by a cottonwood tree; the sign here says YARD SALE—FRIED BREAD.

A dark-haired woman comes outside to shake hands. "I'm Felicita Lucero," she says, nodding to the piled-up tables and boxes. "My husband. I told him we have to sell some of this stuff!"

"I'm Olivia," I tell her as I walk toward a box of books.

"He reads those mysteries all the time. We have to sell a few."

"I'm a book freak, too," I say.

I notice a large, shallow basket made of twigs. Wide and oval-shaped, the basket could hold magazines or mail on the counter between my kitchen and dining room. "What is this basket made from?" I ask.

"Willow," Felicita says, turning to point behind her. "They grow over there by the ditch. I made that one."

Turning the basket over, I find no price tag. "Is it for sale?"

"Oh, of course. Fifty cents?"

"No," I say. "I'll pay you a dollar, at least. It's beautiful!"

She shrugs and turns to go inside. "When you're through, come in for some warm bread and lemonade."

She welcomes me into her yard, sells me her handwork for almost nothing, offers me the books her reading husband has consumed. If these are such private people, they are also very warm, and trusting.

I pick a couple of mystery novels—*25¢* the handwritten stickers say—and place them in the basket. I knock at the front door; Felicita's voice and the warm, yeasty smells call me inside.

She offers me a chunk of bread just out of the oven. She puts the torn bread on a paper plate and hands me a plastic honey dispenser. I squeeze the honey on, take a bite as I look around the room. White plaster walls and the same kind of bancos Alex has in his house divide this large front room from a darkened living room and the kitchen. Her husband waves to me from the kitchen doorway. Two small boys scuffle at his feet, get up, run to the living room.

"Our grandchildren," Felicia says, moving her arm in a gesture that tells me everything I need to know: they're spoiled, she adores them, they wear her out.

"This is delicious bread. I'll buy two loaves," I tell her. She hands me a damp cloth for my sticky fingers, then a glass of icy lemonade.

The front of the house is a kind of shop, I realize. They sell silver jewelry, wood carvings. On the wall are two portraits of men in uniform. When I put on my glasses, I realize one of the photographs is faded, the other bright and new.

"Your relatives?" I ask.

Felicita sets her chin in her hand. "That's my brother, he died in Korea. And my nephew. My sister's boy. In Vietnam last year."

I shake my head, unable to tell her how much I understand and share this grief. "It never ends," I say.

"I know," she says.

I give her a ten dollar bill. When she reaches for a change box, I tell her to keep it. I head for the door.

"Is this part of the pueblo?" I ask.

"Yes. But if you want to see the church and the main part," she says, following me out, "just turn right up the road there."

"Oh, I see. Thank you, Felicita."

"Come back and see us," she calls.

My basket of books and warm bread is beside me on the seat as I drive toward the cluster of houses. A man stands in front of a cinderblock wall that borders the dusty courtyard of the church.

The pueblo is a gathering of low adobes. A neighborhood, a place where families live. What in the world did I think a pueblo was, I wonder, as I get out of the car. There seem to be rounded, beehive ovens in almost every yard. I ask the man what they are called. *"Hornos,"* he tells me. But the rounded ovens don't distinguish this little village in any vastly exotic way from Branchview Court. Why do I find the ordinary things in people's lives so astounding? Did I think I'd find some new life forms, some *escape* from the ordinary? Leona bakes. Alex takes walks. Patrina goes to business school. My client plays the flute. This Isleta woman, Felicita, has a husband who reads mysteries . . .

And children play. Ah, there's the trouble. Those scrambling grandchildren of hers. And the children darting and dancing beneath a tree in the bare, dusty center of the pueblo. Coming upon them so unexpectedly, after seeing the portraits of those dead soldiers, I feel the potential for panic in this reminder of lost things. Their laughing voices hurt my ears.

This is a Saturday, I tell myself, as if literal reality matters, as if I can stop myself from remembering Gary and the Branchview Court children on weekday mornings when they were too young to go to school—the way there seemed to be glorious extra spaces around them, as though the morning could go on forever. Later, after lunch, they were different, as if they sensed the vacant spaces would soon fill up: older children home from school, fathers back from work. Their mothers, possibly preoccupied with morning tasks but always nearby, would shift their attention after lunch to the others' arrival. These young pueblo children, with their shining blue-black hair and round dark eyes, are playing with that same sense of morning spaciousness, even though it's not a weekday. I can feel it. I know it. What I didn't know—at least not when they were happening to me—was that the ordinary things were the miraculous ones. . . . And now, to think that I have started again on my birth-control pills. One round pill a day, to keep the babies away. Forever!

I feel the panic in my skin, but I walk calmly back to the car. I have felt this before. It happens over and over again, but at intervals, like childbirth contractions. I'm learning to ride it out. Moments of disintegration do not go on forever, *can't* go on forever. I should know: I waited long enough to disintegrate out here on the desert.

On the road leading from the pueblo and toward the town of Los Lunas, I spot a thatch of cattails growing way out in a field, beside an irrigation ditch. I can just see cattails in a huge pot! I could buy a big vase from one of the Indian women at the Palace of the Governors. Forget that! I could make my *own* pot or vase. Sure. Why not?

I park on the side of the road and make my way across the field. I snap off the brown-tipped stems until my arms are loaded with a dozen or more, then I stop to watch water spiders skating on the murky surface of the ditchwater. This is good. I've taken my test; I've visited the pueblo and survived the children. Now I stand here to view the dusty cottonwoods across the way and take one more opportunity to look up at the sky and search for a word to express B L U E. I turn my face up to the sun and take in a deep breath.

Suddenly tires screech on the road. I jerk around, certain that a crash will follow and my old blue car will be the victim. There is no crash. A pickup truck has come to a halt behind the car. Relieved at first when I see three Indians getting out of the truck, I freeze a moment later. They are drunk. Definitely not out to pick cattails, they stagger across the field toward me. My eyes are so bad. The Indians are fairly close to me before I slip my glasses down from the top of my head and see the obscene things they are doing with their hands inside their jeans. Somehow I must keep at the front of my mind the fact that they are drunk.

I'm going to die! Having just decided to fill up a pot with cattails, I am now going to die.

"We fuck you, lay-dee," one calls out in a rasping monotone.

The others laugh. The spokesman elaborates on their plans. "One, two, three. Fuck the shit out of you."

Easily over two hundred pounds, each of them. Together the three of them probably weigh seven hundred. I have no reason to question the sincerity of their intentions; I merely maintain a stranglehold on that one premise: They are drunk.

I've made some terrible mistakes, I am telling some unseen presence, maybe God, who lives with my mother in Potsdam. Maybe the god of marriages who lives on or near Branchview Court. Maybe the goddess of mothers, with whom I've only just recently begun to negotiate. I can't make up for Gary, I tell the goddess of mothers. But the god of marriages, this god I can negotiate with . . . maybe. "Firewater!" I shout, stepping down from the rise of the ditch bank, edging nearer to the yellow-red whites of their eyes. "Jim Beam!" I yell as I back toward the car. "Have Jim Beam!" I smile.

This is their land I'm trespassing on, and what do I do? I drop subjects from sentences with some insane notion that less grammar means better communication. No wonder they're intent on doing me harm! I laugh as I walk toward them. Oh, I'm so funny. I know what's coming next. Tears, shrieking. I figure thirty seconds. I figure I have thirty seconds before I am no longer effective in my own defense.

"Jim Beam," they say, looking inquiringly at each other. They turn to follow me, quickening their stumbling pace. I give them a wave of my hand as if urging them to follow me to the car. I'm still walking but stretching my legs just as far as they'll go.

This is my body, an instrument of *my* pleasure, not theirs. Oh, please, I say to the goddess of passion. I didn't understand. I ignored you for so many years. A wave of nausea hits as I hear the grunting sound one of them makes as he tries to speed up. I think of the sounds, the smells, the pain I may be in for. I think of my body. There must be a way for me to get to the driver's side. I take off running. I dash around the front of the car, almost slipping on the gravel but still smiling. As I lunge for the door and look up, they're running too.

God, gods, goddesses, wherever you are. This wouldn't be right. This just wouldn't be right.

All these cattails, bundled in my arms! I want to fix up my

place—that's a good sign, isn't it? I refuse to just dump them on the road. I jump in the car with my cattails. They spill across the steering wheel, onto the seat, the floor. One almost gets caught under the gas pedal when I start the car. I see a sweating hand press against the glass as I look left and release the emergency brake. The hand looks to me the way a water spider's wonderfully efficient floating feet must look to fish cruising in the irrigation ditch. Are there fish in ditches? I'm not cruising.

I peel out. They'd catch me on the highway for sure, so I swerve in and out of ditch roads and hide in a clump of cottonwoods. I shut off the engine. I wait. Just as I start up the engine again, almost ready to pull out on the highway, I see the truck. I sit in terror, afraid they'll hear the engine, but they haven't seen me. Their truck goes weaving on up the dusty road. I'm shaking and crying so violently that I bite my tongue, and that makes me cry all the more. Ahh, God.

As I sit on the patio with a glass of wine, my hands are no longer shaking, but my entire body feels fragile, somehow, as if the terror is still inside me. The hot summer sun sets reluctantly, hanging like a golden apricot in a pale-pink velvet sky, descending behind a neighbor's rooftop, apologetic for leaving me, continuing to light the sky long after I can see its perfect shape, a comforting afterimage, in my eye.

I need to call someone. It seems logical that I would call Alex, yet I resist the idea. Maybe I'm protecting my wounded pride. I'm afraid he'll be angry and disappointed in me; after all, I ignored his patient warnings about Shiprock and *that* sacred ground. I know better, yet I'm a thief; I know the rules—STAY OUT!—yet I go out on reservation property. But those men weren't telling me to get off the reservation. I was afraid for my *life*.

It hits me now: I wanted to live! I am thinking of Andrew the day I drove away from that house. I am smelling those musty clothes I unpacked from the box. We were dead people and now we're both beginning to live! It's Andrew I need to call. I need to tell him what has happened, keep him posted, weave another thread into our tattered connection.

"Were you hurt in any way? You should call a doctor."

"Oh, no," I explain. "Not at all. I'm okay. No, it's what I discovered. . . ."

I am patient for once with the technical questions that follow: How far was the car from the shoulder of the road, how deep was the irrigation ditch, where was the truck in relation to the car? He asks me to wait while he goes to turn off the television.

"I've been looking at this whole trip thing," I say when he returns to the phone. "You know. These catastrophes since Gary died."

There's silence on the other end of the line.

"Well, I wonder if I've preferred this," I say.

"Yes!" he says. "Yeah, go on. . . ."

"I think I feel closer to Gary when I'm in these insane situations. It does feel better in a way. A hitchhiker stealing my purse. The car blowing up. Indians trying to rape me."

We both laugh at my list, but our laughter is serious. "I know what you're saying, Roberta . . . Olivia . . . whatever. Some kind of adrenaline rush."

"Yes, exactly. I think I've needed to push myself away from comfortable things. I pushed *you* away. And you pushed me away, too. . . ."

We pause. Suddenly I ask him out of nowhere: "Andrew? Are you seeing anyone? A woman?"

He doesn't hesitate but a split second. "Yes. Are you?"

"Alex. The one I've told you about. How about you?"

"A woman in my group of parents. Leslie. A terrific person."

I am not angry. I mean, if I'm seeing someone, why wouldn't he? And, I mean, good people, strangers, can help each other. Medicine Men. And Medicine Women. But the blood is rushing to my head and draining to my feet. Who is she? Does she have thin ankles and no overbite? Rush and drain. Rush and drain. Maybe he's feeling the same thing, but maybe not. Tears are running down my face.

"I feel so guilty, but then again, I feel like these new people in my life are kind of like, I don't know, life preservers, who were there when I needed them."

"Same for me," he says.

"Andrew? I figured out tonight. . . ." I am barely whispering, clearing my throat. "I figured out that I don't think I want any more catastrophes."

"I know, baby."

"I don't think I want to be loco anymore," I whisper.

He is speaking so slowly, as if breathing between each word, "Roberta, I love you, hon. We both miss our little boy."

My chest feels as if something is coming loose inside—knots untying, ice melting and breaking off from ribs. Everything is shifting around.

4

One round pill a day to keep the babies away. I swallowed one this morning and almost choked on displaced grief. Yet I am taking them faithfully.

Alex and I have yet to talk about what has happened to us since I started my period. On Monday he helped me list the house next door to my first clients. We had lunch together on Tuesday. And on Wednesday, as we see each other in the hotel parking lot, he tells me he'll be working at his cabin all weekend. Instantly I envision us bathing in a stream, running through a wooded thicket to a rustic cabin where we fall upon each other. . . . He watches my face. He's thinking it, too. Yet neither of us will break this silent wall of uncertainty that has come up between us. We stop on the sidewalk at the Water Street entrance.

"So," I say, waiting to see if he invites me to join him. "Is Joe going up to work, too?"

"No, I'll go by myself," he says.

An instant later I think how unfair that was, probing around in this less-than-honest way to discover if he is taking a woman along, knowing that if he asks me to join him I'm going to be ambivalent at best, given all that's happening between Andrew and me. I am falling into a way of thinking that has nothing to do with us. I am actually asking myself if this man is reacting to waiting a month for the pills to take effect: *Can't wait the month till the pills make me safe. Can't have it now, doesn't want it at all.* Alex, of all people, does not fit that category! What is happening to me?

"I want to talk to you. This is making me crazy. We can't just let this go. . . ."

"All week, I've been so relieved but so sorry, Olivia-uh?"

"I felt so caught by the possibility—and the impossibility," I add, actually adding nothing. He has summed it up for both of us, the passing of our small, uncertain chance, an accident we only halfheartedly wanted to avoid.

"But we need to talk about so many things," I say at last. "I want to know about the woman whose brother was dying and I want to tell you about Andrew and. . . ." I'm ready to spill everything right here in the street. I have to stop myself.

"This afternoon?" he suggests.

I nod in agreement and relief. Already the air around us feels lighter as we go in the Water Street entrance. In the office, Alex hands me an envelope. "Olivia has news for us!" he says.

"What news?" I ask him, devastated that he would do anything so tasteless and insensitive as having me announce that my period has started. I'm going to kill him. . . . At that instant I look down at the envelope he has given me and realize it's from the New Mexico Department of Real Estate.

"Your exam," he says, devilishly.

He never forgets how to play, I realize, admiring in spite of my almost fatally accelerated heart rate and my deadly intentions toward him only a moment ago. Coyote the Trickster incarnate.

"Alex," I say. I tear open the envelope, laughing. "Oh, my exam! I got ninety-eight percent! I can't believe this," I say, truly joyful, more gratified by this affirmation, this odd measurement of myself than I could ever have expected.

Alex and Joe and Patrina are clapping and coming over to hug me, but suddenly I look at Alex. "Wait a minute," I say. "How did I get this so soon? They told us the scores wouldn't come in for weeks or even months."

"I have a friend who runs the computers."

"Alex! I don't want someone helping my score along!"

"Olivia, no. He just puts them in the machine! He can't change your score."

"Small town, small state, huh?" I shake my head at him, my friend with friends in high places.

He laughs, holding his hands in the air, innocent as can be.

"It's yours, Olivia. Fair and square. I have the same friend," Joe assures me. "But I *am* beginning to think you ought to go to law school! Shit, I only got ninety-seven on that test."

I give him a friendly shove.

Patrina is waving her hands to get our attention. "I have news, too!" she says eagerly.

"What, Patrina? Tell us!" I say.

"Ramon and I are expecting a baby. I'm just six weeks, but we're already so excited."

"Oh, Patrina," I say, hugging her. I look at Alex over her shoulder. "This is wonderful!" I say. Alex is silent.

One round pill a day, to keep the babies away. What did I expect? There wouldn't be any other babies?

"Olivia," she says. "I am already feeling the morning sickness." It's almost but not quite as if she's saying "morning seek-ness." I smile affectionately at this trace of her accent lying across her words like a lacy filament.

"I guess this baby's in a hurry to get your attention!" I tell her.

"Bebé!" Alex says, grasping Patrina's thin shoulders in his hands, bowing toward her then backing away. *"Muy bueno."* He says something else in Spanish that I can't pick out. He starts toward the door.

I keep trying to smile, my joy for Patrina real but so tainted with confusion that I will need some time to sort it all out. Seeing Alex's expression, I'm wondering about his reaction as well.

I follow him out to the parking lot.

"What's wrong?" I ask him.

"Hijo, what timing," he says.

"I know. I don't know what to think except I'm so happy for her."

No wonder we feel small, overshadowed by the purposeful, intentional rightness of Patrina being pregnant. We are grieving for the *idea* of a child, each of us in our own way.

"So, Ramon and Patrina will have a baby," Alex says, looking up at the roof of the La Fonda, not looking anywhere, really. "They have been so sad about Yolanda."

"Yes," I say. "They have been sad."

I am almost biting my tongue, wanting to tell Alex that he will be a father someday, as wonderful a father as his own father, Max Romero. I want to tell him that, even for all his kindness, he will stop finding women like birds with broken wings and instead he will meet someone strong and beautiful and whole. He will know it is time to stop worrying about his lost childhood and his sense of misplacement or mistaken identity. It will be time to begin his life. But I can't get the words out because I am still *in* his life, this Detour Life, just as he is still in mine.

"Let's take a walk," I suggest. I feel as if I need fresh air, even though we're standing outside. "Walk with me over to the title company."

"You go ahead," he says, kind of bent over.

"Here," I say. "Let's sit in my car for a while."

"Sí," he says. "Thanks, Olivia."

We get in the old blue car. I quickly roll down my window. He rolls down his.

"I feel sick to my stomach," I tell him

"*Hijo!* Me, too, Olivia," he says, rubbing his hand across his chest. He looks at me. He really does look pale. "Are we having the morning sickness?" he asks.

We laugh together now, on the soft edge of tears, knowing Patrina and Ramon will have their baby and restore the balance for all of us queasy people. But it's not enough to know that. Alex needs to believe. He needs to believe that I have secret women's wisdom; he has to believe in my medicine if he's going to feel better. As if any two women have ever agreed on what to do for it, I tell him: "You know, Alex. There is really only one cure for morning sickness. You have to eat!"

"Unnh, I don't know, Olivia," he groans.

"No, really. You have to eat." I start the car. "Let's go to Santiago's," I tell him. "We need a breakfast to cure the 'seekness.' "

I drive us over to Muñoz Café. Alex rests his hand on my shoulder the whole way there. I think he trusts my medicine.

We sit side by side at a round table outside on the patio, shady in this early-afternoon light. Santiago is working inside; a young waitress takes our order. "Two orders of hotcakes," I say.

She looks at Alex. He is hunched over and still so pale.

"You think so-uh?" he asks me. "Pancakes?"

"Just what the doctor ordered, Alex. Blue corn, with unsulfured molasses, please," I say to the waitress. "Oh, and fresh-squeezed orange juice, too."

She goes back inside. I take his hand, pushing his fingers against my face. "I know my way around, Alex. Leona's training is paying off."

He grins, responding to my touches. "Around where?" he asks, smiling, bringing his other hand to reach behind my neck and pull me toward him.

"Muñoz Café!" I laugh. My chair starts to tip and I get up to push it closer to his.

He puts his arms on the table and rests his head there, looking at me. "This is changing my whole life, Olivia. Maybe I was going to change anyway, but it's changing since I met you."

"You want to have children. You want a family, a home."

"*Sí.* You should have seen me a few years ago," he says, looking away. "You'd never believe I'd say this. I was all over the country. I didn't know what I was going to do from one minute to the next. I wanted every woman I saw. . . ." He raises up, pushes his chair back from the table, his arms behind his head, his long legs stretched in front of him.

His physical presence—his black hair, his eyes, his legs—his actual physical self seems to fill up the front of my brain. All my wise insights about his future are fluttering around at the back. I must reach back, past his presence, to speak: "I know more than I'm letting on," I say, intensity tightening my throat. "I'm smarter about us than I want to be. I don't want to be honest. Do you know what I mean?"

The waitress brings our plates. Alex's color has improved considerably. She notices, hesitates, until he looks up at her. Persuaded, she walks away.

"Being honest, that's hard to do," he says. He pours the hot syrup onto the layered stack, letting it run in golden rivers down the sides. He takes a bite, bends his head forward over the plate to catch the drips, looks up at me. "How are you smart?" he asks.

"I know we've changed each other. I know we will have to go to other people. I know you have mended the pieces of me. . . ." My voice gives way, surprising me. I hadn't seen this rush of emotion coming. "It's not easy, knowing these things."

"Olivia," he says, dabbing at his mouth with a napkin. "I always have wanted to make people happy. My parents, my sisters. My sisters were older, they were crying about boyfriends. I was the little brother, I would tease them and do things to make them laugh." He is eating like there's no tomorrow, scooping in another mouthful of pancakes, washing it down with orange juice. I take a nibble of mine. They are good! I take another bite.

"But, ay, that night with you. When I read the stories and all? *Hijo,* I knew I could help you. . . . I don't know how. I just knew. I felt so important in your life. I mean, important! Lover, friend, all that, but something else."

"You were important, you *have* been," I say. Noticing my verb tenses, I add, too late, "You are!" I swallow orange juice, feel with my tongue as the pulp touches the top of my mouth, gets crushed by my tongue, and slides down my throat as I swallow.

"It just happened, sort of came over me. It felt so powerful." He stops eating for a moment. "The woman you asked about. Her name was Lupe. I thought I was helping her, going with her to see her brother. He had leukemia. But it ruined everything for us. She didn't want to see me anymore. After he died, she said every time she looked at me she thought about his dying. She thought I just felt pity for her."

"Did you?" I ask him.

He looks down at his plate. "*Sí,* I did. She was right."

He is moving the flat of his fork all around his plate, lifting it to his mouth, taking every last drop of syrup onto his tongue. So delicious, watching him; I can taste the delicious last drop of the syrup from his plate.

I can't resist the question, not now. Like passing a mirror in a restaurant, how can I not look at this reflection? "Do you feel pity for *me?*"

"No. Not pity." He leans back from the table, draining his orange juice glass, making a tongue-swipe at the pulp on the inside surface. "You are this person who keeps getting better. You get stronger. And I keep feeling like, well, *hijo,* like I did something and I'm not sure what I did, but I knew I was doing it and I liked doing it."

"Like a drug," I say. I slice the remaining stack of pancakes into bite-size pieces, preparing the plate for my onslaught, knowing as I do it that Virginia always told me to cut only one bite ahead, two at the most. *Ponk!* I puncture one little tower with my fork and pop it into my mouth. He is watching me. I chew slowly as he takes my shoulders and leans over to kiss me. The man is tasting my pancakes with his tongue.

"I think I could get hooked on that," he says.

"You seem to be over the morning sickness."

"You gave me a miracle drug!" he says.

I cannot stop smiling because at this very moment I have learned what I have never known before. The thoughts are so intimately tangled in my mind that I don't really hope Alex will understand, but I tell him anyway. "In order to be playful," I tell him, sitting straighter in my chair, as if to deliver a lecture, "you have to be alive at all levels, different states of being!"

I'm amazed I even thought it up. Yet this convergence of seemingly diverging states of being is probably the reason most people, including me, have found playfulness—and what? spontaneity?—to be tinged with fear and confusion. I smile and stab another stack of pancakes, aiming this one directly into his mouth—open wide.

"That's probably the reason we have drugs!" I add. "The fear, the confusion of being sad while we're happy and good while we're bad and sick when we're well and . . ."

Suddenly we are both so serious. As if we know more than we can bear, we are staring at each other. Alex has turned sideways from the table and is facing me, resting his arms on his thighs. "I can't figure it out," he says.

The waitress clears our plates, leaves the check, but we cannot look up to acknowledge her.

"You want your marriage to make it," he says.

"I do want it, yes," I say, almost choking as I speak.

"We both want it, *sí,*" he says. "It's important."

"Not because it's a marriage, though. It's that Andrew and Gary and me were one thing, one piece. But now we've been torn by the war, and . . ."

I can feel Alex relax. Even though we aren't touching, I know the moment when he just relaxes. "It's spirit," he says quietly.

"What?" I ask. My voice is almost musical with pleasure. He knows I like what he has said. I see the corners of his mouth turn up at almost the very instant I am feeling this pleasure. He knows me the way a child knows his mother; he can work on me the way Gary did. He knows my other pleasures, too. But then, nothing is ever simple.

"Spirit. Strong spirit. In us, Olivia-uh? We have mother and son in us. We have some of that . . . like you said, all states of being?"

As if my very chest cavity has opened up to let him in, I want to crawl over to him and lay myself across him. I want to rock back and forth. I want to trace with my hand the top of his head, the curve of his skull, the angle of his jaw. I want to rock him. I want him to rock me. But what would be left of either of us? Who would we be? I wish I had read a story that would fit us, but the Indian storytellers didn't seem to bother with a lot of details about the wifestealing. The wife who returned did not tell her story. Old Coyote Man said the woman just left and then came back again. One thing and then another. I rest my elbow on my knee, my chin in my hand.

"The spirits will stay with us," he says.

"If we treat them right," I say.

"Sí," he smiles.

He pulls me up by the arms and reaches into his pocket. "My treat," I say proudly, thinking of my sale. I quickly pull a twenty-dollar bill from my purse and toss it extravagantly on the table. We leave and lean against the sun-warmed adobe wall beside the café. We talk about spirit, yet we've never been more conscious of each other's bodies: I put my arms around his waist; he rests his chin on my head; I talk into his chest.

"We have to treat the spirits right," I say. "Some kind of appropriate offerings." I picture us walking to the foot of something made of sandstone or down underground. "Piñon nuts and blue-corn tortillas. Some kind of feathers," I say, playful in spite of this unsettling moment.

"Parakeet feathers!" I say, looking up at him. "From the bottom of the cage. Already fallen. No plucking allowed."

Alex laughs from down in his throat, a deep releasing of sound. "Who ever heard of this offering, Olivia?" he asks, leaning his face into my ear.

"Nobody," I say, grinning. "This is the secret Spider Woman never told! Great wisdom. Great secret medicine."

"Piñon nuts and blue-corn tortillas and parakeet feathers," he says, laughing again. "We'll do it-uh?"

This isn't easy. This isn't playful. I thought once we talked the heat would go away, but the touch of our arms, the brush of our faces spark small wildfires. People really do make choices; life doesn't just happen to us. I want to tell him that I can live two lives. I want to tell him that I will mend my torn fabric and then embroider him above my breast. But I can't.

We are in the car. I'm driving him back to the hotel parking lot.

"O. Mi amigo," I say as I stop the car. I lean my head on the steering wheel and look over at him.

"O. Mi amiga-madre-amor," he says, in that rapid way he speaks to those who are fluent, when he knows no translation is necessary.

5

Knowing Alex has gone to his cabin, I find myself focused, released somehow into the mundane privacies of my own life. More than once I find myself summarizing: Andrew is in Virginia and Alex is at the cabin. No one home but me.

On Thursday, almost hourly, I have desperate thoughts of Alex—tender, jealous, erotic—and then I let our lunch at Muñoz play through my mind again. The thoughts pass in cycles. Then the industrious energy that has taken me over returns. I type up flyers about the house I have listed; I will send them to other realtors. I canvas a three-block area of the neighborhood, checking first on the office map to be sure I'm well outside of Joe's red zones. I call the owners and schedule an open house for Sunday afternoon.

On Friday morning I come into the office at eight, to answer the phones and organize a file drawer for myself. After lunch I drive to the Safeway and buy a ten-pound bag of pinto beans. I sort the beans on the white plastic patio table, scooping them out by the cupfuls, separating the dusty, withered ones into a paper sack and placing the fat, shiny ones in a big dented aluminum pot that came with the apartment.

The beans and the fine soil that clings to them are like old friends. I watched my mother and her sisters sorting legumes and grains when they got together in the winter. They sat around the table, with the bare, gray sky visible through the high window—high for me, I realize now, since these are very early memories that have returned to me.

They talked over barley, rice, peas, white navy beans, and even pintos, though they called pintos "brown beans." I remember learning to count by collecting the various beans as they dropped to the floor. And earlier yet I remember my grandmother, my mother's mother, scolding her for allowing me to play with the beans, the peas, the barley. "She'll choke, Virginia! She'll put one of those beans up her nose!" I remember my mother, in her offhand way, telling her mother, "*You* deal with her. She'll ask you questions and you'll forget why you ever tried to tell her anything." Sometimes they cooked for days, and when they made brown beans they also baked cornbread. The kitchen was always warm. They have gathered around me.

At the sink, just the way those women did, I rinse the beans and set them on the counter for an overnight soak. I go out to the patio with an empty coffee can, shovel some sand into the can, and stick a few of the beans into the dirt. I bring them inside, run some water over the soil, and set the can down.

I'm staring out the window, then looking down at my hands. I don't know what has happened. I mean, I can't explain to myself why this morning I had every intention of holding that Sunday afternoon open house and why now, late Friday afternoon, I am dialing the phone number of that lovely young couple and canceling the whole thing.

"Could we just postpone it a week?" I'm saying. "Something has come up. It's a schedule conflict. You know how that is."

I don't know why they're so nice about it, either, but they're actually expressing relief. "It gives us more time to work on the yard," Peter says.

"Yes, Olivia," says Denise, from the extension phone. "We'll have time to take that old barbecue grill to the dump."

"Don't forget you're seven months pregnant, Denise. You take it easy," I tell her.

They laugh; they like my concern. We hang up. As I stand at the sink, I know: I need some time, a couple of days. I can do some handwork. I can make some good shapes out of clay. I know this, but I don't ask myself why. According to Leona, "One doesn't ask oneself those kinds of questions."

Sometime Friday night or early Saturday morning I dream about a nighttime fire that looks like the Great San Francisco Fire looked in my American History textbooks. Threatening to consume rows of wooden buildings, this fire bounces like a ball, from one strangely familiar yet anonymous structure to the next. As soon as it bounces upward, the-fire—in whatever house it's been in—goes out, but then the houses are changed, aglow. They pulse, lovely neon skeletons in pink, orange, green. In the dream I'm not worried about the fire hurting any of us because we're watching the fire. Alex, Leona, Joe—we aren't in our houses; we do not feel its heat. But we see it, and in some way we know the fire. The only disturbing or puzzling part of the dream, I realize in the morning, was not the fire but the fact that I kept batting the fireball; I kept batting it toward a building across the street. When I turn, in my memory of the dream, to look across the street, that building is the house on Branchview Court. What does *that* mean, Leona would ask me if she were here.

On Saturday morning I drain the sandy water from the pintos and add fresh. I put them on the stove to simmer on very low heat. In town I buy a potter's wheel and one hundred pounds of clay—in four twenty-five pound bags—from Leona's supplier. I consider putting a down payment on a kiln, but I take my fire dream to be an omen or at least a clue: For the time being, anyway, I should stay away from incendiary devices.

Leona comes over to provide a brief lesson about the role of air bubbles in the failed firings of pots, vases, and sculptures. "Wedge, wedge, wedge!" she says, cutting off a couple of slabs with a wire attached between two wooden handles. I join her as we slam the cold, hard clay against my kitchen table. Then she returns the clay to the plastic bag, leaving the cutter for me on the counter.

After Leona goes home, I can't go near the clay. All the noise and dust her wedging has created hangs in the air, an echo of itself. I feel incapable of such energy and motion. I sit in a chair at the dining-room table, an outsider, craning my neck to peer in at the bags of gray littering the kitchen. Whatever made me think I could do this? Beginner's luck? One clay ball and now I'm a potter? The cutter swings from my hands like a metronome: You and clay? You and clay?

I think suddenly of my Trip-Tiks, how I had to have them when I first started on the road. I wonder: If I just had a map, a guideline, a plan . . . *Real artists don't need a plan,* the negative, whining voice begins. *If you were an artist* . . . "No!" I say. "No. I *do* need a plan." It's okay, I tell myself. I'm a beginner; I have to start somewhere. I had to learn to read. What were the first things I read? I started with fairy tales, right? Okay. Fairy tales.

I get up and walk to the kitchen, the cutter in my hands. "You cause trouble," I say to that negative voice. "This is for you." I pull the wire taut. *Snap!* I am awestruck by my destructive capacity, and my willingness to use it. I throw back my head and laugh. "Hah!" I say.

I slice off hunks of clay. Three, four, five of them. I give them all a role. "Goose Girl's goose," I say to a piece with an upturned triangular corner that reminds me of tail feathers. "The Fairy Godmother's pumpkin," I tell a squat mound of clay that at first aspires to be Cinderella's glass slipper. "Be who you are," I growl.

Slunk! Off goes another piece. Each time I cut off another slab of clay I feel I'm meeting a stranger. The wedging goes on—noisy, slam-bang warm-up. Then something happens without my being able to really observe the process and I settle, soften myself around the clay like a nesting hen relaxing onto her eggs. I work the clay as if petting it. I use the rounded tip of the potato peeler as I finish off the goose's feathers. Later I look up and realize I've finished altogether with the Grimm fairy tale series—they're lined up on the round white table on the patio. Then I'm mashing the rolling pin onto a ball of clay and rolling out what turns into Old Coyote Man's buffalo robe and Spider Woman's web. Better, I think. Much better.

At some point, long after dark, I begin to weep with fatigue. "My back, my hands. Ohh," I groan. Bent over the sink, I let the water cool the swelling around the cuticles of my fingernails. "I never even got on the wheel," I whine, tapping my tongue against an aggravated hangnail. I could almost laugh as I drag myself to bed. It's three o'clock Sunday morning. The pintos are still simmering. Every light in the house is burning.

I wake to such a stench of body odor that I cannot believe it's me. My armpits smell like onions, or something equally earthy and ripe. There's a bite to this smell. I take a shower and change into clean clothes. I can still smell it through the deodorant. I kind of like the odor in a secretive, private way, but I do wonder what sort of juices this potting work generates, if the juices aren't juices but poisons, and if they are escaping quickly enough.

I'll *run* them out, I decide. I eat a breakfast consisting of a big flour tortilla spread with my mush of pinto beans, salsa, chopped onions, grated cheese. I add one fried egg, over easy. *Huevo Montevideo.* I roll it all up and chomp, my body screaming for these carbohydrates and fats. At noon I leave the apartment.

Walking up Camino del Monte Sol, I'm already impatient to get back to the clay, but some instinctual beaming device in me is saying: Keep going, not there yet. I continue walking and soon I'm at the top of the hill. I stand before the Wheelwright Museum and the old Laboratory of Anthropology. Just like a divining rod, I am pulled toward the edge of the parking lot, into the *chamiza* bushes and on.

I walk quickly, as if I know where I am going, and soon I'm at the rim of the mesa where the laboratory founders, having all the choices they must have had back then, probably said casually, "Well, here's a great view. Let's build here." I find when I look up I see a circle of sky, and as I bring my eyes lower, a border of mountains, and lower still, red-brown earth and earth-brown buildings nestling within a great curvature of earth. I am looking at a bowl of earth. Maybe not a bowl but a deep-dish pie plate, the kind my mother, Virginia, used for apples when they came in fast, when every roadside vendor on every country road outside of town was selling apples—so cheap they'd give them away at the end of the day. Something important, something related, is waiting for me here, but I can't see it yet. Bowls, deep-dish pie plates, the abundance of apples, beans? I don't know what it's about.

I hurry down the hill on Camino del Monte Sol, desperate to talk about what I have seen and yet hoping that I meet no one. Not yet. I have witnessed something I cannot put into words. I need time to discuss it with the clay. Leona calls a greeting as I come into the courtyard, but I wave quickly and slip inside.

I stand in the kitchen. The early-afternoon sun highlights dust and drying clay on the countertops, splatters and drips left by the sponges on table legs and walls. I am grateful. The room is ready for me.

I go to the counter and place my hands on some chunks of clay left over from my night's work. First one piece, and then another. I close my eyes, feeling for angles that will let me sculpt mountains, or apples, or bowls, but soon I abandon that project altogether, pushing those pieces into a corner by the sink. Instead my eye falls on a big, uncut chunk of clay that I had left on the table. I carry it to the wheel. I hold it there to check its size. Too big.

Ignoring the requirements of balance for now, I pound the piece on the table until it seems there couldn't be an air bubble left on earth that would dare to enter this clay. I make it warm. I make it round. I return it to the wheel. I drag a chair to the wheel and sit down. I take a deep breath and push the pedal. The ball is so large in my hands, but it's soft and I can feel its center. I work for a wide base. I notice that I am breathing on every other rotation. In . . . and out. In . . . and out. Reaching into the center of the clay with my potato peeler, I begin scraping out pieces a little at a time. I let each coil of clay fall to the floor as I excavate the center. But it's also growing taller, one foot, two feet, almost three! Oh! Almost forgetting to breathe in the excitement, I catch myself and return my focus to the rhythm of the wheel. In . . . and out. One rotation, two rotations. In . . . and out. I caress the sides as they rise, until, no longer a deep-dish bowl or even a pot, it has become a vase. As in a dance, I wave my hand above it with a drizzle from the sponge. Lifting, encouraging, round and round I go, asking the sides to raise themselves higher, like wings.

I look up from the wheel. Calm and sure, my foot off the pedal now, I get up and bend over the wheel to look inside. The lip of the vase kisses my chin, its primal odor immediately gritty on my tongue. I position my feet flat on the floor, cup my hands carefully around the base of the clay, eyes closed, feeling the wheel's slight rotation, left then right, on its bearings.

I slip my cutter underneath to release it from the wheel.

Damn! Leona said to be sure a pot isn't too wet before I cut it off the wheel. It should have dried for awhile. No stopping now. Slowly, I slip the vase onto a tin cookie sheet and carry it to the dining-room table.

I hold my breath, watching the slick wet clay, amazed that its ghostly gray form is not collapsing before my eyes. Oh, no! It *is* collapsing! Actually, it's slightly tilted now. The curve on one side has a folded place, a weak spot, but there it stands.

Like a mote from the clay-dust floating in the sunlight, a thought sifts into me: Andrew may never know about this vase and all that's gone on here. No one can know.

I take a step or two back, tilting my head, watching the vase. It looks so extravagant—its broad, bowl-like base, the long neck that widens out toward the top. Already *I* feel distant from it, wondering if I even made it.

I'll never have the words to tell him. I'm not even sure what to tell myself.

I scrub the kitchen, noticing with no small amount of wonder that my knees bend when I am washing the table legs and that my forearms flex as I wring out the rags and sponges at the sink. I shove the wheel to the corner, pushing with my strong legs. I will work again with the clay, here in my own place. Maybe when you have an apartment and a job you make decisions about who you are and what you can do, what you need and when you need it.

I go to bed early, while the summer sun still floats in the sky. My sleep is long and deep but filled with dreams toward morning. . . .

. . . "Is it you?" I ask the young man. "Is it really you?"

"Hi ya, Mom. Yeah, it's me."

"I can't see you very well," I say.

"Yeah, it's kind of dark."

"That's silly," I laugh. "The sun's already up!"

"Funny, huh?"

I laugh again as I touch the skin at his neck, the bulge of muscle that comes down in a curve from behind his ear.

"Mom?"

"What, honey?" It's so easy with us, easy and natural. I am full of warmth and some sweet kind of light, and I just can't stop smiling.

Call me by my old familiar name. . . . Speak in the easy way you always have. Laugh as we have always laughed.

What voice was *that?* Reverend Sherman Ellis read that thing at the service. He isn't going to read it again, is he? "This is a dream, isn't it?" I say. "Oh, God, no." I am groaning. "Not a dream. Please."

"Don't worry about me. Okay, Mom?"

Ahh, there he is, there's my boy's voice.

> *Death is nothing. . . . Whatever we were to each other, we still are . . .*

"No," I am screaming, then whimpering. "No, please . . . let him stay with me, just a little longer."

> *Play. Smile. Think of me. . . . Life means all it ever meant. . . . There is absolute, unbroken continuity . . .*

Oh, yes. He's bending over me, that way he has of giving me hugs that don't crush our body parts together. "Oh, come here, you," I say, giving him a big bear hug, and I am filling with light and a piercing joy, and then he's gone and Reverend Sherman Ellis's voice is reading on and we're at Arlington, and even those sentimental words, so unacceptable before, are all right now: They're true.

> *Call me by my old familiar name. . . .*

"Gary," I say. "Hi, Gar. . . ."

Lost and found. Lost and found. Everything is round if we remember.

6

I ride in the passenger seat of Leona's 1955 mud-colored Lincoln, on our way to a pottery and crafts center in town. We're going to fire the vase I made during my weekend with the clay. I am holding my vase in a box on my lap, its neck reaching up past my face. I seem to be holding my breath as well.

"Don't worry, Olivia! Your vase will be fine, and if it isn't, you'll make another one."

"I know," I say. "But I like this one."

"The larger kiln may even be better for such a big piece. Balance the heat."

"I know," I say.

She fired eight of my pots and figures in her kiln at home, but then there was a two-week delay while she went up to Trinidad, Colorado, to visit her sister's ranch. My tall vase has had to wait. When Leona got home on Sunday, there was a gas leak in her apartment. She smelled it. Even after the repairmen left, she refused to use her kiln.

"I won't turn on that kiln for a week!" Leona said. "Fumes."

We glazed my vase on Monday, painting it with a bluish mixture she called *cobalt* and a combination of whites and pinks that she mixed and gave no name. Today, Tuesday, I cup my hand on the vase and tip it sideways within the box to take a look. It may have survived the bisque fire, but the sag is still there. I run my fingers over it, feeling the wrinkle, the place where the clay just sort of folded down on itself. But that makes it all the more important to me, this imperfection, this flaw. . . .

"Leona?"

She looks over at me, tiny behind the wheel of her old, well-cared-for car.

"Thank you for teaching me."

She smiles that soft doughy smile of hers. I smile back. I nestle the vase against my chest, the box heavy in my lap.

A serene young man named Allegheny greets us as we come in. His skin is very tan, but flushed with the heat of his work. It seems he tends the studio and prepares the kilns for firing. Inside the kiln where my vase will go, the dusty ash of previous firings coats the bricks. Allegheny removes a shelf, then turns to take my vase from me. I feel my heart racing as he sets the blue-black form inside. The glaze forms peaks as it comes up from the wide bowl base and reaches to the neck; its sides are rough, split from the earlier bisquing fire. The vase leans to one side, over that folded spot, over that place where it might have given way altogether—and still might, I think with dread. A big round pot of Leona's sits confidently on another shelf, a brilliant reddish glaze dripping down its sides.

Allegheny places two more pieces on the remaining shelf.

"My vase will be dark blue," I tell him.

"Partly," Leona corrects me. "Things change in the firing. And we used some white."

"Yes," he says. "Cobalt and white is always exciting."

"Oh," I say, jumpy, nervous.

The pots are waiting; they sit passively, as if they're in a steam bath. I want to say something to them as Allegheny closes the cover: This is what it takes, I want to tell them. This fire is just what it takes.

"Thursday?" Allegheny asks.

Leona nods. That's two days from now! Sweat pours from my head; it trickles from my temple, past my earlobe, down my neck. I reach up and slide my hand inside my shirt collar. We drive home.

On Thursday, I make no appointments that will take me from the office. I answer every phone call, while Patrina studies for her business-law class.

Leona calls late in the afternoon to say she has the vase. "It came through fine," she says, and I can tell she has been praying for it.

My vase has survived! I dash home from the office, stopping long enough to take a towel from my bathroom shelf. As I am leaving the bathroom, my face in the mirror stops me for just an instant. The woman I see is flushed in the cheeks, brown eyes shining with a wild kind of light, white teeth gleaming in a smile radiant with energy. Is that woman me? I push a loose strand of hair from my forehead, just to be sure. The woman's hand raises when mine does, drops to her side, comes up again in a fist-punch motion that says, "We won."

"Leona?" I call through her screendoor. She comes into the living room, holding the vase out away from her for me to see.

"Oh! The blue is so much nicer than in the glaze powder," I say. "And the base is rounder, wider! I'd forgotten how sturdy it was!"

"The first of many," she says proudly. She looks questioningly at my arm.

"Oh, it's a towel," I say. "I thought I'd wrap it in a towel to bring it home."

I spread the towel on the sofa. She comes over, sets the vase lengthwise. Both of us, bent over the cushions, fold the sides up over this creation of mine and pat it into place. Outside in the courtyard I notice the gleaming surface peeking at me beneath the bumpy terrycloth. But, almost superstitious, I pull the towel across it and go inside.

I uncover it slowly, sitting on the sofa, to discover a blue that is almost black in the lines and bubbly places that form within the blue, and gradations of palest pink to gray in the creamy white glaze that swims down the sides. I turn it upside down on the cushion and find my scratched-in signature: OLIVIA. I set it beside the Boy Child with Book on the counter between the dining room and the kitchen. Then I take it to the patio and set it on the round white table. The hard, shining glaze flares in the sunlight: cool deep-blue-creamy-white fire.

Finally I place the vase in a corner of my bedroom. I sit down on the bricks, next to the cattails stacked beside the wall. I insert them carefully, one at a time, remembering that they are not mine, remembering that I have stolen them from the Indian reservation at Isleta. I am making amends. I am forgiving the three men who wanted to hurt me, forgiving us all for our carelessness. Carefully I make sure the cattails press their soft selves against the walls for support, so the vase won't topple over.

The next morning I make a pot of coffee and invite Leona over. I take her back to my room. I point to the vase, slightly tilting, its brilliant white-and-blue glaze catching the morning light.

"This is a precarious way you've chosen to display your work, right on the bricks, without a stand," Leona says. "Lovely, really. But risky."

I shrug my shoulders and smile at her. "I think I've let my need for the adrenaline rush inhabit the vase!" I say.

She thinks about that for a moment, then laughs in a slow series of airy exhalations and assenting nods of her head.

I reach over to touch the rim of the vase, intending to demonstrate for Leona its relative stability. Instead I get a shock of static electricity and jerk back my hand. It sounds as if something has cracked inside the clay. I look at Leona. We watch the vase for a moment but it neither falls apart nor teeters on its base.

As we walk from the bedroom, Leona stops once to glance back at the vase and then at me. She takes a sip from her coffee cup and starts down the hall toward the living room. I remain a moment longer in my magical room, time passing, August slipping through my hands.

The Fiesta will begin this Friday, the final weekend in August. People aren't just talking about Fiesta, they're obsessed. The newspaper is filled with "history," official and unofficial tales of past practical jokes and outrageous revelry. Suddenly nothing is the way it's been.

After breakfast on Monday morning Leona brings out her Fiesta dress, a gaudy purple affair with alternating tiers of fabric, silver braid, and white lace. The blouse has puffed sleeves and a neckline that scoops low enough, when she models it for me, to reveal the crepe-skinned ravages of her neck and bosom. "You must go to Zozobra with me!" she exclaims with uncharacteristic animation. She washes her dress, starches the skirt, pleats it on a broomstick propped beside her front door. It sits slumped, a headless kitchen witch, in the morning sun.

At the office I ask about New Listings for the week—a kind of sacred calendar that Joe has been posting like a religious object every Monday since I've been here—and he just laughs. "It's time for Fiesta, Olivia!" he says. "It's time to let go of ordinary things!"

I've only recently embraced the idea of living with ordinary things. Am I out of sync?

Joe is in charge of a reception for the ambassador from Mexico—the Fiesta's guest of honor this year. He's had Patrina on the phone calling Washington, D.C., checking schedules, confirming hotel reservations, handling the guest list. She's had no time for our usual conversations, and when she does talk to me she talks about the Fiesta. She tells us that her mother and two of her sisters have arrived from Mexico for a visit. She speaks of the enormous amount of cooking going on at her house. She has prepared a dish called *posole.* She and Alex trade recipes; they speak rapidly in Spanish, leaving me to only guess what this superstition-laden concoction might be. When I ask her, "What about your morning sickness?" she just waves her slender hands in dismissal of the whole idea, as if even morning sickness were too ordinary for Fiesta. "Magic *posole!*" she says as she hands me a foil-covered bowl. "It's for good luck, Olivia!"

I do not repeat the word with my usual linguistic enthusiasm. *"Pah-soh-lay,"* I mumble.

Alex barely glances at the final paperwork on the escrow for my first sale. *"Bueno, bueno,"* he says impatiently. He's so charged with energy. "We'll go to Zozobra? You need to go with me, Olivia-uh?" He bobs his head up and down.

"Leona asked me to go with *her,*" I tell him. We've been so careful with each other. We haven't been lovers all these weeks, and my month on the pills will end tomorrow, and Andrew is making plans for a visit in just a few weeks. . . .

"Hijo. Leona?" he groans. "Well, she can come too-uh? A woman alone isn't necessarily safe in the wild Fiesta crowd. So much drinking. So much dope!" He practically salivates in the telling.

I really haven't thought this through. "We'll see," I tell him.

This crackling Fiesta energy seems to come from a mixture of sources. Actual superstition, the nagging feeling that a person really shouldn't miss seeing the past year's sorrows go up in smoke, as if not going might somehow put one at risk for the coming year. And a willing suspension of disbelief, the urgent and hopeful desire to *believe* that such a cleansing might be possible. As I walk home in the afternoon, I am thinking: Burning gloom? How could I possibly miss such an occasion?

I sink into the cactus wood chair. This apartment is empty! I get up and walk the floor, trying not to listen to the echo of my shoes on the bricks. My cattails are in the vase in my bedroom. The closet has clothes, the bed has sheets. But the army blanket is still on the window, a corner pinned up with a safety pin to let in light. I have no photographs, few books. The statue of the Boy Child with Book sits among my fairy tale figures on the counter between the kitchen and the dining room, dwarfed by the expanse of bare walls, nearly hidden by late-afternoon shadows from the ficus tree Joe brought over from a repossession sale. At least Saint Christopher hangs on the wall; I guess he protects the empty spaces, too.

The saucepan slips from my hand and bangs on the counter as I'm trying to scoop the *posole* from the bowl to the pan. The empty sound repeats itself in a brief, flat collision with the walls. I wipe off the counter. I stir the remaining *posole* as it heats on the stove.

Then I realize: It doesn't matter what *things* I move in here! You don't really move into a house until you have a housewarming! I will buy new clothes for Fiesta weekend, I decide. I will invite Alex and Leona to dinner at my place before we go to Joe's reception and the burning of Zozobra.

Yes. I'll do it.

I sit down at the table and eat as if starved, spooning the magic *posole* directly from the saucepan to my mouth. I read this morning's *New Mexican* as I eat. The burning of Old Man Gloom is not something they do everywhere, according to the paper, but it is a variation on many ancient rituals. I like that. It makes me feel good, knowing the world has room for new things—or fresh variations on the old.

Alex arrives first, an Indian blanket thrown over his shoulders, a black turtleneck shirt and jeans underneath. He wears a beaded headband and leather moccasins. His eyes are a little glazed; I can smell the marijuana. I cannot imagine what Leona will do when she sees him. Theirs is an uneasy truce. She may admire his native garb, or she may see only the mindless *man* she has warned me about. No wonder he smoked before he got here.

He hands me a package, a gift for my housewarming.

Leona floats in a few minutes later in her purple broomstick pleats. She nods to Alex, actually smiles at him. An elaborate silver bracelet winds its way up one of her arms. A heavy silver and turquoise necklace she tells me is called a "squash blossom" cuts into the soft skin of her neck and crushes her breasts. I am stunned but envious, too, on seeing a thin lavender ribbon tied girlishly in her gray-blond hair. At least I have on a denim skirt—size fourteen, not sixteen!—and boots, a turtleneck, a sweater.

She hands me her gift and seems to bounce on tiptoe as she turns to Alex. He's watching her with the look of a man who anticipates being injected any moment with a deadly poison. But he bends to kiss her outstretched hand. She curtsies. Alex spreads his arms beneath his blanket like some ancient warrior god and we walk arm in arm to the patio, a threesome. In costume, at least, Alex and Leona are instant friends. What was it Joe said to me last week? "One thing we Easterners have to learn, Olivia. Everywhere else is just everywhere else, but Santa Fe . . ."

I serve sole filets baked in a light wine sauce and arranged on the sand-colored pottery platter Leona has brought as a gift. "Mmm," Alex responds as I bring out each item. I serve green beans and slivered almonds in a Nambé bowl—metallic, silvery, shaped like a bird's wing curving in flight. Alex brought the bowl. And in a Zuni basket I bought at the Indian Market, I serve Leona-rolls—her recipe, my baking—and cover them with a square of woven turquoise-colored cloth. "Perfect!" she exclaims as she takes a bite. I caress these shapes and textures. They are mine; I recognize them; I can share them.

Our first stop after walking down the hill is the New Mexico Room at the La Fonda. Joe greets us at the door. His fiancée is here with her parents. Keely stands beside Joe in her elaborately embroidered Mexican peasant blouse and long red cotton skirt; next to her are her parents.

"Keely's name is short for Kilene, a family name of some duration," her neurosurgeon father informs me.

"Interesting," I tell him, heading for the buffet table, too full to actually eat anything.

I glance around the room. There must be a hundred people here. For a moment I've lost Alex. I move toward the bar and see him bent over, whispering intently to Leona. I'm glad to see this amiability between them; I walk their way.

Suddenly Alex and Leona turn, and Alex's voice gets loud. They are striding toward Joe and Keely. They are shaking their fingers in Joe's face. Leona places her hands on her hips, pleats quivering, as she leans into the fray. I move closer. The buzz of conversation stops.

"Why was only one Indian man invited to this party?" Alex demands. The deep, flat intonations of Indian speech are a part of Alex's repertoire I haven't heard before. Only his loud voice gives this away as an imitation.

The Mexican ambassador wanders over, his wife at his side. I stretch my neck to see beyond the shoulder of a man who's moved in front of me. Joe looks puzzled but is trying to smile, glancing at Keely, then back to Alex.

"This lady: Artist," Alex says. The way he spreads his blanket it's as if he has produced tiny Leona out of thin air.

"I am an artist!" Leona says. "Do you see any *other* artists in this room?" In spite of themselves—I do it, too—everyone looks around as if expecting to see nametags labeled ARTIST, INDIAN . . . "Is this any way to represent the community for the ambassador?"

"All gringos and politicians," Alex roars at Joe. "And mestizos!" he says, and spits on the floor. Wait a minute, *Alex* is mestizo!

Joe throws back his head and laughs. The laugh is loud and guttural and infectious. He bends at the waist, raises up, still laughing. "I'll get you next year, buddy. I'll have your *ass,*" he says to Alex. They told me what Joe did to Alex last year, but I have forgotten what it was. They punch each other's shoulders and do the handshakes they always do. Laughter ripples through the room as conversations resume.

They've surprised me again! I never see their jokes coming. But even as I laugh, too, at this little identity joke, I feel outside of this celebration, an amputee watching dancers. Something is missing, but my missing parts aren't evident on the outside. I sit down in a chair along the wall. I don't even have a family name of some duration, not the one I go by here, anyway.

Joe takes Keely's arm with one hand; with the other he grabs Alex by the blanket and turns him around to meet the ambassador's wife, who has by now gone a bit sallow around the eyes. Leona bubbles with laughter like the champagne in the glass she lifts from a passing waiter's tray. She nods to me and holds the glass to her lips. Her silver bracelet gleams in the light. Leona knows how to play, even without her artwork.

Now Alex is waving me over. He introduces me to the ambassador, then resumes conversing in Spanish with the ambassador's wife, Taffy, short for Tafoya—a family name, of course.

"And *your* name again?" the ambassador asks from beside me.

I feel I have to tell him. "Olivia Cosmos Montevideo."

"What an interesting . . ."

"It's a long story," I say, directing his attention to Leona, who then dazzles him with her knowledge of the silversmiths of Taxco and primitive Mexican folk art.

I am exhausted from trying to talk, smile, eat, breathe. . . .

We leave the hotel, honored guests and all, to walk the mile or so to Fort Marcy Park, where Zozobra will burn. The crowd in the lobby surges outside toward the Plaza. Strolling mariachi bands and street-corner folksingers make music. There's even a marimba band with steel drums. People are dancing. I'm swallowed up in a river of bodies; my midsection has become rubbery. I'm caught suddenly in the rhythms, my body moving in a kind of wavelike trance, my head poking forward and back. I feel free, outside in the air like this. The music, the flowing crowd.

The Indian women are vending on the sidewalk by the Palace of the Governors, just as they have been every time I've come by here. Tonight they sit beneath the glare of electric lights instead of sunlight, on chairs behind tables instead of blankets that might be trampled by the crowd.

The music keeps on, drifting down on us like rain. Singing voices—some in Spanish, some in English. Instrumental sounds—harmonicas, guitars, flutes, and drums. It all fades as we walk up Washington Avenue, subdued now by the night's quiet. Friends relocate one another, no longer bumping and pushing indiscriminately but clustering together as they walk in the sweet, smoky air.

"What's that smell?" I ask.

"Piñon logs are burning," Alex says.

"Santa Fe will smell this way all winter," Leona adds from the other side of Alex. Then she moves on, speaking to a group of people up ahead.

"I should have known that smell," I say, smiling at Alex, remembering our mid-summer fire.

He drapes his arm over my shoulders. My hand—beneath his blanket, on his back—remembers his body. His skin quivers beneath my fingers. I look at him from the corner of my eye.

"Olivia," he whispers, looking at me, bringing his head down close to mine. He takes my arm and pulls me closer to him; our awareness of the changes to come is only stoking this fire.

"Olivia!" a woman's voice shrieks as we near the park. I see Patrina waving her arms, moving along in the circle of her family.

"Patrina!" I shout, my throat squeezing out a high note at the end. And that's all. Like girls, it's important that we shout each other's names.

"Patrina," Alex says approvingly, not to greet her himself but as if to acknowledge the powerful connection I have with her. His ability to be separate and yet connected is amazing to me, and admirable.

"Patrina! Patrina!" I keep hearing. "Olivia! Olivia!" the voice keeps answering. Soon the echo of our voices, vital and full of joy, is drowned out by unearthly moans, and I see the ten-foot effigy of Old Man Gloom, an oversized head, a ghostly, shapeless body, lit up by spotlights. The grimacing face stares out over the crowd, its mouth an unsynchronized parody of the voice shrieking and groaning through the loudspeakers, vibrating, overtaking even the loudest conversations. Someone is dancing around on the ground in a kind of cavorting frenzy, but I cannot take my eyes from that face. I know that face, the face of gloom.

Leona buys tamales from a woman at a table near the fence. Alex passes me his flask of whiskey. I decline both the tamales and the whiskey, wondering how Leona and Alex can eat and drink at a time like this.

They unwrap the yellow paper, peel back the whitish corn husks, and sink their teeth into the meal and meat and sauce. Their eyes reflect red and yellow flames.

Zozobra is burning now. These are *my sorrows,* burning right now! The voice in the loudspeakers is so convincing that my throat constricts. I bring my hand to my mouth, thinking I might vomit, but it is sound I am holding back. I am battling to restrain my voice. I want to groan with him. Loud. Strong. I want to push the sounds through my throat and out into the smoky air.

"How do you get the job as the groaner?" I ask Alex, yelling up to his ear.

"Same guy every year," he shouts.

Maybe next year.

A woman ought to be heard on this loudspeaker. Old Woman Gloom would call up all the witches who burned at medieval stakes, but this purifying fire would give the custom new meaning. It's a custom given a Spanish name by Anglo men, anyway. Why not add to the multicultural heritage? Burn a woman. Zozobrita, I name her, inventing my own word.

But wait! Zozobra already *has* a feminine ending. Old Woman Gloom is already burning. I wipe tears from my face; I cover my ears with my hands. Alex has seen this; he is watching me.

Zozobra burns, then glows, as the ashes, momentarily suspended in their ghostly shape, begin to break up in the breeze. The voice on the loudspeaker has already gone silent when we leave the park and begin the long walk home.

"Olivia! Olivia!" Patrina's voice echoes.

"Good night, Olivia," Leona calls from her apartment doorway. "Thanks for dinner."

"Olivia," Alex whispers as we go inside. "Oh, Olivia, we're on fire."

"So hot," I whisper back.

Yet we stand for only a moment, holding each other, and then we're moving. Not turning on lights, or locking doors, or even making conversation, we are moving in this heat, swaying in each other's arms, pushing away, twirling back. He flings me toward the living room.

I stop twirling and look at him, silhouetted, as he stands in dim light from the French doors in the dining room—his long hair, his blanket still hanging from his shoulders. Suddenly I raise my arms above my head and turn my head toward him. I stomp my foot on the bricks. I stomp again. He turns toward me and raises his arm, stomps his foot. I move toward him, moving fast but placing each foot. *Stomp.*

As I reach him, I stiffen my arms at my sides, bring both feet together. *Stomp.* "What's this dance we're doing, Alex?" I ask, slightly winded.

He stomps his feet and swings his blanket around me. I stomp a circle around him as he turns. "The Fire Dance," he says.

I fall against him, exhausted. We walk toward the patio door; I turn the knob as Alex reaches above me, pulling it open. But as we step outside, the night air gathers insistently around us, suddenly cool as September. It tells us what we already know, that the fire is banked, that tomorrow really will be different from today.

Mañana comes as I sit on the sofa in the living room, my mind still blurry with the night's burning images. Not wanting to sleep, I've stayed here since Alex left last night. Now I go to the kitchen phone and dial Andrew's number in Arlington, Virginia. I whip the long cord behind me as I step out onto the dewy bricks of the patio. I can see him, standing there in his T-shirt and blue jeans, or sitting on the edge of the bed pulling on his socks. Not even knowing that the burning has taken place, he will pick up the phone in a state of innocence and grace. "Hello, Andrew? This is Roberta," I'll say. "I'm still here!"

But the phone keeps ringing. It's almost eight back there. He could be mowing, or jogging, or already gone to his parents-of-lost-children meeting, or with his woman friend—yes, I tell myself, that is a possibility. I'll call him tonight.

I sit at the round plastic table on a dew-damp chair. I watch the dawn's pink-and-gold arrival, the light spreading across the sky, above my neighbors' rooftops, above us all. If I sit very still, I can imagine that a moment like this is when images become visions for an artist. Or words become poems, or notes become symphonies. It's a transforming moment, but deceptive in its exhilaration. I suspect this is when the work only begins. I think about Alex's story of the Woman of Hard Substances, ragged old thing, living underground in her turquoise-lined kiva. The Sun God brings her offerings. Then she's no longer old but clothed in a dress and moccasins of bright white deerskin, but she runs the course of her life to do it. She does it every day.

I want to paint or sing or recite or sculpt this transforming power—now. I want some sort of creation I can bring forth—here. I'm stuck in the ordinary, though. Contracts. Bills. Phone calls. Memory ought to help. Disturbing and unreliable as it is, surely it's one thing that's kept me going. I'm scattered, fragmented; the people I love are all over the place. But in a moment like this, when it all seems so amazingly connected, couldn't I just send out a message, write a letter, make a call? I did make a call—to Andrew—but that's not it. I mean a message to OUT THERE. A telegram, maybe. Yes, I *could* send a telegram. Yellow paper. Black print. Western Union. So many people have received news of soldiers' deaths in telegrams, but our bad news came with the doorbell and, besides, this is a *good* telegram, to cancel out some of the bad ones.

TO: ANDREW AND GARY AND HAROLD AND VIRGINIA, SAILING THROUGH THE UNIVERSE STOP

I don't want them to stop. It's just telegram language for period. For a while there I wanted them all to go away, but I kept on remembering. And the new ones, building my memories now—I don't want to forget them, either.

TO: ANDREW AND GARY AND HAROLD AND VIRGINIA AND ALEX AND LEONA AND PATRINA AND JOE, ALL OF US SAILING THROUGH THE UNIVERSE STOP

TO: GARY ANDREW MASTERS I DO REMEMBER YOU, SON STOP

I REMEMBER ALL OF YOU IN THE BEATING OF MY HEART, IN THE PULSING OF MY BLOOD, IN THE MOMENT BY MOMENT WAY I AM GIVEN TO LIVE STOP I REMEMBER YOU STOP AND I LOVE YOU STOP SIGNED:

The name. One privilege of creating something, however plain and homely, fumbling and unsure, is that right of authorship, the thrill of attaching one's name. I scratched my name on my vase; I can scratch it here, too.

SIGNED: OLIVIA COSMOS MONTEVIDEO.

That signature would be incomplete. It sounds like an alias, yet it's real. It's just that there is more.

SIGNED: ROBERTA PATTERSON, ROBERTA PATTERSON MASTERS, OLIVIA COSMOS MONTEVIDEO.

Is that it, then? I imagine a telegraph operator wearing a green eyeshade in an old western movie asking the question: "Is that all, ma'am?" I can almost hear the *clickety-clack* of his telegraph machine. Read it over. Play it back.

This is not all. This is when the work begins.

IV

THE SPIRAL

You do not have to be good.
You do not have to walk on your knees
for a hundred miles through the desert, repenting.
You only have to let the soft animal of your body love
what it loves.

—"Wild Geese" from *Dream Work* by Mary Oliver

1

Andrew calls on a Sunday in mid-September.

"Did you buy your plane ticket yet?" I ask.

"No, not yet," he says. His voice is deadpan.

My mind races with implications that I don't want to investigate further: He's decided not to come out and visit me; he's going to marry his friend Leslie; he's . . .

"I might as well tell you the good news, Roberta . . . Olivia . . . whatever. I can't come out there when we planned."

"You can't come out?"

"You might as well know. I found a growth on one of my testicles."

I draw in my breath.

"I was driving to work," Andrew is saying. "It was raining. You know how muggy it gets here in the rain. But it was cold outside, so I was wearing my coat, but then I got hot sitting at the exit ramp, there at North Parking."

"Yes," I say. "I know where you mean." I can see the gray morning sky, headlights of cars streaming into the steadily filling sea of cars in the Pentagon North parking lot. I can see it all.

"I reached down to pull my pants leg, you know, pull my pants out of my damn crotch. Something just felt funny. The way my . . . the way my balls felt."

Andrew's balls wouldn't just feel "funny"—not this man's balls. He was surely in stark terror, already dying, planning his funeral.

"I unzipped my pants. I was sitting there palpating my goddam testicles, Roberta. It's seven o'clock in the morning. I'm at a stop sign at the exit to North Parking and I'm not even hearing the horns behind me. I'm breathing all this hot air and my body smells and I'm finding this pea-sized little knob on my left testicle."

"Andrew . . ."

He felt the left testicle, then the right, convinced that if he returned to the left just one more time he would find that the lump was no longer there. I have done that with my breasts, feeling for matching glands buried in the tissue, always finding them, so far.

I hear ice clinking in a glass. He's drinking scotch. The scotch is loosening his tongue, but his voice keeps breaking, stopping, then going on.

"So I went to work and I kept running to the restroom. You know how far the restroom is from my office, you've been there. Half a mile down the corridor, it seems like."

He and Joe Malone always said they needed roller skates to work at the Pentagon.

"I wasn't in my office much that morning. It was last week. Between running to the bathroom and trying to get . . . trying to get. . . . Now look, Roberta. I was upset. The only person I could think to call was June, because she worked for a surgeon back when . . ."

Back when Andrew lived with her for six months, back in the days of the Bedroom Wars. I feel the stab of jealousy, but it's so insignificant compared to all we've been through since, I just shrug, shake my head. "I know," I say.

"Thanks, Roberta," Andrew says, the voice of a man who holds the governor's reprieve in his hands.

"I love you, Andrew. I'm sorry all this is happening."

There's a long pause before he goes on.

"I tried all morning to reach her. It was Thursday and she does 'errands' on Thursday, they said. Whatever the hell 'errands' are. Does she have a beeper? Hell, no. I remember that surgeon had a pager. You could catch him on the golf course or washing his Jaguar, but when I needed this woman, I couldn't reach her. . . . Sorry."

"It's okay," I say.

"I ended up calling Doc Balsamo. He took me right away."

"The last time I was in there he said he was retiring," I say, remembering the general practitioner who took us as patients almost twenty years ago. A newly married and already pregnant couple, we gave him some good laughs, but he always seemed to laugh with us.

"He scheduled me for surgery with another guy in two weeks. He'll assist."

I figure the time lag. "So that's *next* week?"

"Yeah, I guess it *is.*"

Andrew's story is about love. About NEED. The definition of those words is so simple now: being there. And if you aren't there, what are love and need? Not even habits, not even anything at all. What I am feeling now takes over my body. I feel like the cartoon characters Gary used to watch on television. I walk over to the wood-framed mirror on the dining-room wall, expecting to see some changes: biceps enlarged, eyes dilated by a red glow. But I look exactly the same. A little pale, maybe, jaw set, mouth in a tight, thin line. Andrew NEEDS me.

Andrew is losing control of his voice. "What happened to us, Roberta? What happened to that gorgeous kid. . . ."

Who's to say? What happens to any of us, I wonder.

"I'm getting off now, Andrew. I'll make reservations. I'll be there."

As soon as I hang up the phone I am pulling clothes from the closet, from the drawers, and flinging them into my suitcase. This won't be easy, I keep telling myself. Leaving one life and returning to the other, with the troubling expectation that each might be there when I get back. Such an uneasy balance, I tell myself, dialing Alex's number.

"I'll drive you to the Albuquerque airport," Alex says, upon hearing my hurried narration.

"Oh. Alex. I think I just about have to drive myself," I say, almost feeling his hands on my shoulders as he begins his persuasions. . . .

"You'll worry about the car. You'll be tired when you get back. I just *want* to take you, Olivia."

I'm weakening, such a clutter of thoughts in my mind: a flight across the continent, so little air space in that plane, so few hours to cover so much distance. "Alex, I need to drive to Albuquerque and park the car and carry my suitcase."

"I know, Olivia. Okay. I'll miss you. I hope Andrew wil be all right."

"*Gracias,* Alex."

"The house will feel haunted, but don't be afraid, okay? Gary will come back to you, but you don't need to be afraid. . . ."

Something flips over in the pit of my stomach, chill-bumps form on my arms. "Alex! Do you have some sick need to put a curse on this trip?"

"Hey, Olivia, I'm telling you what I felt after my grandma. You felt it with your father, didn't you-uh?"

I do know what he means, though I don't even want to think about it: my first time back in Potsdam after my father died, the way the house seemed the same yet so different. I cut our talk short. "I know what you mean, Alex. Really. While I drive the car and fly in the airplane, I'll be getting ready for Gary," I say. "For his ghost," I say.

Ghost. Everything explodes in me when I say it: terror and expectation, sorrow and joy.

The pilot is announcing our "descent" into the Washington area. We are landing.

Riding into the terminal area, I am asking myself how I could have forgotten that passengers at Dulles International arrive in little buses from the satellite landing areas. I should have opted for the Dallas layover and flown into National instead of the nonstop flight that has put me into this sprawling piece of Virginia countryside. It would have been less of a drive for Andrew, too. This bus ride, this extra and unexpected leg of the trip has given me time to think about how long it's been since Andrew and I have actually seen each other. Will I see in his face the anger that the telephone hides? Will he see in my eyes the fear that my chatter disguises?

These Coming Back Fears are setting upon me in stages, each stage requiring its own time for depressurizing. Or is it decompressing? Each state the plane flew over. Each foot of altitude we lost as the plane came down and landed. Every second that passes as the bus rolls up to the terminal. Coming back is like the bends. Someone needs to lock me in a chamber, read my gauges, tell me if I'm ready for this.

As I walk into the passenger area Andrew is waving to me from behind padded plastic ropes. He looks utterly familiar, as if in some strange way I am looking into a mirror.

Everything about him is familiar. The pattern of the blood vessels in his tired eyes. The texture of his brown hair, the way it waves only behind his ears. The menthol scent of his shaving cream, the soft bulge of his genitals as he holds me, the wide half-moons in his fingernails as he takes my jacket and tote bag. I must be equally familiar to him. We are primitive, knowing each other by shape and scent, but we're unable just yet to mark the occasion with language.

"Where's your baggage claim?" he says. First words out of his mouth: "Where's your baggage claim?"

"Oh, here," I say, eagerly thrusting my ticket pouch toward him. First words.

We look all around, craning our necks to find the color-coded arrows which will lead us to Baggage Pickup.

"You're gorgeous," he says in the car.

"I am?" I ask.

"Gorgeous," he repeats.

"I lost some weight. I seem to walk a lot."

He has this way of laughing, almost as if he's laughing to himself.

"What?" I ask.

"Roberta . . . I'm just glad you came. I'm surprised. I never thought I'd be glad to go under the knife. . . ."

"You would have come to Santa Fe, wouldn't you?"

"That's just it. I would have gone out *there.*"

I think he's saying that I've brought something with me. I think he feels that he needed what I have brought. I might as well tell him Wonder Woman has not really arrived: "I'm afraid to go in our house."

He nods his head, and now we're quiet, each of us wondering what next.

The Beltway is snarled with traffic. We're waiting for the Arlington Heights exit. "Almost there," I say. It feels natural to reach over and pat his thigh; it's what I always did when he was driving. But I jerk my hand away, remembering suddenly about his growth. "I'm sorry! Did I hurt you?" I ask.

He looks over at me as he changes lanes, then brings my hand back to rest on his leg. We drive on.

"Roberta?" Andrew inquires minutes later, as if checking to see if I'm still in the car. "Your coming in this time of day put me in a bit of a bind."

I look at him, wondering what he means. Getting off work an hour early can't be *that* inconvenient. "Don't tell me Jack's complaining about you picking me up!"

He smiles. "Hell, no," Andrew says. "I'd never tell him. No, hon. It's the neighbors. I told them you were coming home. They'll be driving in when we do. . . ."

I am dumbstruck. "Neighbors?" I say. Nay-burrs? Do I know this word? This is a word so powerful it makes my pulse race, my eyes tear, my hands shake.

"They asked if they could come over. You know, just for an hour or so. I said give us a little while. . . ."

I hadn't thought of neighbors. Good manners would tell anyone you don't barge in on a couple in Andrew's and my rocky circumstances. Couldn't they have waited till tomorrow? Couldn't Andrew have *asked* them to wait? Has he no sensitivity to my exhaustion, my emotional state upon returning. . . . Given *his* emotional state, I ought to be glad he found the airport.

We are turning onto Bent Twig Road. It's almost dusk, this evening in late summer on the very edge of autumn. I feel the dense quiet of trees, lawns, green places where children play and dogs roll on their backs. Wooded areas hover in a speckled borderland beyond the road. Some people have already come home and put on their baggy gardening clothes. They stand outside, in their front yards. They hold hoses with screw-on nozzles, making arcs of spray. They bend over flower beds, turning damp earth with spades in their hands, possibly planting bulbs for the spring they've heard will come.

We are turning onto Branchview Court. I see our house, split-level model. And our neighbors' houses, ranch models, some with upstairs additions. But my *neighbors* are coming, my neighbors are coming! I have entered another level of decompression.

The Reverend Sherman Ellis is parked in front of our house. He gets out of his car as we drive up. "Roberta," he says, bumping me with his pot belly as he pulls me to him. "Roberta, I'm so glad you're back." His voice is familiar to me, with its soft traces of his southern Virginia roots. I see him surrounded by little children, seated at the front of the church during Children's Time, asking questions that Gary often tried to answer. "How many of your parents tell you to give money to the church?" he asked once. An eager if poorly informed participant at three, Gary raised his hand and said, "We don't got any money." Laughter then; tears now. No wonder I ran away. I can't do this! We walk inside with Sherman. I breathe in, trying to sort out impressions as they collide in my mind: The kitchen table is smaller than I remembered it, and the bay window looking out on the backyard is bigger than I thought, and the screened porch is neglected, with cobwebs in the ceiling corners and a layer of dust on the chairs. I have no time for sorting out. Mary Sue and Paul Groves, bringing gifts of food, appear at the back door. They come inside to arrange the table. Andrew and I sit down in the living room, and in come the Findlays, with more food. Soon someone turns on the table lamps because it's already dusk, and the light warms us up. They couldn't *wait* to see me. I savor the texture and flavor of their gifts. I know Terry Findlay's lasagna, baked and frozen as long as six months ahead of time; I remember the brochure she waved at us as we stood on the sidewalk the day their freezer arrived. Frozen Food! we all marveled. I tell her about my memory of her freezer. And there will never be pecan pie like the pecan pie Mary Sue makes from her "mama's" recipe. I tell her so. People pour in, animated versions of shapes I have carried with me inside my head, my heart. We are catching up on the months of my absence, yet remembering is what we are really about. We remember Gary playing with their children, riding squeaky trikes, splashing in plastic pools. We remember when he turned away, grew surly; some of their sons have turned away from them, I find out, finally able to hear what they must have been telling me before, when it was all happening. Mary Sue and Paul Groves and their two teenage daughters have gathered around me. Their son Paul Junior is away at college, I discover. Their son. . . . I can't keep myself from crying, but then neither can they. They feel our loss. It is their loss, too. We can share it.

My body tingles from our neighbors' embraces as we see them off from our porch step. Andrew closes the door as I turn toward the living room. We sit on the sofa, rotate on the cushions to face each other. Touching hands across the sofa back, as if we hadn't really looked at each other at the airport or during the party, we make an almost clinical examination of each other. He takes my hand and looks at the back, the palm. I touch the side of his face, smooth his errant eyebrows, first left, then right.

"You okay?" he asks.

"You look better without those muttonchops," I say, touching his clean-shaven cheek.

"When did you get glasses? I like the green."

"After I cheated death driving across the country!" We laugh.

"You have lost weight, Roberta. You look good. Damn good."

"I do? I have? Well, yes, I have," I say, blushing, looking down at myself. I'm embarrassed at Andrew saying these things. I feel as if Alex must have reshaped me like a blob of clay; what if he left some identifying thumbprint or scratched his initials on the soles of my feet? I look quickly at my watch. "They were here three hours!" I say. "It didn't seem that long."

Can a chunk of your life be given back in three hours?

We mutter things to each other about getting my suitcase and locking the front door and calling my mother to tell her I've arrived. I push off of his leg as I get up.

We walk to the kitchen, thinking to put away food, clean up dishes, but our neighbors have left nothing undone. The dishes are all washed; the food is stowed in the refrigerator; dishtowels are drying on the rack. Grateful for the reprieve, we start on up the stairs. We stop at Gary's room. The door is open, the bed neatly made up. I lean my head on the doorjamb and Andrew waits, probably not sure what I will do.

"You've kept it just the same, haven't you?"

"I cleaned up, vacuumed and dusted."

"But you've been taking care of it," I say, putting my arms around him. Thank you, I try to say, but I am sobbing. It seems as if our tears, mingling this way, are a faucet someone has turned on after a long dry spell. We sputter and choke as the pipes fill up.

"I couldn't even open the drawers until a few weeks ago. I still haven't gone through the closet . . ." he says. "But I've been in there."

"I don't know how you stood it."

"Neither do I."

"We'll do it together. We'll do the closet together."

We go on to our bedroom, taking courage from each other's presence. I pull a nightgown from my undisturbed dresser drawer. He watches me undress. I watch him as he pulls on his pajamas.

"Wait," I say. "Can I feel where the growth is?"

"Jeez, Roberta," he groans.

But I see him trying to stop a smile as he sits on the bed and I bend over him, cupping his genitals in my hand. The fuzzy wrinkled skin shrinks up as I touch it, as if I'm an alien presence to which it is no longer accustomed. At first the two walnut-shapes inside escape my grasp, but then I find the hard little rise on the left side. "No," I say, when I feel it. "Oh, no," I say. I feel such disappointment and failure, realizing I somehow expected the growth to disappear once I was here.

I notice him swelling, stiffening. I close my fingers around his erection. "What's this?" I ask, pushing him gently back onto the bed. "Did you ask the doctor about this?" He laughs, trusting this bashful pleasure he is feeling, pulling me onto him. We fall into a brief, giddy moment of discovery and exploration, amazed that we remember each other. Strangers again, we sleep on our own sides of the bed, and pull back, startled, when we roll into each other in sleep.

2

We're up at five-thirty in order to be at the community hospital by seven for Andrew's pre-op routine. Doc Balsamo told him this hospital would just naturally give him better care, more personal attention. That may have been true twenty years ago when Gary was born here. Now I have my doubts, considering the surgery Andrew is having. What if there's something really wrong, I keep thinking. What if this is cancer? Can this little neighborhood hospital, a three-story brick building surrounded by maple trees, take care of him then? What if . . . I could actually *lose* Andrew. The idea has plenty of time to take hold. Surgery is scheduled for eight-thirty, but I'm still sitting in the waiting room at eleven forty-five when Doc Balsamo and the surgeon come out the double doors. The patient ahead of Andrew had to have longer surgery than planned, they tell me.

"An awfully long procedure," the surgeon says, looking briefly at me and then down at his puffy, green-paper slippers. "Totally unexpected. Your husband is next."

"Next?" I ask, horrified at what a state Andrew must be in. "You mean Andrew hasn't even *had* his surgery yet?"

"He's down the hall, Roberta," Doc says. "Why don't you go talk to him? He's already sedated. We'll be knocking him out here in a few minutes."

"Is he upset?" I ask as we walk through the double doors.

"Let's say he hasn't been especially pleasant."

The surgeon pads on down to the nursing station near the elevator. I'll deal with *him* later, I decide.

Andrew sees me and smiles. He seems strange, not drunk, not

sleepy, but missing some cues. "Poor guy in front of me was in all morning," he tells me quickly. I can hear the terror in his voice, like a child who's been acting up and wants to be good: He *wants* to, but it's too hard. "Remember Bill Greene? They went in there to just take a look. . . ."

"Okay, Andrew," I say, hoping I can get him off this grim track.

"They ended up taking Bill's whole lung. You know what that means?"

"They're not going to take your testicles, Andrew! They wouldn't *dare,"* I say, doing a bump and grind with shoulder and hip. I want so much to kid him out of this, yet I lay my head on his chest and next thing I'm weeping. "You *have* to be okay," I whisper.

"Roberta . . . Olivia," Andrew says, awkwardly stroking my hair, getting his plastic hospital identification bracelet tangled in my hair. I'm crying and pulling against the bracelet. The more he tries to help, the more tightly I am ensnared.

"Calm down, Roberta," Doc says as he frees my hair. I stand upright again, my hand on Andrew's forehead, looking down at him while he looks up at me. "You two are a disaster waiting to happen."

We do seem to have the stability of two six-year-olds; on second thought, six-year-olds would do better than this.

"We're ready for you now, Andrew. I mean it this time." Doc gets at the head of the gurney and tries to roll it down the hall.

I block the way. "Doc, should *you* be doing this?" I ask. "Where are the orderlies or whatever employees who ought to be wheeling the patients?"

Doc takes me aside. "Roberta, you're as white as a sheet. Go lie down in his room. I'll come and get you."

I know I should move out of the way, but I feel I can't leave Andrew.

"Go on. Give him a kiss and get the hell out of here."

"Doc!" Andrew says, his paper shower cap askew, his eyes only half focused. *"No*body talks to my wife like that." He rolls his head off to the side, his temporary bravado apparently forgotten as soon as it appears.

Doc and I laugh. I kiss Andrew's forehead. My hero.

The surgery is over at two. I have gone beyond worrying by

then. I am in the hospital admissions office, complaining, inappropriately, to a fuzzy-haired woman who has three pinky rings on her left hand and two turquoise rings on the middle and index fingers of her right hand. Doc Balsamo finds me and leads me to the elevator. "He's in Recovery now," he says. "No cancer."

As soon as he says it, I have the luxury of indulging in what I know is trivia. "Andrew was so exhausted," I say. "I'm sure there'll be complications. Just from being so agitated, so tired."

"Roberta . . ."

"This was *not* emergency surgery. They could have delayed it until tomorrow."

"Roberta, Andrew's fine," he tells me in the elevator. "It was a benign growth. No signs of trouble," he adds, pulling my gripping fingers from his arm. I realize I have probably bruised him, the poor man; he's past sixty.

"I'm sorry," I whisper, rubbing his arm. "Thank you."

My irritation and fatigue have evaporated as we walk right into the Recovery Room. No longer questioning the relaxed procedures of this small hospital, I am instead grateful for the informality that lets me be looked after this way, allowed in where I don't belong.

Andrew is too dopey to talk—he's pale, sleeping with his mouth open. Doc and I discuss the good news.

"I was sure it would be okay," Doc says. "I tried to tell him. . . ."

"I think there was more going on than worrying about the surgery."

"Yes," our doctor says, looking back, with me, at the twenty years he has been observing us but knowing things *I* don't know about the months since I've been gone. "I'm glad you're here, Roberta," he says.

"I'm just glad *you're* here," I say. "Putting up with us."

"I'll send you my counseling bill," he says, grinning.

Later in the afternoon an orderly brings Andrew back to his own room. Groggy, lying on his side, he looks one hundred years old, the skin at his neck lank and folded over on itself. He faces the window. He's saying something about the light at the window. The sky is gray; the darker gray of tree branches floats outside the window like charcoal lines on a sketchpad. "I'm okay, Roberta," he says suddenly.

"It was benign. Nothing at all," I assure him.

"This time of day . . ." he mumbles. "Driving home."

"I know," I say. "You'll go home tomorrow."

"Driving home," he says again.

He's commuting home, I decide, translating his cryptic messages. He's joining the stream of headlights on the Beltway, merging, continuing as part of the flow.

A nurse comes in. She turns on the light, takes his blood pressure, his vital signs. She gives me the thumbs-up signal. She leaves without turning off the light.

Andrew looks toward the window and rolls suddenly from his side, to his back, to his side, as if in a spasm of pain. I bend over him, my hand on his shoulder. Every time he turns, his abdomen must be drawing up, pulling at the stitches in his scrotum. "Don't jerk that way," I tell him. "Lie still."

He groans

"What's wrong, Andrew? What is it?"

"Light's gone."

"You mean the sun went down?"

"Yellow."

I look at the window. The light of the room is reflected, yellow, on the cold glass of the window. I wonder what he's thinking. What does "yellow" mean in his half-drugged mind? Is it warm? Is it an oozing, infected color? What?

"Gary," he says.

He's thinking about Gary. Tears run down his face. All of a sudden he grips my hand and sobs—weak, suture-restrained spasms.

"My God, Roberta," he says. "I'm going to live."

"So am I," I whisper.

He's squeezing my hand until it hurts.

"Why?" he asks me, as I free my hand and pull the blanket up around his shoulders.

"Why are we going to *live?*" I ask, leaning over him.

He nods his head, eyes closed.

"Because . . ." I straighten up. With one hand I hold up my forehead; my other hand massages the small of my back. "Because we don't have any choice," I say, smiling, shaking my head. Is *this* what I was trying to tell Patrina that day in the office? Is this the one option, going on because we don't really have any choice? Oh, brother. I do hope I remember to tell her!

He's sleeping now. I sit for a while beside his bed, then leave him and drive on home. It's already after nine when I pull in the driveway of the house on Branchview Court. I walk upstairs and change into a pair of Andrew's pajamas. I walk into Gary's room, standing there in the darkness for a minute. Then I take his red plaid flannel bathrobe from the closet and slip it on, rubbing my hands along my arms. It feels so good. Clean pajamas from Andrew's dresser drawer and a robe surely washed after Gary left for Vietnam, yet I can smell them both. I can smell my husband and my son. The air is thick, warm, tangy with the scent of both of them. I sit down on Gary's bed and wait.

Before long, I am switching on a lamp, opening a drawer here, a box there, not sorting or searching but placing my hands on the familiar shapes that remain of my son. I find a pair of wooly socks he left behind; I put them on. I find a pile of school papers; I trace my finger along the jagged, right-slanting tilt of his writing. A half-sheet falls from the pile, torn at the bottom edge.

DEAR MOM AND DAD,

WE ARE

At first I dig into all the drawers and sort through every scrap of paper, desperate to find a more complete version of this note we never received from Gary. Surely he wrote a second draft, I tell myself. Maybe he was analyzing our problems: WE ARE a mess. WE ARE going to need some help. WE ARE. WE ARE. I walk back to the bed, holding the piece of paper to my chest. But that's not close enough. I put the scrap of paper inside, next to my skin, just above my breasts. I press it there, hard as I can. We are. We were. I lie down and sleep.

* * *

Coming Back is a tactile experience. I am making coffee and touching things. I cannot just sit at the kitchen table, I have to run my hands over the wood. After all, I *wiped* that table. I can't go to the basement and simply start some laundry, I have to rub my bare feet on the irregular surface of the concrete floor. I *swept* that floor. I painted it, too, and Gary once peeled away the paint where a big bubble had formed and we had to repaint. . . . Down on my knees, I search until I find that spot again and trace its shape with my fingertips. I walk outside. Not satisfied to just look at the azaeleas, I have to swish my toes through the soil beneath them. But now I smell the mulch and fertilizer Andrew's been feeding the soil in my absence. In a split second I decide the following: If I go to the hospital this morning and he's still really alive, I will always be grateful for his lawncare; if he's dead, if something horrible has happened in the night, I'll feel sick for the rest of my life every time I smell the fecund odors of the earth. Madness. I rush back indoors.

In Gary's room I empty the drawers. But once I've taken the papers, the socks, and a few broken toy parts from the drawers, I cannot vacuum the lint from the corners. The old Electrolux will choke on those tiny bits of lint. Andrew must have felt this reluctance each time he came in here: It doesn't seem right alone. I will wait for him.

I move on to the kitchen. I empty the shelves and drawers, arranging their contents on the floor in separate piles I'll be sorting later. I vacuum with the edge tool, getting into corners, sneezing from curry and ginger and cayenne pepper spilled on the spice shelf. I pull away cellophane from rolls of Rubbermaid shelf paper I must have bought at least four years ago; it's a color called Harvest Gold. I like the color. I like the work. Measuring, cutting, smoothing it on with my arms outstretched, I have a rhythm going here. The morning sunshine warms my back as I sit on the floor to cut more paper.

The spell is broken when the doorbell rings; I drop the scissors and they clatter onto the floor. My heart is thudding in my chest. Vowing never again to live in a house with a doorbell, I pull myself up, gathering Gary's robe closer around me, tucking my hair behind my ears. It's one of the new neighbors who has moved in since I left. She hands me a casserole and says, "Welcome home." A card for Andrew is attached with tape to the Pyrex lid.

"So how long did she stay?" Andrew asks as we're driving away from the hospital later in the morning.

"Not long, since I was speechless and looked like death warmed over! What a nice thing to do, though."

"Yeah," Andrew says, moving stiffly in the passenger seat. He leans his head against the seat back, quiet for a long while. I know he is glad I'm here because he reaches over and tucks a limp strand of hair at the back of my neck that has fallen from my hastily pinned top-knot.

"Don't be too shocked at the kitchen," I say, remembering the mess. "I kind of lost interest in my shelf lining after she left. Then I was almost late coming to get you because I took a shower."

He shrugs.

At a stoplight he turns to look at me. "Were you okay last night? Did you have any trouble sleeping?"

"I slept in Gary's bed," I say.

He studies me as the light turns green and I turn onto Bent Twig. "Sometimes I ended up in there, too."

"Tomorrow or the next day we'll go through the closet together if you're up to it."

"Maybe Arlington on Sunday," he adds.

"I'd like that."

Andrew sleeps most of the day on Friday. Saturday is warm and sunny. We wake up early and go to Gary's room after breakfast. Andrew runs the vacuum cleaner in the drawers while I fold clothes and place them in boxes. We decide that we will give Gary's drafting table, lamp, and chair to David next door. We find a salt map Gary made of the Manassas battlefield; chunks have fallen off, colors have faded. We both touch it longingly with our fingertips, where Gary has touched it too, but by the time I take the trash out in the afternoon, the map is there along with the broken toys and unmatched socks and school papers.

Later I bring hot chocolate upstairs as Andrew is waking from a nap. He sits propped up in bed and I stretch out on floor pillows as the almost-autumn sun warms our room. We plan our visit to Arlington for tomorrow, his doctor's appointment on Tuesday, his return to work later in the week. Finally, he sets the cup down and looks at me. "You'll go back to Santa Fe."

"I have a job. I kind of like it," I say. "Do you want to stay here? I keep feeling like I'm packing us up."

It's not all bad for him here, I am thinking. He has a different life, now, I remind myself. He doesn't play in the band. He doesn't drink scotch. He runs on his lunch hour at the Pentagon. And there's his friend, Leslie. He's not living the same life as he was. I can feel myself winding up into a tight coil of panic.

"I was close to a lot of decisions before you got here," he begins. "I was going to retire. I was going to sell the house. Then I realized I couldn't do that without you. We needed to talk."

"You're going to leave the job? Fantastic!" I say. Then I see the look on his face, the look that says I haven't heard it all.

"I know now I was afraid to see you. I figured we'd fight or I'd freeze up again and not talk. I guess I thought it would be exactly like it was before you left."

"I think I thought that, too."

"I was going to tell Leslie she and I could be together. Her husband's moved out and got an apartment in the District. They fight all the time. You think *we* did the blame thing? Oh, man." He shakes his head. "I was going to say, hey, my marriage is dead in the water."

The hot chocolate is going cold and sour in my stomach, but I am not afraid of this question. Well, I *am* afraid of it, but I'm more afraid of not asking it. "Do you love her?" I ask.

"Do you love Alex?" Andrew asks.

I nod my head. I hold out my hands in a questioning gesture.

"How was it?" he asks.

"Andrew!" I say. I'm shocked and uncomfortable but kind of glad he's asked. I shrug my shoulders. "Good," I say at last, nodding my head. "Damn good." I can't help grinning. I sit up and pull one floor pillow to my chest. I want to tell him that Alex and I are drifting apart—and we are—but what if we drift back together? I can't say it yet.

He's watching me, not saying a word. Old Coyote Man, are you wondering what this wife of yours has learned? "How was it with Leslie?" I ask.

"Good. Really good," he says. He tries to rearrange himself on the bed.

"Do you love her?" I ask.

"Of course I love her. I feel for her. Their daughter was killed by a drunk driver. The little girl was eleven years old, just walking near a park. They have another kid, a boy who's fourteen. They don't know what to do with each other, the three of them. They're all tangled up. They can't eat dinner together, they can't talk about it." He looks at me for a long moment. "I'm really good with that boy, Roberta. He talks to me. I talk to him, but. . . ."

I scoot over and kneel by the bed, my arm across Andrew's chest. We hold each other, thinking of Leslie and her sad, tangled family. "You want to help, but you think they're going to have to work it out?" I ask.

"Yeah," he says. "Just like we are," he says, kissing my ear, and then my neck.

"I'd never have believed we could do it," I say.

I pull back from him and go around to the end of the bed. I slide slowly onto the bed so I won't shake him around too much. I lean back against the headboard. He raises himself, pushing the pile of pillows behind him. We look at each other, as intense and somber as we've ever been, knowing we haven't worked it out yet, knowing we might have begun.

In the morning, when he's made it down the stairs from the bedroom, one step at a time, and we're doing the stairs from the kitchen to the garage in this split-level house, I decide we should not be going to Arlington National Cemetery.

"You shouldn't go out in this rain," I tell Andrew. "Look, it's as gray as ash out there. You'll get a cold. You've just had surgery."

"Olivia!" he says, using my new name as a challenge to my courage. "Are you afraid to go to Gary's grave?"

"I'm afraid I won't *stop* going. Like before."

We get in the car.

"It's just the rain. It seems so maudlin to go in the rain," I say. I feel cold inside, as if my bones are cold, the chill coming from the inside out.

"We may be a lot of things, but we are not maudlin!" Andrew informs me.

"Crazy, maybe," I say, as I jerk out of the driveway in his sputtering Volkswagen. "But not maudlin. You're right."

"Jesus, Roberta. Hold the clutch in. . . ."

I look at him, my hand on the gearshift. How dare he tell me how to drive? I drove all the way to New Mexico! I raise my eyebrows with exaggerated indignation. "Do you know what I can do to you and your stitched scrotum with this gearshift and clutch?" I ask.

He holds up his hands, looks out the passenger window and kind of laughs to himself.

"I can *jerk* this car. . . ." I feel a smile spread across my face. My face feels young, somehow. I feel like my hair's blowing, even though the windows are up. I feel like my hair's tied back in a ponytail that will never stay put and the curls are always pulling loose and fuzzing around my face when it rains. I feel warm, from the inside out.

"This is like when we were going out, in college," he says, right on track with my thoughts. "When I let you drive my car. Remember?"

"I remember a lot of times in your car, Andrew."

We smile at each other, remembering. It helps get us to the cemetery.

The rain has brought the sky down lower, making Arlington seem smaller, and oddly friendly, like a park, with the emerald green of the grass and trees, the canopy of the clouds.

"You okay, Roberta?" Andrew asks as we shuffle along the black, rain-shiny pathways. The water is soaking into the grass and the excess runs in rivulets beside the tarmac paths.

"It sure feels familiar," I say, my arm at his elbow as we walk. "Up one more section," I say.

"Uh-huh."

"Can you do it?" I ask.

"Sure," he says.

And now we're here. At first we just reach for each other and hold on. We laugh at the way the rain is soaking us and how old we've gotten—we were *never* going to be forty, and now he's forty-three and I'll be forty in January. I have to help Andrew get down on his knees to touch the stone. We read the name aloud to each other and to all the others listening for our voices. "Gary Andrew Masters. Arlington, Virginia. March 19, 1952, to May 20, 1970."

"James Lee Storey," I continue. "Warrensburg, Missouri. April 3, 1950, to May 19, 1970."

Andrew looks at me, probably worried that I am going to begin the long roll call of Gary's entire section. But I am not. I couldn't stand the pain. I would be here reading all day and all night and I would never stop. But just this one, this neighboring boy, I had to read his name.

"One time . . ." I say, weeping. "When I was here, you know . . ." I can't get the words out: One time when I was here I met his parents, and they were just like us.

EPILOGUE

1991

Sometimes a storyteller must look closely at her listeners' faces in the firelight. Tonight, before we walk into the darkness and away from each other, before I offer you the final part of my story, I must tell you facts. Different from story, facts will make it easier for you to hear my final words.

Here are the facts: Andrew came to Santa Fe that fall of 1970. During his first days in Santa Fe, we talked a lot about narrow escapes. Equity from selling the house on Branchview Court paid for the apartments on Camino del Monte Sol. We bought the building with that equity and what we called Andrew's "Quit Money" from the federal government. He had taken his twenty-two-years' worth of payments into the retirement system, forfeiting the portion the government would have paid him in *another* twenty years. A narrow escape indeed.

We are still together and live now in a hilltop house north of Santa Fe. I graduated from the university in Albuquerque with a degree in history and went on to finish law school, but I never joined a law firm. As you can imagine, knowing my story as you do, I kept looking for places for families to live—safe places. I've learned that safe places exist, but not for very long; if one place is safe, the one next to it is not. Health and Social Services is my beat, and I just keep looking.

Leona continues to work in clay, and now she rescues animals. Andrew and I did not see this coming, caught up as we were in resewing the quilt of our life, but several years ago she moved out of the apartment on Camino del Monte Sol and into an old adobe in Española. She saves birds mostly. People bring her hawks; once she nursed an eagle back to life. We don't know when she decided to do this, and she has never explained it to us. Andrew and I look in on her now and then, but the feathers and dander cause him to sneeze, so usually we bring her to our house for a meal or even an overnight stay when her volunteer assistant can keep watch on her flock.

A few years after Andrew moved to Santa Fe and Joe married Keely, Alex met a young woman named Julia Esquibel. She was a schoolteacher, and her people were ranchers from Vaughn, New Mexico. Alex married that beautiful woman; she is still teaching, and they live now on the family's working ranch.

They have three children, and I am the godmother of their daughter, my namesake, Olivia. She spends a week or two with us every summer. She calls me long-distance sometimes and says, "Olivia. I miss you! You're my fairy godmother!" Alex tells her I know secret women's magic that I will teach to her, and he's right.

Alex is a man with peace in his heart, but when we spoke last week about the new war, when we gathered in front of the oil-drum fire at the College of Santa Fe for an all-night vigil—all of us; Alex and Julia brought the children, too—he said he hoped he hadn't run out of anger if more protests are going to be needed. I reminded him that those of us who remember must be the healers. We must tell the healing stories. Anger is only one of our medicines now.

I will be sixty years old next year.

Maybe, knowing these facts that I have told you, you will be patient enough to indulge me this one, last bit of telling. Maybe the pieces will fit for you now if I go back just one more time.

It was December of 1970, and we were renovating the apartments. The day I am thinking of was a Wednesday. Not the day of the Winter Solstice, December 21st, but a day near to it. Snow had fallen but had mostly melted away in town. Andrew had been working for weeks, tearing off broken roof tiles. That morning the workmen began early, cutting red tiles with a loud saw and pounding them onto the roof above our heads. Tommy Baca, the carpenter, was sawing boards and pounding nails in the vacant apartment next to ours; strumming guitars and singing voices from his Spanish-speaking radio station blared through the walls: *"O. Mi corazon!"* Oh, my heart. Andrew and I were sitting at the dining-room table, drawing up flower-bed plans and going through seed catalogs, when we looked at each other and knew: This would be the day of our ceremony.

We did not greet the day completely unprepared. Eddie Braceros had told us we would need a ceremony around the time of the Winter Solstice.

"Sí. He told me the same thing, Olivia," Alex had said the week before, when I asked him for ideas. He seemed to hesitate as we stood in the stairway at the hotel. He was coming in and I was going out. It was snowing outside; the tracked-in snow had made a mush on the floor of that high-traffic area. People kept bumping us with the down-padded sleeves of their parkas, making *shush-swush* sounds.

"Okay, well, thanks anyway," I said, and started to walk away from all the confusion.

Alex took my arm then and pulled me over, away from the door. He was wearing his jacket with the sheepskin collar. I put my hand against the sueded leather on the sleeve to steady myself, then pulled it quickly away. "Alex?" I said.

"I don't know why I'm acting like this, Olivia-uh?"

"It's okay," I said, almost laughing at the way we were so careful with each other—wanting so much to honor whatever distances we needed to keep, constantly crossing the boundaries.

"Eddie and me, we already did our winter ritual. I met him out on the West Mesa, near the old volcanoes."

"Oh," I said. "Oh, that's good!"

"Last week," Alex said, looking down, but smiling. He knew I understood. Going to the other side of Albuquerque for his ceremony, Alex had traveled a long way.

"You have your own journey," I said.

"Sí," he said.

His boots made a soft thumping sound on the stairs as he stepped up, one step at a time. I watched him walk away. He turned, and I saw his hair fall across his eyes. Then I walked on down the stairs.

★ ★ ★

Eddie had been vague about what Andrew and I should do for our ceremony, telling us that we would, of course, involve the Mother, the earth. "Of course," we had said, so mystified that neither of us asked him any more questions. There would be a feast, Eddie had said. We would have a time of darkness and a finding of the light.

So we asked around. "What's a solstice ceremony?" we asked.

Leona said she had taken winter picnics to the valley between Taos and Santa Fe when she wanted to mark an important occasion. "The great wide place, the *llano,* might give you room to find perspective," Leona said.

Patrina recommended a favorite restaurant of hers, for dinner later on in Taos. She said we should, of course, stay the night, her brown eyes widening in emphasis, maybe even caution. "Of course," we had said, wondering why. We called her that morning and she made reservations for us at both a restaurant and a rented cottage.

We were on the road by one, feeling bewildered and excited all at once. We had never created a ceremony. You must remember, we were such beginners then. The day settled on us slowly, unpredictably, like silt in the river that follows the new highway, what most people here call the low road to Taos.

We picked our spot, a turnout with a view, and hiked out toward a grassy area patched here and there with snow. Someone had told us that we would be able to see a hundred miles or more, and it seemed we could. Mountain peaks to the north were brilliant white against the December sky. I remember the way the land was red-brown close to us and the plants were every gradation of muted colors from gray-green to rust-red. Patches of snow looked almost blue in the light. But in the distance, as my eyes tried to take it in, the grasses and weeds and silvery trees all blended in with the soil and snow and turned a soft gold. Maybe I imagined that, the soft golden sweep of the land.

Andrew and I were still getting reacquainted, and the one-hundred-mile view drew us closer to each other, as those great spaces can often do. As he carried our picnic basket, Andrew looked so different to me. He was wearing cowboy jeans, as he called them. Levi's. Working on the roof and jogging every day had made him tan; when he smiled his teeth looked whiter than I had remembered them. He said I had changed in his eyes, too. "Your face has lost its baby fat," he said, cupping my face in his hands. "Your eyes are round, but the rest of you has kind of lengthened out." From stretching, I thought then. The past year had been quite a stretch. But we recognized each other, changes and all. There in that big wide space it was easy to see who we were.

The Florida oranges I had brought gave a great display of spraying juice that sparkled in the cold sunshine as I sliced them. We sucked the juice from the orange slices and bit into tamales still warm in their foil wraps. As if waiting for the ceremony to happen to us, we lay back on the army blanket, turned on our sides to sip coffee poured from the thermos and munch on Pepperidge Farm cookies—the thin kind lined with chocolate. We held each other and laughed, a little nervously, at our unimaginative approach to this day that Eddie and the others had deemed so important.

I sat up and patted my hands on soft bulges created by tufts of grass beneath the blanket. That grass grew tall as it wanted when it grew at all. It turned the intensity of its muted green up or down, according to the whims of the summer rains. It slept beneath the cold winter snow. No one would mow that grass.

"Sometimes I wish Gary were buried out here. Closer to us," I said.

"At Arlington, I figure they're all there together, like buddies."

"Um-hum. That's true, too."

"I want to say this, Olivia," he said, rolling over to face me. "I'm not worried about Gary anymore. You know what I mean? Worried?"

"*I* worried that we'd forget him," I said. "Like we would have some awful lapse and that would be it. No more Gary. It felt awful, but I don't worry that way now."

I wondered then: Is that what the ceremony is about—remembering?

Then Andrew said, "You know what kept going through my mind at Arlington . . . God, were we really there in September? Anyway, I kept wondering: Where are all the rest of them?"

"The other soldiers? The ones who died?"

Andrew rolled onto his back, propped his arms behind his head. "No. The ones who made it back."

"The ones who came back."

"Yeah. Where are they?"

"Good question," I said. "Well, there's Pete Monroe, Gary's sergeant. . . ."

"You're right. I'll write to him," Andrew said, nodding his head.

"You will?" I asked, smiling, as we gathered up our things.

We stopped twice more along the low road to Taos, once to wade in that frigid river until our toes ached up to our shin bones, another to look for seed pods and grasses. I picked some hardened sunflowers, round and firm as dishes in my hands. We picked others we didn't have names for, so we gave them descriptive titles to show our respect: Round Spiky Blossom with Cotton Fluff at Tips, Grass Rough as Cat's Tongue on Upper Edge. I pinned a couple of stems in my hair, hoping that was what Eddie meant when he talked about Mother Earth being part of our ceremony. We drove into town about sundown. I was hungry and suggested we eat before going to our room at the place Patrina had arranged.

The restaurant owner greeted us as we came in, waving away any concern about our later reservations, making good use of this chance to cater to early-arriving guests. "Is this a special occasion? I noticed the flowers in your hair. . . ."

I looked at him. Andrew said, "Yeah. The flowers look good."

"The grass . . ." I reached my hand up to touch my hair.

"No, Olivia," Andrew said. "Leave them. It's nice."

I looked at the owner of the restaurant, wanting to tell him the occasion, considering what to say. He stopped me before I could find the words.

"Dolores," he said, pushing his hands on his chest the way Alex's mother Aurora had done. "A sad occasion. I am sorry."

"Well, it's the solstice," I told him, feeling all the remembering come over me. "You know, light and dark. And our son died in the war, in May. . . ."

"*Sí*. Oh, yes. You will eat here as my guest," he said, spreading his arms. "And I will light a candle at Our Lady."

Our Lady? Andrew and I looked at each other.

"Our Lady of Guadalupe. My church," he said.

"Yes!" Andrew said. "Our Lady church."

"Thank you," I said. "Definitely, a candle at Our Lady. That would be very nice."

Holding his palms out to us, he said, "It is something I can *do,* you see."

My legs felt shaky, my hands, even my throat. My body felt drained in the trembling way I would have felt if I'd been crying. "I must be hungry," I told Andrew.

"All that fresh air and sunshine," he told me.

We ordered *chili verde* and *chili rellenos* and *sopapillas* with honey. Our feast. But as the plates were being cleared and the waiter brought coffee, I had the strange sensation of going from color to black-and-white. The red stripes in the serape on the wall across from us were no longer red.

"Andrew. Something's wrong here."

I noticed him getting up suddenly from the table. When I woke up, people were carrying me to the benches at the front of the restaurant. I was nauseated. "I'm fine," I said, as they urged me to lie down. "I really am fine." I threw up my dinner.

An ambulance took me to the Holy Cross hospital just down the road. Andrew followed in the car. "I'm fine," I told the ambulance attendant. "It's a very emotional day, I've never done a ceremony. . . ." He had long hair, shiny silver in the eerie inside-the-ambulance-on-a-dark-night light.

Within minutes of getting to the hospital I had EKG wires attached to my chest, an oxygen tube in my nose, an IV in my arm. A technician was taking blood. Andrew was talking to the doctor outside the curtain. "Andrew," I said, whining. "Call them off!"

The doctor's name was Brisbane. He was about our age, with a little gray in his hair. He was dressed in cowboy jeans and a red plaid flannel shirt. He didn't go in for white coats, he told us. "Just the name tag," he said, pointing at the plastic pinned askew on his pocket. "Your husband says you use *two* names."

"Either one is fine," I said. "I'm fine. You can call me Olivia."

"I think that's interesting. Your names. Well, anyway, we're going to keep you for a while, Olivia. Your husband says you've had a rough year. This could be the stress catching up with you. What do you think?"

How do Andrew and I find these hospitals and these doctors, I wondered. Doc Balsamo and now this laid-back fellow. I smiled at the doctor. "I guess I bailed out."

"Still looking for that great escape," Andrew said.

"Hey, it worked," I said. "I got, what, a two-minute break?" I was joking, but I knew then that Eddie had prepared me for the darkness, that I had gone there for a while and now I was back.

Andrew kissed me. The doctor watched us with unabashed interest.

"We're running all these tests partly because I have the time and you've got the insurance," he said. He turned to the chart. "We're going to send some blood work to the lab. That will tell us a lot. So get comfortable. So far this looks like a syncope episode—fainting—after eating a heavy meal." He meandered off.

Andrew and I settled in, nesting birds. He brought a crumpled newspaper and crawled up on the bed beside me. We read about the Vietnam War and New Mexico politics, equally irrational topics from our perspective. The ambulance driver peeked in. We waved to him. "This is nice," he said, observing our cozy domestic moment. "I'm glad to see this," he said. We were the only patients in the emergency room. Were Wednesdays just slow nights at Holy Cross?

"So," Doctor Brisbane said, back again, arms folded on his chest. "You've just moved to Santa Fe, is that right?"

"We're new," Andrew said. "How about you?"

"I'm from Idaho. Had a fellowship at the med school in Albuquerque. I interned there."

"But your practice is in Taos?" I asked.

"Santa Fe and Taos. Great skiing. Good place to live. My wife's a potter."

"I'm learning," I said. "I've made some pots."

He recorded what he'd read on the tapes from my EKG. "Have you read M. C. Richards?" he asked, the printouts draping through his fingers like ribbons.

"I'm reading her book!" I said. *"Centering,* it's called."

"Great book. She lived around here. No, maybe she just did a workshop. Anyway, my wife met her someplace. I read the book."

"I'm just a beginner."

Dr. Brisbane looked up from the paperwork. "I admire artists," he said wistfully.

"Yes," I said, wondering if he needed some reassurance. "The Indians would consider *you* an artist. The medicine men are artists."

"That's true," he said, unable to suppress a big, wide, boyish smile. "I like that, Olivia."

A man was yelling from somewhere outside. The doors clattered open. The doctor closed our curtain as he left us.

"I'm paralyzed in the leg. I'm trying to tell you I'm paralyzed."

"What's happening?" I asked Andrew.

He put his arm across my shoulder. "Take it easy. I'll see." He got up.

"I'm paralyzed. Get it? I fell," the voice said.

Andrew came back from the curtain. He was whispering. "It's a guy about, oh, twenty-three? He's in a wheelchair. Maybe he's drunk. I don't know. They lifted him onto a bed. Dr. Brisbane is talking to him now."

We went back to our newspapers. The yelling began again.

"I fell. Telling you one more time. I got fucking shot in 'Nam and I'm paralyzed in the leg and I fell."

Andrew and I looked at each other.

"Yep. I got that," Dr. Brisbane was saying in his unflappable voice. "I'm ordering an X ray because I think you've *broken* the leg."

"No way!" the voice yelled. I could hear his distress getting worse.

" 'Nam," I whispered to Andrew.

"Yeah," Andrew whispered back. He was looking down, shaking his head.

I believed the voice of the young man when he said his leg was paralyzed, didn't feel. He might have been in shock, but I don't think he felt his leg anyway. I don't think he knew it was broken until the doctor mentioned it. This pain was in his heart.

"I take a fucking bullet in sixty-eight and now you're telling me I broke it? You hear that, Laney?"

I heard a woman's soft voice. I heard a man's voice. They were trying to talk quietly to the young man while the doctor examined him and cut off his jeans.

"Yeah. Cut 'em off. Okay. I was at a party drinking, doctor. I was going out to my car, to sleep it off. Using my crutches, should've had my chair, but I fell on the goddam ice. Had to crawl back to the house and bang on the door. I swear it was just like 'Nam. Crawling along. Just like 'Nam."

The voices of the people with him began to mutter.

The doctor opened our curtain and came in. He removed my oxygen tube. He asked the nurse to remove my IV. He was pleased with my blood work.

"Since you don't have a doctor yet, I'd like to check on you down in Santa Fe next week, Olivia. I think you'll be just fine, but let's have a follow-up."

By now Andrew and I were barely concentrating on the doctor's instructions, both of us staring intently across the emergency room at the young man on the bed. His girlfriend, Laney, was leaving. She was saying she had to get ready for her job. She said she was sorry; she was working "mids" that week. Midnights, probably. A waitress or something like that, I decided. Trying to scrape by like those young people Gary hung out with. I looked up at the doctor.

"Oh! In Santa Fe. Yes. I'll come to see you next week," I told the doctor, taking his card.

The older man was apparently the father. He had the same blondish hair and freckled look. But the father, in his denim jacket, plaid shirt, boots, was leaving. I don't know why he had to leave. But he looked troubled. He seemed troubled by his son. Maybe he was a rancher and had to get back. . . . Maybe he and the boy's mother had had problems and split up, and maybe the boy had been on drugs and. . . .

"I ain't staying all night in *this* place."

The doctor left us for a moment and walked across to the young man's bed. "You're staying," he explained. "Surgery in the morning. You'll be admitted as soon as the X rays come back."

Andrew and I were gathering up our things. I was wiping off the goo left by my EKG wires and buttoning my sweater. I ran a comb through my hair. I gave it a quick flip, and a stem of Round Spiky Blossom with Cotton Fluff at Tips fell out. I had forgotten all about the grasses and the dried blossoms. I looked at Andrew. He picked up the stray and handed it to me as I took the others from my hair.

The doctor had closed the curtain on the young man's area and returned to us.

"Could we see him?" I asked.

"You sure you want to do that?" Dr. Brisbane asked. But he looked at me and shrugged with indifferent permission as he walked toward a couple who was rushing in the door; a feverish child in footed sleeper pajamas lay limp in the father's arms.

Andrew and I pushed back the curtain a few inches and peered in at the young man. His eyes were bloodshot from drinking, and probably from smoking marijuana. His hair was mussed, falling in damp strands across his forehead. I stared at the unlined skin of his face, the stubble of a beard. I heard the ambulance attendants wheeling in someone else from outside.

"My name is Olivia. This is my husband, Andrew," I said, handing him the fistful of dry grass and flowers from the *llano*. He stared down at the brittle plants in his hands, then at me. I saw where the salt of his tears had streaked his face. All the yelling, all the crawling, all the pain.

"Who the hell *are* you people?" he demanded.

"We're parents," I said. I pulled up a chair for Andrew and one for me. We sat down at his bedside.

"I'm having surgery in the morning. I fucking need my *rest,*" his voice cracked. His lashes were damp. His father had left. Laney had left. The child in the other bed was now shrieking at Dr. Brisbane.

I put my hand out. I wanted to touch the young man's forehead, I wanted to brush his hair back from his forehead, but I didn't. I touched the sheet that covered his shoulder.

"Our son died at Pleiku. In the Highlands," Andrew said. "Where were you?"

He looked intently at Andrew, then at me. The emergency-room lights were bright and harsh. I got up and turned off the bright light by his bed. I sat down again and waited.

"Da Nang," he said at last, giving us the name of his unit, rattling off numbers and functions that I no longer heard. I heard only our voices humming beneath the noise of new arrivals to the emergency room of Holy Cross hospital in Taos, a place for the wounded and re-wounded, a place for the healers to come. We had come. We were there. My story is told.